Dear Reader,

Have you had your vacation yet? Even if you can't get away for a while, why not take the phone off the hook, banish your family and/or friends for an hour or two, and relax with a long cool drink and one (or all!) of this month's *Scarlet* novels?

Would you like a trip to London and the English countryside? Then let *The Marriage Contract* by Alexandra Jones be your guide. Maybe you want to visit the USA, so why not try Tina Leonard's *Secret Sins* and *A Gambling Man* from Jean Saunders? Or perhaps you'd like a trip back in time? Well, Stacy Brown's *The Errant Bride* can be your time machine. Of course, I enjoyed *all four* books and I hope you'll want to read them all too. So why not stretch that hour or two into three or four?

One of the aspects of my job which is both a joy and a challenge is getting the balance of books right on our schedules. So far, I've been lucky because each of our talented authors has produced a unique *Scarlet* novel for you. Do tell me, though, won't you, if you'd like to see more romantic suspense on our list, or some more sequels, or maybe more books with a sprinkling of humour?

Till next month,

Sally Cooper

SALLY COOPER,
Editor-in-Chief – *Scarlet*

ALEXANDRA JONES

THE MARRIAGE CONTRACT

Enquiries to:
Robinson Publishing Ltd
7 Kensington Church Court
London W8 4SP

First published in the UK by Scarlet, 1997

A copy of the British Library Cataloguing in
Publication data is available from the British Library

ISBN 1-85487-966-9

Printed and bound in the EC

10 9 8 7 6 5 4 3 2 1

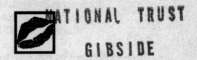

CHAPTER 1

London 1988

Olivia Cotswold thought the City of London a very drab, depressing place on a Saturday morning. The awful weather didn't help. It was rainy, windy, and altogether the kind of Saturday morning to be breakfasting in bed with one's soul-mate. Failing a soul-mate, the *Financial Times* – perhaps. Without the life-throb of its workforce, commuters resident elsewhere at weekends, the city appeared to be in heart-block.

Deep in thought and raindrops, Olivia turned into Cheapside and then Paternoster Row with its sooty-red buildings steeped in publishing history.

It was like stepping back in time. She was able to imagine all those Dickensian inky-fingered hacks and clerks with their green eye-shades and wire spectacles poring over huge manuscripts, tomes and ledgers, quill nibs scratching away with furious gusto in the making or breaking of a 'name' in the precarious world of publishing . . .

Currer Bell, alias Charlotte Brontë, literary con-

1

tribution *Jane Eyre*; George Eliot, pen name of Mary Ann Evans, with *Middlemarch*; Mary Wollstonecraft; Mary Shelley with *Frankenstein*. . . Where would English literature be today, were it not for some long-sighted, caring publishers wrapping themselves around those great giants of literary history?

That world, the world of books, was in her blood. She, like her father, lived and breathed the Lamphouse Cross, Publishers, Paternoster Row, Est. 1854. But times they were a-changing, mused Olivia, entering her father's old-fashioned domain. No designer potted plants surrounding impersonal pristine reception areas here, no fast, functional lifts, glass-walled offices, or all the rest of the 'upwardly mobile' trimmings of eighties-style 'Yuppie' culture. Lamphouse remained musty, fusty and unchanging amid its worn leather armchairs and good old Victorian solidarity – and Olivia liked it that way.

'Good morning, Dankers,' she greeted Pa's uniformed doorman cheerfully, shaking out her umbrella on the chequered tiles of the entrance hall. His real name was Dankford, but ever since she had been a little girl and had first accompanied her father 'on business', Mr Dankford, of avuncular demeanour and Dickensian attitudes, had been known to her as Dankers.

'Good morning, Miss Olivia – though there's nothing good about the weather on this particular morning, is there? Let me take your umbrella; it will dry out nicely beside my radiator,' he greeted her respectfully, and very carefully relegated her bedraggled brolly to the safety of his side of the security desk, while filling her in on the minutiae of life at Lamphouse – as if she wasn't already aware of it! 'Sir Harold is upstairs in his office, and Miss Birdie has morning coffee percolating to its usual high standard, ready and waiting, Miss Olivia, for the cold, wet and needy.'

'Thank you . . . is anyone else in this morning?'

'No, Miss Olivia. Your father did not require anyone else to be present at your meeting.'

'None of the senior editors or managers?'

'None, Miss Olivia.'

'Not even Legrand?'

'No, Miss Olivia, not even Miss Davina. Sir Harold has instructed me not to put through any telephone calls, either. He is incommunicado as far as the rest of Lamphouse's staff are concerned.'

'Ominous, huh, Dankers?' Olivia queried.

'Yes, Miss Olivia. It appears so.'

'What mood is he in?'

'As always, Miss, Sir Harold remains implacably in charge.'

'Hmm!' said Olivia, heading for the old-fashioned cage-lift to take her up to her father's offices. She banged it shut and through the ornate grille-work said to Dankers with a smile in her voice, 'You are most tactful, *Mr Dankford*, as always! Pa is probably like a bear with a sore head. He's never, to my knowledge, given up his Saturday morning round of golf to come in to work – my mother will vouch for that.'

'Yes, Miss Olivia.'

She went on up in the lift and, with a clang of iron

3

gates behind her, stepped out on to worn red corridor carpeting. The smell of coffee beans assaulted her still-dormant senses. 'Birdie' Gough, her father's personal secretary, had indeed got her coffee-machine on the go for the cold, wet and needy!

Olivia poked her head around the door. 'Hi, Birdie – no peace for the wicked, eh? Not even on a Saturday.' She took off her wet mackintosh and hung it up on Miss (Sybil) Gough's ancient coat-stand, which probably had the worm by now – all those busy little bookworms crunching through woodwork as well as yellow parchment . . . Ye gods! thought Olivia, there must be stuff on the shelves of Lamphouse dating back to the Battle of Hastings, never mind the Crimea.

Birdie's chaotic office always made her sneeze. When she opened a desk drawer it took at least ten minutes to find what she was looking for. One couldn't move an inch without knocking over piles of old books, ancient manuscripts, new manuscripts, typescripts, timetables, Almanacs, atlases, charts, dictionaries, encyclopaedias, calendars and take-away menus. Birdie's store of knowledge was prestigious.

Pint-sized Birdie Gough, however, could always find everything – given enough time. She blended perfectly with her surroundings; one was apt to overlook her in the floor-to-ceiling mess. A little brown sparrow perched on her nest, Birdie, like Dankers, had been with Lamphouse for so long, she probably knew more about the publishing business than Sir Harold himself – she certainly had a more retentive memory.

'Hello, Olivia. Just as you like it, black and hot . . .' She dabbed condensation off the coffee-filter machine with a tea-towel and a tender touch. The upmarket coffee-maker had been a fiftieth birthday present from 'the firm', together with a kilo of Kenyan coffee beans. Birdie could now keep up a constant supply for Sir Harold without having to traipse in and out of their offices in search of the communal coffee-jar, kettle, and the 'excuse me' beady eye – 'Excuse me, but who's "borrowed" the special brand of expensive freeze-dried I keep in my office for Sir Harold, and why are you all standing around gossiping when there's work to be done?' The new coffee-machine was too large and cumbersome to 'borrow' on the back of a Despatches trolley without Birdie's being aware of the thief.

'So, what's cooking with Pa this miserable morning? Olivia inclined her head in the general direction of her father's office.

Birdie hiccoughed into her coffee. 'I'm going to miss everyone,' she muttered, slamming the half-full scalding mug into a filing drawer and pretending she hadn't said anything out of turn.

For a fleeting second Olivia half-believed that her father had sacked Birdie, the way she was behaving. The rest of Lamphouse might have become computerized and high-tech – but not Birdie. She categorically refused to have anything to do with 'computerized publishing', encompassing PC monitors, hardware, software, floppy disks, fax machines and so on. *Her* age-old typewriter had withstood the test of time, and so too had her fingertips and

5

memory; she wasn't having 'any of those new-fangled machines which blew up at the press of a button, power failure or thunderstorm' cluttering up *her* office only to finally erase all data in their man-made memory owing to a computer virus. God had given her brains, memory and her stenographer's diploma – she'd use them still!

Birdie had won the argument with Davina Legrand, senior editorial manager at Lamphouse. The new fax machine had been installed directly at Sir Harold's elbow and Birdie's over-filled metal cabinets had remained in situ, repositories for all sorts of things besides editorial files and authors' profiles – coffee-mugs, sugar packets, teaspoons, toothpaste, and heated rollers for last-minute hairdos.

Olivia, her attention focused on Birdie's wonderfully antiquated lifestyle, while her hands warmed themselves around the solid feel of hot ironstone, frowned. 'What do you mean, miss us? Where are you off to, Birdie Gough?'

'Nowhere. Nothing! Forget I said anything . . .'

The intercom on Birdie's desk buzzed and she switched to Sir Harold's voice asking peevishly for the third time, 'Is my daughter in yet, Birdie?'

'Yes, Sir Harold –' she pulled a face at Olivia '– she's just arrived and is having a cup of coffee to warm her frozen hands . . .'

'Send her in at once, Birdie. I haven't got all morning to hang around here while Olivia takes her own sweet time. I've a round of golf to catch up with!'

Birdie pulled another face and jerked her head

towards Sir Harold's private domain, whispering to Olivia, 'Golf, in the pouring rain?'

'Oh, yes!' Olivia replied blithely. 'Even in a snow-storm – you should know!' She went on through into the holy of holies. 'Good morning, Pa, though there's nothing much good about an extraordinary general meeting on a rainy Saturday morning in old London town, I feel.'

'Don't know why you're looking so damn cheer-ful!' he growled, swivelling his great big leather armchair to face her, when previously his gaze had been fixed upon the tall grim building directly opposite his window – now just a derelict depository for unsold educational books.

'And *I* don't know why you're looking so down, Pa,' Olivia said with forced cheerfulness. 'What's happened during my little trip to Frankfurt? Is your ulcer playing up again? Poor you, you ought to go to the doctor instead of pushing yourself so hard, especially on the golf course.'

'Olivia, I've decided to sell out to MacKenzie. I thought you should be the first to know.'

She almost fell into the vacant chair in front of his desk. 'What?'

'MacKenzie Publishing have made me an offer I can't refuse,' he said in his infuriatingly bombastic way. No beating around the bush, no round-the-table discussion with anyone – the boss was the boss and always had been the boss!

Everything seemed to spin around her, even her larger-then-life father, sturdy, bald and impressive in his golfing plus-fours, Harris tweed jacket, checked socks to match his canary-yellow sweater and golfer's cap reposing on his enormous desk. Olivia didn't like his tie, a horrid dark green knitted affair, no doubt one of her mother's making. The only bright splash of colour in the room was his sweater. Apart from that, her father went well with his surroundings, everything in shades of green, brown and grey, everything outdated, just like a Victorian parlour. Dark oak-panelled walls, heavy green velvet drapes complete with tassels at his office windows, the huge green tooled-leather desk, the worn brown leather armchairs, shelves and shelves of forgotten leather-bound tomes, drab oil portraits of his Cotswold ancestors staring down with implacable blind eyes upon this, the latest Cotswold generation on the brink of selling them all off. Olivia put her hand to her head, her thoughts in disarray. 'Oh, no,' she said in horror. 'Not MacKenzie!'

'Why not MacKenzie?' he asked, brittle and business-like, the barrel of his yellow chest enhancing his sun-god image, around whom his lesser satellites spun, without whom they would all shrivel up and die.

'Because . . . because they're American, that's why.'

'They're Canadian, actually.'

'They're . . . they're vultures!'

'Vultures with plenty of dollars, American *and* Canadian.'

'Precisely!'

'Meaning?'

'They have no soul – no . . . no heart for the real

8

publishing side of this business, only for making money.'

'What's wrong with that? That's something we haven't been doing for a long time.'

Olivia got up and began to pace in front of his desk, her neat office suit and white blouse, her 'working gear', feeling damp and crumpled, her feet in their inadequate shoes numb. The kind of day for wellies, she thought abstractedly, and thick woolly socks . . . 'I can't believe I'm hearing this, Pa. Have you told the rest of the firm?'

'I will do, on Monday.'

'Is that fair? You've single-handedly already decided everyone's future. Don't be surprised if you have a riot on your hands, Pa, since you're unable to read your workforce after all these years.'

'How d'you mean?'

'Most of them have been here as long as long as Birdie and Dankers. What about them? You know that MacKenzie will bring in their own staff, make ours redundant. They don't publish what we do – good English literature, educational and informative works and . . . and . . .'

'Booker Prize material. No money in relying on one major best-seller a year, Olivia. We both know that.'

'So you're selling us out to a company who only buy in pop stuff, porn and big "star" names? Never mind that most of their authors can't write ABC without involving a ghost-writer!'

'I realize you're worked up about this, otherwise you'd be fairer to our partners from across the

9

Atlantic. North American publishers know what they're about, and what the general public want, dear girl. Which is more than can be said for Lamphouse at this precise point in time.'

'Tautology, Pa! There can be nothing *but* a *precise* point when referring to time . . . Do MacKenzie *really* know what the general reading public want? What about you, what about me? Where do we stand in all this?'

'I'm retiring . . .'

'You're only sixty, for God's sake, Pa,' Olivia said in exasperation, 'hardly a has-been in the publishing world. Some publishers go on well into their eighties – your old buddy for instance, Lord Clandenberry.'

'Still struggling to keep body and soul together. Not for me any more, Olivia. This business is not what it used to be. I'm tired of trying to make ends meet, of trying to stay in profit for the sake of . . . of what? I ask myself. I'm tired of the rat-race and tired of my ulcer. Your mother and I have decided to retire gracefully to the villa in Antibes. I can play golf and sail to my heart's delight for the rest of my life – *that* is what life is all about. The *appreciation* of the money one has earned through a lifetime of hard work, to *enjoy* one's retirement before it's too late.'

This wasn't her mogul emperor father speaking, self-professed workaholic and worshipper of the mighty dollar. Olivia sensed a dichotomy of viewpoints here. 'Then it's Ma who has decided you get out of the rat race, huh – or else?'

He looked sheepish for once. 'Well, I wouldn't exactly say that. . .'

'Great! So Ma's fed up of being a grass widow – I can't say I blame her. She deserves to see more of her dearly beloved husband after having devoted her entire married life to Lamphouse. Divorcing you for marital negligence I could understand. What I can't understand is why you want to take Mac-Kenzie's money and run, never mind the rest of us. Why won't you even consider another offer? Clandenberry-Hogan's, for instance, or even Charles Longbridge plc, or even . . . ?'

'Because none of them can match MacKenzie's offer.'

Olivia was not in awe of him any more; her awesome father had gone down considerably in her estimation. All this, for the sake of the proverbial mighty dollar. 'I never thought you were the kind of man to desert a sinking ship, Pa.'

'That's why I'm depending on you, Olivia, as my second-in-command.'

'*Me?*' She looked blank. 'Why me? What about Legrand?'

'MacKenzie's seventeen-and-a-half-million-dollar bid for Lamphouse gives you a place on their board of directors. We will retain our name and own identity under your direction, as MD of the New Lamphouse Company. Just one of the many stipulations of the MacKenzie-Lamphouse contract our solicitors are in the process of finalizing.'

'Oh, no – oh, no, no, no!' Olivia came to a standstill before his desk, arms taut on its leather-tooled surface, supporting herself against the shock of such a downright, blatant betrayal – seventeen-and-a-half-million-dollars' worth of betrayal. 'Why couldn't you discuss all this with me first? Why did – *and still do* – you take me for granted? Why wasn't I consulted first, and made aware of your monumental decision to opt out and put me in the hot seat? Up till now I have just been a junior member of – quote – *The Firm*, which was always just *you*, the big boss who never ever listened to one word from his underlings. I didn't even warrant a place at the boardroom table, unlike Vinny Legrand! But now, because *you* wish it, I'm to do your dirty work by picking up the pieces of the *old* Lamphouse Cross while defiantly waving its new banner for the benefit of the MacKenzie clan. Forget it, Pa – no deal. You're not being fair to anyone, least of all me.'

He answered none of her accusations, but stated dictatorially, 'I think *you* are absolutely the right person to take Lamphouse into the twenty-first century, Olivia. Not I, and certainly not Davina Legrand. I'm too old-fashioned and too set in my ways to change now. I want *you* to take my place as the head of the New Lamphouse Cross. Your so-called junior position here has nothing to do with anything. You are my daughter, and you know as much as, if not more about the business than anyone else, including Birdie Gough! After all, you've had to live with Lamphouse all your life, just like your mother. Who better to carry on the family name and its publishing traditions than my own daughter, schooled from the bottom up – the best way in any business: roots to crown?' he finished on a theatrical outburst.

'I wasn't born yesterday, Pa! The moment I cross swords with Stuart MacKenzie, MD, MacKenzie UK – which I foresee will happen on our very first day across the boardroom table – I will be *out!* How long do you think they'll honour such a contract? MacKenzie don't even honour an author's *book* contract the moment that author becomes a liability to them! How long do you think *I'll* last in that kind of uncertain atmosphere? Lamphouse's motto has always been "Truth, Fidelity, Honour". MacKenzie operate on sales figures and little men in grey suits who are not going to listen to my own personal "gut feelings" about a book or an author if there's no money in it for them. I would *never* be able to work under such pressure. And I'm certainly not kowtowing to a *nouveau riche* publishing company who can't speak English, let alone spell it!'

'Then that is your funeral, Olivia, and you'll have to find an editor's job elsewhere. Lamphouse is being sold lock, stock and barrel, whether you want to be part of the stock or not.'

She had expected no quarter from him. Once he had made up his mind, nothing would deter him. The reason for his past successes, the reason for his present downfall. Her father was too cut-and-dried, with no long-sighted vision, only tunnel-vision. He was a proud and stubborn man at the best of times, a complete mogul at the worst – ask her mother!

Olivia said, 'You have the casting couch, Pa. I'm out of here. Whatever you want to tell the rest of the firm on Monday is up to you; I shan't be there. I

13

think you're making a big mistake. We can come through this somehow, without American or Canadian or even Australian dollars. We're British, for God's sake, and we've been here a lot longer than any of *them*.'

'We *can't* hold on, and that's the truth! This business has become multi-national, so let's *think* multi-national. You are my trump card, Olivia, my only child and Lamphouse's heiress. With you, Lamphouse has a chance of surviving into the next millennium; without you, it will be just another old has-been publishing house come Monday.'

She checked on the threshold of Birdie's outer office. 'Blackmail, Father!'

'Perhaps, but I have no other option. Lamphouse has its back to the wall. I was relying on you to carry us all off with flying colours this evening.'

'This evening?'

'MacKenzie's grand book launch for Faye Rutland at Quotes – have you forgotten?'

Yes, she had forgotten, deliberately – she had had no intention of taking up the invitation. As I said, count me out. I loathe publicity stunts at the best of times, and Faye Rutland, Porno Queen, is no novelist. MacKenzie are using her name to bolster their sales figures while all she'll be thinking of is hers – mega bucks for silicone implants.'

'Will you do this one thing for Lamphouse, so that we might be seen as a firm still in the swing of things, not someone about to go under?'

Olivia thought about it for three seconds flat – she had been the one to turn down Faye Rutland's ghost-written novel, *Mitzi's Manhattan*, as being too trashy, too raunchy and downright unprintable as far as Lamphouse were concerned. 'No, Pa, you'll have to go it alone, or get Davina to fly the flag in the face of MacKenzie's seventeen-and-a-half-million-dollar offer. After all, you made *her* your senior editorial manager – and she isn't even your daughter!' Olivia left her father's office.

There were some things a woman of principle could not do, like licking the boots of a mercenary seducer from across the big pond, Olivia thought in angst on the tube back to her flat in Fulham.

She fumbled in her bag for the front door key to let herself in, and could hear her phone ringing in the background. It might be for her, or it might be for Amanda, the girl she shared the house with, although each retained her own separate flat.

Amanda was a photographic model for TV adverts – washing-powder, yoghurt, fish-fingers and gravy-mix, Amanda had starred in them all. She was now in her 'Mumsy role' era, simply because she was a bit past it at twenty-six and a few kilos overweight. Amanda had been a child superstar, having won the 'Miss Perfect Complexion Soap' competition when she was only three. She had been hoping to work her way up the advertizing ladder to high-powered executive cars, rather than stay in the domestic scene all her life, she had confessed to Olivia over a shared bottle of wine when they had both been feeling a bit down, but her hopes were diminishing fast. It was a bubble-gum fight out there, she had told Olivia: the bigger the bubble,

15

the stickier its deflation. Once you got past it, they asked you for all sorts of bodily commitments, from lip enhancement to boob rejuvenation, and she wasn't prepared for all that. What you see is what you get, she had told her agent. Olivia had been able to empathize with Amanda at the time, the red wine going a long way to help bond their friendship, though it hadn't fully cemented it – she and Amanda still only cagily gave each other house-room and definitely respected each other's privacy.

Clad from head to toe in shiny wet-look black PVC, Amanda clumped downstairs in her heavy-heeled knee-length boots. 'Hi, Olivia! I'm off to do a shoot for singin' in the rain.' She sucked in her breath. 'I wish! Breakfast cereal, actually. The type which sticks like amalgam to your kid's fillings, and mine. Your phone's been ringing for ever. I'm thinking of getting you an answerphone for Christmas,' she added by way of an unsubtle hint.

'Sorry,' Olivia mumbled darkly. 'Must be distracting while you're trying to learn your lines.' She cast a covert glance at the latest boyfriend – not bad, if first impressions mattered. Something which could not be said for the majority of Amanda's previous attachments. Still, it was none of her business whom Amanda hung out with; Amanda herself was OK. She was kind, caring, funny, dependable, minded her own business, had a limited attention-span, spoke her mind and always told the truth. There was a lot to be said for that kind of person – especially when they lived under the same roof.

Olivia recalled the number of times *she* had been

16

driven insane by Amanda's continual unanswered phone calls. 'Maybe we can club together and get one between us.'

'Great idea!' The TV advert girl smiled and promptly forgot about it. She went on her way. Olivia closed the door behind Amanda's boyfriend and his sexy walk, and went on up the stairs to her own flat.

Windblown, tousled, thoroughly wet and fed up, she just wanted to unwind for the rest of the day. She had to work out her own future, now that her settled life of working for her father had been knocked on the head – by him! He had always assumed too much, especially with her! It had been a hard week, with all the whispers in the air about Lamphouse going under, about Lamphouse being 'in the custard', about Lamphouse 'up for grabs' – all true now. Didn't they say there was never smoke without fire! But as usual she had been the last to know the truth. Nothing but the truth from the mouth of the mogul himself, now, today, this Saturday morning, when he had given her his *absolute* decision to sell up and get out.

However – and she was very firm upon this point – if he thought he could dictate every inch of her life, for the rest of her life, without so much as a please or thank-you, without even previous discussion or mutual agreement, then he had another think coming!

Olivia continued to rage inwardly. The *New* Lamphouse Cross! Meaning, of course, an imprint of MacKenzie Publishing, USA & Canada. Over my dead body! thought Olivia, banging the post-war 1946 vintage bathroom heater – and she must remember to have a word with her absentee landlord concerning his defunct water heater! She washed her hair furiously in tepid water: Harold and Maggie were, and always had been, suffocating parents to say the very least. 'When are you going to settle down, Olivia?' 'When are you going to have a steady relationship, Olivia?' 'When are you going to get married and give us grandchildren, Olivia? You *are* twenty-five, you know. You'll soon be thirty, too old to have any – a woman doesn't remain fertile for ever, you know! Unfair to give birth when you're too old and career-jaded to care . . . your father would like a grandson to carry on his name and the fortunes of Lamphouse . . . blah, blah, blah.'

Yes, Mother! Never mind, Harry's 'grandson' can be certain of one thing only – his name won't be Cotswold!

Well, Lamphouse's fortunes did not seem to be relevant any more, not in the light of her father's final statement as to where *his* business was headed. As for herself, she wrapped a towel round her wet hair and headed back to bed, hoping that later the water would be hot enough for her to soak away the bad taste of the MacKenzie takeover bid in a bubble bath, without passing out from carbon monoxide poisoning before she resurfaced.

Olivia had hoped to settle down on her bed for the rest of that gloomy Saturday, correcting and editing some manuscripts, a bit of telly, a little snooze, a lazy afternoon, which she had earned after working flat-out for nothing! Nothing, meaning the sell-off of her inheritance! But her mind was too alert, too hyped-up, buzzing with all the stealthy little after-thoughts which kept intruding . . . *'You are my trump card, Olivia, my only child and Lamphouse's heiress. With you Lamphouse has a chance of surviving into the next millennium; without you, it will be just another has-been publishing company come Monday . . .'*

'Dash it all, Pa!' Olivia scrambled off her unmade bed, left in an untidy heap due to her unscheduled early Saturday morning trek into town after the eight-thirty telephone summons from Birdie.

Cinderella will go to the ball! Olivia searched out something to wear. A little black dress with a plunging back V, or rather no back at all, which said it all. Keep it simple, Olivia, she warned herself; you want to be seen as 'class' by the MacKenzie clan.

Too late now to book a hairdressing appointment; besides, the wind and rain would undo the effect of any expensive hairstyle before she even got through the revolving doors of Quotes Literary Club. Olivia managed her damp, tousled, towel-crinkled hair herself – not that there was much anyone *could* do with a short, straight bob! she told herself. She used the hairdryer and steam curling-brush to iron out any stubborn kinks which had sprung up through lying on the bed in an abandoned fashion with a damp towel wrapped around her head. Mercifully, her hair was easy to manage: it did as it was told, it was earlobe-short, it was relatively dark – chestnut, actually – and it was now *absolutely* straight – a sleek bob would have to suffice. She added some long dangly earrings for good measure and examined the finished product in the mirror – not the exotic Legrand image at all! She was just Olivia Penelope Cotswold, heiress to a failing empire, slim, trim but nothing terribly special.

Good enough for those whose tastes were the pits of MacKenzie-Rutland publishing! she told herself on the way downstairs on high heels very different from the dreadfully dull low heels or office flatties she wore during the week.

Olivia hailed a taxi along the Fulham Road.

In for a penny, in for a dollar, Olivia Cotswold, she told herself on the way to Shaftesbury Avenue: Stuart MacKenzie, here I come, if only to save Birdie's coffee-machine from everlasting redundancy.

CHAPTER 2

Olivia decided that on this occasion strategy would be the better part of valour, and decided to play the evening *her* way!

'Darling! So glad to see you. Your father said you wouldn't be coming.'

Davina Legrand was an ambitious redhead of pre-Raphaelite proportions, a lustrous 'Bohemian' woman in her colourful ethnic clothes. With her porcelain complexion and classic cheekbones, sapphire blue eyes, generous mouth and size DD personality, what chance, Olivia wondered, had any other woman in the room?

'Now that you *are* here, come and meet . . .'

'No, thanks, Vinny, I've already met everyone – over and over! I'll do my own circulating if you don't mind.' Olivia found a vacant bar-stool and ordered a gin and tonic with lemon and ice.

Davina shrugged, and shouldered her way into the throng of animated bodies, leaving Olivia to pick at a dish of salted peanuts.

Olivia couldn't help thinking how tough it was being the only offspring and heiress presumptive of a well-established, well-respected publishing house. Even tougher when the publishing house was bankrupt and the man in power took his next-of-kin so much for granted: Cinders *will* pick up the pieces!

How?

Everyone in business was having a tough time lately, the pundits of gloom prophesying a deep recession in the wake of the past few 'boom' years. It certainly appeared that no one had any money left to spend on books – and books, after all, were her bread and butter. Could she envisage Faye Rutland as the would-be writer of a *Pride and Prejudice*, *Sense and Sensibility*, *Jane Eyre* or *Wuthering Heights*? *Like heck!* Olivia continued to muse. She would stake her reputation as a Lamphouse editor that *Mitzi's Manhattan*, of the bodice-ripper genre, would not pass its sell-by date.

Yes, but – a little inner voice said, Faye Rutland's book might have kept Lamphouse solvent for a bit longer: longer still if Lamphouse's publishing lists included more glitz and glamour and less serious stuff.

So, let's compromise, Olivia, she told herself: find a genre that grabs public attention without compromising your principles or conscience, and go for it as if there's no tomorrow!

Easier said than done. If an editor or publisher knew what that genre was, then *everyone* would be on to a winner and there would be no lame or dead ducks on the present publishing front – to wit, the Lamphouse Cross, Paternoster Row, Est. 1854!

Olivia looked into the glitzy façade of bar lights,

optics and mirrored glass and saw herself reflected. She also saw Stuart MacKenzie staring her way, and in that second too, inspiration struck like a bolt out of the blue, like a trumpet call from the Archangel Gabriel, like a laser-beam of revelation, leaving her trembling with intense excitement.

Dream on, Stuwey! She smiled to herself and started counting out cocktail sticks, placing them side by side on the bar, for the excited tremor within her had nothing whatsoever to do with Stuart Mac-Kenzie's covertly sexy concentration on her back, but everything to do with hitting the publishing jackpot – without MacKenzie!

Such a simple, clever, sensible, brave and wonderfully classic idea had come to her in that remarkable moment of insight, call it destiny even, that she wondered why no one had thought of it before . . . or maybe they had already, and she was being a fool to herself.

She did not think so; this time she was certain she was on to a winner! Olivia hoped no one would shoot her down in flames (to wit, Legrand), and pick her bright idea to pieces at Lamphouse's next board meeting.

The problem was, Lamphouse's board meeting on Monday was more of a full staff meeting, inasmuch as Sir Harold would be discussing Lamphouse's merger with MacKenzie, with little time or room left to discuss new internal policies. If only Pa had trusted her enough to have confided in her before, if only he had mentioned his intention to sell out to Mac-Kenzie, there might have been a chance for Lamphouse to survive without MacKenzie dollars even at this, the eleventh hour, Olivia agonized to herself.

Alone on a bar-stool, in a corner farthest away from the MacKenzie-Rutland entourage, she knew her 'touch me not' signals had been read and understood. In a way she was sorry.

On the other hand, principles could not be compromised. Lamphouse's motto had always been 'Truth, Fidelity, Honour'. Her father had wanted to show her off to the MacKenzie clan as the Crown Princess of Lamphouse Publishing (not in the custard, oh, no!), and whatever father wanted, daughter did – but this time it would be *her* way!

Maybe she could get Legrand to listen to her 'radical change of internal policy and bright idea concerning a whole new range of fiction' and Legrand could persuade the mogul (whose ear she always had), to change his mind about selling off Lamphouse, lock, stock and barrel?

Olivia looked beyond her own scintillating reflection squeezed between the gin and whisky optics on the opposite wall, and once more caught the eye of Stuart MacKenzie in the mirror of both their destinies. She kept her smiles to herself; her strategy appeared to be working. Every time she had chanced to look across the room, he had been looking *her* way. It was as if he could read the blurb on the back of her own bookcover.

Olivia Penelope Cotswold, RIP – Rejects Interesting Partnership. Read my lips, boyo: I've better things to do with my life, like launching *a brand new range of books for Lamphouse readers – no, not just*

Lamphouse any more, but supermarket, hypermarket and global market customers – to knock Mitzi's Manhattan into the shade!

Olivia thought he raised his glass to her, but just at that moment Faye Rutland swayed heavily into his left shoulder. All attention to the Crown Princess's back-view was diverted to Rutland's champagne-damped cleavage.

Olivia forgot about counting any more cocktail sticks, and also forgot her second gin and tonic; she had to grab her father's attention before it was too late. She leaned precariously off her stool to retrieve her shoe which had slipped off, and picked up her evening bag in a very purposeful way, eager to talk business with Sir Harold, alone and in private. Unfortunately, once more Legrand pounced.

'*Darling*, Harold has asked me to ask you to socialize, mingle, tingle, smile and wrangle but don't ever let MacKenzie know Lamphouse is in the custard, that sort of thing.'

'I thought they already knew, hence the seventeen-and-a-half-million-dollar offer . . .' She could have bitten off her tongue. The look on Vinny's face told her no one at Lamphouse knew of the sell-off yet and wouldn't know until Monday morning, Vinny was as ignorant as the rest. Olivia feigned lightheartedness to cover her confusion. 'Whoops, there goes another firefly bug! Pa was going to get everyone together on Monday to . . . um . . . break the bad news.'

Davina shrugged and took out a cigarette from her ethnic tapestry bag. 'Well, I guessed as much – we all did. That's why I offered my talents to Stuwey a

25

couple of months ago. He's offered me a place on the MacKenzie board as their rights director in Toronto – with a salary to match.'

And that's why, Olivia supposed, Legrand was (had been) senior editorial manager at Lamphouse (underpaid of course), while she was still working her way up the corporate ladder. One thing could be said for her father: Sir Harold Cotswold did not believe in nepotism until the heiress presumptive had learned the ropes! Vinny obviously had what she hadn't.

No good now relying on Vinny to persuade the old mogul to change his mind about Lamphouse, and certainly not prudent to let her know of any bright ideas she might have had concerning how to save Lamphouse from MacKenzie clutches; Legrand would only pinch them, use them as her own and earn herself another pay rise! Olivia leaned across and took the cigarette out of her ex-friend's fingers, dying to say *Traitor!* to her face, but unable to.

'What are you *doing?*' Davina snatched it back. 'You don't smoke, remember? It's bad for your health, anti-social, burns a hole in the ozone layer, it's a disgusting and filthy habit – and why is Stuart MacKenzie staring at our backsides not Rutland's boobs?'

Mirrored walls continued to scintillate optics in front and the scene behind. Davina grinned. 'Lean on, Faye, and you'll end up in Stuwey's champagne glass yet again . . . *yes!*' Davina bent over her cigarette, lighting it with an Art Nouveau silver lighter before handing the death-weed to Olivia. 'Filthy habit, smoking, but then, so was your father's ultimate betrayal. Shall we talk about it?'

'No, Vinny, you weren't supposed to know till Monday. Do me a favour and don't say anything to the others – promise?'

'I promise. Hey, come on, cheer up, it's not the end of the world.'

'It is for Lamphouse.'

'Get a life, Olivia.' Davina drifted off again, to her new boss's side.

So much for loyalty. Olivia felt she couldn't really blame Legrand. She stubbed out Davina's cigarette, which had made her feel sick and dizzy – or was that due to Stuart MacKenzie's being in the same room but on totally opposite sides? He really was very handsome – very, *very* handsome!

All her preconceived plans to play him along by playing hard to get seemed silly now, almost childish. He was a man who gathered women of the Vinny Legrand mould the way a rolling stone gathered moss. Stuart MacKenzie could buy anything, everything and anyone with his seventeen and half million dollars going spare – he had already bought Vinny, hadn't he?

Olivia wondered who Stuart MacKenzie thought he was! How *dared* he smile and raise his glass to her in that supercilious fashion, his thoughts plastered all over his handsome face? *Facts are, girlie, your days are numbered, time is running out fast. You can't hope to compete with our mega-sales authors – even your own team have come over to my side! So why not lie down and die gracefully, Olivia Penelope Cotswold, because we've got the budget, you've got the prestige, let's do a deal and be friends – huh, girlie?*

27

Over my dead body! Olivia searched wildly for an escape route. The evening had suddenly turned doubly sour for her. She really did feel like Cinderella, only it wasn't the glass slipper she had left behind, but Lamphouse, her inheritance.

Press and paparazzi, critics and reviewers were drawn up in battle formation on the other side of the room. Bright lights and repartee bounced off the gilt, white and blue décor of Shaftesbury Avenue's famous Literary Club. Under the glittering chandeliers Faye Rutland, latest bestselling 'authoress', posed, preened and parried in words of one syllable. '*Pardone?*'

'Miss Rutland, is it not true that you have used your name to sell copies?'

'*Pardone?*'

'New York ghetto to nude pin-ups to pornographic movies?'

'No nude peen-ups, no porno movies, all lies!'

'What about supermodel to actress?'

'Yeah, that bit issa true!'

'And your third husband, is he not connected with the New York Mafia?'

'Sorry?'

'He is your agent and manager?'

'We are a dee-vor-ced!'

'Miss Rutland, is it true to say that not one word of *Mitzi's Manhattan* is from your own vocabulary or pen, but that of your ghost-writer?'

She turned to her agent (not her ex-husband), almost head-butting him. '*Al diavolo! Mi porti al mio albergo, per piacere!*'

The agent turned to the MacKenzie's publicity department and roughly translated for their gob-smacked benefit, 'She wants to know what kind of a hell of a party this is before she goes back to her hotel.'

MacKenzie PR looked to their MD. Stuart shrugged.

Olivia, an expert in body language, from the perimeter of MacKenzie affairs suddenly felt sorry for Stuart, his hands in the air as much as Rutland's.

She didn't know him, had only met him this once, eyes meeting from across a crowded room, the remaining information on his identity faxed through on her father's fax-machine. So why was she making preconceived judgements about him? He was also the successor to an empire built up by *his* father – MacKenzie senior, Toronto, New York and London. Children of dynasties had a hard ride, never mind the nepotism bit.

Olivia stopped panicking about Lamphouse's future. She took a deep breath and turned back to Roger the barman. 'Another gin and tonic, please.' Her good ideas and sudden inspiration could wait until Monday, by which time she would have been able to sort them out with greater clarity and perspective. No good rushing into things headlong.

Now that Stuart MacKenzie had suddenly become recognizably human, everything else had become as clear as daylight. She was *going* to win the battle for Lamphouse! Not only would it keep its own identity, its own place, its own readership, its own authors and its long-standing loyal staff, Birdie and Dankers (forget Davina), she would fight like a tigress, tooth and nail, over the boardroom table (come Monday) to hold on – *yes!* She clenched her fist tightly.

MacKenzie Publishing might have paid Faye Rutland a million-dollar advance for *Mitzi's Manhattan*, but so what! Rutland was a passing phase, like Mitzi's own life-cycle, nothing more than a fluttering moth in her shimmering silver gown slit down the back and the front and held together by creative imagination alone – someone else's at that. Faye might hotly deny to press, paparazzi and critics that Mitzi's life-cycle was nothing to do with her own autobiography, but the fact remained, Faye was a fraud! Waist-length bleached blonde hair provocatively scooped to one side and held back with a huge diamond clip artistically placed above her left ear, an artificial beauty-spot highlighting the corner of her tremulously smiling Scarlett O'Hara mouth, Pearl-drop tooth-caps ready to gobble up Stuart MacKenzie the moment his pen poised over her multi-million *denaros*, Faye's brain suddenly exploded. She threw a tantrum and temperamentally tossed her last signed book across the room. '*Quanto costa?*' She flung up her hands in despair. '*Mi porti al mio albergo . . .*'

I think she's had it! Olivia half rejoiced and half felt sorry for Faye.

Pouting from the exertion of having to sign her name over and over with a gold nib flourish rather than a sexual summit meeting, Faye wilted on a final gasp. '*Mi porti al mio albergo, per favore . . .*'

Ms Average Writer had *every* chance! Miss Rutland might be able to preen and pose but she did not have the staying power committed authors had to have, nor could she write to save MacKenzie's life. Mitzi was just the well-packaged product of present-day society's vulgar excesses: something ephemeral and unbelievable, here today and gone tomorrow. Without being unduly unfair to Faye, Olivia felt that, as a publisher's daughter, if asked what *she'd* like to change about how publishers operated, she'd say – give a good writer without a star name or image an equal opportunity to get the hype and not the hump.

Quotes' resident butler approached her with a card on a silver tray. 'I have been instructed to hand this business card to you, Miss Olivier.'

'Thank you, Jarvis.'

He bowed and ambled off.

Olivia, intrigued, picked up the gilt-edged intro-duction card on which someone had written in a precise, flowing hand, 'Penny for them?' She turned it over – Stuart MacKenzie. She tore it into neat little pieces and put it into an ashtray.

She hoped he had been watching – she knew he had. She could see him now, mirrored in the bar frontispiece, without even turning round to see what was taking place behind her back.

'Decent people ought never to be in the publishing rat-race, Roger,' she said to the barman, who topped up her drink with an unscheduled dash of gin. 'It compromises their principles. Would you pay a million pounds for a serial killer's memoirs?'

'Oh, yes, Mizz. There's a helluva lotta living to be done on a million bucks! My girlfriend wants a new three-piece for a start, then a microwave.'

Oh, God! Olivia went back to twiddling a cocktail

stick in an olive. She was in the minority, quite obviously, so what hope was there for her?

The literati-glitterati were still coming and going through the revolving doors of Quotes' plush foyer. Olivia found it interesting to note that bona fide authors were in short supply. Most probably because the majority of bona fide authors were unable to command Rutland's scale of advance, and, green to the gills with jealousy, probably thought it wiser to stay away lest they murder both Rutland and MacKenzie.

Olivia paid greater attention to common opinion. 'Oh, look! There's George! No, ducky, I said George, not Jaws! Though I dare say you could call him that, too. Talent? Some hopes! MacKenzie must be mad paying Rutland a million advance. An artform of Russian roulette. Sado-masochism? You could say that. He wouldn't know talent if it got up and socked him in the jugglies! Who? Why, George, of course! Poor old bean, he *is* rather past it. I didn't say pass me anything! We're talking about old George – from Parkers. No, ducky, not Parkhurst. *Parkers! Parkers* Literary Agency in St Martin's Lane for the last one hundred and fifty years, like old Parker himself. They've recently been acquired by the Mattick Group . . . oh, what's the use, he's as deaf as a lamphouse . . . did I say that? Lamppost then! Well anyway, old George is deaf as a post and blind as a bat, so it's no good showing him anyone's MS. No, not Mizz Anyone! Jeremy, what about taking orf for Groucho's where we can hear ourselves think? Good idea, ducky.'

Literary agents began to disappear faster than

Rutland could sign her name – but she had no need of them any more. Old soaks fell about the gilded stools and blue-leather club chairs, spilling their drinks on the royal blue pile and the names of the infamous into the ear of anyone who had amplified hearing. Damp overcoats and scarves tossed anywhere; huddled little nonentities, *sans agent*, went for the crumbs like incontinent mice in dark corners. Olivia continued to reflect on her own overdrawn cheque-book of love-hate relationships.

Her father was in animated conversation over a glass of whisky with Charles Longbridge, his old publisher friend. Lamphouse's editorial contingent were close at hand, butch basenotes drowned by screechy voices shouting out false staccato greetings among the popping corks and paparazzi flashbulbs, kings to the right, queens to the left, jacks everywhere.

Olivia got off her perch and sidled ten paces up to her father and Charles Longbridge. She wanted to tell King Harry that the Crown Princess had a bad headache and must get back to Fulham right away, but she would come to St John's Wood tomorrow to have Sunday lunch for a change with him and Ma, since she had had a vision tonight on how to save Lamphouse from MacKenzie . . .

Her father never even knew she was there; he was too busy talking golf. 'How about some a game tomorrow, Charles?'

Charles Longbridge ruefully contemplated a sausage on a stick before biting it in half. 'Dammit all, Harry! I'm so ashamed of my handicap . . .'

Olivia did not hang around to find out any more about Charles's handicap.

She felt as if she was drowning in a tankful of piranhas, everyone and everything stripped to the bone in seven seconds flat, bare drumsticks falling to the floor along with vol-au-vent shells, canapés and crudités. She knew she ought not to socialize on an empty stomach!

Feeling far from well on too many double gin and tonics and a couple of olives, she headed for the cloakroom. No better in there. Olivia took some deep breaths. Claustrophobia and panic had set in with a vengeance; she knew she had to get out, but there was nowhere to run to on the merry-go-round of literary quotes queued up before her in a long line of bladder excesses.

The old light brigade were in full force tonight, baggy turn-ups and Oxfam skirts, jumpers and cardies about to be quarantined, horsy shoes and horsy mouths opinionated under the hot-air hand-dryers. 'Bryan says the stampede is on to grab the big names; America is on our doorstep. Archie says there's only going to be four major publishing houses left in London, and all of them will have American dollars ploughed into them 'ere long. I hear Lamphouse are being taken over by MacKenzie USA – Useless State-of-the-Art . . .'

All those severed heads bobbing around in front of the vanity mirrors, backcombed, uncombed and fringe-combed hair falling into washbasins, plugging them up. Olivia wondered why she had decided to come to the ball at all . . . Funny how one's ears felt all blocked up and everything sounded foggy and misted up in your head when you were about to faint . . . 'Hey . . . are you OK, Olly? she heard a concerned voice from far off.

Olivia got a grip on herself. 'Yes . . . yes, I'm fine . . .' She took some deep breaths and splashed cold water on her face. The would-be first-aider drifted off and the voices took over again.

'Sounds like a second millennium cold-war to me, Gwends.'

Gwends furiously brushed her dandruff. 'All right, Vick, have it *your* way! God help the mediocrity when their hardback sales fall below the million mark – dollars, not Deutsch.'

Vick banged the tampon machine. 'Paperbacks, not hardbacks!'

'Who gives a tinkers? We're in the custard – paper, hard or flexi, we're nothing but yesterday's sog! Pulp fiction, here comes *Mitzi's Manhattan*, I'm redundant. Think I'll go and breed llamas on the Isle of Dogs.' Gwends shut herself in a loo.

'Darling . . . Olly . . . so nice to see you here tonight! You look ravishing, sweetie! Love the little black backless number, darling! But then, you can carry it orf – no bra needed, huh, sweetie? Lucky old you! Someone said you were the Lamphouse editor to turn down *Mitzi's Manhattan* when already it has passed the one hundred thousand sales mark – and that's just hardback! Bet you're kicking your own ass, huh, sweetie?'

That was Pandora Symes, Lamphouse's rights manager, all treacle and pterodactyl claws, and no doubt soon to follow Legrand across the big pond. Olivia carefully wiped away smudged mascara with a tissue before fighting her way out of the grip of the press-gang.

She wanted to settle her tab with Roger for her gin and tonics – she had lost count of how many – as only champagne was on the house; spirits had to be paid for. If ever she ceased to be a publisher's daughter, she thought she might try being a publisher's doggy-bag. 'Quotes' continued to bombard her from behind.

'Historial fiction is dead, but romantic fiction is still alive and kicking.'

'Captive audience, darling.'

'Rutland has about as much talent as a cheeseburger.'

'Did I hear someone say cheeseburger?'

'Hi, Marji! See you've got yourself a TV cookery slot. Good show, darling!'

'My new agent – absolute godsend, darlings. One hundred and one ways with an olive.'

'Is that from Faye's bestseller?'

Just one more minute, Olivia promised herself, and she would be able to walk to the foyer without collapsing in a faint-hearted heap at Stuart Mac-Kenzie's expensive Lobb feet, an embarrassment she would *never* live down.

'More champagne, Miss Olivier?'

'No, thanks, Jeeves, champagne gives me a head-ache.'

'It's Jarvis, actually, Miss Olivier . . .'

'Of course – and I'm Olivia. How are you, Jarvis?'

'Terribly well, Miss Olivier.'

'Good. Have you noticed Mizz Rutland's silicone implants lately, Jeeves – I mean Jarvis? Olivia felt the gin in her head and told herself not to touch another drop.

'Can't say I have, Miss Olivier. Your good father, Sir Harold, has asked me to ask you to kindly be at his table on Monday, one o'clock sharp, Miss Olivier, when the usual luncheon table in the Club Members' Dining Room will be reserved for six instead of two.'

'Six? Who are the other four?'

'Apart from your usual twosome, Sir Harold and yourself, Miss Olivier, there will be at your usual table, Mizz Davina Legrand, editorial manager of Lamphouse, Mr Jeremy Webber, sales director of MacKenzie, Toronto, and Mizz Genesis March and Mr Stuart MacKenzie of MacKenzie Publishing, USA and Canada.'

'Genesis March? Is that a name or a Zodiac sign, Jarvis?'

'I believe it is an American name, Miss Olivier.'

'That explains a lot.'

'She is, I believe, the American rights director of MacKenzie Publishing, New York.'

'Thank you, Jarvis, for such a comprehensive run-down of my lunch companions to be.'

'You're welcome, Miss Olivier. It is better to be prepared than unaware. I am at your service at all times.' He bowed, a quaint, old-fashioned figure faintly at odds with his surroundings.

Soon he'd be calling her Laurence, thought Olivia. And what a drag to have *Them*, the enemy, for lunch on Monday. What else had her father crammed into

Monday's agenda, apart from a round of golf in between *hors-d'oeuvres* and dessert? Did she really want to baby-sit Lamphouse for the rest of her life? Answer – *I don't know!* Could she make it to a taxi and not be missed? *Yes!*

Olivia settled her tab. Time to go home, she told herself. The evening had been a disaster as far as she was concerned: a foregone conclusion.

'Cast-iron boobs,' someone remarked over her left shoulder. 'Like the prow of the QE2.' She knew they were not talking about her; the most she could boast of was a 34B.

'Diamond studs where her retracted nipples used to be.'

'How do you know?'

'I'm her ghost-writer.'

'Good God, darling. Would you like to come and talk to me about tit? I'm an agent.'

'A Mafia *patrone* and her *Lola* centre-page profile says it all.'

'Says what?'

'A wedding shot of her posing in a thong and a pair of galvanised buckets by some funky Italian designer, size ten pins.'

'*Lola* interviews are the kiss of death.'

Disjointed conversations zipped past Olivia like insects on an M1 windscreen, all of them deadly and bloody.

'Whoever trained her to walk to heel, it's obscene – the book, I mean. Sex, sex, sex; it's so filthy they knew it would be a bestseller before she'd even written it.'

'That's why she got a million bucks.'

'How many dollars to the pound these days?'

'Oh, yes! About a pound! Take the pips out first, but don't take the stones out of the avocados otherwise your guacamole will turn black before you can say Mexico. Bye for now, cherubs, must circulate before I coagulate.'

'Bye Marjoram, be seeing you . . . Marji Crane, cookery book on *rolling pins*, ha-ha!'

'Talk about pickled olives, she's so sloshed she's almost embalmed.'

'Can't tell her bream from her skateboard.'

'Gwends, who's the cutie in the lickle-ickle blackmagic number and legs up to her armpits?'

'Where?'

'She *was* in the loo, now she's over *there* . . . oh, no, she's gorn again! She was here a minute ago! Bin propping up the bar all evening with a face like lonely tripe left out in a monsoon. She's over there, I see her now, talking to King Harry.'

'She's his daughter.'

'Who?'

'Olivia Cotswold.'

'The one in the backless . . . you know, number? Is she . . . ?'

'No, she's perfectly straight.'

'Sad! Bit of an outsider, then. Boring-boring.'

'Oh, look, Vick, there's Vinny! You've always fancied her a bit, haven't you? No, go on, admit it!'

'Admit what?'

'That you fancy Le grand Legrand, you old dyke! She's coming this way – no she's not, she's gorn the other way.'

'Is she?'

'Is she what?

'You know!'

'Who?'

'Vinny!'

'Course not! Anything in clan tartan gives her an orgasm. Wonder what Stu looks like in a kilt and sporran.'

'Organic?'

'Sporadic, I'd say!'

'Oh, ha-ha, very funny, Gwends.'

The 'page-boy' sorority of various precarious publishing houses continued to observe from the sidelines. 'Oh, look! What's he doing now? Oh, brill! Stuwey's just written another *billet-doux*, Who's it for *this* time? As if we didn't know! Oh, lor'! Jarvis is taking it to Olivia, *again*! She's still trying to appear detached from the common rabble – oh, look, she's picked it up orf the butler's tray, oh, *look!* Just look at the look on her face! It's priceless! Olly's playing Elizabeth to his Mr Darcy!'

Page-boys and the Gwends-Vick partnership doubled over applauding Olivia, who had torn up Stuart MacKenzie's second overture before dropping it neatly into an abandoned Buck's Fizz.

'How about that for a double snub in the crutch?' said Vick to Gwends. 'Well done, girlie! I do *hate* macho men who think they can grab a woman by her cuspids, grunting, me Tarzan, you Jane, let's pick nits.'

'Vick!' Gwends said irritably. 'You're taking an awful lot of interest in Olivia Costwold.'

'God, Gwends! Is it PMT time or *what?* I'm only *looking!*'

Olivia headed for the carpeted foyer and cloakroom.

She almost got her eye knocked out by a long-lens camera. 'Miss Cotswold, is it true that Sir Harold, your father . . . ?'

'I know who my father is.'

'Right! He's just sold out Lamphouse to MacKenzie for seventeen and a half million dollars, hasn't he?' Someone tried to stuff a micro-recorder in her mouth. 'That's about twelve million pounds, isn't it?'

'No comment!'

'Your shareholders will want to know the truth. Market share indexes . . .'

'Indices. Lamphouse is not a public company; the only shareholders are my father and I. I already know the market share index – turkeys are selling at a dollar to the pound,' Olivia pushed open the cloakroom door, wanting to get her coat, wanting to get away fast when Faye Rutland, with a glazed look in her eye, came from the opposite direction.

'*Pardone* . . . !' Faye wobbled on her galvanised bucket heels, long red talons splayed out for balance. She found the wall behind her, steadied herself, '*W*hy am I apologizing to 'Arry's daughter!'

'Excuse me, we haven't been properly introduced, have we, Miss – er . . . ?' Olivia extended her hand into the flushed face of London's latest literary brain.

'Rutland!' she snapped, losing her sexy drawl and reverting to her native Brooklyn roots. 'Faye Rut-

41

land, Mizz Cotswold! Lamphouse rejected my best-selling book, but I could give you one now . . .'

'I'm sure you could, Miss Rutland . . .' The cameras and recorders came hovering shoulder-high. Olivia did a little circle and backed Miss Rutland inside the ladies' loo again, away from prying eyes and micro-recorders, 'A shame you can't give them away – the books, I mean. Excuse me, I want my coat . . .' She handed over her cloakroom ticket to the attendant.

Faye Rutland continued to emulate Mitzi sprea-deagled on the centre-fold of destiny, only this time she had her clothes on, just about, 'Since Lamppost could not afford the asking price, that is rich coming from you, Mizz Cotswold! *Pardone!* Did I say Lamp-post? Such a confusing name; I'm reminded of what little my little doggy does to lampposts. Do forgive me!'

Olivia smiled; the smile became a grin. She shrugged herself into her coat, '*Touché*, Faye! Sorry I turned you down, but you're right, Lamphouse *can't* afford you. You'll be much better off with MacKenzie.'

Olivia felt that all she could do now was bow out gracefully. No good being churlish over a stupid book. If MacKenzie didn't mind paying mega-bucks for bottom of the slush pile, that was up to them. Faye Rutland's book might hit the general reading public on publicity hype, but there were always those who treasured their library lending cards. It was all down to free market forces and choices.

To her surprise Faye Rutland grabbed her hand and shook it with enthusiasm. 'Let us be friends instead of sworn enemies, Olivia. This silly writing

lark is too much like hard work for peanuts. Mac-
Kenzie approached *my* agent for *my* 'story'; we didn't
approach them. If they want to make money on *my*
name, it's no skin off *my* nose! Call me some time – I
believe Lamphouse is now an imprint of MacKenzie
publishing.'

The leaks in the plumbing system of publishing
appeared to be everywhere, no doubt from the Mac-
Kenzie crowd themselves. Olivia said, 'Not yet,
Faye. Nothing has been signed and sealed as yet.'

'We can have lunch together and talk about such a
silly business, Olivia. I don't understand it, and don't
want to, either.'

You and me both, Faye – but Olivia kept her
thoughts to herself. 'Thanks,' she said, without
any desire to offer free editorial advice to Faye
Rutland, who moved off then, riding the waves of
intruding cameras and micro-recorders hovering
outside the ladies' cloakroom, straight back to the
lighthouse on her horizon. No doubt Stuart Mac-
Kenzie had offered her a free ride home in his
chauffeur-driven limo. Olivia felt that her 'hard to
get' plan had worked a little too well. He hadn't even
bothered to walk across the floor to deliver his own
cryptic little messages to her, the coward!

'Taxi, Miss Olivia?' asked Quotes doorman from
the Dankers school of portering.

'No, I'll get the Tube, thanks.' Olivia stepped out
into the dreary October night, wondering to herself
why anyone thought publishing was a glamorous
business.

CHAPTER 3

Inside the warm, steamy atmosphere of Quotes, Faye flung her mock baby-seal stole at Stuart. 'Cotswold's daughter is one helluva screwed-up little bitch!'

'Because she's got more sense than to sign you up for a million?' He draped the stole over her bare shoulders.

'Why are you being such a butt-end to me, Stuwey? I've done you a favour, or should I say *favours*?' she pouted, and he relented. None of this was her fault; she was just too stupid to realize she was being exploited.

'Sorry, honey, it's late and I'm tired.' He wondered if he could catch up with Olivia Cotswold.

'Let's go, my place, Stuwey. I'm fed up signing my name for nothing.'

'A million dollars' worth of nothing,' he drawled.

Faye examined him through narrowed green eyes: six-two, eyes of blue, in his pin-stripe charcoal-grey suit and shot-silk racing-green shirt that complemented rather than clashed with his eyes, Paisley waistcoat and trendy tie to match, he put the rest of the male population in their tuxedos to shame. Tall, dark and handsome, rich beyond a woman's wildest dreams, he was fully aware of his impact on the female gender. Stuart MacKenzie was a man to enjoy – in bed, preferably.

'Look, sweetie, you told me this was going to be a party! So where's the music, dancing and undead? All I've been lumbered with is a load of *rigor mortis* addicts talking about a hundred and one ways to embalm themselves. This isn't my scene, Stuwey – not when I've got a *real* party to go to with the Rolling Stones. You publishing lot are a real pain in the tush! Just write me my share of the profits; my agent'll tell you where to send the cheque.'

Even that kind of put-down was not as cutting as Olivia Cotswold's turning her beautiful back on him when he had raised his champagne glass to her – now *there* was a classy lady who was *truly* worth chasing a million miles! Quietly keeping her own counsel, dignified and enigmatic, her haughty aloofness from the noisy rabble around her, and her apparent obsession with cocktail sticks, had fascinated him. *She* had no need to stoop to conquer; she had already done that. Without a word spoken except in the mirror of their mutual thoughts, he knew he already worshipped her.

Stuart smiled his handsome lazy smile and said to Miss Rutland, 'Honey, we have the option on your next sex revelation, so when can we expect the first draft?'

'I'll let you know, sweetie.' She took his thrusting sun-tanned chin in her red-nailed clutches. 'I'm promoting more exciting things right now, Stuwey. I got other sponsors besides you, so let's discuss any further advances at my place, huh?' She kissed his beautiful lips.

He responded with lukewarm grace, 'Some other time . . .' adding a condescending tap on the rump. 'Buzz off, Faye, I'll get your ghost-writer to sign for you. She at least can spell – sort of. We'll let you know when you've earned out your advance.'

'You publishing guys are all the same: all you talk about is books,' she said, not taking offence. She liked a man who held doors open for a women. Trouble was, that was about all she ever did get from him. 'Get a life, Stuwey, before it's too late.' Faye couldn't get out of Quotes fast enough.

'Bye-bye, blackbird,' Stuart said in her wake. He went in search of Legrand. 'Have you had long enough to think about my offer, Vinny?'

'Yes.'

'Is that a yes of acceptance?'

'Yes.'

He smiled, and gave her two smacking kisses, one on each of her classic cheekbones. 'Thanks, Vinny, you're a great gal. Bye, honey, must go, see you on Monday . . .' Then he turned back and nonplussed her completely by asking, 'What's your friend's taste in flowers?'

'My friend?' Davina looked fazed.

'Harry's daughter.'

'Olly . . . oh, no! Don't do it, Stu! She's still in mourning for Lamphouse. Let her come to terms first with her paternal crisis. Olly's suffering from

WPS – Wounded Pride Syndrome. Not much fun, I suppose, to find you aren't an heiress after all . . . OK, OK! I can tell by that gritty look in your steely eye that you wish to be spared the details . . .' She picked off a long blonde strand of hair from his smart lapel. 'If you really want to restore man's millionaire image in the eyes of poverty-stricken woman, Olly adores red and white chrysanths.'

'Where do I deliver?'

'Paternoster Row.'

'Private address, Vinny!'

'Classified.'

He sighed. 'I *want* to send her some flowers.'

'How sweet!'

'Without the whole office gawping and miscon-struing things,' he added, painfully aware that Davina was laughing at him. He wished now that he hadn't asked her for Olivia Cotswold's address. He had thought Vinny and she were close friends; obviously he was wrong.

'Whose office, yours or Lamphouse's?' Vinny asked innocently.

'Does it matter?'

'Why didn't you ask her yourself tonight? She was right here.'

'I did.'

'On the back of a calling card? She isn't that gruesome face-to-face.'

'I wanted to, but couldn't get away from my team, or Rutland. Besides, Olivia had a distinct touch-me-not look, so I guess I was just . . .'

'Chicken?'

47

'Wary of putting a foot wrong.'

Davina almost laughed in his face. 'Poor Stuwey! I must tell Olly she'll have to be nicer to millionaires, otherwise she'll end up as the world's oldest bouquet-catcher.'

'Don't do this to me, Vinny!' he said sternly.

'Mind you, she *can* be pretty intimidating when someone's put her back up. I remember once how she whacked my ankle with her hockey stick when she thought . . .'

'You're not going to give it to me, then?'

'Depends what you mean by that remark,' she said through the smokescreen of her cigarette, her languid smile mocking.

'Sorry I asked.' He started to move off towards the exit, looking quite downcast.

Vinny Legrand relented for the sake of her new job and raised salary from the MacKenzie Corporation, USA & Canada, soon to launch themselves into the UK. 'Far be it from me to divulge classified information and the secret haunts of my old school chum, Olly's a very private person. Having been thought of as a traitor once tonight, I don't fancy Olly's cold shoulder a second time around, so ask the club registrar, or get old Jarvis to look it up in the membership book – he's a dab hand at lucrative bribes.'

'Thanks! You're a pal.'

Davina groaned. 'Why am I doing this for her when she hates me?' He gave her another hasty goodnight kiss before going in search of the club membership book.

'Oh, no, sir!' said the all-night flower-lady on the

corner of Shaftesbury Avenue and Charing Cross Road. 'Chrysanths is funeral flowers, you don't want none of them to send to a lady! And never no red and white together. Bad luck is red and white together, them are funeral colours. I got some real fresh mauve and white orchids, sir, right orf the Jumbo this minute from 'eathrow, all the way from Bangkok.'

'Perfect!' he said with a big smile.

Olivia woke up early on Sunday morning. Despite the hangover she was determined to get to the launderette before the machines were all hogged. She took two aspirin with her coffee, did her laundry and then her weekly shopping at the all-day, every day corner store. By ten o'clock she was all done on the domestic front and decided to catch an early tube to St John's Wood where her Ma had roast lamb and mint sauce on the menu.

'You're very early this morning, darling. I've only just sent your father packing in his plus fours along with Charlie Longbridge and Lord Epson of the Clandenberry ilk. Need I say to where? Not that I'm complaining about your early arrival, I'm glad of the company. Be a good girl, darling, and go and pluck some fresh mint from my herb garden – if there's any left after Muffin has been at it.'

Muffin was Maggie's precious pooch, a Yorkshire terrier who devoured everything in his path, including unwanted human beings. The dog was as zany as her darling mother. After Olivia had picked the fresh mint for mint sauce, she tried out her vision for the future on Maggie, the recipe for a publishing coup

49

that had come to her like a bolt out of the blue while under the influence of juniper berries and Stuart MacKenzie's sexy eyes.

'Absolutely brilliant, darling, but hasn't it all been done before?' asked Maggie who, being a grass widow, read a great deal of everything, including, *Learn to Play Golf*, a Lamphouse publication by Harold P. Cotswold, while contemplating a sequel to it: *And Beat Him At His Own Game* by His Wife. 'Best talk to your father about it,' Maggie added. 'He's the brains behind the business.'

Olivia did, when he eventually arrived home at two o'clock in the afternoon and the lamb had congealed to lanolin and her mother had wailed, 'Dearest, do take off your muddy shoes first! You're late, Harold, and don't tell me you and your team-mates haven't been propping up the club bar with your shaggy dog stories. You might have given us waiting women more consideration, Olivia's been here since ten-thirty.'

'Why, isn't she feeling well?'

'Not amusing, Harry! That is precisely the kind of attitude you have displayed over the years to antagonize the both of us, as if we didn't matter one whit . . .'

Olivia whispered, 'Shush, Ma, don't put him in a bad mood now. Just give him a glass of wine while I dish out.'

'Not likely,' said her mother. 'After the whisky he's imbibed, all he'll get from me is an Alka-Seltzer. Harold . . .' she took off her pinny '. . . Olivia has something to say to you regarding the saving of Lamphouse.'

Olivia wished her mother had not precipitated her

quite so fast into her visionary package-deal concerning Lamphouse. Afterwards her father said, 'Splendid idea, Olivia, a very plausible one too. MacKenzie will be very impressed with you.'

'MacKenzie? I though this was for us – Lamphouse?'

'Lamphouse as in imprint of MacKenzie, you mean?'

'You're still determined to go over to them, then, despite my good ideas concerning a new image for Lamphouse, which I know will work?'

'Not a question of "going over to them". We have no other option. If you decide to launch an entire new "2000" range of women's fiction incorporated in a brand new package deal, which means an astute marketing strategy, then you'll need the wherewithal to develop your ideas.'

'I'm sure the banks will listen to us far more sympathetically with our new proposal, Pa.'

'Too late, I've already pledged myself to the MacKenzie deal. I'm sure that Stuart will listen, applaud and fund you over and above the seventeen and a half million already on offer as soon as Lamphouse becomes an imprint of theirs.'

So! The great mogul, her father, had made up his mind and nothing would deter him, not even her last-minute salvage operations concerning a whole new concept of Lamphouse books and readers. Her Pa was bent on taking his money and running, or rather yachting, to the South of France. Olivia noticed that her normally garrulous mother had little to say on the subject either.

Sunday lunch with the parents had its usual non-productive outcome, both of them wrapped up in themselves, Ma with her chutneys and jams for the WI, Pa with his eagerness to retire and play golf and sail for the rest of his life. Olivia returned to Fulham.

She found a note from Amanda, scribbled on the back of an old Chinese takeaway menu. '*A gorgeous chap in an even more gorgeous car called while you were out, and left these gorgeous orchids for you. Said he had been trying to ring you all week. What have you been up to, you naughty girl?*'

So why didn't you get in touch with me last night, Stuwey, personally speaking, that is? Olivia thought with a sly little smile. She opened the cellophane-wrapped flowers and his third calling card dropped out. '*Sorry about last night, but business got in the way. How about dinner some time, so that I can explain?*'

'Explain what, Stuwey?' she said to herself with a big smile. 'You've just said it all, haven't you?'

In the absence of a vase – she had hardly any call for one; it was a long time since anyone had given her flowers – she placed the orchids in a jam-jar on her sitting-room windowsill.

Olivia was at her desk in Paternoster Row by eight-thirty the following morning. Birdie did not arrive until ten to nine. She came into Olivia's office still with her coat on, bearing a long, narrow, presti-giously wrapped and labelled box of flowers. 'Olivia, Stuart MacKenzie's chauffeur just left these with Mr Dankford at the front desk – they're for you.'

'Keep them, Birdie. Orchids give me asthma.'

'You sound as if you already know what I'm talking about.'

'I do. Yesterday.'

'From Harrods?'

'From a flower-seller in Shaftesbury Avenue.'

'It was a good raunchy-launch, then, Saturday evening?'

'Horrendous. I wish I'd been as sensible as you and stayed away.'

'Want some coffee?'

'Love some.'

Birdie took the orchids away and brought the coffee. At nine-thirty her father arrived in his chauffeur-driven Daimler Sovereign, and the morning got under way.

First there was a gathering of Lamphouse's board members in the dark oak-panelled boardroom with curtains and tassels and Cotswold predecessors as replicated in Sir Harold's own office. He dropped his bombshell to sell out to MacKenzie, which was not totally unexpected, then he made Olivia take the chair.

She stood up and said to Lamphouse's senior staff, 'Pa has just told you all about the MacKenzie bid for Lamphouse, which he has decided to take, and of his retirement. I have been offered a place on the MacKenzie board of directors. I have decided to take up the offer. I can't promise anything at this point in time, but I want you all to know one thing for certain: I *will* fight for Lamphouse's *complete* survival. We *will* keep our name, we *will* keep our separate identity, we *will* keep our own staff, we *will* keep to our motto of "Truth, Fidelity, Honour", and we will *not accept* any staff redundancies unless they are made voluntarily. That's all I can tell you, pending a further meeting with MacKenzie's directors. You can count on me every step of the way through this changeover period, as I will need to count on you. I need your support, confidence, trust and faith during what might prove to be a difficult transition period. I promise to do my best to smooth out the bumps along the way and not let any of you down. I will do my utmost to keep Lamphouse alive and kicking into the twenty-first century, you have my word on it.' She sat down.

'Dib-dib-dib!' Davina Legrand started to clap in a very put-down sort of way.

'Get lost, Vinny!'

Davina said for the benefit of no one, since she too was deserting a sinking ship, 'A speech from the heart, Olivia. But you already know where I stand in the spirit of things yet to come. All I can say is, good luck *this* side of the pond.'

'Thank you, Vinny.' Olivia said with dignity. 'I had wished for your support in all this, but failing that, I too wish you luck in your new high-profile director's chair under the MacKenzie banner, New York.'

'Toronto, actually.'

'Wherever. I'm sure Stuart MacKenzie will appreciate your undisputed talents in recognizing a good deal the moment you spot it.'

They smiled, the panther and the tigress, respecting each other's latent power behind the female executive smiles.

At one o'clock Olivia found herself back with her father and Davina Legrand at Quotes.

A more subdued atmosphere prevailed this Monday lunchtime, as opposed to Saturday night's glitzy launching of the Catwalk Queen-turned-Actress-turned-Best-selling-Novelist.

Jarvis approached them in his stealthy, informed manner. 'Sir Harold, Mr MacKenzie and his guests have not yet arrived. Would you care for a drink at the bar first, sir? Or shall I instruct the *maître d'* to escort you to your table forthwith?'

'Drinks at my usual table, Jarvis.'

'Very good, Sir Harold. May I take your overcoat?'

Olivia headed for the powder room while her father and Jarvis sorted them all out.

She looked at her reflection in the mirror and saw that her mascara had smudged; not surprising after her emotional speech as the newly appointed MD of Lamphouse – one gigantic leap from humble junior editor to Lamphouse's senior member all in one short weekend. No wonder she was shaking like a leaf, her face now looking like a panda's.

She renewed her lip-liner and filled in with lipstick. Legrand never wore make-up – didn't need it: Vinny was so gorgeous to start with, make-up would only detract from her Leighton's *Hesperidean* image. No wonder Stuart MacKenzie had offered her a place on his board – in his bed too, no doubt! Olivia examined herself critically in the full-length mirror. The white lacy collar of her blouse looked decidedly jaundiced under the fluorescent lighting; it was also a bit off-centre. She adjusted it to a centimetre of perfection so that it sat nicely over the lapels of her black jacket, a little shiny through wear and tear and hot brown paper pressings with the iron – something she had picked up from Ernest, her father's chauffeur. Ernest's 'mam' still pressed his chauffeur's uniform under brown paper, and perfect it always looked too.

However, *her* outfit was a bit past its sell-by date simply because she had never, to that extent, cared about her outward appearance before her sudden and swift promotion to the higher ranks of publishing. So nepotism did work, after all! She now had to think of a new 'Olivia Image' – *if* she was to become Lamphouse's high-powered MD. Shiny suits just would not do. She ran the brush over her hair one last time, then, with butterflies in her stomach, went boldly out to meet the enemy.

This time it was not Faye Rutland she almost knocked flying, but Stuart MacKenzie's briefcase. He and his party were standing in the foyer close by the cloakroom door.

A stupid place to put a Ladies' Room, off the main foyer! *Why* couldn't it be downstairs where the men's loo was? Olivia, wildly embarrassed, felt she ought to mention to Quotes' management that some women liked their privacy. 'Sorry . . . !'

He turned round and smiled, his hand extended in a chummy greeting. 'Olivia, isn't it? Olivia Cotswold. Hi, great to meet you at last.'

'Hi . . .' Her voice seemed like a silly squeak in her head.

Of course he knew who she was. Hadn't he sent Jarvis over to her with two cryptic little messages on his business card – '*Penny for them?*' and '*Nice back!*'? And what about all the orchids, enough to pollinate the entire insect kingdom of London? 'I don't believe we've been introduced, Mr . . . er?'

'MacKenzie – Stuart.'

'Oh, yes, of *course*! How silly of me not to realize.'

He did the rounds. 'Genesis March, MacKenzie's foreign rights director, New York, and Jeremy Webber, sales director. Can I get you a drink, Olivia?' A dark eyebrow formed a perfect question mark, 'Gin and tonic, lemon and ice?'

So, he *had* been observing her every move last Saturday evening, very carefully, it appeared! 'Just tonic water with lemon and ice, Mr MacKenzie. My father, however, has already ordered it – he's been waiting for you since one o'clock.'

At thirteen minutes past, her pointed remark hit bang on target. He seemed a little flustered all of a sudden. 'Gee, I'm sorry we're late . . . the traffic was heavy . . . um . . . coats!' He looked to his own people and while they sorted themselves out with Jarvis in attendance, Olivia took her seat at her father's table.

The club had two dining rooms for club members, one for smokers and one for non-smokers. Sir Harold's table was in the smokers' room. Three feet away from the white damask tablecloth and Quotes cobalt-blue slipcloth matching their napkins, he sat comfortably at ease, flipping through the MacKenzie contract while smoking a fat cigar and drinking his pre-lunch whisky.

Davina also smoked, elbows on the table, a large gin and tonic in front of her, cigarettes and fancy lighter beside her. 'Why are you smiling like that, Olivia?'

'Like what?' Olivia studied the menu.

'A cat at the cream.'

'Oh, no reason . . . Pa, I think I'll have Quotes' avocado special as a starter, followed by pork stroganoff, jacket potato and selection of steamed vegetables.'

'You *look* as if you haven't eaten for a week,' was his wry reply, reaching out for his whisky glass without taking his eyes off the printed word on his lap.

'As a matter of fact I eat very well, Pa. Yesterday I lunched with you and Ma, *if* you recall. I told you about my salvage operation concerning Lamphouse, but you blocked your ears, remember?'

'What salvage operation?' Vinny asked.

'Too late, dear friend,' Olivia said, and it was just as well Stuart MacKenzie and his team appeared at that moment. Her father stood up to shake hands with the MacKenzie crowd, a hundred and twenty pages of their contract hastily shoved out of sight under his chair.

Greetings were affable, the mood around the table over-enthusiastic, each trying to impress the other. Canadian, American and Brit conversations slipped past Olivia for the better part of lunch. She felt like an ostrich walking on thin ice, a label round its neck: '*I do the splits, too.*'

The wine-waiter kept up a constant to-ing and fro-ing between their table and the club's cellars. Stuart MacKenzie reminded her of her father in the way he ruled the roost. Olivia put her hand over her wine glass; she was staying teetotal throughout this particular meal. The meal itself did not require analysis, but Olivia concentrated on every morsel on her plate. Stuart, who sat between Legrand and herself, whispered in her ear, ever so smoothly, 'Did you get the flowers?'

'Oh, yes, thank you. But I'm allergic to orchids so Birdie Gough took them off my hands – from under my sniffly nose, I should say.'

'Birdie Gough?'

'Pa's PS.'

'Sorry?' He seemed to have difficulty understanding her.

'Pa's Personal Secretary, or Personal Assistant if you wish me to be politically correct.'

'Oh, right!'

'Birdie's been with us forever. She's a bit old-fashioned. Naturally, she'll be staying with us forever – poor old thing is counting on it. She's most loyal. All Lamphouse's staff are, apart from one mercenary exception,' Olivia could not see Davina's face because Stuart MacKenzie was in the way.

'You prefer red and white chrysanthemums, then?' he parried, the whisper of his smooth words reflected in his speedwell-blue eyes.

'Red and white . . . ?' Olivia choked a little on her glass of tonic-water, the bubbles tickling the back of her throat. She put down the glass and searched for a handkerchief in her bag, which was hanging by its strap on the back of her chair. Legrand was too busy chatting to the Jeremy chap on the other side of her, otherwise Olivia felt she might have grabbed her by the scruff of the neck and plunged her face down into her crabcake entrée. She collected herself and said to Stuart MacKenzie, 'Red and white flowers together are bad luck, Mr MacKenzie.'

'I had no idea until the flower-person on Shaftesbury Corner told me. Only Vinny said . . .'

'I shouldn't believe anything she tells you, Mr MacKenzie. Vinny always won first prize at school for creative writing.'

'Is that right?' He seemed very genuine, a little crestfallen too.

Olivia wished now that she hadn't been so hasty or so rude about his orchids. 'That's why she's such a good in-house editor. She has the "feel" for books and an author's viewpoints. You're lucky to have head-hunted her so successfully. Lamphouse trains its staff and its authors to a very high standard. And while it can't afford massive advances on the Faye Rutland scale, we do appreciate our authors and staff by remaining loyal to *them* by providing them with a worker-friendly environment, no harassment, and, most important of all, job security. Vinny has obviously mistaken expediency for security and deserves a lot more than the salary you are offering her.'

'You think so?'

'Absolutely. She ought to be getting at least sixty thousand dollars a year.'

His turn to splutter over his wineglass. He mopped

his handsome chin with a Quotes napkin to match his eyes before slipping in another smooth question. 'How about dinner tonight, Olivia?'

'What?'

'Dinner, Olivia, just you and me. We can discuss Vinny's salary in private, as well as everything else.'

Olivia kept as cool as he was. 'I know my father has arranged this luncheon so that we can all get to know each other a lot better, prior to the crucial signatures being added to paper. However, I feel that the place to discuss matters of salaries and takeover bids, Mr MacKenzie, is around a boardroom table. Working breakfasts, lunches and dinners only cloud the essential issues of corporate management.'

'Not always.' He let his piercing blue eyes linger on her in a most disconcerting manner. First her face, searching her thoughts, before travelling downwards to where her lace collar stopped dead against her breastbone, searching out what else she had on offer.

Olivia cleared her throat and concentrated on the next course.

'Don't you ever answer your telephone? Or are you always out?' he asked in another calculated move over the banoffee pie and cream; Olivia had ordered it and he had chosen the same as she. Never having had such a dessert before, he wanted to test her tastes.

'Uh huh!' she said.

'No one gives anything away in England, do they?' he added.

'They can't afford to, Mr MacKenzie. We all have to meet our deadlines and pay our poll tax.'

'I was referring to the secrecy surrounding classified information.'

'Such as?'

'You private address and telephone number – no one would tell me, not even your Pa's PS when I begged her.'

'Birdie's like a second mother to me. Very protective. So how did you find out?'

'That's classified.'

'I think I can guess!' Once more she glared at Legrand, who seemed not to notice.

'I was hoping to catch you up on Saturday night with the Shaftesbury orchids.'

'So what stopped you?'

'You had already disappeared in a taxi.'

'Call me Cinderella.' She realized she was being awfully facetious, but she couldn't help it. He assumed too much, for a start, just like her Pa.

'And then I changed my mind about following you home in case you had a landlady who might have objected to male visitors calling at an inappropriate time.'

A man who held principles about compromising a woman's reputation couldn't be half bad; he went up a notch in her estimation. Olivia said, 'No landlady, only an absentee landlord, Mr MacKenzie. But you were right to be cautious. I'd have given you short shrift after the supercilious way you behaved. To jot down rude remarks on the back of a business card was . . . was cheap!'

'*Cheap*?' He had difficulty in taking on board that remark concerning himself.

'Yes. Very vulgar.'

'Gee whizz! I had no idea I was being that obnoxious – a bit of fun perhaps in a very boring situation. Please forgive me. Nor did I mean to be supercilious. Frustrated, yes! I couldn't get away from Rutland or my sales people to come over and make your very charming acquaintance there and then, but . . .'

'Don't patronize me, either, Mr MacKenzie.'

'Sorree!' He gave her a steady look. 'You yourself were being very stand-offish, you know. There was nothing to stop you from introducing yourself to us MacKenzies – in fact, I asked Vinny to fetch you over to us, but she told me you declined to be introduced to anyone. I realize you must be feeling sore about Lamphouse, but . . .'

'Not sore, Mr MacKenzie, sad.'

'I appreciate that, but you don't have to be sad – nothing is going to change as far as Lamphouse is concerned. The company will just be financially better off, that's all. You know, I called round at your place yesterday morning to try and get you to have a coffee with me before any kind of business meeting. Too late – I was again unlucky. You really are a most elusive person, Miss Cotswold – Olivia?' A dark eyebrow quirked interrogatively.

He was fishing! He wanted to know about her private life, if she had a particular boyfriend. No competition, Mr MacKenzie, she wanted to tell him, but kept him guessing. 'Uh-huh!' she said.

'Your room mate told me you were at the launderette, and after that you were going to lunch with your parents. No point in hanging around, so I left the flowers for you, hoping you'd say yes to dinner this evening. Please say yes, so that I can apologize for my supercilious, rude, vulgar and cheap behaviour – uh – Cinderella?' Deep blue eyes crinkled at the corners.

He spoke with a hint of Scottish accent through his Canadian drawl. He was certainly charismatic, not to mention persistent.

'I hope the Shaftesbury Avenue flowers were still OK by the time you received them?'

'They were fine, Mr MacKenzie. Both lots.'

'Great! What a relief! The old lady selling them assured me each individual bloom came straight from Thailand with its own little plastic pot of water to keep it fresh on the jumbo.'

'How very fascinating,' Olivia murmured, stabbing her dessert fork into her banoffee pie.

'I'm glad she was honest. I hoped to catch up with you later the next day – like I just explained. And then you weren't there. I suppose I could have left them on your doorstep Saturday night, after the party, but I changed my mind about calling so late, as I've already explained. I hate to waste any-thing marginally salvageable – I have this thing about waste, you see, Olivia. On the other hand, I'd have hated you to receive stale flowers.'

Definitely a man of Scottish ancestry! were Oli-via's thoughts. A millionaire publisher who didn't like to waste orchids but could waste an entire mealtime explaining why not when there were far more serious subjects of wastage to discuss, like staff redundancies and bankrupt companies, was something totally outside her experience. She paid him greater attention. 'How very kind of you, Mr Mac-Kenzie, to go to so much trouble on my behalf. No question, of course, about Harrods orchids being super-fresh and in pristine condition, even without their little plastic flowerpots.'

'My pleasure. Will you have dinner with me this evening, Olivia?'

'I don't think so.'

'Have you a good reason not to?'

'Yes.'

'Is it classified?'

She smiled. 'No, not really. I just don't think I could eat another meal so soon on top of this one. It would only be a waste of good money for a dinner not even marginally salvageable, even in a doggy bag. Such wastage would remain for ever on my conscience. After all, you must – or soon will be – relatively broke after seventeen and a half million dollars spent on a non-profit-making investment like Lamphouse, so I fully appreciate how careful you have to be now, when buying orchids, Mr Mac-Kenzie.'

'OK, we'll have a sandwich and a glass of water each,' he said, thereby splintering the tone of their point-scoring.

And about time too, thought Olivia. She wanted to laugh. He was quite nice really. But she still refused to get sidetracked by him, by his good looks and his very subtle sense of humour. She liked a man with a sense of humour.

Stuart MacKenzie, however, was no ordinary man,

she warned herself. He was a vulture with millions of dollars to spend on orchids and bankrupt companies and insignificant little women like her. And after he had finished with stale orchids and company people and insignificant little women like her, he would put his 'has beens' into his multi-million-dollar waste-disposal unit before moving on to his next big deal and touching little fairy-story of a wilting beanstalk and a giant who told a whopping great watering-can of a lie!

He drew her back with a charming smile right in her face. Shielding them with his hand, elbow propped on the table in a little sideways tête-à-tête with her, he left the rest of his company to do their own little bit of wheeling and dealing with Sir Harold. 'What attracted me most about you last Saturday night was your total composure while everyone else behaved like Triffids.'

'Triffids?'

'Plant mutations with roots and arms all over the place.'

'Really?'

'Yes, really. Thanks to the mirror, I gazed not only upon your charming back, but your beautiful expressive face telling me all.'

'All?'

'Oh, yes! It told me here was a lady I'd really like to get to know better – much better.'

'And there I was thinking you were more interested in Rutland's silicone implan⁺s.'

'Faye Rutland didn't even figure in my thoughts.'

'Funny, because I thought the figure was a one

million advance for sheer tripe,' she once more challenged him, since he was intent upon playing word-games with *her*.

'I don't acquire books or authors – that's Miss March and the editors' territory. I only write the cheques *after* the acquisition panel do the dirty on me. They know what sells best; I'm just the bank manager.'

He went up another notch. 'So what else did my thoughts tell you behind my back?'

' "I am Olivia Cotswold and I am my own person and I hate your guts, Mr MacKenzie" – am I not right?'

'Close, but not quite right, Mr MacKenzie.'

'What then, Olivia?'

'I am Olivia Penelope Cotswold – the Penelope bit is very important, you see, as the founding mother of Lamphouse was called Penelope. And I *am* my own person and I hate your seventeen and a half million dollars, Mr MacKenzie, because you think you can buy not only my father, but me too. That's what crossed my mind on Saturday evening.'

'Can I?'

'Can you what?'

'Buy *you* for seventeen and a half million dollars?'

'That depends.'

'On what?'

'Conditions, Mr MacKenzie.'

'Name them.'

'Lamphouse will keep its name ˄nd separate identity from MacKenzie – an imprint only of the major house, and one with full autonomy under my control.'

'Absolutely!'

'There will be no compulsory staff redundancies.'

'None whatsoever!'

'Lamphouse will abide by its motto, "Truth, Fidelity, Honour", meaning that we will not compromise our principles for the sake of a quick and sleazy buck.'

'Absolutely!'

'These addenda to the contract you and my father have drawn up between you must be in writing, signed, sealed and witnessed in the presence of our solicitors – attorneys to you.'

'On three conditions of my own, Miss Cotswold.'

'I'm listening.'

'That Lamphouse has to show a profit after three years' trading figures, exclusive of MacKenzie's financial back-up in those first three years; that you call me Stuart; and that after three years, if I still like you, you'll marry me.'

Olivia took a deep breath. She knew he was not flirting with her any more, but was suddenly deadly serious, the businessman of boardroom seduction now. 'Are you usually a man who arrives at such fast decisions, Mr MacKenzie?'

'Not usually. It usually takes me forty-eight hours to reach a decision. Precisely . . .' he turned back his smart white cuff displaying gold cuff-links of very good taste, and looked at his Rolex watch '. . . five hours from now, I'll have had forty-eight hours to reach a final decision counting back to Saturday night when first I saw your delicious back. I'll pick you up at your place, eight o'clock.'

He certainly was a fast and *very* smooth talker! No wonder her father had fallen under his spell and capitulated!

Still reeling from the rapidity of Stuart Mac-Kenzie's take-over tactics, while telling herself not to lose sight of the main object, the survival of Lamphouse into the new millennium, Olivia spent the rest of the afternoon back at the office in a complete and utter trance before last-minute panic set in, ten minutes before the shops shut. 'Birdie,' she said breathlessly, 'I've got to go. Tell Pa . . .'

'Aren't you feeling well, dear?' Birdie asked sympathetically. 'I thought you were going to stay late tonight to catch up on things.'

'I am catching up . . . I haven't a thing to wear,' Olivia retorted, hoping she wasn't too late for the shops.

CHAPTER 4

Olivia didn't know where she was going to put any more food; she was still full from lunch.

She managed to find a delectable dress at a boutique which didn't close until nine. Midnight-blue, of the softest velvet, with a complete back this time; only her shoulders were revealed, and her legs to mid-thigh. He'd seen her back; now it was time for the rest of her to be revealed, to advantage but with discretion, of course. She knew that her legs were in pretty good shape, especially in high heels. Without being too conceited about it, she'd often evoked admiring glances in that direction from male members of the firm, not to mention male members of the building fraternity when she was on her way to and from work! Yes, she was a liberated woman of the eighties, and no, she was not a feminist, though she considered herself equal with the opposite sex, and yes, she did like to be admired by a handsome man – what woman didn't?

The boutique assistant clasped her hands together in jubilation, giving emphasis to every other word. '*Per-fect*, Madam, *per-fect* on your *pet-ite* frame, yet such *long* legs!'

Eat your heart out, Vinny! Olivia rushed home with only an hour to spare before Stuart picked her up. She washed her hair under the shower because the water was tepid and insufficient for a bath, and she didn't have time for a bath anyway.

The Cotswold sapphire earrings her only jewellery apart from a gold watch, she had just enough time to redo her nails with pearly nail polish before she heard the front doorbell's strident summons sounding like a fire-alarm thoughout the house.

Just as well Amanda was still out on a shoot and not sleeping, otherwise she might have berated the caller for keeping his finger too long on the button! Olivia looked out of her front window, saw a black Ferrari drawn up at the kerb, and told herself to keep calm.

Grabbing her evening bag and coat, hoping her nails were dry and would not leave pearly pink everywhere, she ran downstairs on legs that felt like jelly and yanked open the front door. She greeted him calmly, though. 'Bang on time this time, Mr MacKenzie.' She closed the front door behind her.

His smile was warm and attractive smile – he really was gorgeous! Stuart handed her a bouquet of red roses interspersed with white gypsophila. 'Sorry about red and white together. I hope they don't give you asthma. They looked and smelled so good, they reminded me of you.'

She hoped she did not look as red in the face as his roses. Blushes were a thing she had not experienced since her schooldays.

'A real English rose – you look stunning, Olivia.'

Flattery like that sounded less soppy from him than it might from some other man. His eyes held an admiring gleam, yet he seemed almost shy now that they were alone together.

Stuart MacKenzie, the big boss, shy? Never!

'Thank you for the flowers, Stuart . . .' Oh-oh! She had slipped unconsciously into first-name familiarity with him – what the heck – he looked and smelled good too!

Olivia stepped into the Ferrari with her red and white bouquet, legs revealed to their full extent, feeling that this time she really *was* the Crown Princess, and what a pity Amanda wasn't home to see her with Mr Drop-dead Gorgeous. She buried her nose in the wonderfully scented roses (which must have cost him the earth), while his designer aftershave wafted around the interior of the Ferrari and mixed with her own expensive perfume, a duty-free perk she had splashed out on during her recent visit to Frankfurt.

She tried not to think about what Stuart Mac-Kenzie expected for dessert. Especially when he told her that he had booked a table at Maryanna's, *the* most expensive as well as exclusive nightclub in Mayfair, frequented by royalty and the *extremely* rich and famous.

Nothing wrong with being wooed by a tall, dark and handsome millionaire; she just wished his name hadn't been Stuart MacKenzie!

In the ultra-ultra candlelit ambience of Maryanna's, they drank champagne and danced on a tiny dance-floor and ate huge bowls of *moules marinière* because by now she had used up so much energy she was starving. And still the adrenalin kept flowing.

She learned from their desultory conversations, in between dancing in a very intimate sort of way, that he did indeed have Scottish ancestry. His mother and father were from Sutherland on the west coast of Scotland, but he and his older brother Geoff – pronounced Goff – were born in Toronto. His brother had died of leukaemia at the age of nineteen, and suddenly he had found himself in Geoff's shoes, the old man (MacKenzie senior) having made his pile by now through publishing newspapers. There was nothing much else to say about himself, so what about her?

'Nothing much, either,' she said, pearly-pink fingernails dabbling in a bowl of lemon-water before she tackled the next garlic-stuffed *moule*, the surest put-off for any further seduction scenes which might be on his mind. She was not used to such high-pressured buying techniques; her relationships had usually evolved with slow precision over a pub ploughman's.

'Ok,' he said, wiping his fingers on a lemon-scented hothouse towel, 'you're twenty-five, you're Sir Harold Cotswold's pride and joy, Lamphouse is your inheritance, you went to an exclusive girls' boarding school in Kent, then a Swiss finishing school, then joined Lamphouse as a junior in-house reader, working your way up the corporate ladder to . . . *where*, Olivia?'

'Maryanna's, obviously,' she replied. 'How do you know so much about me?'

'I don't. I'm waiting to find out a lot more.'

'Vinny Legrand, I bet! She gave you my address, didn't she?'

'Nope!' He could say it quite truthfully. Jarvis it was who had done the deed on his behalf by looking it up in the club membership register for an English fiver. 'Come on, Olivia, I'm not that much of an ogre, I promise. Tell me about you and Vinny.'

'We went to boarding school together, and after that she went on to read English Lit. and Classics at Somerville, while I bummed around as Pa's junior tea-maker until Birdie got an executive coffee-maker. That's all there is to know about me. Next question: am I going to be able to reach your high-quota targets as MacKenzie's most junior and inexperienced MD, that's what you're thinking, huh? Answer, would you like to listen to *my* proposals concerning Lamphouse's future – *if* I decided to take my father's place? And only because I *want* to and not because I'm pressured into it?'

'I'd be delighted – but not now.' He held her eyes with intent of purpose. 'I was actually thinking how lovely you look, how prickly-like-a-cactus you are, how well you dance and what a navvy's appetite you have considering how slim and trim you are.'

'I have a high metabolic rate.'

He grinned and reached for her garlic and lemon fingers, which he held too close to the candle flame over which his sexy chin hovered. 'I think I've made a good choice, Miss Cotswold. I think we will make a wonderful partnership. How about we forget the three-year contract and get married now?'

She withdrew her sticky fingers from his grasp and said, 'The choice is not yours to make, Stuart. If I decide to take my father's place as the rightful head of Lamphouse, the contract negotiated with your company is the marriage contract between two publishing houses. It does not include me in any capacity whatsoever, other than as the managing director of the New Lamphouse Cross, an imprint of the MacKenzie Publishing Corporation, USA and Canada.' She took a deep breath and added, 'I am not into seduction scenes of this nature, especially by a married man of thirty-four. I would like to go home now, please.'

He sat back in his Louis Quinze club chair and put his napkin down before leaning back with one elegant pin-striped leg crossed over the other to view her twice over, this time in genuine awe of her boardroom potential.

'Wow!' he said. 'I'm impressed! You certainly do your homework, too, courtesy of Legrand's *Who's Who*. I *knew* you were the right woman to head Lamphouse the moment I saw you last Saturday evening. The iron fist in the velvet glove; you have what it will take to pull Lamphouse out of its Slough of Despond to make it what it *should* be: a *success*, Olivia! Isn't that what this is all about? Vinny has – well, never mind what Vinny has to offer MacKenzie Publishing; she'd never give to Lamphouse what you can. May I just add a PS in self-defence?'

'Don't try and change the subject, Stuart. I don't really want to know any more about your personal reasons for wining, dining, implying and *lying* to me! Let's go, shall we?' Olivia stood up.

'Olivia, I *was* married, I'm not any more. My wife – my *ex*-wife – and I are divorced. It's all over between us; we have no contact and haven't had for five years.'

Olivia sat down again, not because of his self-justification rhetoric, but because she had just seen Faye Rutland in tight black leather leading her entourage across the thickly carpeted floor on her galvanized-bucket-heels, relying for support on the arm of a very famous pop-singer. 'Faye Rutland has just arrived,' Olivia muttered, keeping her head down.

'So what?' He leaned forward again and lifted her chin, forcing her to look at him. 'I'm very sincere about you. I told you, forty-eight hours is all I need to make up my mind about someone – in this particular instance *you*! You're absolutely right for Lamphouse . . .'

'Don't tell me that. I *am* Lamphouse!' she replied in a fierce whisper.

'Never in dispute! What I was trying to say was, you're absolutely right for Lamphouse and Mac-Kenzie. Give us both a chance, Olivia.'

'You're so sure of yourself, aren't you, Stuart MacKenzie?' she replied, reaching for her evening bag. 'So sure, and so conceited!'

'Yes, Olivia, and you should be too!' he said with a sudden edge to his voice. 'You have everything going for you. Just do yourself a favour and start liking yourself for a change. Get yourself some confidence, some conceit, a new friend, and we might be able to carry this thing through together.'

'What *thing*, Stuart?' she asked with icy hauteur.

'I thought you knew already,' he drawled, signing for the bill. 'You for Lamphouse, me for MacKenzie, seventeen and a half million dollars' worth of working partnership, ma'am!' He pocketed his gold-nib pen. 'That's what it's all about, Olivia.'

Olivia supposed she deserved the put-down. She herself had been so carried away by orchids, roses and millionaire blue-eyes, she had started reading much more than had been intended. What a dummy to think that Stuart MacKenzie wanted her for herself!

On the way back to Fulham they were stuck at red traffic-lights for ages. The Ferrari was going nowhere, and neither of them had spoken a word since leaving Maryanna's, when Stuart suddenly broke the silence. 'I didn't mean to appear conceited, Olivia. That is not how I want you to think of me. Neither am I rude, vulgar or supercilious, I promise.'

'So what about cheap?'

'Excuse me?'

'What went wrong?' she asked.

'Guess I was trying too hard to be Mr Nice Guy in your eyes.'

'You can't have it both ways, Mr Nice Guy,' Olivia said, smiling to herself in the powerful darkness of leather upholstery, his high-profile car only the symbol of his male ego given something else to think about. 'You're either rude, vulgar, supercilious and a perfect rotter, or you're not. What went wrong with your marriage is what I meant.'

'Everything.'

'Were there children involved?'

'Nope.'

She didn't know what else to say without seeming to be either a pryer into his private life, or a prude in hers.

'OK, I take on board your comments about me. I'm only as prickly as cactus when I feel threatened, and I don't need a shrink! Now that I know you a little better, I'll go along with your Mr Nice Guy image – for the moment. Thank you for a lovely evening, Stuart. For the roses and the pleasure of your company – you dance nicely too. I'm very grateful you've taken time out from your busy UK schedule to spend so much time on me.'

He gave her a sideways glance which she caught sight of in the driving mirror. 'Have you . . .' he seemed to have difficulty in clearing his throat '. . . a committed long-term relationship, and that's why you don't want to feel threatened by me?'

'Yes,' she replied.

'Ahh!' He nodded. 'These traffic lights stay red a long time. Still can't get used to driving shoulder to shoulder with everyone else on the wrong side of the road.'

'Don't Canadians drive on the left?'

'No, on the right, same as the US.'

'Funny, I'd have thought it would be on the left, same as us.'

'Why would you think that?'

'Canada is in the Commonwealth. Canadians *should* drive on the left out of loyalty to Mother England.'

'Right . . . see what you mean . . .' The lights changed and the ultimate in two-seater sports cars leapt away from Knightsbridge into the Brompton Road.

Outside her digs Olivia said, 'I was talking about Lamphouse, Stuart, my committed long-term relationship. If you meant, have I a steady boyfriend, then you should have said so. The answer happens to be no. We split up several months ago because he wanted what I didn't.' She paused awkwardly, his profile very rigidly defined under the interior light of his car. 'Well, umm . . . that's about it, really. Goodnight, thanks again for a wonderful evening.' She took her bouquet of red roses and left him out in the cold.

Afterwards she wished she hadn't. Afterwards she wished she had invited him in for a coffee or some hot chocolate or whatever else he had in mind for a nightcap.

The following morning Birdie said to her, 'You look awful.'

'I feel it.' Even a little peck on the cheek to say thank you might have softened her image a little in his eyes, were Olivia's melancholy thoughts. Principles, Olivia! she told herself, must not be compromised – at least until you are absolutely sure of him and his motives . . .

'A long night, then?' Birdie was bent on prying into *her* private life.

'Too short! Don't ask! It was rather nice and warm tucked into Prince Charming's breast pocket. He left me at home the moment the clock struck twelve and

Cinderella left behind her "Truth, Fidelity, Honour" principles on a Maryanna dance-floor.'

'No wonder you look so dreamy this morning. Nice gals don't touch the stuff.'

'Maryanna's nightclub, not marijuana! He thinks I'm like cactus, Birdie.'

'He's not wrong . . . did *I* say that about the boss's daughter? Never mind, dear, he sent you these . . . lovely, aren't they?' Birdie sniffed the hothouse gardenias. 'Stuart MacKenzie must have a standing order at Harrod's flower department, so he obviously likes cactus . . . cacti, cactuses . . .'

Olivia, still full of champagne and food from the day before, head in her hands, groaned with battle fatigue. 'Birdie, I don't suppose you've got any Alka-Seltzer in one of your drawers – filingly speaking?'

'Coming up, dear . . . *cactaceous* . . .' Birdie continued muttering to herself on the way out of Olivia's office. 'As if I should be so lucky as to warrant gardenias, with the birth sign of an old goat.'

'Take them home with you, Birdie, they've given me a headache!' Olivia yelled in Birdie's wake. If so much eating and drinking and flower-arranging was on the everyday agenda of a millionaire's customary lifestyle, Olivia decided to pass.

And so it continued for the next few weeks – manna from heaven! Stuart bombarded her with flowers, chocolates, phone calls day and night, at the office, to her flat, fax messages, dinner dates, lunch dates, until that final moment of capitulation when he asked her back to his Yuppie house for a home-cooked meal.

This she had to see for herself: the magical million-aire and publishing guru turned cook!

He sent the MacKenzie limo for her this time, which took her straight to his bachelor pad in the reclaimed Docklands area of London, given a whole new identity by the number of Ferraris, Porches, Jags and BMWs parked on 'individual unit' fore-courts.

The river view from his window was magnificent, the meal superb, *haute cuisine* to its finest degree, the flowers on the table and throughout his cosy but tastefully furnished rooms arranged by a person with an eye for colour, form and effect. The candles were white and the candle-holders genuine crystal so that they scintillated and radiated diamonds of light from earth as well as heaven. Olivia was very impressed, and she told him so on a lingering kiss. 'Beef strogon-off done to perfection, homemade pumpkin pie with apple and vanilla ice-cream, not to mention the oysters and champagne to start with. What are you doing to me, Mr MacKenzie, apart from changing my dimensions?' she wanted to know.

'Marry me?' He kissed the tip of her finger tracing a path down his cheek.

The most beautiful bubbles in the world were talking in her head while he slipped the hugest diamond she had ever seen on her finger. And then he lifted her in his arms, and carried her straight towards his bedroom and the black satin sheets on his executive bed. Just as he was about to close the bedroom door, she hiccoughed. 'Wait . . . I want a glass of water, Stuart . . .'

'I'll get it!' he said hastily, but too late she caught sight of a maid and butler who had come into the next room to clear away the remains of the day.

Olivia sobered up at once. 'You *cheat*, you *fraud*, you *liar*! Put me down at once!'

He dropped her on to his bed, but she leapt up again and started pounding him with his own pillow. 'You never cooked that fantastic meal, did you? Nor did you arrange the flowers or provide the decor or the ambience or the little pink pearly Lady Jane soaps in the bathroom, did you? Did you?'

'I can explain . . .' He ducked the flying feathers seeping out from the black satin pillowcase.

'I don't want any more of your explanations, Stuart MacKenzie!' She had backed him against the wall. 'You cheat! You've got a whole host of butlers, cooks and maids out there, haven't you – *haven't you*?'

'No . . .'

'Liar!'

'Just a housekeeper . . .'

'And a butler!'

'Well, yes, but only occasionally . . .'

Thump went the pillow against his bare chest because she had mistakenly started undoing his shirt buttons while caught up in the throes of a great passion. What luck that she had learned about him just in time! Seduction on the grandest scale ever, he had duped her into thinking he was as domesticated as the boy next door – well, she'd rather have the boy next door, not a rotten, cheating mega-liar millionaire publisher!

She told him so. 'You've got a thing about black, haven't you?'

'Sorry?'

'You ought to be! If you can lie to me about your cooking expertise, what else have you lied to me about, you . . . you cheap fraudster?'

He winced. 'Honey, listen . . .'

'Don't you "honey" me! I'm going home!' She tossed his diamond ring on to the bed. 'Black is a symbol of power for you, isn't it? Black Ferrari, black bed sheets, black dresses – mine! Black underwear – yours! I don't trust a man who wears black silk boxer shorts!'

'I sleep in them – they're comfortable . . .'

'I don't care what you sleep in! A wonder you didn't put your signature to a black-edged contract proclaiming the death of Lamphouse.'

She found her coat and shoes and her bag and on her way out poked her head into the kitchen and said to the plump housekeeper putting the plates into the dishwasher, 'You must let me have the recipe for your pumpkin pie some time. It was quite delicious.'

'Thank you dear, but Mr Stuart made it. He likes to potter around in the kitchen when he's home; it helps ease the stress of his job, he says. Mr Latham – he's my husband – and me come in to "do" for Mr Stuart when he's out of the country or got business company. He's ever so nice to work for. Goodnight, dear, nice meeting you.'

Outside on his Yuppie forecourt without an overcoat, only sweater and jeans, he dangled his car-keys in front of her face, his breath misty. 'Now what have you to say for yourself, Miss Accusation Cotswold?'

'You're not driving me home, that's for sure!'

'Not even a little tiny hint of an apology?' He put his face close to hers and she could taste frosted champagne on the cold night air.

Olivia put her arms around him and her head on his shoulder. 'Sorry.'

'I should think so! See you tomorrow?'

'Yep . . . thanks for a lovely evening, Stuart, the food was delicious. Fish and chips or spaghetti and tomato sauce I'd have expected, not *cordon bleu* stuff.' She kissed him goodnight, and he slipped the ring back on her finger, retrieved from his bed. He had dismissed the MacKenzie chauffeur earlier – and now she knew the reason why! – and as Stuart certainly couldn't drive after all the champagne and wine they'd indulged in together, Olivia said, 'Call a taxi for me, Stuart, before we both freeze to death out here.'

'What's wrong with staying the night?' he insisted.

'Call me old-fashioned, but I think I'd like to face your neighbours with a clear conscience in future.'

He sighed, 'Gee whizz, honey, you're not like any other English lady I've ever met!' And after he'd seen her off in a black London cab, he went back inside and said to the Lathams helping clear up, 'I must remember in future that that is one cute lady with no head for alcohol!'

'It does funny things to us all, sir,' said Mr Latham, polishing the silver cutlery which couldn't be put into the executive dishwasher.

CHAPTER 5

Olivia went again to Sunday lunch with her parents. They were packing up the St John's house to go into genteel retirement in Antibes.

'Darling!' her mother greeted her with over-enthusiastic motherliness. 'You're as thin as a rake. Are you eating properly?'

'Perfectly properly, Mother. I've come to tell you I'm engaged.'

'About time too, Olivia. Your father and I would really love some grandchildren before we're too old to enjoy them.'

'Engaged, I said, not pregnant!'

'I would sincerely hope not, before you're married. But I do hope the wedding won't be too soon, as I have a lot to do right now.'

'One thing at a time, Ma. I want to see if we're compatible, and suited to each other and . . .'

'You're not thinking of living together first, are you, dear, like all young people these days? I find that so hard to accept. A well brougt-up young lady should keep herself for her husband; that's what the honeymoon is all about . . .'

'Yes, Ma!' Olivia said wearily, 'I know. One step at a time, as I said. All I know is, I can't live without him, so if we both decide one roof is cheaper than two . . .' No, that didn't sound quite right either, Stuart was a millionaire, dammit, and could afford half a dozen roofs. 'Um . . . you see, Ma, I love him, I really do. Right now I'd do whatever he wanted.'

'Is that wise, dear? You know the saying: a woman is made to grace, a man is made to chase.'

She didn't know where Maggie picked up such mooncalf tripe. Yes, she did: she read too many sloppy-sex romances instead of sensible-sex romances. There was a big difference. She would have to change her mother's reading habits first, that was for sure!

Olivia had no idea her father had been paying attention to their conversation. He sat in his armchair beside the fire in the drawing-room, reading the Sunday newspapers, unable to play golf due to a strained shoulder muscle, while her mother and she sat on the window-seat. Maggie busy at her needlepoint; Olivia couldn't wait to see Stuart again. 'No morality among the youngsters of today,' her father grunted from behind the *Sunday Times*. 'Who is he?'

'Stuart MacKenzie, Pa.'

'Good God!' Her father rustled up out of his armchair as if he'd been stung by a bee.

'I thought you realized?'

'Realized – realized what, girl?'

'Don't bellow, Harry, we're not deaf,' Maggie reproached.

'Well, he has been sending a lot of flowers to the office lately. I thought you'd noticed.'

'Good God, woman, I thought they were from some other lover of yours, not MacKenzie.'

'Oh, come now, Pa!' She was on the defensive at once. 'He loves me and I love him, and he has asked me to marry him, and I think I'm going to say yes, so there!'

'Are you sure you don't love his seventeen-and-a-half-million-dollar offer for Lamphouse?'

'Lock, stock and barrel, you said. I thought it was already an arranged marriage between you and Mac-Kenzie senior.'

'Good God, girl! I never meant you to take the contract so literally!'

'Hush, you two,' said her mother. 'Can we talk about this, quietly, no publishing histrionics please after such a nice lunch of roast beef and Yorkshire pudding? You ought to have asked Stuart Mac-Kenzie to lunch, Olivia, so that I could have met him and judged for myself what everyone is on about – all this Lamphouse brouhaha, to say the very least. Your father's judgement concerning outside influences is sometimes apt to be biased. Harry, I'm sure Olivia knows what she's doing. I have every faith in her.'

'Thank you, Mother.'

'You know, Olivia, there will always be another home for you in Cap d'Antibes if things don't work out quite right for you?'

'Don't encourage the girl to take Lamphouse, or marriage, so lightly, Maggie,' her father said peevishly, reaching for the whisky decanter on the table beside him.

'Harry, stop that! You've had enough today. You know what the doctor said about cutting down on your drinking,' Maggie warned.

Her father scowled. 'What the hell does the doctor know! I'm the one who's lived in this body for sixty years; I'll look after it the way it's got used to after sixty years. As for Stuart MacKenzie, he's already married, that's how much you know about the man, Maggie!'

She could tell by the tapestry needle that her mother did not know what to say now, the idea of a bigamist son-in-law not quite her cup of tea. Olivia said quickly, 'Divorced, Pa!'

'Which says it all! If he couldn't make a go of it first time round, he won't a second, believe me!'

'That's unfair.'

'Life is unfair, dear girl, and marriage even unfairer!'

'Meaning what, Harold?' Her mother still held her tapestry needle in mid air.

He grunted something about his ulcer and her needlework and that was the difference between the sexes: a man had to support a wife and family his whole life through, whereas all a woman had to do was stay home with her needlepoint.

Olivia thought, oh-oh, here come the marital boxing-gloves, time to go home!

'Not any more, Harry,' said her mother, staying remarkably cool in the face of such a sexist remark. 'Where have you been the last thirty years? It's the woman who holds a marriage together these days, by minding the kids as well as going out to work. Maybe not in my case, but then I was unlucky.'

'Unlucky?' He looked at her over his reading glasses.

'Yes. You might not then have been quite so spoilt rotten by a wife who has indulged your every whim for thirty years, and I wouldn't have had to put up with a grumpy, ulcerated, bald-headed old soak for thirty years because I might have met a Stuart MacKenzie too!' Maggie left the room in high dudgeon.

'Now you've done it, Pa! I'm off . . .' Olivia grabbed her things.

Behind her he mumbled, 'What've I said now?' and then, 'Women!'

At the front door Maggie stood wiping her eyes.

'Ma, he didn't mean it, you know what he's like.'

'I know. It's his ulcer, it always plays up when he's under stress. He's afraid you and I will think he's a failure, you know, because Lamphouse is bankrupt.'

'That's silly, it's not his fault. Publishing today is different from when he took over from *his* Pa,' Olivia said.

'Try telling him that! Anyway, dear . . .' Maggie pressed a damp cheek against hers '. . . bye for now. Bring Stuart to lunch next time, so that your mother can meet him too. And if you do decide to marry him, just make sure he's got enough medical insurance to put him in a home for burnt-out publishers the moment *his* time comes.'

* * *

Birdie came into Olivia's office one morning looking worn out. 'The contracts have all been typed up now, Olivia. Your father wants you to look them over and initial your approval at the bottom of each page to see we've missed nothing before they go to MacKenzie's solicitors.'

Olivia took stock of the sheaf of documents in Birdie's hands and groaned. 'OK, just leave them on the desk, I'll try and get through them as soon as I sort out our spring publishing list . . .'

At four o'clock that afternoon she had reached page sixty-one of the MacKenzie-Lamphouse contract when she jumped up from her desk and stormed into her father's office. 'Pa, can I borrow the car and Ernest?'

'What's wrong?'

'I need to talk to Stuart.'

'Fax him.'

'I need to talk to Stuart face to face – the bastard!'

Ernest, her father's chauffeur, was cleaning the Daimler in the underground car park next door to the Lamphouse building. 'Ernest, drive me to the new MacKenzie offices in Farringdon.'

'The Dame's still soap-sudsy, Miss Ol . . .'

'Just drive, Ernest!'

'Yes, miss!' He grabbed his chauffeur's cap off the back seat and hid his sandwiches in the glove compartment.

The MacKenzie Corporation UK had acquired a brand new modern office building, all smoky glass and designer yukka plants in self-watering tubs and fast new functional lifts. Olivia swept through the reception area and right past the security officer, snapping at him when he asked for her name. Without waiting for him to issue her with a little plastic badge of admittance she got into one of the lifts and pressed the button for the penthouse suite and the MD's offices; more like a hotel and less like a serious publishing house was her angry assessment of the place when she got out on the eighth floor. Olivia surged straight past his PA's desk, and left her with her mouth wide open and still swallowing air. 'Miss Cotswold, Mr MacKenzie is . . .'.

'An A-one bastard!' Stuart was on the phone, Olivia slammed page sixty-one down on his desk, took off her engagement ring a second time and tossed it into his lap. 'You creeping Judas!' And she walked out again.

Stuart said into the phone, 'I'll get back to you . . .' and dashed after her. The lift doors were closing when he got his foot caught. The doors slid smoothly open again despite Olivia's finger pressed hard on G for Ground. 'What the hell was all that about, Olivia? How *dare* you barge in here like this and start throwing things at me without some sort of explanation?'

'You want an explanation? Then hear this! The engagement is off! I have better things to do with my life than waste it on a cheat and a liar! How *dare* you promise me things without any intention of keeping those promises?'

'What promises?' His arms strained to keep the lift doors wide apart, leaning into the lift with a face white with fury, eyes like blue ice. 'What promises have I broken, Olivia?'

'You promised me Lamphouse would retain its identity!'

'Yes, and it will . . .'

'Not if we're to move into this . . . this prissy, tarty, tawdry, characterless building with *your* lot!'

'Ohhh!' He took a deep breath, fighting with steel doors and with her. 'Look, let's talk . . .'

'I don't want to talk to you any more!'

'Yes, you do . . .' He got into the lift with her and tried to put his arms around her.

'Don't, Stuart!' She shook him off. 'Don't think you can fob me off time after time!'

'Sweetheart, a very big misunderstanding, that's all . . . you've got yourself worked up about nothing . . .'

'It's not *nothing*!' The lift stopped halfway, the doors slid back and a contingent of MacKenzie staff tried to get in.

'Sorry, we're not going anywhere at the moment . . .' Stuart pressed the B button for Basement and then turned the key in the emergency slot to Off. '*Now* let's talk about this sensibly, huh? Lamphouse will be far better off, MacKenzie will be far better off, if everyone is housed under one roof – *this* one! It will be more economical for a start. The old Paternoster house is about ready to fall down, it's cramped, dark and highly inefficient – and that's just for starters. I told you Lamphouse would retain its own identity and keep its own staff, and it will. You'll have the entire fourth and fifth floors to house them, twelve thousand square metres of efficient working space.'

'Keep your twelve thousand square metres of efficient working space! We're going nowhere; the old Paternoster building is home to me and *my* staff, Stuart MacKenzie!'

'You haven't been appointed Lamphouse's new MD as yet, Olivia! Not until the MacKenzie Board approve my direction and everything is signed between Lamphouse's solicitors and our lawyers.'

'Oh, so it's blackmail now, *Loot*-tenant? And that's what you are doing: looting from Lamphouse! That's how you say it, isn't it? When it's actually spelled Lieutenant, pronounced in English as "Left-tenant!" Not as Rutland wrote it and *your* editorial panel signed for it. We at Lamphouse speak and write and spell English as in England, not bloody MacKenzie American – or Canadian!'

He raked his hair in exasperation. 'Have you been drinking this lunchtime?'

'What the hell is that supposed to mean?' she demanded.

'It goes straight to your head . . .'

'I have not been drinking! The only time I touch the wretched stuff is when you make me!'

'I *make* you? How?'

'You want to sleep with me, don't you?'

'Yes – but not right now. Not when you're behaving like a spoilt child who can't get her own way, instead of an intelligent woman.'

'Oh, I'm a spoilt child now, am I?' She turned the key to get the lift moving again but his hand clamped back on hers.

'Why are we quarrelling like this? Don't do this to

me, Olivia, please! I *love* you! Keep your wretched old building, I don't care . . . I just want to keep *you*, that's all . . . come here.' He slipped the ring back on her finger before she was even aware of what he was doing, just as before. 'Now let's go back to my office and talk about this sensibly. That was my father on the phone. Rutland's agent is threatening to sue for breach of contract. I don't need you to do the same.'

Olivia asked in a small voice, now that she had calmed down a little, 'What . . . how . . . I mean, in what way are MacKenzie in breach of Rutland's contract?'

'Haven't a clue! Not my department . . .' His arms wrapped around her, holding her tightly, and then his mouth came down on hers, hungrily, and *then* he turned the key to take them up again to the penthouse suite to amend page sixty-one of the MacKenzie-Lamphouse contract, which never actually got amended because Stuart had other things on his mind, like trying to seduce her on his executive couch.

'Stop it, I've work to do . . . !' She tried pushing him off, but ended up with a fit of the giggles and a weakening resolve. He tickled her quite cruelly, hands trying to work in under her blouse, while she tried to keep control and her blouse firmly fastened pending an unscheduled visit from his PA.

'What are you saving yourself for when we're going to get married in any case?' he wanted to know.

'In case I change my mind between now and a pre-nuptial contract being drawn up to my utmost satisfaction, Mr MacKenzie.'

94

Fortunately the fax machine started churning out some paper at that moment. 'OK,' he said, releasing her and smoothing down his tousled hair. He straightened his tie. 'Buzz off, Miss Cotswold; I've had enough of you for one afternoon. We'll continue this meeting later at Maryanna's.' Stuart escorted her to the lift.

On the way back to Paternoster Row, Olivia sat in her father's place on plush grey leather upholstery in the back of the Daimler Sovereign and stared at the back of Ernest's head.

She felt ashamed of the scene she had caused. There *was* such a thing as compromise; he had never promised her Lamphouse would *not* be moved from its present, long-occupied premises; they *were* rather old and drab and dark and inefficient. She was just being sentimental and nostalgic about an old building, which was, after all, only an old heap of bricks;

So why not put it to a democratic vote, ask the firm if they wanted to stay where they were or move into the new, modern, light and cost-effective MacKenzie UK building in Farringdon, with twelve thousand square metres of office space. Birdie wouldn't know where to put herself!

The ring back on her finger, her face aglow with happy and pleasurable thoughts concerning a handsome and sexy, rich and romantic lover soon to be her husband – how lucky could a girl get? – Olivia initialled page sixty-one on her lap. If Lamphouse staff themselves voted to move offices, then they would.

CHAPTER 6

Olivia hardly heard what Stuart was saying; her mind was on other things. Fingers wrapped tightly around the fragile stem of her champagne glass, as though her life depended on something to cling on to, she couldn't help thinking how she missed her plain old lifestyle of a quick cup of coffee and slice of toast for breakfast, or a microwaved plastic lasagne after work.

All this high living was getting to her, and her waistline. Huge 'working' breakfasts of bagels, croissants, smoked salmon and scrambled eggs, full-blown midday lunches, extravagant four-course dinners, champagne morning, noon and night, was really too much for her.

She felt that Stuart was 'buying' her – as indeed he had.

Vinny would laugh at her – whoever heard of anyone growing tired of a millionaire lifestyle! And what about the man himself? Had she become tired of him too? Get a life, Olivia, Vinny would have said.

'You know something?' Stuart said, putting his hand firmly over Olivia's. He could feel the tenseness of her fingers, as if she was clutching at crystal straws.

They sat before a blazing log fire in the Cumberland Country Club, of which he was a member. The ambience of the place was soft, seductive, exclusively chic and wildly expensive: a bottle of champagne started at around seventy-five pounds. A quiet inglenook, lattice-leaded windows and country-house chintzes gave the club a feeling of home from home – Harold and Maggie's home, not hers!

Olivia felt an overwhelming sense of panic. She stared at the bright leaping flames in the hearth, her mind focused only on Lamphouse and its survival. Was she not, in truth, selling not only *her* soul, but the rest of the old firm's too, by allowing herself to be so seduced by its handsome UK director to whom money and people were no object?

The MacKenzie directors had now officially offered her the job as MD of their latest acquisition. It had been like receiving a luncheon voucher for a banquet gone sadly stale, she the poor little beggar girl left to pick up the crumbs.

Was she up to the job amid such high-flyers? Olivia asked herself. Unlike Legrand, she had not been to university to read Classics, world literature or anything else to degree standard; all she had finished up with was a Lausanne diploma in laying the table for a dinner party and flower-arranging! The only reason why she had been offered a directorship of a publishing company at all was because of who she was by birth – Olivia Penelope Cotswold, whose father could pull strings on her behalf. Meanwhile, all she had to offer in return were 'gut feelings' when it came to recognizing literary talent – in someone else.

As if he could read her thoughts, Stuart continued, 'I've discovered the reason for the monumental chip you nurse on your sweet shoulder, my love.' He smoothed that part of her delectable anatomy pressed close to him.

'Chip?' She brought her attention back to he who was still prepared to offer her the sun, moon and stars, as well as blue chip diamonds, in return for Lamphouse's innermost soul.

'Oh, yes, chip! A great big wooden chip, sweetheart, weighing you down in rather a lop-sided fashion. You're still so unsure of yourself, so self-effacing and negative – not the right attitude for the MD of a big publishing business at all.'

'Is that right!'

'Right.'

'Surely Lamphouse is only small fry to you and the rest of MacKenzie?'

'No reason why you shouldn't make it a big fry, Olivia. You're a great gal, with plenty going for you, if only you'd relax a bit and not take everything so personally. The first lesson to be learned: *never* get emotionally involved with staff problems. Leave that to personnel.'

Olivia slammed down her glass of champagne, thereby negating the sure touch of Stuart's warm hand, which had clamped down on hers before she crushed her glass in an agony of indecision. She knew to whom he was referring!

She had spilled champagne on the polished surface of the coffee table before their cosy armchairs, and she fumbled for her handkerchief. Her panic mounting, she just wanted to get out of here, anywhere, feel the fresh, pure rush of cool air blowing through her mind, clearing it . . .

He stayed her trembling hand before refilling their glasses. The ice in which the bottle of Bollinger RD nestled in a silver bucket was melting rapidly from the warmth of the fire. She felt claustrophobic, unable to face all the smart chit-chat at this celebration lunch with the rest of the MacKenzie board boffs – who, mercifully, had not as yet arrived, foggy motorways from London no doubt the reason for their non-appearance.

'Stuart, I . . . please can we go?'

'Go? We've only just arrived – aren't you feeling well? What's wrong, honey?'

'Please don't call me, honey . . . I – I just need to talk . . .'

'I thought that was what we were already doing – in here, where it's warm and pleasant.'

'Walk . . . I – I'd like to . . . to go outside for a bit, that's all.'

'Fine! OK. We'll send the chauffeur to lunch instead; we can talk in the Rolls.'

The reason why they had driven out to the country club in the MacKenzie Rolls was because Stuart hadn't wanted to drink and drive – perfectly understandable. The reason why he had a black Ferrari and not a red one like every other man rich enough to possess such a status symbol was because he had demanded a custom-built black one, and was able to afford it.

The reason why she had chosen to live in a run-down terrace in a cheap part of Fulham and not in St John's Wood, Kensington or Belgravia was because that had been *her* choice, and now that her choices were fast being eroded by a handsome, suave millionaire with a custom-built black Ferrari, designer suits, black satin bedsheets and a degree in desktop seduction, Olivia felt suffocated.

'I'd like to walk outside, in the grounds . . . to clear my head . . .'

She knew she was being awkward, behaving badly, but she needed to get away from people and from publishing.

'OK! You do know it's bucketing down, don't you?' he said in exasperation, before turning to the *maître d'* to put luncheon on hold and to tell the rest of MacKenzie's entourage, *when* they arrived, that he and Miss Cotswold had gone for a walk in the English rain because they were fed up with waiting!

The *maître d'* seemed to understand, the look in his eye conveying that he was well used to the idiosyncrasies of the rich and famous, especially when love was in the air.

The grounds of the Cumberland Country Club were extensive, sharing the Virginia Water lake bordered by rhododendron and azaleas, a riot of breathtaking colour in spring, but, on this rainy, bleak, February day, miserably shrouded in the heavy damp fog which had somehow managed to wrap itself around Olivia's soul.

She was on the brink of telling Stuart to find a replacement MD for Lamphouse: like her father, she too was retiring from anything to do with the Lamphouse Cross. 'Oh, look!' she said, putting off the moment. She stooped to a cluster of fragile snowdrops in the grass. 'How lovely!' She plucked one, her concentration focused upon it – a big decision, Olivia, now or never!

Since, quite literally, bumping into Stuart MacKenzie, she had found him to be *the* most exhilarating, exciting, heady, passionate, challenging and frustrating man she had ever encountered. He who never took no for an answer. She had had no difficulty in her past relationships – not that there had been that many. In fact, there really hadn't been *any* before Stuart MacKenzie had come on the scene and swept her off her feet in such a huge way.

It seemed as if the word 'no' was simply not in Stuart's vocabulary, once *he* had made up his mind.

How long had they been together now – three months out of four? Olivia had lost count of the weeks, certain only of his insidious encroachment upon *her* life. So, what had happened to *her* own free choices?

In plain and simple terms, she had fallen head over heels in love with him – that was what had happened; madly, frantically, passionately and frustratingly, she loved him, no two ways about it.

So, what was she griping about? Olivia asked herself, in view of the fact that Stuart confessed to loving her to distraction too.

She did not particularly like his opulent lifestyle. It

all seemed like a dream, and dreams were unreal in the morning.

And every bubble burst, sooner or later, champagne bubbles faster than soap.

Enormous wealth had enormous drawbacks: the fact that there was such a thing called *noblesse oblige*, wherein privilege and duty were inseparable.

The drawbacks to their relationship went through her mind like a never-ending data-sheet, drawing to her attention the fact that even 'the old firm' had undermined her only last week when her new status as MD of Lamphouse had been publicly proclaimed in the wake of Sir Harold's retirement.

They had put it to the vote. 'Do we or do we not – the Lamphouse contingent – move from Paternoster Row to Farringdon, to share twelve thousand square metres of new, modern, well-equipped, well-ventilated, air-conditioned office space, along with the rest of the MacKenzie American-Canadian clan?'

The democratic ballot box had returned an overwhelming majority vote in favour of the move. Flimsy excuses such as nearer to the Tube, buses and Charing Cross main line station; more modern office premises; cleaner, no allergy-accelerating processes; more space, lots of light and no mice in dark corners – that sort of thing had swayed the punters to take up residence with MacKenzie UK under one roof, all except Birdie and Dankers, ever her staunchest supporters.

She wanted Birdie to be her own personal secretary (following in Pa's footsteps), and Dankers to be given the position of head of security. In the reshuffle of the two houses, the appointment of 'shared person-nel', such as reception clerks, security, front door-men, despatch staff, cleaners and such like had to be approved by MacKenzie boardroom management, who held the purse-strings. Olivia was accused of being 'partial' and 'biased' as far as former Lamp-house personnel were concerned, authors included.

Birdie was different. Birdie was her own person, Birdie had stood up to God in the shape of Sir Harold Cotswold, so the hell to 'Stuart MacKenzie and his Gestapo' as Birdie referred to them.

In essence, then, it seemed to Olivia that she did *not* have a free hand in everything to do with Lamp-house. She had resented the 'former' bit, had pointed out that Lamphouse was still very much in the forefront of MacKenzie interests; it was in *all* their interests to pull along in harness.

She, Birdie and Dankers were classified as old-fashioned odds and bobs, while criticism levelled at her (behind her back) included such personal re-marks as 'No real personality, introvert, proper snob, thinks she's too good for us, Miss Goodie-Two-shoes – you're joking! Sold herself to Stuwey, didn't she? Wonder how many bonks it took to get her MDship? Only reason why she ever got such an elevated position within the company was on account of *who* she knows, not *what* she knows!'

Olivia was well aware of what the new regime, and some of the old, thought of her from the gossip in the loos, lifts, corridors and canteens. She, the unwitting eavesdropper, became the show-stopper the moment she appeared; conversations dried up quicker than a cucumber in the desert.

In trying to separate Dankers and Birdie from being her surrogate parents, they who had come a long way *with* her, through times past, right up to now, when Harold and Maggie had mostly been absent, Olivia took the good with the bad. She knew that Lamphouse and its staff were considered to be a second-rate house in the eyes of MacKenzie staff and management, because Lamphouse had been unable to support itself without an injection of the mighty dollar. She had worked harder than ever to assert *her* rights, and had given tit-for-tat: she told the Mac-Kenzie board that they were guilty of 'ageism' in the marketplace – the over-fifties had every right to life too.

Birdie and Dankers were slotted in, she as Olivia Cotswold's personal assistant, he on the front reception desk.

Olivia had not mentioned such petty details of 'harassment in the workplace' to Stuart, for fear of another management label, that of nepotism.

If Birdie and she, however unwillingly, now looked down on Holborn Viaduct and together shuddered at their new environment, it was not of their choice. If noises off were kept to a minimum behind the double glazing, and the blank computer screen in Birdie's new office bore testimony to the fact that Birdie was not mechanically minded, it was through a democratic majority vote, and not from personal choice.

Meanwhile, all three of them, Birdie, Dankers and she, were fighting tooth and nail to resist becoming three more jobless statistics, ousted out of the company before their time by internal pressures and mean men in sombre grey suits and no humanity in their souls. Progress was sometimes a bitter pill to swallow, Olivia couldn't help feeling.

At the same time too, behind all their recent new management crises and ill-feeling centred around what was 'British' and what was 'American', a tiny thought crept unbidden into Olivia's mind – maybe some of the 'old firm' were to blame too, for being too inflexible, too stuck in their ways, and too proud to kow-tow to the laws made upstairs in the penthouse suite of the new MacKenzie building in Farringdon.

'Penny for them,' Stuart said. They had come to a standstill on the edge of Virginia Water. Even the lily-pads hibernated beneath the surface on such a raw day. He kept the umbrella over them with one hand, a little waterfall dripping off its rounded surface to keep them pressed close within its intimate sphere. With his free hand he tilted her chin, forcing her to look him in the eye. 'You've been acting so strangely these past few days. Tell me what's wrong?'

'Nothing.'

'Something is – not right.'

'Everything is so impossibly right, I have to pinch myself sometimes to prove I'm not in some sort of trance, dreaming the impossible dream. Every time something goes wrong, worries or upsets me, you're there to put it right.'

'Is that so very terrible?'

'Not terrible, just disconcerting – sometimes I do know what I'm doing, Stuart. All my life I had a father who made me feel very inadequate. He wanted a son to carry on his name and his business after he retired. But he ended up with me – a useless girl as far as Pa was concerned.'

'Harry's a chauvinist?' Stuart asked, and made her smile.

'Not a chauvinist, just a great big male-management mogul as opposed to my scatty female "casting-couch" image. Girls get married, start a family, get lost in the kitchen sink of domesticity. Empires and great dynasties have been lost on account of the lack of male heirs. Females only clog up the arteries of civilization, big business and high politics; females have too much emotional baggage to take with them wherever they roam . . . room, I should say!'

'I'm losing you,' he said, his expression quite befogged.

'Boardroom, Stuart! A boardroom is not the place to dump one's emotional baggage – that's what my father used to drum into my mother when she phoned him at work because she'd fused the lights or blown up the iron, or the washing-machine had flooded the kitchen floor. That's why I moved out to my own place, because I couldn't stand his attitude, her tears and their stupid rows.'

'The chip I was talking about, Olivia . . . so, without losing anything of that soft heart of yours, be glad you're a chip off the old block.'

'Meaning?'

'You've inherited his business sense as well as the business.'

'Have I? Aren't you merely handing to me what

should rightfully be mine? Don't suffocate me the way he did, Stuart, and don't patronize me. I'll reach my own conclusions and make my own decisions, as well as mistakes. Just don't do the same to me as Pa did to my mother, just let me find my own level – please.'

He took the sorry-looking snowdrop that in her present dejected mood she had mangled in nervous fingers, and threw it away. 'You've got something else to say, so say it.'

'I'm scared.'

That's good. Fear makes one channel all those negative emotions one harbours into positive ones.'

'You're patronizing me again.'

'I told you about my elder brother dying before his time, and how I, too, became second-best in my father's publishing empire. Parents are a funny species. They want from their children what they couldn't achieve for themselves. Geoff was his ace card; I was the knave in the old man's eyes.' Stuart rubbed his chin, embarrassed about raking up his former 'high' and irresponsible lifestyle.

'Isn't it funny how life duplicates itself sometimes?' Olivia said.

'Sorry?' He looked uncertain.

'Birdie Gough and Geoff, the lost brother you call "Goff".'

'I'm the lost one, sweetheart.'

'The dead one, then! Neither name is spelt according to pronunciation – that's the difference between us. We both speak English, but say it and spell it a different way: Gough as in Goff, and Geoff as in Goff instead of Jeff, and what the hell does it matter anyway, except when you're editing an author's typescript – but you wouldn't know about that side of the business, as you're only in publishing to make money.'

'Olivia?' He seemed pained by that fierce diatribe against him, as well as confused.

'Oh . . . I'm sorry! I didn't mean to sound so whiney! It's just that sometimes we – meaning Lamphouse and MacKenzie – *appear* to speak the same language, Stuart, without necessarily understanding each other.' Olivia pulled a face. 'Is it because we human beings like to complicate our lives deliberately?'

'In what way am I complicating your life?' he asked gently.

'You can take a person out of the country, but you can't take the country out of the person. You and I, at a personal level – do I become Americanized or do you become Anglicized? OK, don't answer that; I know you'll come up with one of your flippant little quips.'

'Are you usually so profound this early in the day?' He smiled.

'I always read the small print first before putting my signature to anything, which includes marriage contracts.'

'So I've noticed.' His well-tailored shoulders hunched against the cold and damp, he took a deep breath. 'Olivia, honey, unfortunately life deals us a crap hand at times – millionaires included. Someone once said, life's a bitch and then we die. Maybe they're right. After Geoff's death my father had to deal out the Knave of Hearts: I'm not proud of my past performances, and nor was he. But all that has changed. There comes a time in a guy's life when he wakes up one morning and realizes what an absolute ass he's been. The old man doesn't believe in me – nor, I think, do you, and that's why you refuse to take me seriously as a future husband. I don't know how to say this in English, but I want to settle down with you, for keeps this time.'

Always, he made her smile. Always he took the serious out of the sanctimonious and made sense of life. Once again Olivia felt herself a willing partner in a way of life she was very unsure of from a personal point of view. Here he was again, thrusting big decisions upon her, weakening her resolve every time he brought up the subject of marriage. At this early stage in the relaunching of her new, high-powered executive career, she was not sure she wanted the trappings of marriage to add to her list of uncertainties.

'Trouble with you, Olivia,' he continued on the analytical theme of their conversation she had started, 'you're too much of a perfectionist.'

'What's wrong with that?' she countered.

'Nothing! It's an absolutely wonderful trait of character – only in my experience perfectionists are their own worst enemies. Don't try too hard, for fear you wear yourself out in mental cogitation.'

'A big word, Stuart!'

'Sure, I read English sometimes.'

'Sorry – I didn't mean you to take my British-American tirade too seriously.'

'Well, I'm being serious now. Never settle for second-best, honey.'

'I've no intention of doing so; Lamphouse is the best in the business,' she assured him.

'I mean myself.'

'You, second-best, Stuart?' she scoffed. 'You're being terribly meek and mild all of a sudden, my darling.'

'Don't mock, I'm serious. My father and your father must have something in common, and that's their ability to rear offspring in their mould. Perhaps "blackmail" might be a truer word. My father believes he's dealt himself a duff hand, like your father believing that a daughter can't do his job nearly as well as a son. Let's prove them wrong, together.'

'How did you know what was on my mind?'

'I think we're both on the same wavelength – I'm a good judge of character.' Blue eyes had lost the sparkle with which he went through life, and she knew he was being utterly serious.

'Believe in yourself first, Olivia, and the rest of the world will start believing you too; you own chances will follow. We're fighting for the same thing, we're here to survive – or not.'

Between them, they had so much emotional baggage in common, it was uncanny. Olivia took his hand, offered to her as a friend *and* lover. They crossed sopping green lawns to the Cumberland, venue of the rich and famous and the plain megarich, who didn't have to prove a thing – unless they themselves chose to do so.

Stuart fell into a category she was still trying to come to terms with. No matter what anyone said, the children of dynamic parents – more so when that also brought wealth, fame and prestige – had it tough! One had to be able to perform perfectly, persevere and prove harder than anyone else not born under the banner of nepotism that might was not right, only dedication to what one *believed* was right.

'I'm relying on you to pull Lamphouse – in the long run, MacKenzie too – through this current rough ride of ours, Olivia.'

In view of his utmost sincerity, how could she pull the rug from under his feet, just as things on the Lamphouse-MacKenzie front were sorting themselves out, Birdie, Dankers and a few others of the old firm excepted? Olivia took a deep breath. 'OK, I accept the challenge. Let's go back there and tell them I'm willing and able.'

'Really?'

'Yes, really.'

'Not so fast – when will you marry me?' he asked half ruefully.

'I thought I was already doing that, by accepting the MDship of Lamphouse under the MacKenzie banner.'

He stopped dead in his tracks, and hers.

First of all he looked at the lowering sky, three fingers pressed to his lips; then the sparkle came back into his eyes and he turned her around, round and around like a spinning-top, to make her dizzy under the soaking umbrella.

'What are you doing, Stuart?' Olivia laughed.

'Taking stock of the goods to make sure I'm not being lumbered with a carousel instead of a woman – you've some strange mental processes going on up here, Olivia Cotswold!' He tapped her head, let the umbrella roll on the ground and took her in his arms, holding her close for a long time in the misty shrubbery of Virginia Water, unburgeoned yet in the forefront of a spring yet to come. 'You've made my day – promise me you won't change your mind?'

'I promise.' She kissed his sweet-talking lips and grabbed the umbrella before they got any wetter.

Stuart really did have a sentimental streak, which she had not recognized at their first meeting – the second, perhaps! Perhaps his American father and Canadian mother, both with Celtic ancestors, had a lot to do with it. Stuart was not at all the hard-faced image of a mogul: perhaps MacKenzie senior was, and Stuart's dead elder brother had been, but the youngest of the trio was – not bad at all.

Olivia couldn't help feeling that the romantic novelists had got it all wrong – tall, dark, handsome and wildly rich heroes were by no means in short supply, nor were they male chauvinist pigs, dastardly heartbreakers, buccaneers or devils incarnate. Sometimes they were just down-to-earth, honest-to-goodness hardworking blokes!

Having reached the momentous decision to give the MDship of Lamphouse her best shot, Olivia gave herself up into Stuart's hands, still hoping to retain her own identity, and that of Lamphouse.

'*Will* you really marry me?' he asked again, his arm

tightly around her shoulders while they paused at the front entrance of the Club.

'Oh, yes . . .' She too was still dreaming.

'When?'

'Whenever you want – July.'

'Why July – why not right now?'

'Too busy. Lamphouse has to get established . . . re-established, before its new MD goes missing: in July we're less busy, the summer list is done. Right now we're in the middle of scheduling it. But no fancy trappings, mind! I couldn't bear all the fuss and nonsense of an expensive wedding.'

'Whatever you want, Olivia.'

Perhaps not a knight in shining armour wielding Excalibur, but the next best thing – in modern-day computerized jargon, the New Roman riding a fax-machine across the pond whenever she required a little heart-to-heart massage.

CHAPTER 7

No doubt about it: she, Olivia Penelope Cotswold, made her mother very happy when she decided to legitimize her swift and heady relationship with Stuart Lyon MacKenzie by getting married among the open-air, free-breathing Mediterranean spruces of Cap d'Antibes.

'*I, Olivia Penelope, take thee, Stuart Lyon, to be my lawful wedded husband, to love, comfort, honour and protect, and, forsaking all others, be faithful, as long as we both shall live . . .*' What a commitment, for life! To vow before God and the assembled company such an undertaking!

The wedding, as she had wanted, took place in July. Birdie and Dankers were flown in especially by private plane, like a couple of rare pandas from London Zoo.

'I've never been so cramped in my life, Olivia,' Birdie had complained, stepping out of the Cessna at Cannes, while Olivia, who had gone to meet them in her father's new Citroën, tried to straighten out Birdie's rumpled feathers and relocate Dankers' lost last-minute EC passport.

114

Vinny Legrand arrived from Toronto to be her 'maid of honour', a euphemism if ever there was one where Vinny was concerned, Olivia couldn't help reflecting.

Lady Cotswold, in her usual zany but forgivable way – trust her! thought Olivia – had provoked the lengthy explanation of, 'Why blue, Olivia? Virgin brides always get married in white.'

'Not this one, Ma.'

'Don't tell me you and Stuart have been living in sin, too?' Maggie looked shocked, the 'too' referring to Vinny.

'With respect, Ma, Stuart and my sleeping arrangements are nothing to do with anyone or anything. I'm a big girl now. However, black satin sheets and communal electric toothbrushes aren't my scene. It might come as a surprise to you and Pa to know that Stuart is an altogether old-fashioned reformed gentleman, meaning, he respects me, and whatever I want – wanted – from our pre-nuptial partnership. Blue suits me. White makes me look like the morning edition of the *Daily Fangs* . . . oh, and no little bridesmaids or long-drawn-out speeches, either. Please tell that to Pa.'

Firmly Francophiled in their peasant farmhouse a short haul away from the beaches of the Côte d'Azur, Maggie had put on her 'offended' expression. 'This really is a most peculiar wedding! One always has bridesmaids at a wedding.'

'Not this one. They'll only fall overboard and I can't chase round the yacht looking to see where, since Vinny will be too busy chasing anything with a large bank balance to keep an eye on bridesmaids. This is an adult affair, with the minimum of fuss and nonsense, please, Ma. Stuart and I want it that way.'

'I hope you and Stuart are going to exchange wedding rings, dear, as a symbol of mutual faith in each other,' was Lady Cotswold's final say in the matter.

Vinny, in the midst of her own confused passions, remembered to steer clear of starboard and kept to port-side at all times by wearing black and white – the white Puritan shawl wrapped around her black velvet shoulders, looked very pre-Raphaelite.

Stuart's best man was his best friend in the firm, the company lawyer, Ashton Dore Cleaver. Olivia met him for the first time under the bower of bougainvillaea at Antibes' Hôtel de Ville, where she and Stuart exchanged their marriage vows and wedding rings. Ashton Dore Cleaver was almost as handsome as the groom. Olivia could see Vinny mentally undressing the smart American lawyer with a view to placing her bouquet in his hands at the very earliest opportunity.

'You look ravishing,' Stuart whispered for her ears only, beneath a bower of bougainvillaea.

'So do you,' she replied with perfect poise, concentrating on them, and not the maid of honour or the best man.

The reception was held aboard the Cotswold yacht, *Penelope*. The wedding-feast was a sit-down affair handled by outside caterers, and took place in the nautical dining-room of rich mahogany and brass fittings, plush seating and an enormous oval dining-table which could accommodate the fifty wedding guests when stretched to its limits. Sir Harold had often entertained aboard the company yacht in times past, and, since his retirement, negotiated to keep it 'in the family', as long as he and Maggie had first rights to it.

Her father's *après-feast* speech mercifully steered clear of the young Olivia Penelope Cotswold wetting her seven-year-old knickers on her first day in boarding school: instead, he bored everyone rigid with Lamphouse's ancient history.

'Today is a significant day in the marriage of two publishing houses, one very old, one very new. I hope Olivia and Stuart are proud of their legacy, and take it from strength to strength. The Lamphouse Cross was founded by my ancestor, Samuel Cotswold, who 'mortgaged' a family heirloom to set up his new business in a somewhat similar manner to my having mortgaged my own precious heirloom, my daughter, to the MacKenzie Corporation, USA and Canada, our future bankers . . .'

Amused titters all round at the analogy, Olivia cringed with embarrassment. It was the first time he had ever professed sentiment where she was concerned, and she could only conclude that her Pa was vastly relieved to be getting rid of her to Stuart Lyon MacKenzie.

Her father was in full swing even without his golf clubs, '1854 – a bit before MacKenzie's time. The Cotswold "heirloom" is now locked up in a London bank vault. I sincerely hope such a fate will not befall my daughter at the hands of our excommunicated

Scots brethren after the English drove them away to foreign shores long before 1854.'

Handclapping and more inebriated catcalls from the wedding guests; Olivia whispered to Stuart behind the wedding cake, 'Forgive him, he's well pickled today. He started with whisky at breakfast.'

'The Cotswold heirloom, a priceless gold Russian Patriarchal Cross set with precious jewels, is not for sale to any antique jewel collectors present from Sotheby's.'

'Get on with it, Pa!' Olivia groaned under her breath.

'In the early eighteenth century, the Russian emperor, Peter the Great, was studying shipbuilding in a place called Deptford – that's London, England to our American and Canadian guests. In Peter the Great's entourage was a Russian Orthodox priest, Father Lampion, who contracted smallpox while in London – it wasn't a healthy place to live in those days, and is even less healthy now – that's why Maggie and I moved to the South of France.'

Laughter and clapping hands all round, from wedding guests well soused like her father. Olivia gritted her teeth and bore the story with a fixed smile while the bridegroom appeared to be enjoying the unusual spectacle of his father-in-law making a fool of himself – and Stuart had promised her there would be no trappings or speeches!

'Father Lampion was segregated from the rest of the Russian court. It was my ancestor as well as Olivia's who nursed Father Lampion in her humble house in Deptford. Penelope Cotswold died of the disease, as did Father Lampion. Penelope left behind a husband and seven children. In gratitude to Benjamin Cotswold and his children for the "sacrifice" they had made on the Russian front, the Russian emperor gave all Father Lampion's possessions to Benjamin – thus becoming the first Robin Hood of St Petersburg . . .

'I jest, of course . . .' Her father mopped his bald, sweaty pate with a table-napkin and asked for the air-conditioning to be turned up. 'Among the priest's personal possessions was the Patriarchal Cross, known as the Lampion Cross. Lampion is an old-fashioned English word meaning a lamphouse or lighthouse – in other words, a beacon to light the darkness, hence our publishing name of Lamphouse.

'Cotswold's precious family heirloom was passed down from Benjamin to his eldest son Samuel, the founder of the Lamphouse Publishing Company, established in Paternoster Row, London, in 1854. Samuel mortgaged the Lampion Cross to raise money for his new venture, and was soon earning enough money to redeem the Cotswold family heirloom with a boom in Crimean war stories.'

Lots of hand-clapping now and raising of glasses.

'Unfortunately,' Sir Harold continued, 'one hundred and thirty-five years on, the Lampion Cross, although still very valuable, is precious only to us Cotswolds who value it more out of sentiment than anything else, as it is a part of our family history. It could not raise the funds required today to bail out my failing publishing company amid the cut and thrust of the modern world.

119

Olivia looked at Stuart on the other side of her father's paunch. Stuart made a cut-throat gesture – she was glad they were both on the same wavelength. So why had they agreed to such mutual torture? she wondered. Why hadn't they just eloped quietly and got married at Gretna Green or Las Vegas?

She knew why; her mother's tender expression said it all, Maggie would have been oh, so disappointed had they done any such thing. Underneath, the parents were really quite proud of her achievement – not the MDship of Lamphouse as much as having the astuteness to catch a good-looking Canadian millionaire. Pa seemed to have forgiven her for not being a boy. Olivia was glad she had made her peace with Maggie and Harold by getting married so publicly; she really had been a devil to them during her teenage years. She brought her attention back to her father's proud speech concerning his family . . .

'Had that been the case, then I would willingly have mortgaged it a second time, and left my daughter to buy it back from her father-in-law.' Harold raised his glass and toasted Stuart and Olivia. 'May good fortune and good health attend you both throughout your lives. I know Olivia will continue to uphold old family traditions of Truth, Fidelity and Honour.'

Harold sat down heavily amid the applause and Olivia rejoiced – until he leaned across her mother to say to MacKenzie senior seated beside Maggie, 'Beat that kind of publishing history, Custor MacKenzie!'

'Ma, I think Pa's a little drurk!' Olivia said in outrage.

'Darling, I think he's more than a little drunk – but he's so happy because his little girl has decided to settle down at last, I can forgive him. Remember the number of times you used to embarrass *him!*' Maggie refilled Harry's glass with the champagne to hand, 'Maybe tonight I won't have to listen to his latest handicap because he'll be too busy being blotto on his own verbosity.'

On the MacKenzie side of starboard, there was the old silver-haired, handsome, self-made multi-millionaire himself, Stuart's father, boasting about his poor beginnings to Harold (who had never experienced a poor beginning in his entire life), and how he, MacKenzie senior, had had to pull himself up by his own boot-straps from newspaper boy on 33rd Street by Pennsylvania Station, way back in Depression days, to where he was today, a self-made publishing multi-millionaire – and gee, Harry, that was some cute family history publishing story about the Lampion Cross, and did it really belong to a Russian Emperor and he'd like to put in his bid for the precious family heirloom as a new-age logo for MacKenzie . . .

Stuart's Canadian mother, Mrs Pears MacKenzie, was a tall, slender, elegant, dark-haired and haughty-nosed woman, whose family were also in publishing. *De rigueur* wedding speeches out of the way, Pears, in a beige silk ensemble by Versace, having crossed over to port-side, wobbled a little on her gold-strap shoes and was instantly captured by Maggie who was sentimentally desirous of showing off Cotswold family photographs, Cotswold personal histories,

121

and Cotswold home cooking recipes. 'Harry's favourite recipe is Clipping Time Pudding,' said Maggie.

No escape route available other than overboard, Pears peered down her hawkish nose at an overexposed photo of Olivia on a pony, aged three years and ten months. 'Clipping Time Pudding?'

'Eight ounces of rice and some beef marrow bones . . .'

'Is that his name?' asked Pears, focused on the pony.

'And four ounces of stoned raisins, one pint of milk, three ounces of sugar, four ounces of currants, a little cinnamon, one egg and a little salt and bake for twenty minutes in a moderate oven . . .'

'Mother, darling,' Olivia steered Maggie clear of Mrs Multi-millionaire MacKenzie and her manicured long red-tipped fingernails that had never cooked anything apart from a multi-millionaire, 'Birdie is dying to hear your recipe for Clipping Time Pudding, being a bachelor girl herself – no offence to Pa's golfing-yachting activities leaving you a grass widow all over again.'

'Let us hope,' said Maggie, 'Stuart won't do the same to you, darling. Big businessmen can never be trusted. You ought to have made Birdie *his* secretary, not yours; she could have kept an eye on him for you. Try knitting as a hobby for him – at least he can do it from his fireside armchair.'

'Yes, Ma.'

'Oh, and I'm so proud of you, darling . . .' Maggie patted the back of her daughter's hand, and lowered her voice after looking furtively over her shoulder

'. . . for remaining *"intacta"* up to your wedding day.'

'*Intacta*, Mother?' Olivia pretended she had not heard of it.

'A virgin bride, dear. Stuart's a lucky man.'

Maggie wandered away and Olivia went to stand beside the lucky man on deck. While a fantastic red-gold sunset claimed the Côte d'Azur horizon, she said to him, 'Poor mother, having to live in a world of her own. She's just desperately unhappy, I suppose.'

'Because you married me?' He looked dismayed.

'No, silly. Don't make light of a serious subject, Stuart.'

'Sorry, sweetheart.'

'Because she married my father and never had a son, and all that. Pa has always made her feel like a failure – even today of all days, I heard him put her down. Do you think Harold and Maggie could ever have been deeply in love with one another?'

Stuart squeezed her hand reassuringly. 'I'm sure they still are. Maggie adores the old mogul, you can see it in her eyes and in the way she fusses over him. She's great – we all think so. "Just look at the mother to see how the bride will turn out, Stuart" – that was my Aunt Clidhah, my mother's sister – I have no worries!'

Olivia rested her head against his elegant bride-groom's lapels, squashing his white gardenia button-hole, and sighed with pleasure. Beneath the setting orb of blood-red sun the group of hired musicians assembled on deck began to play sentimental music for the wedding party.

'Dance?' Stuart asked, watching the nuances of light and shadow playing upon her face, the movement of her lips recapturing the song of an era in which she had participated as a mere schoolgirl.

'Let's just drift . . .' They did just that, in a world of their own.

Some very young and distant relative wandered past and dug Olivia in the ribs. 'Bet you can't wait for tonight! He's real cool, Olly. Hope I'll find a millionaire like him one day.'

'Forgive her, she's only twelve,' Olivia apologized for the young and distant relative. 'Now you know why I didn't want any bridesmaids. I'm exhausted with them all,' Olivia gazed into his remarkable blue eyes and hoped this day would last for ever and the night even longer.

'Me too, but they'll all be gone soon – I hope.'

'They', the wedding guest list from both sides of the Atlantic, had been booked into the famous pink and white Cap d'Antibes Hotel high above the bay. On the rocky, spruce-green promontory of Cap d'Antibes 'they', with any luck, would soon be dispersed among the world's most exclusive yachting fraternity, while her mother and father returned to their stone-washed Provençal villa: Pa could sleep off his joyous champagne and whisky hangover from having lost a daughter and gained a son. Tomorrow would be another honeymoon day, she and Stuart on their way to the Greek islands.

On deck, Vinny Legrand, in her maid of honour, Bible-black and Puritan-white outfit, spoke to someone on a mobile phone, and then erupted like the

Mauna Loa volcano. 'Guess who that was, Stuwey!'

On his wedding day, a beautiful bride in his arms, more than enough champagne to hand, a spectacular sunset turning little white sails to little red sails in the bay, he couldn't have cared less. 'Whoever it was, tell them to go and eat worms in the garden. I'm busy . . .'

'Cashiloggan!' Vinny hissed.

'Who?'

'Cashiloggan! The billionaire arms dealer, lately released from prison, wanting to know why Mac-Kenzie, Toronto, haven't been able to sell his personal memoirs, bought by every other country on the planet, to Israel!'

'Go to it, then, Vinny, that's why you got the job in Toronto.'

Stuart had the supreme knack of delegating to lesser mortals without another thought given. Left to her, Olivia reflected in a kind of abstract way, she would have gone hurrying and scurrying to grab the phone, fax and big deal out of Vinny's hand, just to make sure it all went through smoothly.

How she wished she had his talent, wished she could be as laid-back as he was when it came to megabucks wheeling and dealing. Even at her wedding it was going on in surreptitious little whispers up and down deck, MacKenzie big noises never far from a phone or fax and the smell of money. In Stuart's book, however, it appeared there was no big secret to being a millionaire; it was all to do with attitude, and luck – tons of it!

Vinny grabbed Ashton Dore Cleaver's arm as he rocked over the side in the throes of sea-sickness, even though they were anchored and going nowhere for the moment. 'Ashton, I want your legal advice . . .'

'Is that what she calls it?' Stuart asked, and he and Olivia burst out laughing.

Maggie once more drifted by in her creamy-pink lace dress and her picture hat with artificial pink silk roses, looking more like the bride than the bride herself.

'Darling,' she said to Olivia, 'come away from the rail; the sunset does nothing for your complexion. You look positively mauve in this light – I told you not to wear blue! But you're not as mauve as your father. The old mogul emperor in his deckchair has turned right royal purple while the sun goes down on his retired golf-bald head.'

'Isn't she something?' Olivia said to her husband, both of them chuckling once more. Families were *such* an embarrassment, and at weddings were, in tennis championship language, the pits!

The honeymoon was a joyous experience for Olivia. Stuart was patient with her inexperience, delighted with her innocence and, under his expert tuition, Olivia became the passionate, fulfilled woman she was born to be.

Tender, passionate, fun and exciting, Stuart made every day – and night – of their honeymoon into a perfect memory. Olivia was so glad she had married him – the perfect lover she had always dreamed of, and had subconsciously been waiting for.

CHAPTER 8

Midhurst, Kent, 1990

The four-week honeymoon cruise among the Aegean islands over, Olivia returned to the workplace looking suntanned, relaxed and infinitely happy.

Birdie remained out of her depth in her bright new twenty-first-century office with computer screens and undefiled desk drawers. She brought her moans to Olivia – her coffee machine was redundant on account of Canadian-style coffee-vending machines in all corners, which belched out not only coffee in all shades and sweetnesses and temperatures, but also tea, cocoa, hot chocolate, milk shakes and fruit juices: Birdie couldn't compete; no one wanted her fresh-brewed coffee beans any more!

Maybe, Olivia thought, that was because Birdie didn't filter them properly and it was like drinking volcanic sand. She didn't like to hurt Birdie's feelings, though, so she said nothing except, 'Why is your hand bandaged?'

'Scalded myself, didn't I!' Birdie turned tail and scampered, straight into Brodie Forrester, head of sales. 'Watch where you're going, Mr Forrester! No one's allowed in here without an appointment . . .'

Always po-faced, he ignored her. 'I've brought you the printout you wanted, Olivia.'

'Thanks, Brodie. Birdie was just bringing me a cup of coffee; sit down and join me while we discuss the latest sales figures.'

Dankers, meanwhile, had been shoved into a smart new dark green and gold-braided security officer's uniform, to stand behind a smart new reception desk and dish out impersonal little plastic pin-up identity passes to anyone who desired to step beyond the lobby desk and into the hallowed inner precincts of the MacKenzie Publishing Corporation, UK.

His running battle continued with the other Mac-Kenzie men on the desk, who did not like his 'personal touch' of drying off wet umbrellas amid their in-house high-tech security TV monitors. 'They' had complained to management, in Olivia and Stuart's absence, about Mr Dankford's old-fashioned ways and smarmy attitude.

Dankers, in turn, objected to the 'new, baby-faced, jumped-up, ex-armed forces, policemen, and macho brigade throw-outs, who only thought about their pay-cheques at the end of the day, never mind treating people with respect and dignity – "Oi, you there . . . yeah, *you*, with the briefcase under yer h'arm! Come back 'ere and register yer name while we takes a good butchers in that case. Here's a clip-on ID if yer wanna see the Sci-Fi chap in editorial" instead of, "Excuse me, please, sir (or madam, as the case may be), may I be of assistance? Who is it you wish to see? Oh, that'll be Mr Norry Wilmot, editorial manager of sci-fi fiction, fourth floor, sir/ madam. Would you, please, just sign your name here and I'll pin this little badge on you – just so as you don't get lost, and I will ring up straight away to ask Mr Wilmot's assistant to escort you safely to his office . . ." '

Dankers did a very good interpretation of a ventriloquist and his dummy, Olivia had a hard job to keep a straight face while Dankers put forth his case of 'personal harassment' to management. But the fact, though exaggerated, remained – those nice little touches from Dankers cost nothing – 'like it had been at Lamphouse in the old days, Miss Olivia'.

She pulled strings on Danker's behalf: he was working for his pension, having been with Lamphouse for forty years, aiming to go the whole hog to fifty; he was not far off a golden handshake; don't make him leave now, tail between his legs. Dankers was the politest doorman – sorry, security officer! – of the lot. She herself objected to being greeted by a reception clerk – sorry, security officer – with the words, 'Oi, you there, before you get in that lift, come over 'ere and sign yer name!' She did not know from where in-house security officers were recruited these days, but courtesy cost little. Dankers, in view of his long service as a front-of-house doorman, ought to have been made officer in charge of MacKenzie internal security, and then *no one* could argue with him, thereby bringing peace to the new establishment.

'Remember, we are at *their* service, they are not at

ours. We earn our living from them, they are our bread and butter, so treat them with respect – i.e. the general public, which includes authors!' Olivia had pointed out to the board. Once again she was accused by MacKenzie directors of 'nepotism'.

Being Mrs Stuart MacKenzie was going to be a rocky ride, to say the very least. Instead of performing her real function as Lamphouse's managing director and senior editorial consultant, she was now Big Chief Peacemaker. She told Stuart that her post-honeymoon in-house experiences were *not* part of her marriage contract. He didn't want to know about the petty internal wrangling of his staff. 'Tell personnel, not me.'

She couldn't really blame him, she supposed, and wished *she* could remain as detached.

The next few months went by so swiftly, another New Year was upon them before Olivia became aware of it. Fully caught up in her role of Lamphouse's MD, she had never had so little time to herself, nor had she ever worked so hard.

The whole economic situation was depressed – the pits for the book trade, according to Birdie who liked to do her Cassandra bit in foretelling the gloomy future where Lamphouse was concerned. 'Couldn't come at a worse time,' Birdie said, 'seeing as how Lamphouse is trying to make an impression with MacKenzie, ha-ha!'

The fight to keep the book market afloat, let alone remain at healthy profit levels, was all about fight the good fight. Olivia worked over the figures of Lamphouse's six-monthly profit and loss returns. Shades of the early eighties all over again when Lamphouse had almost gone under, along with a great many other companies, it seemed that, as soon as they managed to get it right, down they plunged again, boom and bust.

Or get it right, Olivia, she told herself over fruitless hours of juggling with royalties, advances and escalating printing costs; it seemed that more money was going out than coming in. The only way to reverse the trend was to cut back on the big advances made to authors – tough on the authors, but it had to be done.

Stuart came into her office one morning in February, the gleam in his eye warning her that he had another little card trick tucked into his pristine shirtcuffs. 'Honey, how would you like to move out to a place called Kent?'

Still trying to come to terms with in-house management, stroppy authors who did not meet their deadlines yet still demanded their full advances, as well as Faye Rutland-type hype, not to mention manuscripts sent to the bottom of the pile because all submissions were required to be readable typescripts, double-spaced, and to the best of one's ability correctly spelled and presented, Olivia swivelled round to face her dearly beloved husband, for better or worse, and tried to appear as though she was in perfect control. 'Say that again.'

'A first wedding anniversary present, sweetheart.'

'Hey, slow down, Stuart! What's all this about? In case you've forgotten, we got married in July – last July . . .' A hasty glance through her diary brought her to February 1990. Olivia wasn't too sure herself whether she'd skipped a month or two, or even a year or two; Stuart had taken her unawares, which he had a habit of doing, of course.

Sweet of him, though, to even remember there was such a thing as a wedding anniversary. Her father had never ever remembered anniversaries and birthdays, and had left 'all that kind of sentimental stuff' to Birdie to organize. Olivia, however, did think that Stuart was being a little premature in his good wishes.

'Kent, I think we should buy it,' he continued to insist.

'The whole county?' She knew she was being facetious; he didn't.

Stuart waved an estate agent's handout under her nose. 'Midhurst Manor! It looks like a great place for us to live. Within easy commuting distance of London, twenty-eight acres of land – most of it is in the valley below as the house itself is built on a little hillock, but we could keep horses. I know our first wedding anniversary is in July . . .' he didn't and he hadn't, but Olivia forgave him '. . . but I don't want to lose the place. By the time the sale goes through, it probably *will* be July. If you want to quibble over incidentals, let's call it a birthday present.'

'My birthday's in September; it's only February.'

'Well, then, February is a kind of anniversary month for us – last February you said you'd marry me, or have you forgotten Virginia Water? Come on, sweetheart, can't you accept the fact that I *want* to do this thing for you – for us?'

'I'm sorry. I'm being very ungracious, but why not just say what *you* want, Stuart?'

132

'OK, I know you grew up with horses – no reference to Sir and Maggie – but you know what I mean.'

'Do I?'

'Yes, cracks in the walls and ceilings, reclaimed river frontage, shrinking gardens, not to mention foundations. Yuppie land is falling apart. Not a good investment, I admit it now. Money down the drain; the sooner we get out, the better. Midhurst Manor looks rock-solid, something we should think about for the future. You know, children, raising a family and all that . . . huh?' His voice petered away when he saw the look she gave him. 'Well, one day we'll want a family. I know you're busy right now.'

Olivia looked at the estate agent's handout – Stuart had done this thing off his own bat, without her prior knowledge. Now he was sneakily removing her from her executive desk to relegate her to a kitchen sink and children, just when she was about to prove her worth as head of Lamphouse!

He was so devious. Why had she failed to see it?

Not only was he devious, he was also possessive, jealous and afraid she might outstrip him, professionally speaking, hence her removal to Kent!

She was angry with him. He ought to have consulted her first. She had not been aware of his desire to move out to wide green open spaces – another step towards taking away her own choices.

She dismissed him, and his subject. 'Sorry! No green wellies and muck and mud for me. I'm a city girl.'

'And I'm a city guy, who grew up in the shadow of the tallest building in the world – no, not my father, but the Sion Tower, until Dallas overtook it. Sixteen auto-route systems carving up downtown Toronto, that's the city I grew up in. So give us a break, Olivia!'

They went to look at the house. Olivia fell in love with it immediately. It needed a lot of work, inside and out! The late owner, Brigadier-General Sir Gerald Urquhart, Bart., had faded away gracefully in a Tunbridge Wells nursing home, thus ending the illustrious line of old colonial baronets while leaving the manorial property in a very sorry state of repair.

'The asking price of £450,000 is quite cheap for a property of this sort in this area,' said the estate agent. 'A property of this sort in good repair would fetch £750,000.'

'But it's not, is it?' Olivia parried. 'Far from it.'

'Granted, a lot of money will have to be spent to restore it to its former glory, but it's still a bargain,' said the estate agent, well aware of the black Ferrari parked in the yard; he had always assumed they came in one colour only, red, so it was obviously American and Americans had mighty dollars to play with.

'No worries,' Stuart said nonchalantly.

'Woodworm in the rafters and beams, sir,' said the agent, coming clean for the sake of his professional reputation.

'No problem,' said Stuart.

'Requires a new roof – Kent peg tiles come expensive these days.'

'No problem,' said Stuart.

'And a lot of tender loving care to stop it slipping down the hill, sir, madam,' said the honest salesman, beginning to rub his hands, nose twitching as it sensed a sale coming up.

'No worries,' Stuart said, squeezing Olivia's hand while they walked round the house, poking, prodding and examining the rotten window frames, warped beams, worm-eaten oak panels and beautiful cedar staircase left to rot. 'Do you like it?' he whispered in her ear.

'Love it.'

'Told you so!'

Breathtaking views from all four points of the compass had captured their attention, and imagination. A splendid panorama across the Weald of Kent, and no immediate neighbours. Olivia knew she could be happy here. The whole place exuded an aura of tranquillity, of time at a standstill, a sense of permanence – well, semi-permanence. Right now everything required a lot of tender loving care to salvage it from the brink of a demolition order.

Yes! She breathed in deeply. Here was a place on which she could bestow a lot of tender loving care, given the chance. Money, of course, was no object as far as a MacKenzie was concerned: '£375,000,' she offered the estate agent.

'I shall have to get back to the old Brigadier's trustees on that account, madam – there *is* someone else after the property.'

Rubbish, thought Olivia, they all said that! There was no one else after Midhurst Manor except Mr and Mrs Stuart MacKenzie.

'Vacant possession, which means no long chain of buyers pulling out at the last minute. The new owner

135

could move in here within a matter of weeks. We shall have to accept the best offer, sir, madam, I don't think the trustees of the estate will go that low . . .'

'£390,000, and that's our final offer. Here's our card. Ring us on Monday morning, otherwise we withdraw.'

Stuart looked amazed, unable to get a word in edgeways between the agent and his wife.

Over the weekend he was in a ferment in case they lost the house on account of her – she had taken words out of his mouth; he hadn't had a chance to make his own offer. 'We *can* afford the asking price, you know!'

'Yes, I know,' Olivia said smugly, never before seeing him in such a panic over losing an acquisition, 'but we have to call their bluff. Wouldn't you like us to save ourselves sixty grand?'

'Of course – but are you sure about this?'

'You're not used to English estate agents, darling,' she told him, 'they're worse than sharks, they're piranhas. I wish you'd been as willing to offer Pa a higher price for Lamphouse.'

That shut him up.

On Monday morning the estate agent rang her at the office to tell her that the trustees of the Briga-dier's property were willing to accept their offer.

'There!' she told Stuart. 'Now you can put that £60,000 I've just saved you into my personal ac-count.'

'Fagin!' He grinned. 'No worries – knew I was right about your business head. How about a cele-bration lunch, just us two without the mob?'

'No, I'm too busy. Birdie and I are sharing sandwiches today.'

This time it had been *her* choice, Stuart had become her grateful green-wellied partner.

Their plan was to stay on in the Yuppie house in Docklands until the building work and redecorating had been completed on Midhurst Manor. But things did not go according to plan, even for the young upwardly mobile Filofax professional still willing to take risks on the property market.

In the following weeks they spent so much time on the phone and fax machines, talking to architects, solicitors, planning authorities, building inspectors, builders, roofers, carpenters, joiners, decorators, plumbers, electricians and garden landscapers, that in the end they decided that, instead of using up valuable office time, energy and temper, it would be less inconvenient for them to start living in the house and be on the spot for such discussions, and commute to the office every day. They would take it in turns to stagger their office hours.

Olivia resigned herself to a life of upheaval and inconvenience for the next few months.

She was unprepared for the disasters from hell.

Not even her husband, who took away her breath by the sheer pace at which he went through life, could compete with the hassle to follow. Off to London each morning in the Ferrari or the chauffeur-driven Rolls, back every evening for dinner – if lucky; more often than not they were stuck among the red cones of motorway jams and unscheduled in-house commitments. 'Sorry, Olivia, honey, won't be home tonight

. . . sorry about dinner . . .' or else they got a last-minute directive from MacKenzie senior, or one or other of them was flying off somewhere in the pursuit of business – MacKenzie senior again.

The Yuppie pad, now sadly past its heyday, had become a token of the past. They still hung on to it for the moment, renting it out to a couple younger than themselves, who failed to see that the real Yuppies, like ephemeral butterflies, had faded away on a wing and a prayer.

Stuart still had regular meetings with his father in New York, or the big noises at MacKenzie, Toronto, keeping the flagship sailing sweetly by flying Concorde across the Atlantic, while Olivia still had her own functions, meetings and author launches in town.

Olivia and her beloved husband became like ships in the night, passing each other and passing out on the pillow from sheer exhaustion, the hectic routine of their days spent at office desks, boardroom tables, in the backs of cars, on planes, while the never-ending banging of builders making a brand new Kentish peg roof over their heads all took its toll.

He mumbled sleepily one night, 'Can't remember the last time . . .'

'Last time for what, Stuart?'

'Nooky.'

'Horrible word!' she said, and promptly fell asleep with her head on his chest.

CHAPTER 9

Olivia had to put the brakes on Stuart's bright ideas when he suggested a swimming pool and gymnasium to add to their complex plan of current building work yet to be completed.

'A swimming pool is a waste of time in England where the sun only shines one day a year. And if you think I want to look out of my brand new Kentish farmhouse kitchen to a solar pool-bubble in the back garden, you've got another think coming, darling! Besides, we live on a hill.'

'Indoors, I mean, all very discreet. It'll blend with the architecture of the old manor house, I promise. We could have a Jacuzzi, sauna and solarium.'

'Oh, yes? And when have we time to relax in a Jacuzzi or a sauna, husband dear?'

'Now!' He had a wicked glint in his eye. 'No one banging around today . . . except me . . .' He chased her across the builders' rubble and into an old barn where Olivia took refuge, laughing.

Afterwards, she said, 'I suppose the next best thing to making love in a Jacuzzi is making love in a body-wrap of muddy straw!' She ruffled his dark hair and

139

picked out bits of mouldy straw before slapping back his flat cap as worn by the archetypal country gent. 'I think I prefer you in green wellies, Barbour, cords and cap instead of the sleek, sexy exec in a Savile Row suit.'

'And I prefer you with nothing on at all,' he chipped back.

They had to have a housekeeper. Olivia found Mrs Dannymott by placing a 'Wanted' notice in the local newsagents. Mrs Dannymott lived in Midhurst Village and turned out to be a treasure beyond Olivia's wildest hopes and dreams. This, after all, was an era of equal opportunities, minimum wage directives and no one to 'do' any more in the way of household duties, bar Rent-a-Vac.

Mrs Dannymott didn't mind, she was of the old school of housekeepers – she had 'done' for the old Brig. Plump, cheery, and utterly obliging, rather like an apple dumpling, Mrs Dannymott agreed to 'do' a few hours each day except Saturday and Sunday.

In the days to follow she left supper ready on the Aga hotplate so that Olivia wouldn't have to worry her head about cooking for 'hubby' after a long day in the office – the sweet woman! Olivia cherished her new housekeeper.

Neither was there the need to keep two chauffeurs, now that Stuart and she had combined their motor transportation. The MacKenzie Rolls and its chauffeur were dismissed – too ostentatious, Olivia had said; the locals would think they were jumped-up pop stars.

Ernest and the Daimler (unrequired in Antibes where her father had his yacht and his new Citroën to get him and Maggie around), were installed at Midhurst Manor. Ernest slept in a little bachelor flat above the garage, his joy being 'Mister Stuart's Ferrari', which he was forbidden to drive, but still polished to perfection every weekend. Next they wanted a handyman-gardener and soon found an obliging local who answered to the colourful name of Andy Grafter.

'Andy Grafter?' Stuart said jokily. 'You're not serious?'

'I am!'

'No!'

'Yes!'

'No!'

'Yes!'

'Don't you just love the country and its local Anglo-Saxon populace, sweetheart?' Stuart said when he realized she was not making up the garden handyman's name. He put on his Wellington boots and went out to inspect the big hole the builders had made for his indoor swimming pool and private leisure complex.

If there was one thing Olivia could not come to terms with, it was Stuart's twenty-first-century millionaire's mentality. When it came to extensionalizing and vandalizing an old property for the sake of self-indulgence, she was decidedly Victorian in her reproaches. Next there would be a super-duper house-warming party to baptize his extra-extensionalized ego, read swimming pool!

141

'Honey, sweetheart, Olivia . . .'

'Don't you honey me, Stuart! The old Brigadier would turn in his grave if he knew what you were doing to his property.'

'A pity he left it to go to rack and ruin then, huh?'

Oh, well, thought Olivia, calling a truce, they would both have to muddle through as best they could.

One morning Birdie took up an irritating stance on the threshold of Olivia's office overlooking Holborn Viaduct. She sniffed, and when Olivia did not respond, hissed, 'Are you busy?'

'You can see I am.' Olivia looked up in exasperation. She was tired, her eyes were sore from reading unreadable manuscripts, typescripts, spread-sheets, swatches of material, paint-colour charts and wallpapers; her head ached with the noise and banging still reverberating through it from they who monopolized her home, which still looked as if a demolition order had been slapped on it. All she wanted in the work-place was a little peace and quiet.

'There's someone here to see you . . .' Birdie made big eyes and gave a little jerk of her beak to indicate that there was someone standing right behind her.

Olivia drew her diary of the day's events towards her, 'I wasn't aware you had booked an appointment for me this morning, Birdie – I've a board meeting in ten minutes and then a . . .'

'No appointment, Olivia. It . . .' Once more Birdie appeared to have a twitchy left shoulder. 'It's a spur-of-the-moment thing . . .'

'What and who? Look, I'm sorry, but I can't see anyone right now . . .'

'Olivia, it's a lady-in-waiting!'

'Then she'll just have to go on waiting, sorry . . .'

'A *real* lady-in-waiting! Birdie appeared to be getting very hot around the collar. 'You know!'

Olivia said, 'No, I don't know, Birdie, so please stop talking in riddles.'

'*Violet!*'

'Who?'

'*Memoirs of a Shrinking Violet*, published by Lamphouse in 1932.'

As that did nothing to stir the boss's memory cells either, Birdie added for Olivia's benefit, *Youngest Lady of the Bedchamber*? You know! Lamphouse has published her royal memoirs before!'

'Oh . . . oh, yes, vaguely . . .' From Lamphouse's old cuttings book which Dankers used to keep at Reception and was proud to show her when she was but knee high to a grasshopper. Olivia said in a surreptitious whisper, 'Surely she's long past her sell-by date, Birdie?'

Birdie glanced nervously over her shoulder, and then hissed like a frantic fruit fly, 'You can't put Royalty on the slush pile, even if they haven't got an appointment!'

Birdie herself was suddenly removed from blocking the doorway by the emergence of a big-boned, strapping woman in headscarf, dark glasses, pearls, tweeds and brown brogues, seventy-five years old if she was a day. Under the cosmetic disguise she retained a vibrant and youthful air. She carried an unmistakable designer handbag over her left arm, and a portmanteau in her right hand. 'Good morning – you don't remember me, I suppose?'

'No, I'm afraid I don't . . .' Olivia was at a complete loss.

'Not your fault, we only ever spoke over the telephone. Lady Constance Arbuthnot-Fordyke-Toynbee, pseudonym Violet Fordyke, Miss Legrand.' She squeezed Olivia's hand in a grip that brought tears to Olivia's eyes, which said a lot for a gracious lifestyle, vitamins, work-outs and an undying belief in one's own self, thought Olivia – her ladyship's, not hers.

'We discussed the "subjects" in question over the telephone,' continued Violet, 'and you said you'd be delighted to take a peek in view of the writer's name and status. Violet – that's me – has now completed two incomparable memoirs, the first entitled *Living With Royalty*, and its sequal, *Dying for Monarchy* – about the hazards of a British Republican system.'

Lady Constance Arbuthnot-Fordyke-Toynbee dumped her capacious portmanteau on the desk, opened it, extracted a gold cigarette case and lighter, lit her cigarette and in a puff of smoke produced a sheaf of papers. 'Here they are . . .' She slapped them on the desk. 'First-hand knowledge of European monarchy as I knew it, and still know it: Portuguese, Spanish, Greek, Romanian, Russian, Norwegian, Dutch, Belgian and British, they are all there, *in flagrante delicto*, so read your heart out.'

She snapped shut the portmanteau of royal secrets and was about to depart with the rapidity with which she had entered, when Olivia gathered her senses.

'Excuse me . . . er, your ladyship . . .' A quick

glance at the state-of-the-art parchment and embossed coat-of-arms was not enough to reassure her. 'I think there has been some misunderstanding. I'm not Miss Legrand, but Mrs MacKenzie – Olivia MacKenzie.'

'Where is Davina?'

'In Toronto.'

'Can't be helped, I suppose. Where is Sir Harold?'

'In the South of France.'

'Typical of him, ever the handsome publishing playboy.'

Hardly, were Olivia's frenetic thoughts concerning her retired bald-headed father, not as I know him . . .

'Who are you – I mean your position, here, Mrs MacKenzie?'

'Managing director of Lamphouse and senior editorial director in place of Ms Legrand who is now with our Toronto office. I'm Sir Harold's daughter.'

'I knew you were a Cotswold the moment I saw you. You have his chin – at its worst, thrusting and aggressive in defence of your own realm, at best dignified. You'll do . . . take a peek at the scripts, my dear. Violet would like a firm yes or no – preferably yes, by the end of the week, when I shall be returning to Paris. Goodbye . . .'

'Lady Violet . . . I mean Constance, I'm afraid we are not taking any more unsolicited manuscripts for the time being,' Olivia said desperately.

The large (pre-war) lady-in-waiting paused on the threshold, blew smoke almost into Birdie's open mouth, still standing in the open doorway, and smiled behind her heavy dark glasses and manifold wrinkles. 'You will appreciate, Mrs MacKenzie – Olivia – that I am not just *any* unsolicited manuscript! I am Violet. An author who coined millions for Lamphouse during the thirties, forties and fifties. When my revelation of *A Royal Affair* was bought by millions, Lamphouse basked in my glory.'

'I did not mean to . . .' Olivia began, but was cut off in mid sentence by the author of *A Royal Affair*.

'In case your father never told you, I am an illegitimate descendant of his – no, don't look so shocked, my dear, I meant the Conte de Pira Angelloni, not Sir Harold's! Pira's family were connected to the Italian Napoleons, and his affair with my mother, the daughter of an English lord, caused a great scandal at the time. My father put her on the stage of the Folies Bergère as a dancer, where she was quite an attraction, I believe. Pira was poor, you see, and quite faithless. Mother shot him in a strategic part of his anatomy for being unfaithful to her whilst she was heavily pregnant with me: I, therefore, remained the only product of that unfortunate liaison. There is more to the family saga, but it's all in the book. So match that for fame and notoriety – if you will!'

Olivia could not. She had no defence, and so she paid more attention to the redoubtable illegitmate descendant of dubious European nobility.

'Lamphouse still needs me, Mrs MacKenzie. Your father ought never to have sold out to them. However, one should never cry for yesterday, only for tomorrow. Give him my regards if he's still level-pegging it around the golf course – I always used to beat him at his own game! Must, dash, my dear, I'm off to Harrod's.' She shouldered Birdie out of her way and departed with her aristocratic portmanteau and designer handbag.

Olivia slumped into her office chair and breathed deeply. Birdie was about to creep away when Olivia barked, 'Not so fast, Birdie Gough!'

'I was just going to get you a cup of strong black coffee, Olivia . . .'

'Don't you ever do this to me again! I felt such a fool. I had no idea who she was, why she was here and for what reason, except that she's utterly and totally insane! Now I'm lumbered with some dated memoirs no one would lose sleep over let alone fork out for.'

'*Royal* stories, Olivia . . .'

'*Shut up*, Birdie! Thanks to Vinny, *I'm* now lumbered! She could at least have warned me. It sounds as though she agreed to accept them prior to her departure to Toronto.' Olivia flung out an exasperated hand at the crested typescripts, most professionally presented, it had to be said. 'So what do I do now, Birdie?'

'Publish them and make yourself famous too!' said Birdie cheerfully. 'No harm in earning Lamphouse a royal death warrant!' Birdie trotted off to fetch the coffee.

Olivia felt guilty watching Stuart packing his suitcase prior to a trip to the States. She sat at her dressing-table in the big bay-window with new leaded-lights and seasoned-oak frames. The master bedroom was now redecorated and refurbished in keeping with its manorial stateliness, and so too was Stuart's adjacent dressing-room. His suitcase on the four-poster bed, he rummaged through the chest-of-drawers in a bid to find his underwear.

Olivia did offer, 'Can I help?'

'I can manage.'

'Your socks are in the bottom drawer, underpants in the next one up, ties are in your wardrobe and your shirts are . . .' in the linen-basket still, but she kept quiet on that score, hoping he had sufficient clean ones.

She had wanted to do it all herself, but the new bride's intentions had gone sadly awry. She had wanted to be a good wife to him, as well as a responsible business partner. She had wanted to attend to his everyday domestic comfort and welfare, as well as the decor and refurbishment of her home. Time and tiredness did not allow for such indulgences: life in the 1990s was tough on a working woman.

Compromise was an opt-out, but they had compromised. An interior designer had taken the strain. A shake and a nod, and the thing was done – no real satisfaction in that.

Olivia rubbed night-moisturiser on her face, her honeymoon suntan now only a distant memory. Her skin felt flaky and dry from spending long hours under artificial office lighting. She tried to make some conversation, as a means of still keeping in touch with him, even though they were both tired enough to crash out at a moment's notice.

'You should have seen Birdie's face when Lady Constance Arbuthnot-Fordyke-Toynbee, alias Violet, bodily removed Birdie from blocking her path. It was the best Rugby tackle ever! Lady C. must be at least seventy-five if she's a day! I started to read her Memoirs of royal reminiscences, 1952 to 1972. *Living with Royalty*, about her affair with a Russian Grand Duke. She lives in Paris now. It makes fascinating reading, and certainly broke up the train journey home.'

'You caught the train home?'

'Yes, why not? You had the Dame, remember.'

'We ought to have kept the Rolls and the Mac-Kenzie chauffeur.'

'Not necessary. I like the train. Gave me time to read all about Violet's several other colourful affairs and marriages. What a life she's led! Did you know she even became a volunteer – Royalist Forces – during the Spanish Civil War? After which she was parachuted into France by the British to fight with the French Resistance because she could speak several languages, including German. She is of course quite definitely dotty. Ought I to publish them? I mean, it's a bit sycophantic, isn't it? Lamphouse is knee-deep in good and bad material, so why should I be drawn to the memoirs of "Violet", just because of her minor royal connections, very minor, assuming it's all true. Apparently, she's been published by us before, pre-World War Two and in the fifties.'

'Up to you, I don't know anything about books,' Stuart replied shortly.

149

'Is that all you can say? You're not very chatty this evening, are you, my darling?' Olivia protested at his couldn't care less attitude. It was not like him at all. He was usually so with-it, bubbly and charismatic: Stuart was like a glass of champagne. When the bubbles went flat, so did she.

'What else can I say?' he countered. 'No, you shouldn't, yes, you should; it would be a great feather in MacKenzie's cap to publish the memoirs of a dotty old lady with delusions of grandeur?'

'Lamphouse, you mean!'

'Same difference. Publish blank pages if you like, if you think an aristocratic name will make any difference to the profits of the company.'

'You've been talking to your father!'

'Not recently.'

'You're making me feel very guilty, Stuart.'

'Why?'

'Your attitude for a start.'

'I should be the one to feel guilty, making you travel by train because I'd hogged your Pa's Dame! I hope you went first class.'

'*Our* Dame! Why first class? I like slumming it!'

'So I've noticed.'

'What's with you, Stuart? Travelling on a train with other people gives me a chance to read the day's workload as well as listen to other people's conversations – very entertaining to say the very least, even if they are *ordinary!* I can't read in the back of the Dame or the Rolls because reading in a car gives me car sickness! I'm *ordinary* – so what's wrong with that?'

150

'Nothing, except, I've told you before, people like us can't always do as they please. You *think* you're ordinary, but you're not! Someone like you, in your position – dare I say it – a millionaire's wife, beautiful, unprotected and guileless, can easily be hijacked and held to ransom.'

'Oh, poof! You're getting carried away by your bang-bang, all-guns-blazing American background.'

'Canadian, actually.'

'Not to mention your flashy superiority.' She turned around on the dressing-table stool. 'You're making me feel *very* guilty!'

'Why?'

'For not packing your suitcase for you, dammit!'

'Why should you?'

'Because I forgot about your clean shirts.'

'No problem.'

'You told the estate agent no problem, and look what we've got – problems galore! Burst watermains, no electricity: I forgot about your shirts. I forgot to tell Mrs Dannymott to put them in the washing-machine . . . I'll go and do it now since they've re-plugged us to the re-connected mains . . .'

'Forget it! It's nearly midnight, they'll never be dry by morning.'

'I'll put them in the tumble-dryer.'

'Forget it, Olivia! I'll buy some new ones at the airport.'

'There you go again! "I'll buy some new ones at the airport!" The poor woman's answer to everything: marry a rich man! Don't make me feel so guilty, Stuart, I can't be everywhere at once.'

'I'm not asking you.'

'Then what are you implying?'

He didn't reply, and that made her madder still. She flung the tube of moisturizer amongst the scent bottles and 1920s Art Nouveau silver-backed dressing-table set which had belonged to her Cotswold grandmother, and said, 'Why are we nit-picking like this?'

'Nit-picking?' Nakedly gorgeous, he went into their ensuite bathroom, condescending and hurt by a mismanagement wife. 'Who's nit-picking, honey?'

Olivia sank back down on her dressing-table stool; suddenly she was living life as her mother had lived hers. Suddenly she was not a person any more, but a wife: a wife who went everywhere in the wake of her husband, did everything according to his decree, a partner who was not a partner any more but a dictator because a marriage certificate and a wedding ring had made her his acquisition.

Well, get wise, Stuart!

This was not marriage number two in his Filofax, about to hit the rocks, but one that was going to survive – until death did them part!

Olivia followed him into the en-suite untiled bathroom (they were still waiting for the tiles to arrive); she paused on the threshold, temper rising, a temper she never knew she possessed. 'Don't walk away from me when I'm talking to you.'

'You were not talking, sweetheart, but aggressively arguing.'

'And what are you doing?'

'Shaving . . . so I don't have to do it first thing in the morning. My flight leaves at seven.'

'I've taken the next few days off so that I can work from home and be here for the swimming-pool men in your absence.'

'I'm only going for three days, honey.'

'Don't call me honey!'

Three days – time enough for Noah's flood to take place.

Olivia warned herself about becoming a nagging housewife, something a man hated. She had read about such harridans in all the novels she had ever perused from a critical in-house reader's point of view.

'Stuart, I love you as if there was no tomorrow, you know that.'

'I love you too, sweetheart.'

'I've . . . OK, never mind, but I *want* to take you to the airport myself.'

'Not necessary; we have a chauffeur who gets paid to run us around.'

'There you go again! I want to be a proper wife, Stuart – proper meaning ordinary. All my life, life itself has whistled to my father's tune. I don't need that kind of lifestyle any more.'

'Then why did you marry me?'

'I want to be here *for* you – *without* the trappings of wealth!'

'Then you should have married someone else, Olivia.'

'What are you trying to say, Stuart?'

'What are *you* trying to say, Olivia?'

'I'm trying to say that I believe in an adult working partnership, but that a privileged lifestyle isn't necessarily one that makes for happiness. I'm trying to say that our kind of life doesn't have to lose sight of the essentials, like, I'm still a person who wants to keep her feet on the ground in case the bubble bursts. I'm trying to say, if that happens, I won't feel quite so let down and won't ever blame you for not keeping your promises. OK, I'm not the eternal optimist, I'm a workaholic too, in case you hadn't noticed. I know that once we stop working for a living, you and I and the whole rigmarole of Lamphouse-MacKenzie, our privileged lifestyle and millionaire status will disappear overnight. Life is tough out there, Stuart – my Pa *didn't* teach me that. I learned it for myself.'

'You're preaching to the converted, honey,' he replied.

'So now, I will go and wash your bloody shirts, dry them and iron them, so that they'll be all clean, nicely dry and aired, according to my mother's heartfelt decree after thirty years of marriage without a dirty shirt in the linen basket,' Olivia told him flatly.

'You and your mother read too many hysterical novels!' He grinned in the shaving mirror. ' "Stroppy"! British informal slang meaning bad-tempered or hostile, quick to take offence, 1950–55, from ob-strep-er-ous, the "o" remaining unexplained. Oh, but I guess it's an American version not published by Lamphouse, and so they don't want to know. You're overtired, and definitely pre-menstrual.'

She threw his slipper at him.

It was impossible to remain hostile towards him!

He was a latter-day twenty-first-century man, almost, who knew all about dysfunctional feminine moods, and how not to cope with them.

Olivia flopped into bed, drew the sheet up to her chin – not black stain any more, but non-iron cotton-terylene floral, black satin having been relegated to the back of the linen cupboard in case Mrs Dannymott got the wrong idea about them – and thought – let him buy new shirts, damn him!

She turned on her side and made a good pretence of being fast asleep when he removed the suitcase from his side of the four-poster and flopped in next to her. 'Olly, are you asleep?'

She jabbed him hard with her elbow. 'Don't call me Olly or honey – I hate you for making me feel so inadequate.'

'You're wonderful . . . come here and let's prove it . . .'

'Go to hell.'

'I love you.'

'I don't love you.'

'Yes, you do.'

Yes, she did! She turned over and faced his smooth chin and smiling eyes and knew she was going to miss him like hell on earth, even if it was only for three days.

CHAPTER 10

At five-thirty a.m., Ernest, who slept over the garage, was still asleep when Olivia backed the Ferrari out into the yard. She felt eyelid-stuck with tiredness – Stuart could exist on five hours' sleep; she could not!

She wished now she had let Ernest take him to Gatwick.

But she had wanted to see her husband off like a good little housewife.

In Gatwick's shopping mall he who usually had all his clothes tailor-made and thought nothing of paying thirty dollars per pair of Bloomingdale socks bought himself three pre-packed shirts, and didn't seem to mind that there were no Armani labels or that the sleeves might not fit his long arms.

They kissed for fully five minutes in the executive lounge and then his flight was called and he was gone from her, the slick city businessman travelling first class – what else?

Olivia returned to Midhurst. Stuart had given her *carte blanche* where the Ferrari was concerned, and no greater love hath any man for his wife, Olivia

156

couldn't help thinking when she parked it in the new garage and slammed shut the steel doors. Ironic too, she mused, that the Ferrari got a roof over its head before the mistress of the house!

It was eight-thirty and the day was still young, but an awful lot of people seemed to be about, all noisily arguing amongst themselves. She had been hoping to steal another three hours at least in bed, but now it seemed any such hope was gone.

At first glance there appeared to be several hundred people claiming her own private little patch – a mere dozen when she sorted out her angry statistics. The new gardener-cum-handyman, Andy, brandished a spade in a most threatening manner, while Ernest shouldered the heavy metal steering-lock from the Daimler, both of them in defence of Mac-Kenzie territory.

Olivia, in a panic, shouted at them before they did someone mortal damage with their instruments of trade, 'Hey . . . stop that, you two!'

Ernest and Andy retreated. Olivia turned to the group of trespassers. 'This is private property, what are you all doing here?'

A bearded man in his late sixties, Olivia hazarded a guess, became the spokesman. Rucksack, walking-stick and heavy walking-boots poised over the crater at his feet, he said, 'Mrs MacKenzie, sorry to be a nuisance, but this is a public right of way.'

'Are you sure?'

The bearded man thrust an Ordnance Survey map under her nose. 'The old Brigadier knew of it – the right of way across his land. We seem to be stuck in our tracks, which is contrary to the articles of law governing footpaths and rights of way.'

On the brink of the crater, Olivia too, was stuck.

She glanced at the yellow-penned highlighted right of public access picked out on the OS map. 'I think there must be some misunderstanding, Mr . . . er . . . ?'

'Grieves: Theodore Grieves, Mrs MacKenzie, chairman of the local Ramblers' Association.'

'Oh . . . oh, I see.'

'There seems to be a hole in front of us, which was not here in the Brigadier's day.'

'Yes . . . I mean, no! I don't know how this was overlooked by our solicitors and planning authorities, but do you think you and your ramblers can come back another day – when my husband and I have sorted out your right of way across our property?'

'Public property, Mrs MacKenzie, according to ancient common law rights granted to the people of Midhurst in the Magna Carta.'

'I dare say. But as you can see, Mr Grieves, none of your ramblers can go anywhere for the moment, in view of . . .' a damn big hole, Olivia wanted to say, but changed it to '. . . in view of an architectural mishap.'

'Perfectly understood!' Theodore Grieves doffed his flat cap, smiled benignly and instructed his fellow ramblers to turn around and follow another path through to the valley bottom to reach their objective – he did not specify what objective.

Olivia went indoors and picked up the wall-phone

in her recently renovated farmhouse kitchen, complete with Aga, rustic quarry-tiled floor, state-of-the art wall units in solid oak and work surfaces of germ-free marble, and dialled Stuart's lawyer, the architect, then the land registry office, then the planning officer, then the estate agent.

Each time she was fobbed off with the same answer – Mr, Mrs or Ms So-and-So were at a meeting.

Olivia huffed a sigh of discontent on her kitchen workstool; she had done the same – or rather, Birdie had done the same to prospective complainers on her behalf: Ms Cotswold was at a meeting, even when she was actually wining and dining or being wined and dined at vast expense.

She took up the cudgels once more and drove the Ferrari to the nearest reference library, and there looked up 'ancient rights of way' appertaining to Midhurst Village and discovered that Mr Theodore Grieves and his ramblers were perfectly within their rights, no doubt about it. An ancient bye-law permitted public access from Midhurst Village across Midhurst Hill to the valley on the other side, cleaving a footpath through the manorial lands, which unfortunately meant the new indoor swimming pool and private leisure complex. Short of building a footbridge over the roof of the envisaged new extension to the main house, Olivia did not know what the answer was to the latest MacKenzie construction dilemma.

She sent a fax message through to MacKenzie, New York, informing Stuart of the current crisis involving a Mr Grieves and the local Ramblers'

Association, desirous of rambling all over their property. Olivia asked Stuart to ring or fax her, ASAP.

And, just in case he didn't go straight to the MacKenzie building after stepping off the plane, she rang the Plaza Hotel and left a message for him to ring her as soon as he checked in. He always booked in at the Plaza, simply because the family home was way out on Rhode Island, and the Plaza was not far from MacKenzie's offices on the Avenue of the Americas. To which venue Stuart was always shuffled back and forth in the stretched limo. Stuart seldom slummed it anywhere!

His call came through at four that afternoon, around nine o'clock in the morning in New York, just about the time city offices opened. 'Hi, I've just received your message – in fact I've only just got in from JFK. I'm still at the reception desk. Haven't even booked into my rooms as yet, or unpacked an unsweaty new shirt . . .' Did he sound just the slightest bit huffy? Olivia wondered. 'So, what's up?'

She told him, while wondering at his stamina – how could he start a new working day three thousand miles away, with so little sleep and so much travelling under his belt? Amazing!

Stuart said, 'Then we'll sue – don't worry about it, sweetheart. We'll sue everyone involved, estate agents, lawyers, architects, planning authorities, for not putting us completely in the picture prior to buying.'

'You can't sue your best friend, Stuart. Remember, you were all for Ashton Dore Cleaver to handle the sale for us. Putting business his way, you called it! We ought to have gone to a local solicitor who knew what he was doing.'

'OK, so I'll kick Ashton's butt – he's in London. I'll get him to sort it out when I get back.'

'That doesn't solve the problem of ramblers still rambling over your swimming pool complex. Even if we abandon the idea of the pool it still gives them right of way across our land.'

'Leave it with me, honey, it'll be A-OK, I promise.'

'A-OK! And don't call me honey.'

'Sorry: I'll be with you the day after tomorrow. Meanwhile, don't worry.'

Somehow he managed to put the world right, every time.

Olivia had done to him what her mother had always done to her father – the unforgivable. She had phoned Stuart in his workplace to gripe about domestic situations instead of handling them herself.

But how?

Marriage was a two-way partnership; had she gone behind his back and made a wrong decision, he would have had every right to criticize her; in fact, she'd phone ADC herself, right now, and tell him what a real hash he had made of their conveyancing. Stuart had probably had too much champagne when he put the papers in Ashton's hands. So much for mixing business and pleasure!

A sharp ring on the front doorbell followed by a thump on the sturdy door-knocker made her dump her coffee mug in the sink. Olivia put the phone call to ADC on hold; better still, she'd fax him, later. She went to answer the front door.

'Hello, I'm Annabelle van der Croote,' said a pretty blonde woman with a basket on her arm.

Olivia dismissed the sudden thought that she might be a colourful gipsy selling pegs. 'Hi . . . how can I help you?'

'You're Mrs MacKenzie – Olivia?'

'Yes.'

'Hi, Olivia! I would have called sooner, but Max and I didn't know if you were in or out. The ramblers said you were in, and so did Mrs Dannymott . . . I hope I haven't called at an inconvenient time?'

'Not at all.' Olivia stepped back. 'Come in, nice of you to call. It so happens I've taken a couple of days off work . . .' She held open the heavy oak-studded front door wider. 'I was just having a coffee break by myself; I'd be glad if you'd join me.'

Annabelle dumped her basket of fruit and vegetables in the hall. 'All fresh and home-grown. Anything supermarket I wash twenty times to get rid of hormone implants and chemical impurities. The kids – we've eight – are allergic to everything, including peanuts.'

She continued to divulge her family circumstances while following Olivia into the kitchen. 'I'll only drink your coffee if it's decaf. We're all vegetarians close to becoming full-blown vegans.'

'Sorry, no decaf,' Olivia stated helplessly, she and Stuart needing the 'buzz' of caffeine first thing in the morning to get them to work.

'Know the feeling – been there, done that – Max

and me. He sends his greetings. He's Dutch – South African Dutch, actually. I'm English. Max is a commodities broker with an office in London. You might have travelled up – or down – with him on the train. We're your nearest neighbours, in the valley below.'

For some reason, Olivia felt strangely drawn to Annabelle van der Croote, who divulged her life history very openly and without any snobbish reservations.

Annabelle pulled a wry face. 'What a lovely kitchen! Wasn't like this in the old days. More often than not he used to stable his horse in here – that's when he was able to ride without falling off it. For the last twenty years though, he had a drink-drive problem. But he *was* ninety-two when he finally pegged it – as any of us should be so lucky!' She hitched up her long skirts and draped herself neatly on a high kitchen stool. 'I was talking about the old Brig.' She hunched her shoulders in a playful, little-girlish way.

Olivia didn't doubt it.

'Lovely, lovely views!' She eyed the scenario outside the kitchen windows. 'I'm an artist – when I'm not doing other things: I heard Midhurst Manor was being restored to loving perfection by its caring new owners. It's about time we had a Lady of the Manor to preside over us. Don't mind me, Olivia, I'm just so pleased to have you as a neighbour and potential friend.' She leaned precariously off the stool to shake hands late into the relationship. 'I hear you're in publishing – Lamphouse, or something like that, Mrs Dannymott said.'

'Yes.'

'Books or newspapers?'

'Books for me, both for my husband. The Lamp-house Cross is an imprint of MacKenzie, USA and Canada, but both publishing houses are under one roof now – in Farringdon.'

'A double marriage, how super! I'd hate to work with Max. All he talks about is the price of animal feed, sugar, tea, coffee and wheat from Nebraska to Nanking! All very boring. It must be wonderful to be in something as clever and glamorous as publishing. I bet you meet some exciting people – of course you do! You married one of them, a millionaire – or am I wrong about that?' She peered into Olivia's face expectantly.

Olivia smiled; she was very pleased to be recognized as a person in her own right and not the wife of the millionaire publisher, Stuart MacKenzie, who had acquired the Manor House, but she knew the attraction always had to be with Stuart and his millionaire image. 'Would you like a glass of milk as we have no decaf?'

'Great! Lovely! Thanks! Don't mind us locals, Olivia. Gossip goes gathering in a small village; we knew all about you before you got here. We're veggies – have I said that already? I can bring you home-grown vegetables every day. Max and me, well, me mostly, we're into organic gardening in a big way.'

'Really?' said Olivia helplessly.

'I hear you've got problems with old Teddy?'

'Teddy?'

'Theodore Grieves and his ramblers.'

News certainly did travel fast around here, thought Olivia.

'Don't let Teddy pressure you into giving up your privacy. He had a running battle with the old Brigadier over the same subject. Our local ramblers just try it on . . .' Annabelle rested a milky-smooth arm along the edge of the sink and leaned forward in a conspiratorial fashion. 'You have *nothing* to fear, Olivia. Ancient bye-laws are a funny thing. I trained as an articled clerk before I got fed up with it. I'm an artist and sculptress now, well recognized locally. Art is not something you merely fall into, but is there from the very beginning. I'm not a clever person, a bit thick according to Max. I'm more of a creative person, even in bed – all those kids to prove it! But I tell you for a fact, don't let old Theodore and his ramblers get the better of you, they *have no rights!*' Annabelle wagged a warning finger.

Her words seemed like colourful beads strung along the length of her sentences, breathlessly divulged in little gushes of information. She sat gracefully sipping milk like a fairy wanderer from under a red-spotted toadstool. A wispy creature with her Tinkerbell voice and airy-fairy scatty manner to match, she looked cool in her high summer red polka-dot pinafore over a white body-stocking and red and white spotted calico hat with a turned-back brim. Amazing, Olivia reflected, how she could have given birth to so many children and still retained her slim-trim figure.

'No rights?' she asked. 'How do you mean?'

'Easement, Highways, Prescription and Use of Restrictive Endorsement concerning the Property Act of 1925,' Annabelle gushed forth like a clear crystal torrent.

'That's going back a bit, isn't it?' Olivia hesitated to ask.

'New laws only ever hark back to old ones. Parliament can't be bothered to update everything and get their facts right, especially concerning the more obscure feudal bye-laws regarding our countryside. They're so archaic, most have fallen by the wayside – so to speak. Parliament merely keeps on adding bitty postscripts to ancient history to update all the gobbledegook they then have the nerve to pass off as law. Loopholes are there, if you care to search for them. Ever heard of intermediate rights of way?'

'No.' said Olivia.

'You should have.'

'How?'

'On the plans of the property. Didn't you look at them properly?'

'Stuart gave them to his lawyer to look at properly.'

'OK, but you two should have looked at them yourselves. An intermediate right of way, also known as an "easement", is somewhere between a private and a public right of way. The land on which Midhurst Manor was built was granted to the Baron of Midhurst by King John of Magna Carta fame. The Baron gave what is called in legal jargon "an intermediate right of way" to the villagers of Midhurst. This meant they were "allowed" as opposed to "granted" access across his land in order to collect firewood from the forested area in the Vale of Midhurst to the northwest of your property. This "right of way", therefore, belongs by immemorial *custom* to the inhabitants of Midhurst, but is not "theirs" as a right *legally*, other than to gather firewood.'

Olivia paid greater attention to the artist and ex-articled clerk, who appeared to have been sent from heaven.

'Theodore tried it on with the old Brigadier, who was too old and sick to argue about it – probably forgot about the old "right of easement only" in the deeds of the Manor. What I'm basically trying to say, you can disallow or revoke the right of way across your land because the ramblers are not out to collect firewood from the valley opposite, but are using it as a footpath for their own personal pleasurable pastime – that of going walkabout to no real purpose.'

Annabelle had taken a great load off her mind, but she had to be certain there were no more 'loopholes'. 'Wouldn't we have to prove it in law?' Olivia asked.

'Nope – it's already written into the law regarding easements. Don't worry! The reason why I know so much about this property is because my father's the village solicitor – next best to being the village idiot! I was the idiot, being articled to him after I left college. Father was Sir Gerald's solicitor, so he handled all the Brig's legal affairs. However, having said that, Teddy and his lot *might* decide to collect firewood, and then they *would* have legal rights to the inter-mediate footpath crossing your swimming pool leisure complex.'

'How did you know we were building a swimming-pool?' Olivia asked, still in some confusion, adding, 'It isn't a complex, it's just a private indoor pool for our own use.'

'All planning applications have to be approved by one's nearest neighbours, who have a right to object if it inconveniences them in any way. Doesn't necessarily mean that the authorities will take their side. The local planning department sends notices around the Parish like a kind of "O Yea, O Yea" proclamation.'

'Is that right?' Olivia felt very ignorant about such things; she was a city girl, after all.

'Max and I raised no objection, we're too far away. As long as your swimming-pool doesn't present a problem to us – draining off our water-supply, that sort of thing – and is not an eyesore, we couldn't care less. My father, Henry Blackwood of Blackwood and Partners, is, as I just said, the local solicitor. You should have gone to him with your conveyancing. Us Blackwoods – although I'm now a van der Croote – know more about Midhurst than anyone else around here.'

'We didn't know about him – Henry Blackwood and Partners. We gave all the papers relating to this property to my husband's lawyer, who is also a good friend of his.'

'Well, as I said, medieval laws appertaining to places like Midhurst Manor can be quite complicated,' Annabelle stated.

Which said it all, Olivia supposed; it would have been better to have gone to her father's solicitor at the Inns of Court in London, who had handled everything to do with Lamphouse. But she had trusted Stuart, and Ashton, to know what they were doing.

'Not to worry,' Annabelle added. 'If Teddy insists on making a fuss, ignore him.'

'Is that possible?'

'Oh, yes. Teddy's all gas and gaiters. It would be just like him to make you keep the right of public access open by bringing back firewood from the forest. If he and his ramblers decide to revert to that kind of strategy, tell them you're relocating the "easement" elsewhere by resiting the Baron's beaten track further down the hill.'

'Are we allowed?'

'Well, you'll be quite within your rights. You see, since Baron Midhurst's day, a perfectly good road has been built from the village, which joins it to the Vale and the Wealden forest, so anyone wishing to collect firewood – ha, ha! – can go via the road. Simple! Just tell Teddy and his ramblers to push off along the public highway to collect their firewood – which is illegal anyway, since the forest now belongs to the Forestry Commission and is part of the Kew Gardens Trust.'

Olivia could have hugged her. 'Thanks, Annabelle, you've taken a load off my mind. I don't think I could have faced any more legal wrangling over Stuart's wretched swimming pool.'

'My pleasure,' she said. 'Anything else you want to know about public footpaths, easements and rights of way, just ask.' She scribbled down her phone number on a piece of kitchen towel. 'Normally a right of way is indisputable once it has been thrown open to the public for a number of years, and, during those years it has been in constant use by the GP – general public. But you can always argue the toss that in the last twenty years the Brigadier was senile and didn't know what was what, thereby allowing Theodore Grieves and his ramblers to take advantage of the "easement" clause mentioned in the deeds of the property, by turning it into a public footpath for pleasure instead of purpose – which was not its original function.'

Annabelle next talked about her family of many children while Olivia did the listening. When she was leaving Annabelle extended an invitation. 'When Stuart gets back from the States, Max and I would love you to come to dinner one evening – if you don't mind the chaos of our home.'

'We'd love to, Annabelle. But it'll have to be a Saturday evening. Weekends are the only time we get to ourselves – and even then, not always. Stuart is never in one place for long, he travels all the time with his job.'

'I understand. But don't forget, if you want a chat any time, I'm only down the hill – in more ways than one! I'll ring you about our dinner-date. Bye for now, Olivia – must collect Lois and Bryce from playgroup.' She skipped off with her empty basket and suddenly the place seemed remarkably dull and lacklustre, until the foreman arrived.

'You're late today, Mr Rapps. Where's your workforce?'

'Got another job on, ma'am, but we'll be back termorrer. Have to take the work where we can gits it, and that's why we're not always on the job – this particular one, I means. We have ter stagger the jobs.'

'Is that right?' Olivia smiled and made him a cup of coffee. 'Do you think we might at least get the house completed by Christmas?'

He sucked in his breath. 'Not easy, but we'll do our best.'

'Four more months, Mr Rapps, surely not? You've already been here three – in fact, ever since we moved, in, which was last May. We're talking only bricks and mortar, after all.'

'Not *just* bricks and mortar, ma'am, but a lot more besides. We've hit a snag with yer hubby's swimmin-pool.'

'What snag?' asked Olivia in alarm.

'Can't get on with anything more till the foundations of the new extension are sorted out. Seeing that it'll be adjoining the old house itself, it's got ter be done right in the first place, otherwise the building regs officer will be down on us like a ton of bricks. It's fer yer own safety too, all this rural planning thingy.'

Olivia said, 'I think we've managed to sort out the problem of a public right of way across the swim-ming-pool, Mr Rapps – well, we will have, once I've sent off a fax to our lawyer who handled the con-veyancing. As far as I'm concerned – and I'm sure my husband won't mind, either – we shall let the local ramblers keep their right of way across our land by relocating the footpath further down the hill instead of directly past our front door.'

'Ain't talking about no public footpaths, ma'am, but a bloody great cess-pit under.'

171

'Cess-pit?'

'Thought you knew?'

'Knew what?'

'This place ain't on mains drainage. Lots of places in the country still ain't connected, 'specially when they're on a hill. Surprised yer didn't know about it. Didn't yer solicitor point it out from the plans before you bought the place?'

'He might have. My husband and I know nothing about such things. We've left that side of things to those who do know, like your good self, Mr Rapps!' Olivia went indoors, away from such trivialities. She had better things to do with her time, like acquiring good new authors for Lamphouse, which could only be done by time spent on reading and being entertained by the written word, not discussing public service utilities!

CHAPTER 11

It started to rain in the drawing-room, which still had a tarpaulin for a roof. Olivia fetched buckets and bowls to catch the deluge from a real August thunderstorm – no point in screaming, there was no one to hear her.

Cowering under a mackintosh, she passed the buck: Stuart would just have to do some re-talking and rethinking with the planners, mains drainage experts and sewer-pipe connectors; it had been *his* idea in the first place to make a swimming-pool over a cess-pit!

She had wanted to get down to some serious editorial work but in view of the deluge from above and Mrs Dannymott's arrival, the next half-hour was spent mopping up the place and making more coffee and chit-chat concerning cowboys let loose on society.

After lunch of a banana and crispbreads – no point in cooking something just for herself – Olivia got down to some Lamphouse work at the kitchen table, since the kitchen and bedrooms immediately above were all that was fully rainproof.

Five minutes later she had to dash into the downstairs loo. 'Serves you right for not eating properly!' she told her re-emerged lunch.

She put it down to stress.

Stuart returned from New York. Ernest fetched him home from Gatwick.

Olivia told Stuart about the recent cess-pit crisis under his swimming-pool adding to the one of 'easement' over it, and how she had kicked his best friend's butt over the fax machine, which more or less told Ashton Dore Cleaver he was an incompetent idiot for not finding out what everyone in the district appeared to know.

Stuart didn't take it to heart.

'We'll get properly connected to the main drainage pipes, no problem. I'll get on to the planners tomorrow, about a new "easement" which will allow the ramblers to go their own sweet way across our land, but not necessarily within our view.'

'Stuart, I can't live with builders and planners for another minute, let alone another year!'

'You don't have to. If Mr Rapps and his team aren't doing the job, we'll get in another firm. Don't worry about it.'

'Easier said than done. This is England, not New York or Toronto – pity you didn't think of that when shooting your mouth off to your best buddy – just because he happens to be a lawyer! I'm sure American or Canadian laws concerning land and property differ from ours.'

'I have every faith in Ashton.'

'Well, I haven't! We have to re-apply for all sorts

of planning permissions to be connected to mains drainage and . . . and . . . the drawing-room and swimming-pool extension are no nearer to completion than they were three months ago!' Olivia said in exasperation.

'OK! Rome wasn't built in a day . . .'

'We're talking about an ordinary house, not the Colosseum.'

'Look, you're all stressed out for no reason. Shall we go out and eat – save you cooking? Somewhere nice and quiet, just us two?'

'Annabelle and Max have invited us to dinner.'

'Annabelle and Max?'

'Our nearest neighbours – she's really nice, very friendly and without any side. I haven't met him yet. Annabelle told me to ring her when you got back.'

'Then let's go and dine with them, if that's what you want.'

'What do *you* want?'

'Whatever you want.'

'Oh, Stuart!'

'What?'

Olivia despaired. She slumped down on the black suede sofa they had brought with them from the Yuppie house in Docklands. 'I *hate* living in two places at once! I *hate* all your . . . your black furniture! I want to buy *new* furniture!' She pounded the sofa with ferocity. 'Decent, elegant furniture as befits this house, not . . . not Yuppie-style death-by-cremation – or drowning!' She buried her head, ostrich-style, in the black suede sofa bearing the brunt of her onslaught. 'It smells damp and it's getting horribly

175

mouldy stuck here under a tarpaulin for a roof. Black might have seemed sexy and very macho to you when you were a single man, but now I want to have a say in how I want this place to look – not leave it to architects and interior designers and . . . and other experts who don't know *anything!*'

'Go and order what you want, Olivia,' he said brusquely.

'No point, is there?' She rose as if from the dead, her mascara smudged. 'Not for the moment, anyway. Everything will get ruined with the dust and debris and rain! Only half the house has been completed to our satisfaction so far. Even the Spanish tiles we ordered for the new bathroom and our en suite haven't materialized, in spite of the manufacturer's promises. At this rate it'll take *years*, not months, to finish. Sometimes I wish you were more *positive* about our *domestic* situation!'

'What domestic situation? We're married, aren't we? We've got a roof – two roofs – over our heads, sort of. We've got food on the table, good health, we're young, we love each other – don't we? So what's the problem?' He stood in the doorway between hall and derelict drawing-room, still unpacked, still marooned on the highway between being a publishing mogul and a domestically harassed husband. Stuart looked as lost as she herself felt in that moment.

'I need a life beyond publishing,' she said at length.

'Ring the neighbours,' he said, his clipped tones making it very evident that he didn't want to foul up another major domestic decision.

'It's not Saturday till tomorrow.'

'Then make a date for tomorrow evening. Right now I'm off to have a shower in the untiled en suite bathroom before trying to get some kip before getting back to Farringdon in the morning.'

'You're going into the office tomorrow morning?'

'Yes, I've got a sheaf of paperwork to attend to.'

'Just be back in time for dinner,' she muttered before she took up the telephone. 'Hi, Annabelle, it's me, Olivia. Will tomorrow evening be OK for our get-together? I know it's rather short notice, so do say if you've made other plans.'

'Great! Lovely! Is there anything you two utterly detest in the way of food?'

'Liver. We both hate liver.'

'Us too! Wouldn't touch it with a bargepole. The liver is a potentially life-threatening organ as it gives sanctuary to every known germ in the animal and human food chain, before passing it all through the digestive system.'

Olivia was forcibly reminded that the van der Crootes were dedicated vegetarians – would Stuart be able to cope?

'By the way,' said Annabelle, 'I forgot to mention it the other day because you were more concerned with rights of way, but did you know that the manor entails a title?'

'Sorry?'

'Oh, yes, my father reminded me of it when he came to supper last night – he's a widower. Mother died about two years ago . . . anyway, along with the deeds of entitlement to the manor house, provided that it has been fully paid for and is not subject to any hold over it such as a mortgage, your husband can purchase the title of Baron of Midhurst.'

'You're joking!'

'No, I'm not. Through the death of old Brigadier-General, Sir Gerald Urquhart, the title is now in "abeyance" – that's legal jargon for lapsed. The "Baronetcy of Midhurst" is not a hereditary title, but a purchasable one. £30,000 will buy you the right to call yourselves Baron and Baroness MacKenzie – rather like a personal number plate. It's nothing to do with peerages, which have to be approved by an Act of Parliament, but is an ancient "right of status" bestowed with the Manor of Midhurst – provided you have the cash.'

Olivia found it difficult to keep a straight face. 'I think we'll pass on that score, Annabelle. We've enough on our plate at the moment with rights of way, let alone rights of status! Stuart might like to be called the Baron of Midhurst, but I would simply *loathe* being a baroness!'

'Just thought you'd like to know. One more thing: could the Lady or the Lord of the Manor open our village fête in two weeks' time? August Bank Holiday weekend. You needn't decide now, tell us Saturday evening. Little old me is on the fêteful committee of the Parish Council – as if you couldn't guess!' Olivia could picture Annabelle giving one of her little hunched-shoulder shrugs of modest glee.

She made a cheese souffle and took it up to Stuart. He was relaxing in the four-poster in a bid to unwind from the pressures of big business, zapping through four British TV channels as opposed to forty-four American ones.

'I've brought you some supper since it's a long time to wait till Saturday night to sample Dutch vegetarian cuisine.' Olivia bent a knee and made her peace with him. 'Want to hear something funny?'

'What's that, my love?' He wrapped his arm round her waist and almost upset his supper tray. 'Not the one about what the bishop said to the callgirl, like what a good job I married an English cook with a Swiss diploma? À la Lausanne Finishing School-style, of course.'

'You can be quite uncouth, you know,' she replied primly.

'And you, my love, can be a real pain in the butt!' But he did kiss her with passion before tackling the cheese soufflé. 'I've missed you,' he mumbled through the hot cheese.

'Me too.'

'What's the joke?' he asked.

'Annabelle has just told me there's a title that goes along with this property – a status title.'

'Really? What kind of status?'

'For £30,000 you can buy the "Baronetcy of Midhurst", which goes with the property, entitling you to become Baron MacKenzie and me the Mrs Baroness. She was quite serious. Annabelle's father, Henry Blackwood, is a widower, which has nothing to do with being a solicitor but I thought I'd mention it in passing in case you decide to sack Ashton Dore Cleaver. Henry Blackwood handled the old Brig's affairs.'

'Legal or illegal?'

'Be serious for once.'

There was a distant gleam in his eye. 'Interesting.' He carried on eating.

'Oh, no! Forget it! I can tell by that gleam in your eye your transatlantic ego has been stimulated. No way will I let you spend £30,000 to buy yourself a personal number plate like that. If you want to spend £30,000 on an ego-trip, then give it to charity with your name on it.'

'It never even entered my head to go to such lengths to gain recognition, sweetheart!'

'Good! End of subject. So how did the meeting with MacKenzie senior go?'

'So-so. He was more in praise of you than me.'

'Why?'

'Because you've done great things with Lamphouse since becoming its MD. For the first time in recent history it has shown a profit, thus pleasing our little grey men in grey suits.'

'Shall we celebrate?' she asked, nestling her head against his bare shoulder.

Stuart's Yuppie-era black silk underpants were now laid to rest alongside his black satin bachelor sheets in the back of the airing-cupboard. He now slept in just his skin and, like all true transatlantic cousins, showered it a lot. Olivia ran her hand over his firm lean torso, and experienced as always the yearnings of love. 'I can always slip into something more comfortable, darling.'

'What's in the cellar?' he asked.

'Only me.'

'This soufflé is great, so why do we ever go and eat elsewhere, I ask myself, when I have a perfectly good *cordon bleu* chef on my staff? You know – we could always turn this place into a country hotel and advertize it as offering *haute cuisine* by the Baroness!'

'Stuart!' She thumped his shoulder.

'What?'

'I'm chatting you up for your body, and you haven't even noticed! I'm sorry for being a pain over your wretched swimming-pool; just say you love me still.'

'You know I do.'

'*Say it!*'

'I love you.'

He finished the cheese soufflé with relish and then zapped the TV. 'Come here, you abandoned female, and prove you're worth your wages.'

'In gold, Stuart Lyon MacKenzie, *in gold!*' She nibbled his ear with sensual passion.

'The Dutch like to eat well,' said Annabelle on Saturday evening, 'and they do eat well every day of the week – sorry about the mess, but the brood are home to roost. How I hate summer holidays!'

Olivia and Stuart fought their way through a hallway full of muddy trainers, cricket bats, rugby balls, tennis racquets, wet swimming costumes and a variety of animals, some stuffed, others very much alive. 'Meet Max,' said Annabelle.

'Hi! I am zo pleased to meet you. Annie haz told me zo much about you,' said Max van der Croote, big, blond and hearty; only his two barking-mad black Labradors and a huge shaggy English sheepdog were more hearty than he.

'*Aus!*' he commanded. The dogs, Candy, Claude and Jemima, jumped back on to the settee where one of the smaller children sat cuddling a cat. 'I haf never had ze pleasure of shaking the palm hoff a millionaire vith zo much money in it!' Max thumped Stuart on the back and laughed like a drain.

Behind Max and Annabelle, Stuart looked at his millionaire palm, shrugged and made amused eyes at Olivia. She could see him trying hard to keep a straight face, his wicked sense of humour never far from the surface. She kicked him on the ankle and brought him to order.

'Max was a wet-bob in his former Oxford rowing days.' Annabelle preceded them through from the living room to the patio, bearing aloft an elegantly garnished platter of asparagus, hard-boiled eggs and melted butter sprinkled with grated nutmeg.

'Your mother would love her!' Stuart hissed in Olivia's ear.

'Shut up! Be gentle with them!' Smiling fit to crack a plate, Olivia manhandled her husband past the children, dogs and cats, a parrot that squawked and left its droppings on the back of a chair, a budgerigar in a cage and an aquarium full of rare tropical fish. Heaven knew what the van der Croote household kept outdoors – lions, tigers and cheetahs probably! thought Olivia.

Two televisions blasted away simultaneously, one at which two boys were playing a video-game, the other tuned in to a popular Saturday evening pro-

182

gramme.

Annabelle and Max's 'brood' appeared to vary in age from one to twenty-one. Tandy explained how, by tugging Stuart's trouser-leg to gain his attention when he sidled past her and disrupted her view of the screen. 'I'm Tandy – I know you've been invited to eat with us, but *we're* not invited. Mummy said she'd kill us if we spoiled the evening. That's Amy, she's the baby, she's only one and a half. Mummy gets pregnant *a lot!*'

'The baby' was sucking the cat's ears, and marmalade fluff was stuck to Amy's chin.

'That's Lois who's crayoning over the floor; she's nearly five but still goes to playgroup with Bryce, 'cos there's no room for her in the infants school. It's falling down and there aren't enough teachers or money. That's Dicky and Gower playing silly video-games. That's Sally and Sarah, they're twins and they're nearly fifteen. The big one is Ute; she's the au pair who looks after us all because Mummy is always busy making babies with Max.'

Amidst the unbelievable din and confusion, Stuart and Olivia shook hands with all eight plus one – the 'big one': Should have been two, thought Olivia, noticing in which direction her husband's attention was focused. 'Nice to meet you, Ute.' She nudged Stuart forward to take his place outdoors where the table was set because it was such a balmy Saturday evening since he and Ute appeared to be super-glued for a second longer than it took to say hi.

Through the open patio doors Annabelle warned the children to stay away from the table laid out under the blue and white striped patio awning. 'Grown-ups only. I don't want anyone near us for the rest of the evening, except for Sally and Sarah who can help serve and wash up. You can eat up the scraps later. Ute, please wipe Amy's nose, it's disgusting. And please stop her from eating the cat.'

Annabelle was now in the role of war-goddess so Olivia saw a new side to her. Gone was the image of the airy-fairy princess of the other afternoon; she was now earth mother, fully in control of her little earthworms.

It was a wonderful evening for eating outdoors, warm and pleasant without even a wasp to mar the scene; they were kept at bay, Olivia noticed, by the number of mosquito-jars placed under the table and at other strategic spots around the food.

Olivia handed over a box of chocolates and a bottle of wine. 'Just to say thank you, Annabelle.'

'You shouldn't have,' Annabelle said, 'it really is our pleasure to have you and Stuart grace our table.' She added in an aside while Stuart and Max were talking, 'Some women have it all! Not only a millionaire, but dishy with it! Lucky you!'

'I wish Andy – he's our new gardener-cum-handyman – was as good as yours appears to be. Not a weed in sight!' said Olivia, suddenly embarrassed by Annabelle's gushing remarks concerning Stuart. Ute too had shown a marked interest in her husband; it gave her rather an uncomfortable feeling to know that a wedding ring did not necessarily mean he was totally private property. Olivia forced her mind back to what Annabelle was saying.

'Gardener? No way! Max and me couldn't afford a gardener. I do it all myself – with a little help from him.'

Oops! thought Olivia, put your foot in it there, didn't you, Mrs Millionaire MacKenzie!

'I'll show you around the garden later,' said Annabelle. 'It looks lovely by moonlight, but then, don't we all?' She sighed wistfully before adding, 'Behind that high wall is the kitchen garden. The herbs smell wonderful on a hot summer evening like this. I've tried to design it like the one in South Africa, where Max was raised. Of course I'm unable to grow the kind of exotic plants his parents had in their garden, but I'm persevering with the aid of a greenhouse.'

'How do you find the time to do everything when you've eight children to take care of?' Olivia asked in astonishment.

'I don't do *everything*,' Annabelle laughed. 'I only do the things I like. I hate housework, so I leave it all to Ute. I like gardening, so I make time for that. I don't like children.' Annabelle gave another Tinker-bell laugh. 'Only kidding – that's a joke!'

Olivia smiled politely.

'Down here in the valley,' said Annabelle, 'the land is flat – I suppose it would be, wouldn't it? I'd hate to tackle your slopy gardens up there on Midhurst Hill. Only thing you can do with it is terrace the slopes or keep horses and goats, like the old Brig who allowed it to go to rack and ruin. Thanks for the chocs and wine, you two! Golly-gosh, you're spoiling us. Look Max, real Belgian chockies – keep them away from the kids otherwise we won't get a look in.'

'Ja, chickadee! But I guess zis is not Zainsbury zupermarket Chardonnay but somezing extra special.' Max studied the label on the bottle of red wine Stuart had taken from his cellars. 'Not from a leetle farm in Africa, but a very good yar – many, many zanks,' he said in his thick Afrikaner accent, which got broader by the minute.

Olivia had the feeling (she hoped she was wrong), that Max thought they might at least have brought along a crate of champagne, seeing that they were millionaires! Funny, because she never actually saw any of this millionaire money, which all seemed to emanate from an invisible source, paid for by an invisible banker and accounted for by invisable accountants.

'Take a pew, you two, we don't charge,' said Annabelle. 'Sorry about garden seats with manky cushions, but the kids ruin everything . . .' She captured a green caterpillar off Stuart's seat before he squashed it, and carefully carried it in cupped hands to the low garden-wall separating patio from green lawns, flower beds and willow trees. 'I'd be a Buddhist if it wasn't for Max's high Lutheran principles.'

'I'd never have guessed!' said Stuart from the side of his mouth, looking at a vague point in the distance. Olivia kicked him on the ankle again – he was going to end up with a lot of bruises by the end of the evening, she couldn't help feeling.

Max got on to the subject of the end of apartheid and the new reforms promised for South Africa and

Annabelle said, 'I bet you two go to some fantastic parties, and know all the right people! Tell us how the other half lives, go on!' She made her little hunch-backed giggly plea. 'Drop names, *we* don't care, do we, Max?'

Once more Olivia felt acutely embarrassed by Annabelle's gushing appraisal of her lifestyle. She, like Stuart, did not like being treated like a rare species of life-form.

'Dream clothes and fabulous lifestyles, nightclubbing and filmstar authors who invite you to their mansions – do tell!' Annabelle continued to gush. 'Max, you know, is tickled pink – as well as green with envy – about living next door to people who own a Daimler-Sovereign *and* a Ferrari! Tell us how it's done, go on!'

'Nothing to tell,' said Olivia, 'except it's not easy. We both have to work very hard for a living. Stuart and I are just ordinary people – aren't we, Stuart?' She gave him her special naughty smile, her dimples deep.

'Go on with you! Don't believe you!' Annabelle tapped Olivia's hand. 'No one with your kind of lifestyle can be just *ordinary*, can they Max? What about all the high-life rave-on parties your kind of people go to?'

Our kind of people? Olivia wondered where Annabelle got that idea. 'We don't – we're quite boring and dull in that respect, Annabelle, I assure you. Stuart and I are mostly too tired to take up such invitations – not that there are that many.'

'We're just working-class millionaires, Annabelle,'

Stuart replied with a straight face. 'We play chess with paper-money. All unseen, untouched Monopoly money chasing around the world like confetti, and all gone in a trice if any of the big bad wolves touches the wrong button.'

'Let's hope no one does, then,' said Annabelle cheerily.

'Your husband, I dare say, can vouch for that, being a commodites broker,' said Stuart, who hated talking religion, politics and making money, and therefore manipulated the conversation towards another topic.

'I zink ze economy is over-'eating, ja?' said Max with his mouth full. 'I zink per'aps the cur-unch vill zoon come, and we vill zen be in a ver' big recession, ja? Bigger zan it eeze now, ja?' The more he talked with his mouth full, the broader became his accent.

'I don't know much about that,' said Stuart, trying to be as diplomatic as possible.

'Ah, but you muzz know it, Stuwart! Zer is great unemployment now in zer USA, and always, Britain is not far behind! You muzz know of it if you care about vot 'appens to the poor people of your country, and zis one, which *muzz be* your adopted home, like eet iz for me.'

It was difficult to find a level playing field; whichever way the conversation was manipulated, it always got back to the same three subjects out there on the van der Crootes' cosy patio – money, politics and power.

Maybe it was just them, Olivia thought. She and Stuart, a couple of millionaire maggots under a microscope, who got irritable and touchy when people started prodding them to perform like millionaire maggots.

'Yeah, I guess,' Stuart drawled in his lazy way, uncomfortable, and unwilling to be drawn on any subject remotely flammable. 'All I can say is, I reckon the British system is better than most. We're the lucky ones.' He said it cynically, crossing one Savile Row knee over the other. 'The rich men of the world who do our bit too – though some don't see it that way. I count myself working class, though I guess you won't buy that, Max.'

Hell's bells, Stuart, Olivia thought, don't start on *that* subject with Max van der Croote!

Max looked at Stuart in astonishment. 'You ought to be in politics, boy, for such a shit-sentimental streak. Hit 'em an' hit 'em hard, right in the pocket, where it hurts – isn't zat vot zer rich man tells himself – how the poor vill alvays be vith us.'

'I'm a publisher, not a politician.' Stuart turned to Annabelle. 'Great food!'

Olivia was glad he had changed the subject so abruptly. By now she wasn't too sure which side Max was on.

'Nut escalopes in a rich tomato and basil sauce – tomatoes and basil grown by my own fair hands,' Annabelle informed them, and then asked Stuart, 'Is Olivia a good cook?'

'She's a great cook,' Stuart rejoined, while Max refilled their glasses with the MacKenzie contribution to the dinner table. 'She knows the way to a man's heart, for sure!' Stuart gave Olivia the thumbs up before tackling nut escalopes and home-grown tomato and basil sauce.

Olivia praised him, silently, from the bottom of her heart. He had endured every minute of interrogation, circumspection and downright bourgeois hostility with supreme tact. Max obviously didn't like anyone richer and better-looking than himself, and courtesy was not his trademark.

Next came the Dutch rusks with currant sauce. '*Beschuit met bessensap*,' Annabelle said. 'Max's favourite.' She turned to Stuart. 'Can I ask a favour?'

'Sure!'

'Will you open our fête on August Bank Holiday weekend?'

'When?'

'Weekend after next.'

'What do I have to do?'

'It means cutting the red ribbon on the day, and presenting trophies for the biggest and best marrow, best dahlias, best home-made cake, best heifer, that sort of thing. Free beer in the marquee and home-made sausage rolls are the perks of the job.'

'Sounds OK to me,' he said.

'Are you sure, Stuart?' Olivia said. 'You might be in the States or Toronto the weekend after next.'

'I'll work my schedule around Annabelle's village fête, no problem, sweetheart.'

'That's settled, then,' said Annabelle. 'Come on, Max, chop-chop! Make the coffee and bring out one of your ghastly Dutch liqueurs while I cart these dishes away so that the girls can wash up.'

'Let me help.' Olivia got up to assist, but in the

next instant was overcome with a tremendous dizziness. 'Annabelle . . . sorry . . .' She sat down in a hurry, unaware that it was on Amy the baby, a kitten and a dog.

'Take some deep breaths,' said Annabelle, while the other children stopped whatever they were doing to look upon the little scene with profound interest.

'Shall I fetch her glass of water, Mummy?' asked Tandy.

'Yes, please, Tandy.'

'I don't know what came over me,' Olivia murmured at length, the clammy fainting fit mercifully past.

'I do. You're pregnant,' said Annabelle.

'I'm not – can't be.'

'Oh, yes, you are. I *know*, I've been there, done it, got the T-shirt. I know a budding pregnancy when I see one. Taking the pill is rather like a mantra. You do it over and over without thinking, until a moment of exquisite abandonment when concentration and everything else goes by the board, swept away on a tidal wave of lust! Practising safe sex is nothing in the hands of the Lord, believe me. I've been there many times. Lust comes first, condoms later. Congratulations, Olivia, you're about to be a mother, give or take another seven months.'

'Don't say anything to Stuart – not yet, in case it's a false alarm.'

Annabelle went on her way with the handful of dirty dishes. 'I won't even mention you're pregnant to my nearest neighbour.'

Tandy did. She brought Stuart in from the garden,

his hand held fast in her nine-year-old fist. 'Are you all right?' he asked. 'Tandy says you fainted because of a baby.'

'Good lord, whatever gave her that idea? She probably meant Amy . . .' Olivia turned to 'the baby' and gently withdrew the kitten from Amy's mouth. 'It's the heat, Stuart. I felt a bit over-heated, that's all, like poor little kitty here . . .' Overheated and half-mauled damp little kitty fled into the garden in the wake of the dog Olivia had hastily sat upon, the moment it was released from baby Amy's fond but untender clutches.

'Are you sure you're feeling all right?' Stuart asked with a concerned look.

'Don't fuss, darling, I'm perfectly all right!'

He relaxed. Olivia felt she could murder young Tandy! She and Stuart smilingly rejoined Max and Annabelle on the patio with a good excuse to take their leave.

When they arrived home at the unbelievably early hour of ten o'clock, Stuart tore off his tie, kicked off his shoes and flung himself down on the black suede Yuppie sofa with a sigh of relief.

'Thanks a lot, sweetheart, for a most unbearable evening. If I'd stayed there another minute, I think I'd've socked Max van der Crude right on his jutting jaw and that *would've* been the beginning of cess-pit sanctions. What a conceited *prat!*'

'I'm going to bed,' Olivia said. 'Don't forget you made another date with them – at the local fête.'

'A fête worse than death . . . I'm coming to bed

too, sweetheart.' He dragged himself off the Yuppie sofa she had suddenly taken such a dislike to, when in times past, they had shared many an abandoned and glorious hour on it. The effort exerted was only to help himself to a whisky and soda before he flopped down again in front of the TV. 'By the way, I should have mentioned it before, but Ashton's coming to lunch tomorrow.'

'Why?'

'To sort out our current conveyancing problems.'

'Conveyancing, past tense. We've already bought the place. He should have sorted out Land Registry searches *before* we purchased. Ashton in green wellies down a cess-pit or chasing over the ramblers' chosen route with a divining stick will not solves our problems. Just get him to re-do the proper legal work – properly, this time.'

'Yes, ma'am!' Stuart saluted her forthrightness. 'I didn't realize I was marrying a Tartar – sorry, perfectionist!' when she threw a cushion at him.

Olivia went up to bed. Now she would have to think about what to get for Sunday lunch; tea and dinner too, by the sound of it! She wished Stuart had told her earlier. She had been hoping for a nice quiet Sunday alone with her husband, cosily eating cheese on toast and reading the Sunday papers in the four-poster, the only true piece of manorial furniture they had happily inherited.

It had been too big to shift out of the master bedroom, so it had stayed. A token of their own married life, rather as the black suede sofa of Stuart's bachelor-husband days represented his

'Yuppie' era, but, unlike the old Brig's bed, was well past its sell-by date.

Neither of them had minded unduly about the age of the old four-poster – the mattress was brand new.

At the time too, it seemed an awful shame to chop up such a magnificent 'symbolic' bed for firewood. But . . . ! She might even do it yet, she told herself, if hopes of an early peace treaty regarding the 'firewood fiasco' involving Theodore Grieves and his ramblers came to naught. In which case, she'd chuck the lot at him who had invited himself to lunch tomorrow!

Olivia decided to keep it simple and *al fresco* (thunderstorms permitting), in view of all the home-grown salad and vegetables Annabelle had bestowed upon her.

Life at Midhurst Manor was proving to be the kind of Lamphouse saga she herself could never write, let alone edit on someone else's behalf! Olivia yawned, got into the Brig's four-poster with a sigh of bliss, and was fast asleep before the Lord of the Manor had finished his bedtime glass of whisky on the old Yuppie sofa downstairs.

CHAPTER 12

The start of a new working week. On Monday Olivia felt it was her turn to travel first class. Ernest would drive her to the office. Stuart had hogged her father's ex-Dame for too long now, no doubt thinking he was slumming it after she had made him get rid of the Rolls and the MacKenzie chauffeur. Cutting the housekeeping budget, *she* had called it.

Her dearly beloved husband had offered to stay at home to sort out their domestic problems; about time too! Olivia couldn't help feeling.

She had left him fast asleep in the four-poster while ADC occupied the Yuppie sofa with a hastily thrown-over duvet from last night. Ashton and Stuart had stayed up until the early hours drinking, talking and playing chess. She hoped Ashton would not be around when she got home from work; he was not a good influence on her husband – even if they had been 'buddies since fourth grade'!

Birdie picked up on her wishy-washy looks straight away. 'You look awful.'

'I feel awful.'

'Flu – everyone's down with it.'

'In August?'

195

'Flying off on holidays, no end of suspect germs brought back. Just think how many can get inside a jumbo jet!' said Birdie, adding for Olivia's benefit, 'No one left here to do any hard graft except Dankers and me. I'm glad you're back, Olivia.'

'I was here last Wednesday.'

'Seems like a lifetime ago. A lot has happened since.'

'I know the feeling, Birdie. My husband's American lawyer decided to stay overnight. They ignored the subject of public easement over our land and a cess-pit under it, and spent more time discussing a title of status entitling Stuart and me to call ourselves Baron and Baroness – can you believe it?'

At one time Birdie would have taken off on a shrill cackle of amusement. 'No kidding!' she replied soberly.

'For £30,000, Birdie! How about that for a waste of hard-earned money?'

'Pocket money to the likes of your husband – I should be so lucky!' Birdie was all doom and gloom this morning.

'If he hasn't hopped the nest by the time I get home tonight, meaning ADC, I'm giving him some more papers to handle on Stuart's behalf – divorce! I'm beginning to feel like an outsider in my own home, what with ramblers now adding to the rest of Kent's population occupying our space.'

'I know you don't mean it.'

Birdie limped out of the office, but halted on the threshold when Olivia said, 'What's wrong with your leg, Birdie?'

'I fell down the stairs at home – well, only one really, the back step when I was going out into the yard to hang up my smalls. Strained a muscle, that's all, so quit staring at me!' She hobbled off, and Olivia smiled to herself. Birdie sometimes liked to put on the agony of working amongst the MacKenzie crowd!

By Wednesday a lot more had happened – and something important hadn't.

Olivia picked up a home-testing pregnancy kit from a local chemist.

It was negative. She breathed a huge sigh of relief.

False alarm! Annabelle was wrong in her eight times earth mother forecast.

It was all down to pure stress; she couldn't cope *now*, let alone face an unplanned pregnancy creeping on to her agenda, so thank goodness she was still non-productive in the baby line.

By Friday afternoon everyone just wanted to get home, especially herself. Olivia put down the phone on an irate author who had been promised the sun, moon and stars, but who still hadn't seen her beloved first novel on the hardback stand at Gatwick Airport. 'Just wait till the paperbacks take off,' Olivia had said desperately down the phone before opting for the easy way out: she put the author through to sales.

Birdie barged into her office. 'Bloody authors! Don't know why I'm in this business.'

'I know the feeling. So, tell me the worst, Birdie.'

'Question of advances, meaning Violet's. You ought never to have taken her on again, Olivia. She's crazy. Drove your father crazy too, before the war, and she was a lot younger then!'

'I found her *Memoirs* terribly interesting, as well as funny,' said Olivia defending her right to buy the author's work.

'Well, you won't find *this* funny; she wants half a million in advance – pounds, not dollars.'

'Talk to her agent. Make the agent talk sense to her.'

'She hasn't got an agent – never did have one. She handles her books herself.'

'Then *find* her one, Birdie! Don't hassle me on the subject. I've more important items to attend to than Lady Violet, or Lady Constance, or whatever her name is!'

'I'm interested in your private life, Olivia, in case you've never noticed,' Birdie rejoined, 'so what's bugging you today?'

'Nothing.'

'Pull the other leg, it has bells on,' said Birdie.

'Well then, let me put you fully in the picture regarding my traumatic weekend: Tandy, a young friend Stuart and I happened to pick up in the course of this last weekend – no, not golf course, but an obstacle course of drainage problems, wandering ramblers over our land and a vegetarian dinner party on the hottest night of the year – . Tandy managed to inveigle herself into Stuart's heart and he's gone all broody. Ute wished to do the same – with him. Tandy can be excused; she's only nine. Ute cannot; she's the au pair.'

'A hot night, then, when everyone's passions overboiled?

'You could say that. God, I'm so jealous of that

man! Stuart has decided on girls to leave his father's money to, never mind what I want as a postscript to my life. Tandy's managed to get where she has without help from anyone, least of all her wacky mother! And I have every sympathy for young Tandy. Didn't I have to endure a zany mother too, all through my formative years, Birdie?'

'Lady Cotswold never did a bad job on you or your father, Olivia.'

'I know that! I'm trying to relate the story of my *married* life over one countrified weekend. My own personal desires never entered into the picture, Birdie.'

Birdie peered over her bifocals. 'And what might those personal desires be, Olivia MacKenzie, if I should be so bold as to ask such a thing?'

'It's too personal to mention, Birdie, but just let me say, I know what my mother must have felt like when my father drove himself too hard for the sake of the firm!'

'Aha!' Birdie said with great diplomacy. 'The grass widow syndrome! I've never been married, but that doesn't preclude me from sympathizing on your behalf. But believe me, half a husband must be better than none.'

'Thanks! I'll bear it in mind next time he's yawning his jet-set head off while I'm all rarin' to go – and ending up going nowhere because he's suffering from jet-lag!' Olivia suddenly noticed the difference at last. 'Since when have you taken to wearing glasses, Birdie?'

'Since I was fifty-two and got eye-strain, not to

mention RSI, through tapping at a bloody keyboard all day.'

'I forgot your birthday!' Olivia felt awful.

'So, what's new?'

'Oh, God, I'm sorry, Birdie – look, I'll make it up to you, I promise.'

'Forget it,' Birdie panned out her hands, 'you're a married woman now, I understand. What did he buy you for your second wedding anniversary?'

'Haven't we talked since July?'

'If that was when you were last married.'

'Sapphires! Necklace and earrings to match my eyes.' Olivia fluttered her eyelashes.

'Oh, good, keep him at it. He might forget to buy you anything by next July. Man's fidelity usually runs out in the run up to the hat-trick, or haven't you noticed recent divorce statistics?'

'Thanks, Birdie!'

'Didn't mean it. I'm only glad I stayed as I am, a celibate virgin. I didn't really want anyone to re-member my fifty-second birthday, but I treated myself and got enrolled at computer classes. That's how much I love you and yours.'

'Sorry, Birdie, Stuart and I will . . .'

'Ahh-ah! No rash promises, mind!' Birdie held up a warning finger. 'Just let me make you feel bad by telling you I took a crash course in the modern marketplace which has become like a pig-killing exercise for me.'

'OK, you've learned to use the computer, well done! What else?'

Birdie shrugged. 'Nothing much. Like you, I'm

still waiting for one of our readers to dig out a bestseller from the slush pile so that I can have a pay rise.'

'OK, you've got yourself one.'

'Really? You mean it?' Birdie brightened at once.

'Of course I mean it; but only where you're concerned. Don't let a rumour circulate about pay rises being in the air – we haven't found that bestseller yet.'

'If you're compromized in any way, Olivia, I don't mind not getting one. I was only joking, you know,' Birdie added.

'Buzz off, Birdie. I want to ring home to find out if my beloved husband happens to be missing me, or whether or not he's disappeared to the pub with his best buddy. If Mrs Dannymott answers, I'll know the worst.' Olivia kept her hand over the mouthpiece while Birdie gave her the thumbs-up sign.

The following day Olivia received a shock, engendered by Birdie herself.

On her desk was Birdie's resignation.

Birdie quitting – what next? How would she be able to manage without her own personal back-up system? Olivia went into Birdie's office, but she was not there.

'Where is she?' she asked Birdie's young assistant.

When everyone started to look 'baby-faced', as Dankers griped about his fellow security officers, then it was a time to start reflecting upon how old you yourself were becoming: Olivia glowered at the in-house reader eating a chocolate snack bar over someone's precious typescript. She yanked the offending snack from under the young lady's nose and threw it in the wastepaper basket. 'Don't eat over other people's property, Natasha! It's bad policy, on *your* health and *their* presentation.'

Olivia had never sounded so harsh. The poor girl cowered in her chair and Olivia calmed down at once.

Rule number one, learned from her mogul magnate father: never let them see the job is getting to you, and never apologize. If management apologizes to staff, they'll have you over a barrel for ever!

She took a deep breath and apologized. 'I'm sorry, Natty. Things are bit fraught this morning. I don't suppose you know the reasons for Birdie's resignation?'

'It's her eyesight, Olivia.'

'Her eyesight?' Olivia looked at her in-house reader twice. 'I'm sorry, I don't understand.'

'Birdie's got some eye problems. She's afraid she might be going blind. She told me, in this job eyesight is vital. I think she didn't want to let you down and decided to hand in her notice before things got worse. And I'm sorry for eating chocolate over someone's typescript, Olivia.'

Olivia patted the girl's shoulder. She had been in Natasha's shoes once; knew how devastating to personal morale a chilling put-down could be, that uncalled-for reprimand from those who had lost the human touch.

'I'll be back soon,' she said. 'Just hold the fort for me meanwhile.'

Like the effect of a good watering on a bone-dry plant, Natasha suddenly emerged to life. 'Oh, I'll do that for you, Olivia!'

Olivia jumped out of the taxi outside Birdie's terraced house in north London. Birdie answered her urgent summons on the doorbell.

'Olivia, what are you doing here . . . ?' Birdie said in surprise. 'You shouldn't have come after me.'

'Oh, yes, I should!' Olivia backed the diminutive figure of Birdie into her living room. 'You knew I would, so what's all this nonsense about quitting Lamphouse? I require at least one month's notice.'

'I know. But it's in lieu of my pay rise. I felt you'd forgive me, just this once. I really do get fed up of know-it-all youngsters straight from their flashy universities telling me how to punctuate, spell and present a letter when I've been doing it for thirty years – on a typewriter!'

'Point taken,' said Olivia, 'but that's no reason for you to resign so peremptorily.'

'Sorry!' Birdie really did look down in the dumps.

'Aren't you even going to give me a good old Lamphouse cuppa, Birdie?'

Birdie put the kettle on in her tiny kitchen. 'I haven't been shopping, so I haven't any cake,' she peered into the biscuit-barrel, 'only some stale digestives.'

'Fine by me. Look, how about I ring Stuart to get Ernest to pick us up and bring you back to our place? You can stay with us for the weekend and we'll both go back to the office together on Monday morning, to a fresh start?'

'Thanks, Olivia, it's kind of you, but I like my weekends to myself – only chance I get to do the shopping and dusting.'

It was an excuse. Olivia subjected her to a good hard look. Birdie seemed extremely off-colour, pale, wan, very red-eyed and weepy. She was also all steamed up behind the bifocals which she'd forgotten to take off – no wonder she was always tripping over things and scalding herself. 'When did you last have a holiday, Birdie Gough?'

'Last year,' she said, 'like everyone else who takes two weeks' annual holiday plus statutory days.'

'Right, OK, in future you're to have at least four weeks' holiday every year – two in the summer, two in the winter and as many other days off you want, starting from Monday. Take next week off, I can manage. Plus the promised pay rise. Only stay with me, dammit!'

Birdie smiled at Olivia's tone. 'It won't make any difference . . . would you mind carrying the tray into the sitting-room?'

Olivia played mother and poured the tea. 'What won't make any difference?' she asked.

'To the way I feel about them!'

'Them?'

'All those jumped-up snotty-nosed little tartlets who think they can teach their grandmother to suck eggs just because they've been to university or college.'

'That's not the whole truth and nothing but the truth, is it, Birdie?'

'No, it isn't, Olivia,' Birdie said in a small voice.

'I'm listening,' said Olivia. 'And don't try and get away with any half-truths, Birdie. Natasha has spilled the beans.'

Over the next half hour Birdie poured out her troubles to Olivia, who listened, sympathized and felt utterly helpless.

Olivia returned to Farringdon, shut up shop at six-thirty and went to find Stuart, who had already gone home according to Dankers. 'Mr Stuart thought you'd already left, Miss Olivia.'

'*Mrs* Olivia if anything, Dankers! Though why you can't just call me Olivia, I don't know,' she replied irritably.

'Sorry, Mmm . . . Mrs MacKenzie, but familiarity is not my style, especially to my superiors when in the marketplace and . . .'

'Stick to calling me Miss. Mrs MacKenzie is just not our style, Dankers, is it?'

'I don't think it is at all, Miss Olivia.' His lately cultivated po-faced expression relaxed into the old familiar smile.

'So why do we keep calling it *the marketplace*? – as if we're breeding pigs or something, Dankers?'

'It does seem silly, doesn't it, Miss Olivia? Mr Stuart left with Ernest about half an hour ago, thinking that you yourself had gone home. Shall I call a taxi?'

'No, I'll walk to the Tube, thanks. Sorry for mouthing off at you just now, Dankers.'

'No offence taken, Miss Olivia. I reckon we should all shut up shop in August. The heat and fumes in town get everyone down. Goodnight, Miss Olivia, have a nice weekend.'

'Goodnight, Dankers, see you on Monday.' Olivia resigned herself to a hot and uncomfortable journey home by commuter train – unless she went first class.

The last thing she wanted was to be seen as a coward in Stuart's eyes. It would be like admitting 'defeat in der heat!' – as Max van der Croote would say!

Between the sheets on Sunday morning, not a visitor or rambler in sight, it was wonderful just reading the newspapers, munching cheese on toast, and generally slumming it without a thought given to the rest of the day.

Stuart said, 'Sweetheart, I know you're not going to like it, but I've got to go to Toronto for a week.'

A piece of toast halfway to her mouth, Olivia paused and reflected before speaking. 'What you're trying to say is, you won't be available to open the village fête and present prizes next Saturday afternoon? Is that the message I'm receiving loud and clear?'

'That's about it, sweetheart, sorry. A couple of hours cutting red tape is no big deal, honey.'

'Is that all you can say? Honey and sweetheart in the same sentence?'

'No. I can truthfully say how truly sorry I am for not being at the forefront of South African politics and vegetarian cuisine.'

'*Stu-art!*' She thumped him hard with the pillow. 'I *hate* you!'

'Do it for me – if you love me . . .' He cowered behind another pillow, using it like a shield in the face of more feathers flying.

'I *knew* you shouldn't have offered! I *knew* you'd pass the buck! I *knew* you'd find an excuse! Can you tell me what an MD like you truly does for a living?'

'First of all I study worldwide consumer appetites in the way of books and newspapers – including the tabloids – and what is selling off the international best-seller lists quicker than a condom. I pass such information on through the appropriate channels which exist in order to halve my personal agony at having to deal with so much piffle in one day, which would not be humanly possible even for a Superman like myself. So I talk to Superman's father some more, about some more money to hand out to some more people to spend on our behalf. I attend board meetings, I study financial printouts and forecasts, I follow the international stock-markets and share indices and talk to my investment brokers, and my father some more.'

'Shut up, I don't want to know.' She continued to pound him with the pillows.

'I make peace between Toronto, New York and London. I sign some more cheques, go to other people's meetings, fly first class, observe the current trends in advertizing, banking, marketing, PR management, plus a whole lot more. I attend yet more meetings, talk to some more clients, some more investors, bankers, insurance brokers, sales people, printers, book-binders, editors, authors, agents, and I dictate letters to my various personal assistants. I hire staff, I fire staff, I dispense tea and sympathy at all times . . .' meanwhile he had grabbed hold of her and the pillow '. . . I sign some more cheques, I talk some more on the telephone, I send faxes all day long. I receive them all day long. I organize, I delegate, I adjudicate, I pray . . .' He brought his face closer to hers while his arms kept her pinned under him.

'Get off me!'

'For my long-distance wife to understand why I'm not home on time to beg her forgiveness because the dinner's burnt out like myself. I plead with politicians and heads of state, meaning in-house management staff, board members and acquisition panels not to overspend on the current budget else my old man'll beat me up. I smile upon old ladies' committees. I chat up the young ones. I dispense largesse to charity workers and I empathize with faculties who want to know how to become a millionaire in three easy steps and then I talk to my father again . . . don't reach for that pillow, Olivia, or I'll make you eat feathers for the rest of the day!

'Then my father-in-law, my mother, my mother-in-law and Ashton Dore Cleaver demand my attention before I've even got around to talking to my wife and the local branch of the Ramblers' Association. And that's just for starters – don't, Olivia. . . !'

'Glad to see you've got your priorities right. Can you ever expect me to be serious about such an itinerary when your wife gets last but one place from bottom, one notch up from the ramblers?'

Olivia asked, helplessly pinned under him and unable to do anything except bite his ears.

'I'm still listening, sweetheart.'

'How rich are you really?'

'I don't really know. It's all paper money anyway.'

'Precisely! Our gardener-cum-handyman starts at one point of the compass and by the time he gets around to three-hundred and sixty-five degrees, the weeds are growing again – in the same place they started out from. Which leaves twenty-seven point seven-five more acres to go, and that many heart attacks.'

'Your maths was never to be disputed; that's why I married you. But where is all this leading, my love?' He relaxed his he-man hold over her and began to renew his interest in her anatomy.

'Stuart?'

'Ummm . . .'

'What is your definition of love?'

He had to think about that. 'I guess love means being perfectly honest and perfectly comfortable with one's chosen partner. That, and learning how to include "full-time lover" at the top of my CV.' He bit her ear in return. 'The wonderful thing about having a pillow fight is being able to talk about it afterwards.'

Olivia burst out laughing. 'You haven't a clue, have you?'

'Of course I have!'

'Sometimes I ask myself why I ever married such a retarded millionaire,' She caressed his bare chest.

He stroked her hair, the colour of roasted chestnuts, grown long and sleek since their wedding day because he preferred it long. 'I do too – often. Ask myself why I married you.'

'You mean why I married *you*, don't you?'

'I suppose so. Why did you? Apart from the millionaire publisher bit.'

'Because you persisted. And because I hoped to salvage you from your morally irresponsible previous life.'

'Is that all?'

'You tell me first what you discussed with Ashton and Theodore and what's happening on the domestic front and then I'll tell you how I'll commit suttee if ever you find another woman.'

'What's suttee?'

'You're not that ignorant a publisher, surely?'

'I might be.' He gave nothing away between his half-closed sexy eyelids.

'OK. Suttee is an act of supreme sacrifice. It's a Hindu custom where a widow-wife throws herself on the funeral pyre of her dead husband, lord and master.'

'You'd do that for me after I'm dead and gone?' he asked in amazement, raising his head a little from the pillow, speedwell-blue eyes open wide to view her in full perspective.

'Nope,' she said. 'I'm not *that* stupid! I will miss you, though.'

'Why?'

'Because I will. Because I love you. Because there is everything and nothing to say about our partnership because it's so good.'

He hugged her tighter. 'Teddy has agreed to walk a longer route round the swimming-pool. The new "easement" will be placed somewhere out of our sight, just as Annabelle said was strategically possible. The planning committee have agreed to speed up the whole process along with Mr Rapps and his workforce, who have promised to get everything done by Thanksgiving.'

'Thanksgiving? Why Thanksgiving?'

'A time to give, a time of thanks,' he said, ever so casually.

The penny dropped, and she stared at him with horrified wide eyes. 'You didn't – did you?'

'Did I what?'

'Bribe them all?'

He inclined an ear. 'Sorry, sweetheart, didn't quite catch that?'

'Then catch this, Stuwey.' Mouth to ear, she bellowed, '*Theodore Grieves, the Midhurst planning committee, the parish council, Mr Rapps and his builders* – did you or didn't you?'

'Don't know what you're talking about.' He shook his head with wisps of goose-feather-down turning it vaguely grey, though any minute now, Olivia vowed, his handsome head would be stuck in the microwave if he didn't come clean.

'Thanksgiving,' he continued blithely. 'You were the one who wanted it all sorted out before Christmas! I wanted it sorted out before we fly to the States to be with my side of the family. You know how Thanksgiving is a time for the old dictator to gather us all into the bosom of his finances and tell us how

211

happy he is dictating while we're left slaving.'

'Thanksgiving happens to be three months from now, Stuart.'

'I'm trying to follow in my master's footsteps by being prepared for all eventualities,' he said.

'You're hopeless – I despair!' He cradled her laughing head against his chest while she snuggled closer. 'Old dictator and old mogul, can't we change direction, Stuart, and get away from old dictators and old moguls in publishing? Go it alone by forming a new company called MacLamp or something?'

'Not likely, I've never had it so good at my father's expense,' he said.

'You must have been a pretty awful young man for your father to make you toe the line so strictly – ten years on!'

'I've thought about it myself, often. I was the pits. You wouldn't have married me ten years ago, that's for sure. I drank, I raved, I drove my parents and my ex-wife to despair . . . by the way, Ashton's left you, meaning us, a dozen Bollingers and two tickets for Covent Garden Opera. It's his way of saying how sorry he is for the inconvenience his oversight has caused us.'

'I'll give him Bollinger!' Olivia went along with Stuart's change of direction. She knew how the subject of the past, in particular his brother Geoff's death, was something to which he could never reconcile himself, despite all his power-play banter.

CHAPTER 13

People and Places: 1991

Stuart left for Toronto, and the following Saturday Olivia wondered what to wear as the VIP invited to cut the tape at Midhurst Village Fête. It was a hot and sultry August Bank Holiday, with the threat of a thunderstorm in the not too distant future – better take an umbrella, she thought, just in case!

Despite the weather Olivia chose to wear a floral chiffon afternoon frock with long puff sleeves, and a picture hat with a matching chiffon scarf around the crown – all very summery and garden-partyish.

As pre-arranged, at one-thirty Olivia met the vicar at the lych-gate to the church. He would be her guide and mentor for the afternoon. He was far younger and far less intimidating than she had previously imagined. With his round boyish face, gingery hair, jolly manner, and family of young children, Adrian Fairbanks appeared exceedingly human. Which just went to show how looks and preconceived notions of people within their given occupations could be so utterly misleading, thought Olivia.

213

Annabelle had had pre-conceived ideas about Stuart and her – millionaires of star status – and how wrong were they! While she herself had imagined the vicar to be an ancient grey-haired old fuddy-duddy.

Olivia shook hands with the vicar's wife, and Patsy Fairbanks said, 'So kind of you to step in at such a late hour to open our fête, Olivia.' She had in tow their three children, and two large Tupperware-encased cakes, 'I'm manning the home-made cake stall. The kids are eager to join up with Annabelle's crowd, so please forgive us if we appear to be in a hurry.'

Patsy and the children went off down the lane towards the village green where the fête was being held, leaving Olivia to follow on with Adrian. He confirmed his wife's earlier statement. 'Thanks for filling in the gaps in our programme at such short notice, Olivia.'

'My pleasure,' She smiled before glancing through the programme of events to get an idea of what was expected of her. 'I see you're doing a sponsored abseil down the church tower, vicar; how very brave of you!'

He grinned. 'Another way of putting my life in God's hands, you mean? We need all the sponsorship money we can get for a new church roof, so I'm daring the devil.'

At two o'clock Olivia cut the red ribbon outside the refreshment marquee and the fête was officially declared open. From then on she, together with the other adjudicators, went around the various stalls and tents, assessing the merits of what was on offer.

Mrs Dannymott won two first prizes, one for the best fruit cake and the other for her grapefruit and orange marmalade, a pot of which was duly presented to the Lady of the Manor. Mr Dannymott won first prize for his dahlias, second prize for his cucumbers.

The village butcher, Mr Wyman, also a local farmer, won first prize for his heifer called Brutus, while in the local artist's tent Annabelle took three first prizes, one for a watercolour of *The Village*, another for a collage of the *Old Smithy and Duck-pond*, and yet another for a beechwood carving called *Mother and Child*. Olivia did not know from where Annabelle found the time to be so creative.

Max, meanwhile, was thirstily downing beer in the refreshment tent along with other devotees from the village pub, the Midhurst Arms, whose landlord, Arthur Stapley, was offering a free crate of lager (past its sell-by date), to anyone who could guess his colossal weight – down to the last gram.

It was a good way of meeting the neighbours. They invited her to join this and that committee, group or organisation, including MADS – Midhurst Amateur Dramatic Society. MADS were enacting a little im-promptu pantomime of Mother Goose in one corner of the field. Olivia, as the newly installed Lady of the Manor, had the casting vote as to the best actor or actress, and the best home-made costume. A difficult choice – they were all good and witty – but she chose Mother Goose, not only because of the elaborate lengths Miss Loganberry, head of the local play-group, had taken with her costume of hand-plucked goose-feathers, but because she got the most laughs.

Theodore Grieves almost bowled Olivia over by presenting her with a self-published (desktop) copy of his book, *The Footpads of Midhurst Discover New Pathways*.

Deep down in most people's hearts, Olivia felt sure, were two conflicting emotions – how to be recognized when you were not famous, and how not to be recognized when you were. Which just went to show the contrariness of human nature!

'Looking forward to traversing the new easement at the lower end of your lands, Mrs MacKenzie,' he said, quite charming about being thrown off the higher easement giving access to the valleys and hills beyond manor boundaries. Olivia wondered how much Stuart had parted with in the way of bribes to get the old goat and his herd off their backs! But then she knew the price of sweetness when Theodore added, 'Perhaps Lamphouse might see its way to publishing any future books of mine? I do have several manuscripts lurking in odd dark corners, and they're not all to do with rambling across our countryside. I can easily dig them out if you'd care to peruse them for me some time . . .'

Olivia gave him one of her stunning smiles to mask her true feeling – that word 'peruse' always set her teeth on edge. 'I'm so sorry, Mr Grieves, but Lamphouse is not accepting any more material for the time being. We're simply inundated with typescripts for the foreseeable future.'

'Well, perhaps I can submit my writings – they are awfully interesting, you know – to you at some future date, dear lady?'

'Yes, do that!' Olivia moved off hastily without actually committing herself to anything. She did so wish people wouldn't accost her at odd moments and ask her to publish 'their scribblings', just because they knew she was in publishing. Her Pa too, used to get annoyed at such an approach. He'd used to say. 'Most people think they have a story somewhere inside them – and that's where most of them should stay!'

At five o'clock the crowd thinned out on the village green as everyone went off to see the vicar of Midhurst abseiling down his own tower. The local press and TV were there, and got a good shot of Adrian stuck halfway up the tower because his gear had snagged, leaving him swinging in the air for five minutes until he managed to get going again. He landed safely and decorously among the gravestones, amid much hand-clapping, cheering and catcalls, and received a huge hug from his relieved wife who'd thought she was on the brink of widowhood.

Turning to go back to the village green to complete her last presentations of the day as Lady of the Manor, Olivia stumbled on the uneven church path and fell among the tombs of earlier generations. She wasn't quite sure what had happened – whether she had caught her heel, become dizzy, or if a ghost had pushed past her.

When she came to a few minutes later, she was lying on a pew while the local GP, Dr Gareth, fussed over her with his stethoscope. Annabelle, Tandy, the vicar and his wife were all looking down at her with worried and sympathetic expressions. Feeling a real fool, grass stains on her expensive frock, a tear in the sleeve, Olivia struggled to sit up.

'Now, now, Mrs MacKenzie – Olivia, you must take it easy for a while, no good rushing about at the moment,' said Dr Gareth, gently easing her back against the hassock someone had put under her head.

'What happened?' Olivia asked in bewilderment, her face, so pale and clammy before, now bright red with embarrassment.

'Only what is to be expected in your condition, my dear,' said Dr Gareth, repocketing his stethoscope before patting her hand. 'You fainted in the heat – not a wise thing to do at the moment.'

By now Patsy had fetched her a glass of water from the vestry and Tandy had given her back her battered garden-party hat. Olivia began to feel a little better, until Tandy piped up, 'Dr Gareth, Mummy says Olivia's having a baby but she doesn't know it because she's never had one before.'

Once more Olivia could have murdered young Tandy van der Croote for broadcasting what happened to be an untruth – the pregnancy-testing kit had proved that nothing of that sort was happening to her, it was just pure stress!

Dr Gareth seemed to nod in agreement. 'I think so too, Tandy, but we shall have to wait and see.' He addressed Olivia. 'You haven't registered with my surgery yet, have you, my dear?'

She had to confess the truth. 'I've never been ill in my life . . . I've had so little time lately to . . .'

'To look after your health? Won't do, won't do at

all, dear lady! You must take time out from your busy schedule, Olivia. Monday morning, eight-thirty, and no excuses. We'll check you out and make sure everything is ticking over as it should.' Twinkling grey eyes and a fatherly smile tried to put Olivia at ease.

Despite Dr Gareth's most reassuring pewside manner, Olivia felt like a truant schoolgirl. She was only thankful that nearly everyone, including the local camera crew, had dispersed from the vicinity of the church when she had gone down with such an embarrassing thud. Patsy had closed the doors to keep any nosy stragglers at bay. She pulled herself together and said briskly to Adrian, 'I feel such a fool! Sorry for holding things up, Vicar; shall we press on?'

He shook his head. 'Doctor's orders, not to mention my wife's. You're to take it easy for the rest of the day. No more roaming around in the heat this afternoon, not in your condition, Olivia.'

Olivia wished they wouldn't all keep referring to 'her condition'. There was nothing wrong with her except stress. 'I'm really awfully sorry . . . thank you all for being so . . . so kind, but really, I feel fine now.'

Patsy, in her busy, bustling way, said, 'Olivia, I think Adrian can manage to give out the last of the day's prizes for the children's fancy dress competition. You've done your bit, very splendidly too.'

'Very splendidly undertaken,' Adrian reiterated, 'We could do with someone like you on the Midhurst Fund-Raising Committee, to take the strain off

Patsy's shoulders at times – but only when you're feeling up to it.'

'So, let's get on now, Vicar, there's nothing wrong with me, I'm fine . . .' Olivia began again, hating to let them down, even though they had completed three-quarters of the day's itinerary.

'We know that. Having a baby is perfectly normal – for us women.' Annabelle gave her a hand up.

Patsy said, 'You're coming back with me to the Vicarage, Olivia. Annabelle and I know how exhausting these events can be. The show's almost over anyway. We'd love you to stay to supper with us.'

'We want her to come to supper with *us*!' said Tandy, sounding very annoyed about being pipped at the post by the vicar's wife. 'Stuart and Olivia were our friends first . . . ouch!' Tandy turned and glared at her mother who had slapped her nine-year-old bottom for being saucy.

Nothing could be worse than sitting under a tarpaulin with a lonely supper on your grass-stained lap while your husband was six thousand miles away and you most needed him to restore your wounded pride. Olivia accepted the invitation with bashful grace.

A crash of thunder heralded the onset of the storm threatening all day. 'Come on, let's go, everyone, before it buckets down,' said Patsy. She turned back to her husband. 'You'll have to be quick about judging the fancy dress, Adrian; it looks as if rain is about to wash out play, any moment now!' She dashed one way with Olivia in tow, the vicar went another, and Annabelle and Tandy went home to the accompaniment of Annabelle's happy comments about 'just what the garden needs'.

The following morning Olivia was in the middle of having her solitary breakfast and browsing through the Sunday papers, coffee and toast, when a tap at the back door disturbed her solitude. 'No peace for the wicked,' she said to the kitchen clock, before opening the door, only to find Ernest on the doorstep, cap in hand.

'Sorry to disturb you, Miss Olivia, but I came to ask a favour of you.'

'Favour, Ernest?'

'Yes – mmm . . .' He shuffled awkwardly in the doorway. 'It's personal, like.'

'Well, come in and shut the door. Would you like a cup of tea?'

'That's kind of you, Miss Olivia, but I won't take up any more of your time than I needs to.'

'Nonsense!' She got up and poured him a mug of hot sweet tea, the way Ernest's 'Mam' had always put in it his flask when on duty for Sir Harold. 'Go on, then, ask me this personal favour, and I'll tell you yes or no.'

'Well, it's like this, Miss Olivia . . . ummm, Mrs MacKenzie . . . I aim ter get married, but . . .' He didn't finish the sentence but looked at his boots instead.

'But?' Olivia pressed him for the rest of what was on his mind, hoping he hadn't come to tender his resignation; she would be quite unable to do the job of Stuart's chauffeur, given the amount of travelling he did in one week.

Ernest looked up at her with a red face. 'Her old man won't let us get married till we got a roof over our head, Miss Olivia. Neither does he want us to live with him and her mam because they need the rooms for paying guests. Jenny and me don't earn enough to get a mortgage, nor do I want to be too far away from you and Mr Stuart.'

'Jenny? Do I know this Jenny, Ernest?'

Ernest gave a sheepish grin, 'Jenny Stapley, Miss Olivia – her Dad's a bit big to argue with!'

'I should say!' Olivia agreed; well, well, young Ernest was keen on the landlord's daughter, who himself was keen to hang on to her since she helped out behind the bar at the Midhurst Arms. 'She's a very nice girl, Ernest, I'm happy for you both. So, how can I help to solve your problem?'

'I was wondering, Miss Olivia . . . sorry, I mean Mrs M!' He stumbled and blushed in his nervous zeal to appear correct in her eyes. She also knew how shy Ernest was, and didn't want to give him cause for further embarrassment. He was finding it very difficult to get to the point, and she didn't rush him.

'Just call me Olivia, Ernest, I won't bite!' Her eyes twinkled. 'So what's the big favour? You want me to come to the wedding? You'd like to borrow the Dame for the day? You'd like to have the reception here? Well, it's yes to all three, I wouldn't miss your wedding for the world – the moment Jenny's parents give the go ahead.'

'We wouldn't want you to Miss . . . er . . . Olivia . . .miss it neither. Jenny's close to her mam and doesn't want to get married without her there, even though Jenny is eighteen. What I've really come about is the garage.'

'The garage?' Olivia looked blank.

'Well, the flat above it really. You see, Olivia . . .' he suddenly lightened up and straightened his shoulders without all the previous tugging of forelocks bit, 'me and Jenny can get married right away if we got a place to live which won't cost us much. I was wondering, since I got the garage flat to meself, if Jenny could move in with me after the wedding. I know I get it free at the moment, but Jenny and me'll pay you rent for it. If you and Mr Stuart can't see your way to renting the place to a married couple, I wouldn't be able to stay in the job – and I do reckon I'd like to stay on with you and Mr Stuart, who've been real good to me after your Dad left the firm. I don't mind doing a bit extra around the place, helping Andy with the garden and what not, nor any extra jobs Mr Stuart'd like to get done. I'm sure Jenny'd help out here too, when Mrs Dannymott can't get in.'

Olivia couldn't help smiling. 'Ernest, Ernest! No need for any more explanations – of course you and Jenny can have the flat!'

His expression was one of great relief, and suddenly Olivia had the inkling that 'our Jenny and Ernest' might be wanting to bring the wedding date forward for other reasons besides accommodation – and before Jenny's father found out!

'Only I have a better idea, Ernest,' Olivia added. 'There's the old tithe cottage down by the bottom spinney; it's bigger than the garage flat. It needs a lot

doing to it, but I'm sure Stuart will get it all fixed up
for you two. In fact, I know he will, since we'd both
hate to lose you.'

Ernest's grin of gratitude stretched from ear to ear.
'Well, I don't know what to say really, Miss . . . er
. . . the cottage would be real fine for us – wait till I
tell Jenny, she'll be over the moon! Thanks, Olivia!
You always was a grand lady to work for – like what
Birdie and Dankers always said.' He rushed off then
to tell his fiancée the good news.

Later in the day Olivia went outside to see how the
garden was progressing. She came upon Andy Grafter digging deep into what she hoped one day would
resemble an eye-catching rock garden with a little
fountain and stream, terraces and neat pathways.
'Hello, how's it going?'

'Afternoon, Mrs MacKenzie. It's a big job, this.'

'Well, I've come to help out. What would you like
me to do first?'

He took off his flat cap and scratched his head, 'We
could get a bonfire started and get rid of all this dead
wood and stuff, ma'am.'

'OK, I'll get cracking.' She smiled. 'A bonfire
sounds a good idea; it's got really chilly out here.'

'Autumn's jest around the corner, ma'am, and it'll
soon be Christmas an all,' he said.

'Don't mention Christmas! It seems as if I've only
just taken down last year's decorations!'

'Know what you mean, ma'am. My wife says
exactly the same. But if you need a good fat goose
for Christmas, you let me know. My brother rears

224

them blighters, wot are better than a guard dog, they're that vicious!'

It was quite therapeutic working the land: it gave her a great sense of achievement and satisfaction, and freedom! Olivia could see why Annabelle enjoyed gardening so much. Raking and digging and collecting and burning, tugging, pulling and cursing under one's breath because of the tearing brambles certainly got rid of the cobwebs and brought the colour to the cheeks. It also put into perspective the petty frustrations of office routine; nothing like the great outdoors to match an aerobics class – which she had always intended to join because of her sedentary work.

With her face glowing pink and the sparkle back in her eyes, she and the chatty old gardener got on with clearing quite a bit of hillside. A real old Kentish rustic, Andy explained to her the difference between what was Kent and what was Kentish – not that she had been aware of any differences. 'There's them what're born *that* side of the Medway, what are called Men 'n' Maids of Kent, and us what're born *thisaside*, what're Kentish Men 'n' Kentish Maids.'

Only when the bonfire had died down to a sultry glow and it was too dark to do any more outside, did Andy Grafter take himself home. Olivia appreciated his giving up his Sunday afternoon to help clear the jungle the old Brig had left in his wake: Stuart would be pleased to see the improvement they had made to the garden.

Olivia locked up for the night and then spent a long time soaking in a wonderful bubble bath, *The Book-*

225

seller propped up in front of her on the bath-tidy. She promptly fell asleep in the tub and only when the water had turned tepid enough to be uncomfortable did she come to again. Somewhere in the background the phone was ringing, but by the time she got to it, it had stopped. Jolly annoying when that happened, she thought, and made herself a cup of cocoa to take to bed, a poor substitute but a comfort in Stuart's absence.

CHAPTER 14

At eighty-thirty the following morning Olivia went to see Dr Gareth. She didn't have to wait, as she was the first of his appointments. He confirmed that she was in fact two months pregnant, and possibly a little anaemic, hence the fainting-fits. He took a sample of blood to be sent to the laboratory, and meanwhile prescribed some iron tablets.

The district nurse would book her into ante-natal clinics: one a month for the next five months, and fortnightly thereafter – unless her 'condition' required monitoring at closer intervals. With twinkling eyes and his charming smile to temper the severity of his threat, Dr Gareth told her that he'd come after her with a big stick if she failed to keep to her regular check-ups.

Afterwards, on the way to the office, only fifty-five minutes to the big smoke where she had lived all her life previous to her marriage, a 'city-slicker' in the fast lane, Midhurst seemed a world apart to Olivia. From the old London town of Paternoster Row and a trip down Memory Lane, and also as far as a new twenty-first-century London town was concerned,

227

none of it was very appealing any more – not like in her bachelor-girl days. If the city was full of traffic jams, carbon monoxide poisoning, beggars, bombs and brutality now, what was it going to be a few years hence, the so-called dawn of a new millennium? It didn't bear thinking about – she shuddered.

Living in the country had its drawbacks too, like not being on mains drainage, and sudden and unpredictable power failures disrupting your faxes, senses and PCW texts every time there was a thunderstorm. Oh, well, thought Olivia, Utopia was only a dream anyway: Merry Olde England, who could help get everyone to the moon, yet still couldn't provide rural sanitation for her country folk, could be forgiven for her eccentricities – a real classy sign of old age, 'Violet' would say, and still a jolly good place to live!

The Midhurst fête on Saturday afternoon had brought it all home to her. Everyone still carried on living in a kind of *Just William* time warp. It was rather reassuring really; no change meant that things were all still good and acceptable and time-honoured and dependable – like stepping out on an old-fashioned rambler's pathway long forgotten by everyone else except the likes of Theodore Grieves and Annabelle van der Croote. Who else knew what lay beyond the next stile?

Olivia continued to contemplate the back of Ernest's head. She had no idea why staring at the back of Ernest's short-cropped head (he never wore his chauffeur's cap unless it was a for a formal occasion), should precipitate such maudlin thoughts in her about old-fashioned country ways and how good they seemed in comparison to city life, and how lucky she herself was to have a roof over her head, food on her table, loving and caring parents like Maggie and Harold (she'd never thought she would ever say that!), money in her bank account sufficient to pay other people to do her and Stuart's dirty work, with more than enough left over at the end of the week to buy herself a facial and body makeover, and the health farm that went with it, so what had *she*, Olivia Penelope Cotswold MacKenzie, to worry about?

Getting older!

So, she was getting older and wiser, she was beginning to realize the true value of real friendships, not the fly-by-nights who always took and never gave. A few nice people like Birdie, Dankers, Ernest, and all those other 'Olly-supporters' from the firm's good old days – discount Legrand, she told herself, Vinny was nothing but a self-server, who wouldn't be above stabbing Olivia in the back, if it would further her own cause. Friends of the more recently home grown variety: Annabelle, Adrian and Patsy Fairbanks, Mrs Dannymott and family, Dr Gareth and Andy Grafter and a whole lot more from where they came from – *real* people.

Life truly isn't that bad, then, is it? she asked herself in the back of the Dame. You've got it all, Olivia Penelope Cotswold MacKenzie, so don't be so ungrateful!

Thinking about Stuart made her doubly miserable. Somehow, these days, he was always leaving a big gap in her life. He was never around when he should be!

With all sorts of nostalgic feelings and emotions

arising in her, nothing to do with sex, sensuality or desire, but a deep-down warm, loving and romantic feeling towards him who was absent for the greater part of her life, Olivia put such feelings down to all those maternal hormones rushing about her body all of a sudden, all those strange changes going on inside her without any conscious thought from her. All terrifyingly clever, as well as disconcerting!

Her trip to Frankfurt had to be cancelled on account of morning sickness and an absent husband. She had never missed a Frankfurt Book Fair before, she and Vinny nightclubbing the night away and as high as highballs the entire week long! Even so, they had still managed to sell a whole lot of books – personality *counted!* Vinny's, not hers.

Anyway, forget Vinny! What she wanted from her life and her marriage was total commitment from Stuart – *now!* They were about to be first-time parents, so what she wanted from him was a *twenty-four-hour* commitment to family life, fatherhood and estate management, like, knowing wind directions and how to light a bonfire without it all blowing back in your face and setting the place alight.

Men were exceedingly selfish! Her mother had doted on the old mogul all her life and look where it had got her – exile on a French golf course! Stuart might try taking up village activities as a hobby instead of mergers and acquisitions and investments! She would tell him so, the moment he got home. No more the 'two's company' bit; life had changed. They would both have to rethink their lifestyles with a baby on the way, a pregnancy that had descended out of the blue, totally unplanned. What will Stuart say to that little slip-up? she wondered.

But whatever his thoughts might be, it didn't really matter to her any more – they were now committed for life, to bring up their precious child in a very careful way. After all, Pa, the old mogul, and Mac-Kenzie, the old ex-newspaper boy from the corner of 33rd Street, demanded a grandchild to whom they could pass on their publishing immortality – two grandfathers to dish out the dosh, one pretty rich (hers), and the other multi-millionaire-rich (his) – which was a lot more than she or Stuart had started off with themselves.

Not bad for a christening present, babe! she silently told the unidentifiable little person inside her, who was seven months away from a recognizable dinner-date with her.

If there was any one thing she desired to know most in her life right now, it was that Stuart would be there in seven months' time, at the other end of the table, having prepared a good old plate of porridge and ice-cream for her, telling her how gorgeous she looked with a lump to make a camel envious; she would love him for ever and a day, if only he would share this experience of parenthood with her.

He was flying back from Toronto today, and she would see him that evening, Ernest was picking him up from Heathrow, which meant she would have to catch the train home. If absence made the heart grow fonder, she was *definitely* dying to see her husband again!

Olivia breezed into her office, happy with the knowledge that she was incubating another little soul inside herself. Birdie was sorting the mail on her desk.

'What are you doing here, Birdie Gough? I thought I gave you the week off.'

'You didn't seriously expect me to sit at home twiddling my thumbs for a week, did you?'

'No, but you could have twiddled the knobs on *Neighbours*. OK, take a rain-check. It's bucketing!' Olivia shook off the raindrops, asked for coffee, and hung up her raincoat while her umbrella dried out downstairs, kind courtesy of Dankers who still continued to ignore house rules.

'So how come you're so wet when you came in the Dame?' Birdie wanted to know.

'Good question. After Ernest went on a round trip of London via Paternoster Row, he deposited me on our Farringdon doorstep. Then he nipped off with the head of sales and foreign rights manager for a meeting with other heads of sales and foreign rights managers. Then he was off to Heathrow to meet Stuart – a busy day driving about town for our Ernest. So I slipped off to do my own thing.'

'Like singing in the rain? What has prompted such big smiles from you this morning . . . no, don't tell me, your husband's made himself another million bucks by putting lesser mortals out to grass,' Birdie retorted caustically.

'I remembered I had a prescription in my pocket, so I popped into the chemist's around the corner. Then, while I was out, I had a yen to visit the old home again, so I nipped along through the courts, and the rain, back into Paternoster Row.'

232

'Don't mention that name! It brings tears to my eyes for the good times we had there.' Birdie wiped her eyes.

Olivia knew she was only pretending to be mawkish. 'Then you'll know how it is now turned into a reference archive and bookstore for old unwanted tomes such as *Names And Their Meanings* and *Chinese Astrological Charts and their Significance*. Lamphouse, being a beacon in the darkness of our times, is able to shed light on everything. Does that answer your profound question?'

'More than adequate – glad to see you're so cheerful. So what's this about astrological charts and other bunkum? Don't tell me you've become a Zoroastrian?'

'No, nor a Persian parsee, Birdie. I'm talking Chinese – *feng shui*. Which means, good or bad atmosphere – only there's more to it than that. I've only given you my roughly translated version of *feng shui*; the Chinese have a thing about lucky names and places, you see, Birdie.'

'I'm totally in the dark still,' she said.

'Never mind. It's too complicated to explain in one go. I might call in a Chinese *feng shui* expert to tell me where best the nursery ought to be, and what name has a fortuitous aura. I'm also halfway to becoming vegetarian since living in Midhurst. I'm also two-ninths of the way to having a baby, if that has anything to do with becoming a vegetarian. You're about to become a great-godmother in about seven months' time.'

'Well now, that's grand, Olivia! Congratulations – only it's bad luck to say it before the baby's born.'

'Pagan!'

'So is Foong whatever.'

'No, it isn't! *feng shui* is a proven scientific art perfected by the Chinese.'

'I suppose that's why you went in search of a baby book of Chinese names. They say pregnant women do weird things.'

'Eat weird things, Birdie.'

'That too. Me a great-godmother at the age of fifty-two is not what I expected to happen to me, when I've tried to remain celibate all my life.' Birdie passed into the nether regions of her office with all the letters passed on by Olivia which Birdie could answer by herself.

As the morning wore on, Olivia formulated her strategy; it was not going to be easy broaching the subject. From what Natasha had told her about Birdie's eyesight, it sounded as though Birdie might be worried about glaucoma.

In the afternoon she said aloud to herself in Birdie's presence, 'For goodness' sake, what's this . . . a "wasitline"?' She thrust the proof page under Birdie's nose. 'Should it be "waistline"?'

Birdie peered at the print. Even with her new bifocals, Olivia knew she was struggling. 'Don't ask me. It's not my job to correct proofs, Natasha does that,' Birdie was immediately on the defensive. She added, 'Perhaps that's the way the author wants it, a "wasit-line". Wasit here, and if it wasn't, where wasit? It's a very funny book about a woman's struggle with yo-yo dieting – you should read it when it gets into print.'

234

'At this rate, it might never. When did you read it, Birdie? It's not your job, remember?'

'OK, you've got me there. Nat read out bits to me she thought were funny. Nor is it your job to stoop to menial tasks either, so say what's on your mind and stop trying to trap me and trick me by devious methods pulled out of a slush pile, Olivia!'

'Sit down, Birdie.'

Birdie sat down suddenly on the nearest chair. 'OK, sack me!'

'Birdie, forgive me for raising the subject, but I've noticed how you've been bumping into furniture, spilling the coffee, and wiping your eyes all the time while looking as if you've been weeping buckets. It's embarrassing for both of us; people will start thinking you're being ill-treated in the workplace.'

'Huh!' Birdie grunted.

'Did you have your eyes tested properly when you bought your bifocals?'

'Of course! Where did you think I got them from, the charity shop?'

'Close. I don't believe you've done anything positive about your eyesight because you're scared. The other afternoon you went all round the houses to tell me about your other worries like bills and not getting on with the MacKenzie crowd, but nothing about your worry over your eyesight. Glaucoma isn't necessarily the end of a life, if it gets early recognition and proper treatment.'

'How do you know I have glaucoma?' Birdie challenged.

'I don't, but you're behaving as if *you* think you

have . . .' Olivia pushed a card across the desk. 'Here's an appointment, a private one. I rang the eye-specialist on your behalf. You're to see him privately at Worfields Eye Hospital tomorrow morning. I was coming over to Finsbury anyway, to tell you, but since you're here, I'm telling you now. I'll take you there myself, to make sure you're safely deposited on Mr Braintree's treatment list. Be ready at ten-thirty sharp; the appointment's for eleven-thirty.'

'And what about future *private* appointments, Olivia? The last time I saw anyone *private*, it cost me eighty-five great smackers! I can't afford that kind of treatment for the rest of my life.'

'It's the least Lamphouse can do for you when you've devoted your eyesight to Lamphouse for the past thirty years, Birdie,' Olivia reassured her. 'I'll take care of the bills: a great-godmother's belated birthday present from me, and whoever's inside me.'

'As long as it's not a horse's head,' said Birdie, wiping her eyes.

Olivia caught the six o'clock train from Charing Cross and travelled first class because she wanted to be in a 'comfortable' frame of mind to greet her husband, whom she was dying to see again. This past week without him had felt like a lifetime, she had so much to tell him!

Unfortunately her comfortable frame of mind was soon shattered. She had just settled down in an empty carriage, for executive reasons glad to have it to herself, when the door slid back and Max van der Croote loomed large in the opening.

'Hello, Olivia, I thought it was you I haf seen vith your vurking-girl briefcase dashing along the platform . . . I vill join you, *ja*?'

She smiled politely, not overjoyed at the prospect of spending the next fifty-five minutes in his overbearing company. 'Be my guest, Max.'

He shook out his umbrella in the corridor, took off his raincoat and hung it on a suction-hook just inside the door, one he had brought himself – breathed on before he firmly fixed it to South East Network's property, rather like a rubber stamp. Max's still dripping umbrella was placed in the rack above an empty seat. He remained oblivious to the slow plop of drops on to the blue upholstery below, which soon became like a Chinese water torture on Olivia's nerves.

'It takes as long by car as by train, *ja*? Zat is vye I alvays go by train,' he said.

Olivia smiled politely.

Max put his briefcase beside him, and a McDonald's takeaway bag. He removed the pale yellow polystyrene carton of a double Big Mac and French fries, and a sealed beaker of Pepsi-Cola. He placed them neatly on the window-table beside him. Then he got down to tackling his double Big Mac with great gusto, bits of onion and coleslaw garnish squashed outwards like whiskers on the grin of the Big Mac.

'*Ja*, I am a naughty boy! But you vill not tell Annie, please, zat I am liking trash food. For me I am a man who likes *biefstuk*, not English tomatoes, vich to me is like trash-food! Zo, I haf my *biefstuk* ven I ham at vurk, and Annie's vegetables ven I am at home. It is

237

to keep zer peace vith my little woman, *ja*?' he winked at her.

Olivia averted her gaze – it was up to him what he ate, none of her business. But if he was dishonest about his Big Mac appetites, what else was he capable of hiding from Annabelle? Olivia concentrated on the papers in her lap.

Having finished his secret carnivorous diet, Max licked his fingers before taking out of his bulging briefcase a copy of the *The Grainman's Gazette*.

Oh, good, thought Olivia, he's going to read and not talk, but Max's mobile phone bleeped just then.

'*Ja . . . ? Ik denk dat er een fout is . . . ja, ja! De goederen moeten vergezeld zijn van een factuur . . . Ja, ja! Tulpen, ja, narcissen, ja, rozen, ja, fresias . . . alstublieft, sturr een creditnota en een nieuwe rekening . . .*' He finished his conversation and shut down his mobile. '*Gottdampt!* Zese peeple, zey are zo stupeed! Zey do not know vot is a simple invoice even! Ven they do not even read und write, how can zey ever expect to govern a country twenty times *laarger* zan Great Britian?'

Once more Olivia smiled politely.

'I am to send Dutch flowers to South Afreeka for the beeg ANC party to celebrate de Klerk's proposals for the new presidency of South Afreeka, but they are *steel* keeling each other over there – I am hating to say South Afreeka is steel my sad country!'

'Yes,' said Olivia, 'sad, isn't it?' She put away her papers into her briefcase. She had no wish to start a political discussion on South Africa with Max van der Croote, whose accent became more and more apparent the more het up he became, from a commodities point of view.

'This is not our stop yet.' Max looked out of the window. 'Ve have three more to go, Olivia.'

'I'm like a good Baden Powell girl scout, Max, I like to be prepared.'

Olivia spent the next three stops standing in the corridor, six compartments down from big Max, the secret carnivore, ready to jump and flee homeward the moment of arrival at Midhurst Station.

'It looks like you've had quite an eventful week while I've been away.' Stuart yawned and stretched his long arms to the ceiling, which meant the tarpaulin still in situ above the Yuppie sofa.

'If you can call having cauliflower cheese with the vicar and his wife on Saturday evening eventful, then it was eventful. Adrian's writing a book about the Parish of Midhurst and asked if I'd read over his manuscript some time – just to see what a real publisher thought of it! Theodore Grieves did the same to me, only *his* subject was footpaths. I felt that the good turn-out at the village fète, which Adrian boasted about, was because people came to gawp at me – what does she look like, a millionaire's wife? That sort of zoo-thing. I think the whole of Midhurst are a little bit barmy! Must be all the fresh vegetables they consume in such vast quantities. Patsy and Adrian, though, did offer cold meat with the cauliflower cheese.'

'Do I detect a note of dissatisfaction regarding country life, my love?'

'No, I love it. It's me. I'm the odd one out because they treat me as if I'm Tutankhamun's mask or something. The person they're really trying to get at is you – Mr Millionaire MacKenzie. Only you're like a butterfly – here today and gone tomorrow. Thanks for getting out of the fête worse than death, Stuart Lyon MacKenzie! Good timing, I must say.'

'Sorry, honey, but duty called.'

'Dearest husband, darling Stuart, can we take care of Birdie's non-NHS bills? Discreetly, without making her feel embarrassed?' Olivia changed the subject.

'What do you want me to do, write an invisible cheque? Of course we'll pay for Birdie's treatment, no question about it. It's up to her whether she feels she's a charity case or not.'

'That's precisely what I'm talking about!'

'Then you must bring into play all your reserves of diplomacy, tact and persuasion, my love. You can do it.'

There he went again – passing the buck! He was so *good* at it!

'God, I've missed you . . . come here and give me a hug before you fetch my slippers.' He held out his arms.

'Not yet, I've got something else to say.'

'If it's about Teddy Grieves, ADC or ramblers' rights of way, Mr Rapps and cess-pits, everything's being taken care of.'

'Do you think Mr Rapps could get some repairs done on the old tithe cottage down by the spinney?'

'Why?'

'Ernest's getting married and wants a bigger place to bring his bride home to.'

'OK, no problem.'

'And do you think we can make a start on a nursery?'

'I dare say . . . it's like that with them, is it?'

'It's us, actually.'

'Us?'

'Yes, us!'

He semi-twigged at long last and stopped trying to find something worth watching on television. 'Run that by me again?'

'*I'm pregnant!*'

'Gee whizz . . . are you sure?'

'Positive. Morning sickness, dizzy spells, falling among gravestones in a dead faint of embarrassment only to lie stretched out on a pew alongside Dr Gareth's stethoscope. I'm sure.'

'Sweetheart, that's great news . . .' He wasn't quite sure how else to receive such great news after a long-haul flight. 'Did we discuss this major event in our lives?' He hesitated to ask it, a little crease between his speedwell-blue eyes.

'Not exactly. I think lust pre-programmed us somewhere.'

'Mine or yours?'

'Ours.'

Contraception was not exactly a romantic subject to raise at such a moment. During a great silence – his – Olivia jabbed him back to respond to her. 'I know you're thinking about our long-term commitment to Lamphouse and MacKenzie, and how much this house is costing us, and that I planned this on purpose, but I assure you I did not! Motherhood has come as as much of a surprise to me as fatherhood to you. I was ultra-ultra careful to take the wee white bubble-packed pill every night – or at least first thing in the morning if I forgot. But now that it has happened I feel as though it was meant to be, and I'm very happy about it. This is *our* baby, Stuart, for better, for worse.'

He came beside her and put his arms around her, her feet comfortably curled up under her, her eyes on a level with his as she sat in her own favourite armchair salvaged from her parents clearing-out frenzy. He said, 'Then so am I happy about it. Do I detect a note of uncertainty in your voice regarding me? I just don't know what else to say, because I . . . I've never been a father before!'

She hugged him tightly. 'How about, shall we go and get a pint dahn at the old local, along with a steak and kidney pie?' She tried to say it in a real Kentish way but failed miserably.

'How about getting into the old four-poster along with the old Brig's ghost to ask his advice about parenting the next generation?' He yawned. 'Because I think I'm suffering from jet lag, sweetheart, and need some tender loving care.'

'Done!' she agreed wholeheartedly, pushing him aside so that he all but keeled over. She helped him to his feet. 'You shower; I'll get supper.'

He kissed her, tugged off his constricting tie, and said, 'Cheese soufflé?'

'Coming up!'

When she took the tray up to him, she found him

sprawled on the four-poster, his shoes halfway off, dead to the world beneath the 1960s fake medieval tapestry canopy above his head.

Olivia looked at her husband tenderly, drew up a rug over him without disturbing the bedclothes on which he lay, and ate the soufflé herself.

The following day, Stuart, though still feeling jet-lagged, was certainly more with it. They drove to the office together in the Ferrari as the Dame had to go in for its MOT. Stuart had a meeting that morning, but he would come to her office at six-thirty and they would return home together. Olivia rang Mrs Dan-nymott, asking her to leave a meal for three in the Aga hot cupboard.

Mrs Dannymott said, 'Saw you on local telly, Olivia, you looked a real picture. Nice hat – proper Lady of the Manor you looked, dear.'

'Thanks, Mrs Dannymott.' Mrs Dannymott had also seen her in the flesh, but telly was more im-portant – 'celebrity status' to her.

'Hope you didn't hurt yourself when you fell over at the church, dear?'

Olivia groaned to herself – so, local telly had also managed to record her downfall for posterity. What a bore. 'No, I just slipped – silly thing to do. I wasn't used to such high heels.'

'That's all right then, dear. Didn't Adrian do well on his abseil down the tower? He's a proper caution for a vicar, but I like 'em modern and unstuffy – more in keeping with our young 'uns of the Parish – who we want to keep on the straight

243

and narrow, don't you think so, dear?'

'Oh, yes, Mrs Dannymott!' Olivia wondered how much longer this conversation was going to continue. 'I hope there's enough in the cupboard for a meal tonight. I haven't been shopping . . .'

'Oh, that's all right, dear. I'll make a list of what you've run out of and go down the supermarket myself. You can owe me the housekeeping. I'll leave a meat and red wine casserole for you, hubby and guest.'

'Thanks, Mrs Dannymott, you're a real treasure.'

'Not at all, dear. I'd've done the same for the old Brig – only I'd've never got the housekeeping money back from him! Cheerio for now. Have a good rest this weekend, mind!'

Olivia went to Finsbury Park to pick up Birdie.

'Blimey!' said Birdie, getting into the ultimate in sports cars for the first time. 'Bit small, isn't it?'

'Sorry, no Dame today, Birdie, it's had to go in for its MOT.'

'It's not the only one. You shouldn't be doing this thing for me, Olivia, when you've got the business to run. Whose going to supervise things with you and me both away?'

'Don't worry, I've decided to do what Stuart does with such panache.'

'Meaning you're flying Concorde to Kent?'

'Chance would be a fine thing. I mean delegating more – much more. And if the paid-for slaves don't come up to scratch, I kick butt!'

'I hope it works,' said Birdie doubtfully.

When they arrived at the eye hospital she told Olivia not to wait.

'I *am* waiting,' said Olivia emphatically. 'I've got all the time in the world, seven months before the baby's due, if that's how long it takes to talk sense into you. I know you: the moment my back's turned, you'll skip bail.'

'Would I do a thing like that?'

'Yes.'

'I feel bad about you paying for me to see this eye bloke, all private and posh.'

'Then feel bad. You'll be more of a liability to me if you can't see what's under your beak through lack of proper treatment. New glasses aren't going to make any difference, as far as I can tell. Eyesight is one of the most precious gifts we have, Sybil Birdie Gough, so you get in there and look after it!' That kept her thinking instead of opening her mouth again.

At eleven-thirty, on the dot, a nurse came to fetch Birdie, who chipped back over her shoulder, 'Amazing what a fee up front can do when it comes to not hanging around in hospital waiting rooms to see the Big Chief!' She toddled off in the wake of the nurse and Olivia picked up a magazine to pass the time.

Twenty minutes later Birdie reappeared and Olivia put down the magazine. 'What did he say?'

Birdie pulled a wry face. 'Not much. He just peered into my eyes like he was in love with me or something, and then got the nurse to put in some eye drops.'

'What did he *say*, Birdie!' Olivia asked in exasperation.

'Wants to do some more tests first before he'll commit himself. Says he wants me to come in for a few days next week. I can't afford to hang around in a hospital bed while Mr Braindead makes up his mind what's wrong with my peepers.'

'Yes, you can . . .'

'I can't afford it, Olivia!' Birdie snapped back.

'I can, so shut up. I'm going to have a word with him myself; you're hopeless.'

She asked the nurse if she could have a quick word with Mr Braintree. The nurse went away and came back again with a nod and a smile. 'He's got five minutes.'

Olivia was shown into the great eye-man's presence. He asked her what relationship she was to Miss Gough – as if that had anything to do with it.

'She's my godmother, and I'm paying for her treatment, Mr Braintree, so I want the best for her. Is she suffering from glaucoma?'

'Yes, I'm afraid so.'

'Oh!' Olivia faltered. 'Not a blocked tear-duct then?'

'Why would you think so?'

'I didn't . . . not at first. Then I read a medical book about eye troubles. A blocked tear-duct was the least I could have hoped for – for my godmother's sake. Glaucoma's quite serious, isn't it?'

'It is, but it can also be a lot worse.' He got up from his chair and went to a VDU, snapped on a button and a great big eyeball criss-crossed with red and blue lines appeared before her. 'What Miss Gough is suffering from is the early stages of chronic glaucoma as opposed to acute glaucoma. Acute glaucoma is a medical emergency with an enormous amount of pain involved, so we won't go into that, but stick to specifics, as that is *not* Miss Gough's condition. Chronic glaucoma usually occurs in people over forty, when the trabecular meshwork – the filtering tissue at the margins of the eye – become blocked and drainage slows down. The condition cannot be cured, but intra-ocular pressure predisposing to complete blindness can be controlled.'

'How?' Olivia asked.

'Usually by drug therapy. Laser treatment to the trabecular meshwork often improves the situation, but usually only for a time. Surgery, which involves an artificial channel for fluid to leave the eye, offers more long-term relief. A tiny window may be cut in the iris during the same operation.'

'You mean she has to have an operation on both eyes?'

He snapped off the video pictures and resumed his seat. 'At this stage, I am unable to say what will be the best treatment for Miss Gough; that is why I wish her to be admitted for further tests as soon as a bed becomes available. But the sooner we can get started, the better the prognosis. Meanwhile, I should like her to continue with the eye-drops and to refrain from any eye strain whatsoever, to wit, the four R's including religion, which might involve reading the small print of a Bible, Koran or computer.'

The great man had a sense of humour after all, Olivia was glad about that.

'She tells me her work involves a computer,' he said.

'Yes, she's my personal assistant – an invaluable one.'

'In that case I suggest you find a replacement for your godmother, Mrs MacKenzie, until her condition improves.'

There was that word again – *condition*!

He walked her to the door of his consulting room. 'We've caught the condition in time, so let us be thankful for that. Don't worry about your godmother, Mrs MacKenzie, treatment will soon sort her out.'

Small comfort for Birdie right now, thought Olivia. She handed him her business card. 'My godmother will be coming to stay with me for the next few days. I can be contacted at the office, at home, or on my car-phone, concerning when you want her to come in.'

'My nurse will contact you and Miss Gough within the next few days, so get her to keep her hospital bag at the ready. Good day, Mrs MacKenzie.'

'Yes, thank you. Goodbye.' Olivia took her leave of him. 'Home, Birdie,' she said.

'Aren't I coming back to the office with you?'

'Nope. Home! No reading, riting, rithmetic or religion for you, my gal. Not for a bit, anyway. No TV, no eye-strain, no messing me about, got that?'

'Bad as that? So, I'm dying, tell me the worst.'

'Far from it. A few more tests to see whether you need treatment with drugs, laser or surgery, and you'll be A-OK.' She noticed with an inner smile that she had adopted Stuart's optimistic American expression.

'I need drugs,' said Birdie, 'to zonk me out for a million years. Did you know there's something called cryogenics – they do it in the States – where they can freeze your whole body for that many years until they can come up with a cure for your particular ailment? So freeze me, Olivia, it'll be cheaper in the long run than going private.'

'Birdie, I know that you sometimes prattle on as a way of masking your true feelings, but I read you clearly – shut up! You'll be fine.'

'So what do I do now with my life except learn Braille?'

'Take up knitting. You can do that with your eyes closed. Meanwhile, get your bag packed, you're coming to stay with us at the manor house, because I don't trust you to keep your hospital appointment.'

'What a lot of fuss and nonsense!' Birdie sighed.

'Not fuss and nonsense, Birdie, but plain practicalities. You ought to have told me in the first place about the problem with your eyes, and not left me to find out in such a roundabout fashion. For a while there I thought you were going senile, not blind!'

'Don't blame yourself, dear, for living in your own little world since meeting a millionaire.'

A cruel indictment indeed; but she knew Birdie was only speaking from a self-defensive, very scared viewpoint. 'OK, enough said, I'll pick you up after work. Stuart and I are leaving the office at six-thirty sharp, come hell or high water. So get your bags packed and be ready for us to collect you round about sevenish. We're having casserole tonight, whatever time we make it back to Midhurst.'

Birdie got out of the car, held the passenger door wide and asked, 'How do you think you're going to get three people *and* a suitcase into this sardine-tin?'

'We'll manage . . .' Birdie still didn't move out of the road and was in danger of being run over. Olivia said impatiently. 'What now? – hurry up and say what's on your mind, I've got work to do for the next four hours even if you haven't.'

'Where am I going to sleep when you tell me you're living like gipsies?'

'We have a perfectly good guest bedroom – six, in fact. I've never got around to looking at them properly, but they're all habitable and waterproofed, contained as they are under the new roof bit. We're getting there slowly, just don't mind the peeling wallpaper, damp and no mod cons.'

'I'll never notice since I've lost twenty-twenty vision – I'm talking new millennium and not eyesight. If I bump around in the night, don't mistake me for the Brig's ghost and brick me up behind any walls, will you?'

Olivia grinned. 'I might! I'm double-parked and holding up the car behind . . . see you this evening!'

Birdie blew her a kiss. 'I'll bring a couple of hot water bottles – so glad I chose you as a goddaughter, Olivia. You and Stuart are my dream family. Love you, darling!' She banged the door.

Me too, Birdie Gough! Olivia, smiling to herself, straightened the rear-view mirror, remembered something and shouted through the driver's window, 'And don't forget your eyedrops!' before roaring away towards Farringdon.

CHAPTER 15

When she got back to Farringdon Olivia went straight to Birdie's office; it wasn't the same without her. All the way home she had been in a private reverie, first about Birdie, then her parents, then Stuart, and strangely enough, about Vinny Legrand, her best friend turned traitor!

Olivia remembered how she had once envied the educated, mature, assured, gorgeous as well as competent Davina Legrand, who knew how to catch any man she wanted, while she had always been 'the girl in the shadows', the 'dark little puppy, eh, what?', who 'happened to be Vinny's best friend'.

The 'dark little puppy' had next metamorphosed into the 'stroppy' young daughter of the house with no real credentials other than that which came her way through an accident of birth – nepotism, it was called. Excruciatingly shy and tongue-tied on account of always being made to feel second-best, she had never taken herself seriously, and neither had other people. Her own father had never held a high opinion of her, had referred to her as, 'my stroppy young daughter, Olivia, suspended from school last week for playing truant with that Vinny girl – off to some country house rave the pair of them, boys, drink, drop-outs. That's what comes of sparing the rod and spoiling the child: the more you give them, the worse they are . . .'

Not true, Pa! – but he had never heard her let alone believed her, so she had played up to her reputation of being idle, dreamy, careless, 'hasn't got a good A-level result to warrant paying for a university education.'

Not going to university had been her one great regret. Somehow, that degree, in whatever subject and no matter how lowly a division, still lent a woman credibility in the modern marketplace. Until she had met her destiny in the shape of Stuart Lyon Mac-Kenzie. He had given her back herself, her identity, had given her a chance to prove her worth. Now she didn't have to worry any more. Dollars – millions of them – meant far more than all she had lost out on, education wise – so who was she kidding?

Everyone except yourself, Olivia! a little inner voice said.

'Olivia . . . are you all right? Sit down . . .' Out of the shadows Olivia heard Natasha's anxious voice intrude upon the buzzing in her ears and the racing of her heart . . . She took a deep breath, and the nausea and dizziness passed off.

'It's all right . . . I'm fine. Just a bit dizzy from dashing about all over London. Has anything important cropped up while I've been out?'

'Not really. I've been able to cope with most things – oh, but there is one thing. Pandora Symes wasn't in

252

when Vinny Legrand phoned Rights. So she asked to speak to you. I told her you were out too, and she made some sort of quip about too many office lunches being bad for business, but would I pass the message on anyway.'

'Good grief!'

'Is something wrong?' Once more Natasha peered anxiously into her face. 'Can I get you a coffee or something?'

'A glass of water would be nice.'

Natasha fetched it. Olivia collected her wayward thoughts about telepathy – she hadn't heard from Vinny in a long time, and now, on her very own thought-waves, it appeared, Vinny had telephoned from Toronto. 'Did she say what she wanted?'

'Something about an author profile on Violet. She'd like it faxed through to her. She's also managed to get New York interested in the "zany lady".'

'Good old Vinny!' To herself Olivia reflected that is was about time Legrand came up trumps on her behalf and made amends for deserting Lamphouse.

'They think she'll go down in a big way in the States,' Natasha was saying. 'Provided, of course, Violet's who she says she is, and isn't making up all those stories about all her associations with aristocrats and royalty – that's what Vinny said. She wanted to know where Birdie was too. I said she was off sick.'

'Thanks . . . I'd better ring Vinny back . . .'

'She was hurrying off to catch a plane to Vermont or something, for a short vacation. She said to fax her assistant on Monday.'

Olivia looked at her watch. 'Dig out all the gen we

253

have on Lady Constance, alias Violet. Check to see if we've got the proofs back for *Living With Royalty*. Then get on to graphics about the dust cover. I'll be in my office till six, but don't put anyone through to me unless it's matter of life and death – I'm at a meeting! Mr MacKenzie is an exception.' I don't see enough of him as it is, Olivia thought to herself on her way out. She went into her own office and closed the door.

She slumped into her chair and thought, whew! Opening fêtes was a doddle compared to today! She took an iron tablet, felt her stomach, wondered when the baby would start kicking her around too, and made a phone call to Antibes.

Talking to her mother made her remember she hadn't had a bite to eat since breakfast, and, for the baby's sake, decided to do something about it the moment Maggie stopped swooning over becoming a grandmother. She asked to speak to the old mogul. Olivia told him about Birdie, and then asked him and Maggie to extend a 'convalescence' invitation to her in the event of a major ophthalmic operation, explaining how Birdie had to rest and wouldn't do that of her own accord. He agreed to co-operate in any way he could. 'How much cash do you require to pay her private hospital bills?'

'Haven't a clue! Private doctors working with the NHS are extremely cagey about their bills. Anyway, Stuart's promised to take care of that side of things.'

'Oh, good, about time he earned his third share of the company yacht. He got hold of a bargain when he got Lamphouse *and* you!'

'Thanks, Pa!'

Knowing he was soon to be a grandfather had mellowed him, for sure! She got off the phone at last and buzzed her new assistant.

Natasha appeared like a flash at the door. 'Yes, Olivia?' she asked breathlessly, terribly chuffed at being in Birdie's shoes.

'Can you get Dankers, or anyone else on the front desk, to send out for some sandwiches and doughnuts for us? I'm starving . . . I could kill a cup of tea too, before the food arrives.'

'I didn't get a lunch break either,' said Natasha.

'Natasha, did Birdie ever tell you about Violet?'

'No.' Natasha looked puzzled.

'Violet's quite a wonderful character fallen on hard times. She doesn't live in Paris, as she once did, next door to the exiled Duke and Duchess of Windsor – the ex King of England. She is not now married to a Grand Duke of Russia, or an English lord, or an Italian count or even a Hollywood mega star any more. Her lovers outside marriage are also dispersed, dead and gone. Lady Constance now lives in a grace-and-favour place called St Bethany's, a refuge centre for the genteel homeless – or, as she prefers to call it in her book, "a refuse centre for gentiles". This may all sound very depressing, but I assure you it's not: her books are great fun to read – witty, entertaining, informative and with great PI – public interest.'

Olivia took a sip of water and slipped off her shoes under the desk. 'We've got to do this upmarket author profile in order to *really* sell Violet to the States. She's had a great life – she really *did* do all those things she wrote about, she really did marry all those exotic handsome and aristocratic men she wrote about. She really did lead a wild life, and she can take down a great many public people still living. Pre-publication hype sells copies hot off the press, so I'm asking you a publishing hype question: do we blow the whistle on her and say she is now a cardboard city creature, lost and bewildered and rejected by those in high places she once knew – or do we go for the truly aristocratic lady-in-waiting without her fake designer handbags and classy portmanteaux, dark glasses and Harrod's prestige she can no more afford?'

There was no question about it. Natasha said at once, 'Cool! She sounds really cool. Someone my wacky grandfather would really like to chat up in a floating gin-palace. Telling the truth about her having fallen on hard times is hype enough. Everyone will lap up her riches-to-rags story and the dear old wrinkly might even get a free facelift on her first promotion tour.'

That about said it all! Olivia smiled at her new assistant. 'I'm so glad you said that about sticking to the truth. Go to it, Nat, and do your best with the blurb, warts and all.'

On the green hill of gardening enthusiasm, over the weekend Birdie told Andy Grafter what he was doing all wrong, and then went to Stuart to tell him what *he* was doing all wrong.

'What you need is a proper digger – no reflection on the poor old clod you're slowly killing to death, but I mean an earth-shifter like JCB.'

'JCB – what's that?' Stuart asked from behind the *Sunday Times*.

'As in damn great mechanical digger to dig up the hillside. Forget the twee little rock garden, Olivia; you two want to grow grapes instead.'

'Grapes?' Stuart peered out from behind his newspaper.

'The things you drink all the time in pulp form, Mr MacKenzie!'

'I know what grapes are, Sybil Birdie Gough,' he retaliated, and where there was an investment to be made, he always had a gleam in his eye. Olivia could see it now, the way Birdie had captured his interest.

'Don't!' she said. 'We've got enough on our plate at the moment . . . why, what have I said?' when Birdie went off into her high-pitched cackle the moment anything tickled her pink.

'Grapes on your plate . . . OK, seriously, grow vines and get rich. I know you two are already rich, but no one is *that* rich! Every millionaire has to keep at it.'

'Not lately,' Stuart muttered, returning to his newspaper and Olivia kicked him on the ankle, out of Birdie's sight.

'Especially in a time of recession,' Birdie added.

'Birdie has a fixation about times of recession,' Olivia explained to Stuart.

'Maybe it's because my mum and dad got married in the thirties recession and my brother and me were brought up on the smell of boiled marrowbones and dripping. I've had a horror of being buried in a pauper's grave ever since. That's why I keep working for a living, in case you two have never noticed. Youngsters these days don't know how lucky they are.'

'I didn't know you had a brother, Birdie.'

'He got bombed, Olivia, like the rest of the old folks at home. One of Hitler's doodlebugs back in '44. He was eight, I was five. It landed straight on our house in Clapham and they only managed to get me out of the rubble because I was skinny enough to pull through a mangle.'

'Oh, Birdie! That's terrible! You never said – nor did Pa and Ma ever mention a word about it.'

'That's because they didn't know, Olivia, and you wouldn't have known either, except for my life flashing before me in the shape of a white coat called Mr Braindead.'

Stuart cleared his throat and quickly changed the subject back to a 1990s situation. 'England isn't the place to grow vines, Birdie, so I'm not taking you seriously.'

'You're a Yank, what do you know about England? OK, I'm talking to the boss, Olivia, but he's got his carpet-slippers on today – and talking of carpets, I thought every millionaire had one.' Her pointed remark was directed at the bare floorboards and dust sheets under their feet, since the drawing-room was still not yet finished. They were waiting for the parquet flooring to arrive. 'Just take a trip out into the countryside, Mr Millionaire, and open your eyes. See how many Kentish vineyards there are around here. They've replaced the hops, you know.'

'Hops?' Stuart asked, and made Olivia groan some

more. Why couldn't Birdie just shut up instead of putting more and more bright ideas into her husband's head!

'In my day, we'd all get out of London on a working holiday to pick the Kentish hops. But those days are gone, so now it's not beer any more but wine. You've got good sunny slopes. What with the money you save on carpets, you can afford to get some good topsoil. Grow vines, grow grapes, make wine, grow rich – richer.'

He put down the newspaper. 'You're serious, aren't you?'

'You bet! Make life a lot easier on yourself, boy. It'll save you having to weed the rockery in future years when your wife's too busy with the kids and the recession's got everyone in a poverty trap of marrow bones and dripping on the Aga hotplate.'

'You might have a good point there, Birdie,' Stuart said, and Olivia groaned some more.

'Of course I have. I've read enough sentimental manuscripts over the years into the wonders of growing grapes, like, *In The Valley of Sharon*. That was one of Lamphouse's best successes ever, Olivia, about a post-war Jewish family who survived the Holocaust and planted a vineyard on the soil of their new-found country called Israel, and then refounded themselves in California as third-generation viticulturists who became millionaires.'

Stuart and Olivia continued to listen to Birdie with half an ear. Like a drowning person, her whole life flashing past her eyes, she who had never divulged her life history to anyone before was now doing so to the point of boring them to death. Olivia couldn't help feeling immensely sad on Birdie's lonely behalf, because the only family she had was Lamphouse.

Birdie received a phone call about going into hospital on the following Wednesday, when a bed would be available for her. 'Mrs Dannymott's left you a steak and kidney pie in the Aga and I've got the call,' said Birdie to Olivia when she got home from work. Birdie set the kitchen table in the absence of a decent dining-room. 'Is the Lord of the Manor dining with us tonight?'

'No, he's sleeping over in the exec suite as he's off to Paris first thing in the morning.' Olivia sank down on the sofa.

Birdie trotted in after her with the cutlery still in her hand. 'You're doing too much, you know. Just you mind that baby of yours, else you'll end up in a private bed like me. So, tell me, how is the new personal assistant?'

Olivia opened her eyes. 'Good – Natasha's really very good. Got through an awful lot of work for me over the weekend – in her own personal time.'

'That's great news. So now I'm permanently redundant! I suppose you'll give her the hot seat while you're in Frankfurt too?'

'I've decided to skip Frankfurt this year – didn't I mention it?'

'Not to me.'

'Sorry, I thought I had. I really don't feel like going. Pandora of the pterodactyl claws will represent Lamphouse. It's just as well I decided to delegate, Birdie. I couldn't have gone anyway, since you're to go into hospital on Wednesday.'

'Don't make me feel worse than I do already,' Birdie replied.

Olivia heaved herself up. 'I'm going to take a shower and then we're going to eat, Birdie Gough. I'm starving, in fact, I'm so starving, I fancy a sandwich before dinner.'

'I'll make you one. What do you want?'

'Peanut butter and marmalade.'

Birdie's jaw dropped an inch. Then she shook her head, and, muttering to herself, 'So, she's pregnant, at least it's not a charcoal and cheese sandwich,' trotted back into the kitchen while Olivia switched once more from high-powered executive to house-wife.

On Wednesday morning Olivia dropped Birdie off at Worfields Eye Hospital, then went to the office. After work she and Stuart, back from Paris, paid Birdie a visit.

She received the grapes, chocolates, get well card and flowers with her usual blasé attitude concealing a heart of pure platinum. 'Thanks, you two smoochers, what would I do without your tender touches? They're operating on my eyes tomorrow, so I'm not allowed visitors. Considerate of them not to take the mick. I always hated blind man's buff, even when I was a kid in Dr Barnardo's . . .'

'Birdie, when were you ever in Dr Barnardo's?' Olivia protested.

'Didn't I ever tell you? Never mind.' She kissed

their hands and extended her own to the glass of water by her bedside. ' I lived with an old aunt who survived the doodlebugs . . . cheers, all I'm allowed – not even bread to go with it, as I should be so lucky. Only God knows how I feel right now.'

'Oh, come on, Birdie!' Olivia tried to cheer her up. 'You're going to be fine! Just don't be such a pessimistic grouch.'

'Am I a pessimistic grouch – am I?' she looked to Stuart for moral support in the matter. 'Didn't I tell you she was the best one you should marry and not that Legrand woman – didn't I?'

'Yes, Birdie!'

'What are you two talking about?' Olivia asked suspiciously.

'None of your business,' said Birdie, 'except I saw him before you. He came to Paternoster Row one afternoon with your father, all busy-busy like, all smart and smarmy and ready to take over Lamp-house. You and Vinny were in my office and because of the dust didn't see him pass by with your Pa. What he said to me after was, which one's the boss's daughter? I said, the brunette with a lot of sense; marry her, the red one's a vampire. He said, good enough for me, and married you, so you've got me to thank for putting him your way, Olivia.'

Olivia looked him straight in the eye across Birdie's bed and grinned. 'Is that right?'

He said, 'Right!' and made a cross with two fingers above Birdie's head. 'If she says so.'

When they were about to leave Birdie clung on to their hands. 'Let me look at you two – properly this time. I might never see you again in the same light . . . OK, you're both beautiful, buzz off now and give me some space.' She switched off her night light.

In the corridor outside, Olivia, a lump in her throat, her hand in Stuart's, said, 'She's really scared and trying not to show it. She always chatters nonsensical rubbish when she's nervous. I am too. I just hope the operation will work.'

'She'll be fine, sweetheart, just fine.'

'I hope so, for Birdie's sake.'

As Birdie wasn't allowed visitors the following day. Olivia rang up to ask how the operation had gone. The nursing officer in charge said, 'Good, no problems, but we won't know for definite how successful until the bandages are off her eyes.'

'Mr Braintree said that a little "window" might have to be cut into the irises – did she have that done as well?'

There was a little pause while the nurse flicked through some papers, Olivia could hear the rustle of pages over the phone. 'Yes, that was done . . . he's written in her operation notes that drainage of the blocked trabeculae was satisfactory. I can't tell you any more until the bandages come off and we know how good the results of the operation are.'

'When can we next visit?'

'Saturday. She has to lie perfectly still and flat till then.'

'Thank you.' Olivia put down the phone and went outside to do some gardening in order to take her mind off Birdie and other things. Although she had set up a little office to enable her to work from home, in the meantime she felt guilty about taking time off during such a busy period at Lamphouse.

'Hello, Mrs MacKenzie.' The gardener seemed to be a little harassed, looking at the landscape with a bewildered expression, and doing precious little gardening, it appeared, his tools and wheelbarrow not in evidence this morning.

'Hi, there, Andy. Is something wrong?'

'Mr Stuart, ma'am, said you was turning the hillsides into a vineyard, and he'd ordered a mechanical digger to dig up the place. Shame, because it really was coming along nicely, this rock garden. Seems no point in doing any more landscaping, ma'am,. Does this mean I'm out of a job?'

'When did he tell you that?'

'Before he took off for the office, ma'am. I wouldn't have bothered to come in today, if he'd rung me last night to let me know his change of plan.'

'Well, don't you worry about it, Andy. Just you get on with what we were doing – I'll sort out "Mr" Stuart and his big ideas!' The moment the bigger digger gets home! Olivia added to herself on the way back to the house in her muddy green wellies.

Olivia was in the kitchen, a pinny wrapped round her as yet unnoticeable pregnancy, when she heard and saw Ernest parking the Daimler. Stuart came breezing in through the front door in one of his smart pinstriped state-of-the-art office suits which never showed a wrinkle or crease. He flung his briefcase on to the sofa and came on through into the kitchen, ready to give her a big hug and a kiss. 'What, no mercy visits tonight?'

'Birdie's not allowed visitors today.'

'Oh, right . . . I forgot. I just love coming home of an evening to find you here, sweetheart, instead of Mrs Dannymott. It makes it all worthwhile.' He sniffed the kitchen aromas appreciatively. 'What's cooking?'

'This!' She slapped a crisp stick of celery against his proud chin. 'And this!' Another hearty strike with the unfortunate vegetable from Annabelle's walled kitchen garden, and another. He fell back in utter astonishment into the unfinished drawing-room whither he had made his entrance, while she continued to advance upon him.

'How *dare* you start planning vineyards, ordering JCBs to annihilate, in one fell swoop, not only *my* rockery but Mr Grafter's hard slog for the past few weeks, without prior consultation? How *dare* you undermine my confidence in you? How could you take Birdie Gough seriously, when she was not in her right mind about anything last Sunday?'

'Sweetheart, I . . .' He tried to defend himself against her tirade.

'Today is Thursday, the day of her operation, four days since the suggestion was made. You didn't waste much time, did you, Stuart, in taking up the challenge of making new money? Well now I'm telling you, so listen and listen good. There aren't going to be any vineyards or any more fancy projects until this house is fully completed and utterly habitable. I'm not going to bribe Mr Rapps or his building firm with extra cash in hand like you, because then they'll slow down some more, and some more, in the hope of receiving yet more undeclared American backhanders. Get the picture?'

'Canadian . . .' He tried to assert his own rights.

'I'm going to sack Rapps and his men without prior consultation, so there! Can't you see what they're doing to us? My father always told me to look after the pennies and the pounds – dollars to you – would take care of themselves. You're too busy making big fast dollars to be concerned with small pounds. Well, it's got to stop, and I'm putting a stop to it here and now. Either this house is finished within the next six weeks or I'm off to Antibes to live with my parents until it is! Got that, Stuwey?'

'Sweetheart . . . Olivia, calm down,' he said from the arm of the sofa on which she had trapped him. 'You're overwrought, what with Birdie going off sick, her operation, no one to take her place at Lamphouse, the baby and everything else . . .'

She whacked him some more with the raw celery, took off her pinny and stormed upstairs.

Olivia lay down on the bed and zapped on the bedroom telly, trying to calm down – not good for her 'condition' to get so stressed out, she warned herself.

This was the first time she had lost control and lashed into Stuart like that, and she felt a cold shiver of fear. She felt like an innocent victim on a trundle-cart, the fast lane running out on her as she faced the guillotine that might forever sever her ties with him – served her right if he went off with another woman; he had the power to do it.

And that was what unnerved her most about their marriage; he had so much *power*, which only money could buy. It sometimes frightened her to death, knowing he could do just as he liked. He had done it before, hadn't he? He had divorced his first wife, Christine, and left her with lots of alimony and that was about all! What if he ever did the same to her?

It all came back to her, that cold February day beside Virginia Water, how she had tried to put the knowledge of his former life way back into the corners of her mind; she had loved him so much then, still loved him so much. She had accepted his offer of love and marriage without another thought; now she was not so sure. Now *she* was the bewitched second wife, making excuses for him, when all the time in the back of her mind was that day at Virginia Water and the little nagging doubt – what if Stuart was the kind of man who could *never* settle down, and it all went wrong again? What if he was the kind of man who fought shy of fatherhood, his main concern only to make money and still more money? He hadn't exactly been overjoyed by the fact that she was having a baby – *they*, Olivia, *their* baby . . . it was as much a part of him as her!

She tried to relax, her breath coming unevenly, tried to concentrate on the sitcom on the telly, even if it was utterly banal. She fumbled for her handkerchief under the pillow.

He came into the bedroom with a tray on which he had served out the meal she had cooked and prepared for him; quiche, salad and baked potato. 'Thought you might be hungry – got to eat for two now, sweetheart.'

'You don't even know when the baby's due!' she accused, frowning at the TV screen.

'February.'

'How did you work that one out? Seeing that you're never here.'

'Oh, I was here all right. Takes two to tango, you know. Eat up – would you like me to feed you? I'm quite good at spoon-feeding. I do it all the time on MacKenzie's behalf.'

She burst out laughing, a little hysterically perhaps, but it was a step in the right direction. Olivia zapped off the sitcom. 'You're an evil, money-grabbing, horrible, ugly, selfish, hateful swine!'

'I know. But I'm only a chip off the old block. I used to tell that to him who screwed up my own life. Here . . .' he tucked the napkin under her chin '. . . eat up. I'm a workaholic, I admit, but I enjoy what I do, and I thought you did too, being a workaholic yourself. MacKenzie Inc. is not my first love, but I know Lamphouse is yours, my love.' He had the nerve to tell her.

'Don't you *dare* say things like that, Stuart Mac-Kenzie!'

'OK, I retract that. But I have done my fair share of slumming it, and so I have a real horror of poverty now.'

'Don't you dare say that either! You don't know the first thing about being poor. You've always had a rich father to bale you out of "slumming it"!'

'He doesn't – he never has and he never will. The money I make, I make for myself – us. My father's companies are his alone, I'm merely his UK representative. I can pull out any time I like – he's made that very plain. He puts nothing my way, Olivia, other than what I've earned myself. I invest my own money of my own accord, nothing to do with him – that's why Lamphouse is *our* baby! It might be an imprint of his major companies, but it was I who raised the capital to buy your father out, not Mac-Kenzie senior, by *my own* shrewd efforts. If I'm seen as a millionaire "playboy", it's because I've worked my goddamn socks off for it, that's how! No thanks to anyone – except you, who were with me right from the start!'

'Stuart, I know you did it for us.' It had been a part of their pre-nuptial contract.

'Don't say I don't care about you and the baby. I care about you, and the family we want, more than anything in the world.'

'Tell me what went wrong between you and Christine.'

'You know – I've already told you.'

'How do I know you told me the truth? How do I know she walked out on you with another man? Might it not have been that you walked out on her with another woman?'

'Because I would not lie about something like that to you, and you know it! I don't know why you're behaving so unreasonably, unless it's to do with having a baby at the wrong time . . .'

'Who said it was the wrong time? Did I? It might not have been according to plan, but I can manage Lamphouse *and* a baby, so there! No problem for me – though it might be for you!'

269

'Olivia, I refuse to listen to any more nonsense when you're in this irrational frame of mind. Can we change the subject? Your birthday present will be arriving any day now.'

'Oh, no!' Olivia clutched her head, 'I don't want to know about any more of your *schemes*, Stuart!'

'Eat up, then, and I'll cancel the arrangement with the stables. I know you can't ride in your present state of approaching motherhood . . .' She was really glad he hadn't used the word 'condition'. 'It's a racehorse,' he added slyly.

'A *racehorse?*' she echoed in dismay.

'Thorough Arab.'

'What about the vineyard?'

'I thought you weren't keen on vineyards, honey.'

'Stuart, we'll need a hell of a lot more land than twenty-eight acres to keep racehorses and vineyards!'

'No problem. We can always buy up more land in the future. Anyway, that's all by the board now, since you're so dead set against going into the wine business. The Arab stallion is a start. We could race horses, have a stud farm . . .'

'Stuart, I refuse to listen to this madness any more. What's wrong? You can tell me.'

'Nothing is wrong, sweetheart . . . I just feel we have so much potential going to waste here. Rockeries and flowerbeds don't generate any income. Vines and horses do.'

'Now I know why you're a *millionaire damn mogul*, Stuart!' she said angrily.

'What's with you, Olivia? Are you afraid of being Mrs *Multi*-millionaire MacKenzie?'

'If you want to know the honest truth, yes.'

'Why?'

'Because it involves more of you with other people, and less of you with me.'

He didn't know what to say to that.

'Olivia, honey, what is so very wrong about the other side of publishing? You yourself said you wanted another life away from the workplace.'

'Not racehorses and vineyards, Stuart.'

He raked a hand through his dark hair and gave a diffident shrug, his smile one of bemusement. 'Gee whizz, honey, the British have a mighty strange idea about money, haven't they? It's OK if its inherited wealth, never mind most of the guys pinched it from other less fortunate guys, or got it given to them from king, queen or country for being pretty mean on the battlefield against the so-called enemy. And it's OK if you win it on the football pools or gambling lotteries . . .'

'We don't have a lottery in England – yet!'

'And don't have to pay tax on it,' he finished. 'But when it comes to working for it and paying tax on it, then that's considered to be "*nouveau riche*" and totally unacceptable in the eyes of the smart set! Hell, I don't think I'll ever understand the British mentality when it comes to making money and spending it!'

Olivia smiled at his tone, 'OK, Mr Moneybags, point taken. But please can we take one thing at a time? The house first, other things next.'

'I've thought of a name for the baby,' he said.

'What?'

'Ollypenny.'

'What kind of name is that?'

'You know, James Bond and Miss Moneypenny? Olivia Penelope Pears Margaret MacKenzie.'

'What if it's a boy?'

'Well, I suppose we could always call him Stuart the Lyonheart.'

'Are you ever serious about anything, Stuart?'

'Of course. I'm serious about you for a start. Your love, my love, our life together. And all the little things to make you happy.'

'How about a fully renovated, refurbished manor house with a decent nursery by the end of the year? You treat life as one big round of pleasure, Stuart. You take nothing seriously. You don't even take your wealth seriously. To you it's all one big boy's game – spend, spend, just a whole lot of fun to you.'

'That's how it is with me, Olivia. I don't take money seriously, nor the making of it. To me it *is* fun; it has to be. The really serious things in life are life, love, good health, happiness, togetherness.'

'You screwed up once before because you never took yourself seriously,' she reminded him.

'I took myself *too* seriously, darling.'

He hardly ever called her darling, it was not one of his natural terms of endearment. Darling to him was always used in a flippant context.

'I screwed up because I didn't feel I was up to the job, a good son, a good student, a good husband, a good enough lover, a good enough heir for my father to leave his empire to. All those negative feelings made me feel I really was a good-for-nothing layabout, with only a whisky bottle and a divorce settlement to show for it.'

Now where had she heared that speech before!

Echoes of the past, that day by Virginia Water, wondering if she was doing the right thing to take on the MDship of Lamphouse, wondering whether she was making the right choice by marrying Stuart Lyon MacKenzie, who, apart from being a very good lover and financier, had little else to tell her about himself . . .

'Especially when the old dictator used to remind me of it. I was always trying to live up to my big brother, but couldn't quite manage it. So I screwed up because I wasn't being me. Now that I am who I am, Stuart MacKenzie and not the substitute Geoff MacKenzie, things have worked out better for me. Doesn't mean to say they will go on doing so, especially if you do a Christine on me.'

'Blackmailer!'

'No, just running scared, my love.'

'Did you love her?'

'I never really knew what love was until I met you. And, since then, I have never been unfaithful to you.'

She put aside the half-eaten meal, which she had cooked for him, and drew him close. She cradled his head, and forgave him his sins, those she knew about, and those she didn't. 'I never said anything about being unfaithful, I was talking about being *crazy*. I'm sorry for being such a pig to you just now, but you really made me mad about vineyards and stuff when there's so much more to be getting on with.'

A tear dropped on his hand. He mopped her tears

away and kissed her salty mouth. 'We'll forget about my bright ideas if they upset you so much.'

'No, keep your bright ideas, Stuart, life would be awfully dull without them. Only don't go scaring everyone because of your impulsiveness. I love you the way you are, that's why I married you. But I get scared too, more often than not, and I've only you to blame, and only you to turn to.'

He held her close for a long time, then he chucked her under the chin, looked into her eyes and asked, 'Would a classy lady like you have married me if I was an ugly old dosser on the dole?'

'I thought you still were.'

He grinned. 'I suppose I asked for that one . . . but listen to me, please. You're the best thing that's ever happened to me. I'm just here for whatever *you* want, and you'd better believe it!'

CHAPTER 16

On Saturday morning Olivia went to see Birdie in hospital. 'No more than half an hour, Mrs MacKenzie,' the nurse told Olivia when she asked to see Miss Sybil Gough. 'No excitement, otherwise her blood-pressure will send up her intra-ocular pressure.'

Whatever all that meant!

'I promise,' Olivia said, and opened the door to Birdie's private room. She was sitting up in bed, looking very spry in her dark glasses. 'Hi, Miss Glamour Girl, it's me, Olivia MacKenzie, here to publish your memoirs.'

'Now I *am* disappointed. I thought it was Her Majesty come to give me the Order of the Boot,' Birdie offered her cheek for a kiss.

'Nice to see you looking like something out of *Dynasty*.' Olivia put the basket of flowers in their oasis on the windowsill along with all the others Birdie had received, among them, a huge bouquet from the office.

'You noticed my new hairstyle, then?'

'Of course – you look great, Birdie.' Olivia put fresh grapes and bananas into the fruitbowl on Birdie's locker.

'The nurse did it for me in view of visiting nobility,' Birdie quipped, patting her new hairstyle.

'How are you liking it here?' Olivia drew up a chair and sat down.

'So-so.'

'No good?'

'Only kidding, dear. They're treating me like royalty. For the money it costs going private, they should kiss my posterior. I reckon I can get used to the life of a millionaire's godmother.'

'Here's a little present from Stuart and me.' She gave it to Birdie. 'How are you – eyesight-wise, Birdie?'

'Blind as a bat behind these dark glasses, but I'm to wear them for a week. Mr Braindead came and made love to me this morning and says I'm looking good. All the fluid has been drained off and the pressure's gone down behind the eyes, so I should be able to start seeing things more clearly within the next couple of days. I got drops to put in four times a day – well the nurse does that. Hellishly awkward doing it yourself, especially with sunglasses on. So, what's news on the publishing scene?'

'Violet's been offered a whopping great advance from the States for both her books. She wrote a touching little letter to you and me for "still having faith in her ability to entertain the general public"!'

'Nice!'

'Well, aren't you going to open your present?'

Birdie had difficulty unwrapping the little gift-wrapped box. Olivia assisted her.

'What is it, Olivia?'

'Can't you see it?' Olivia asked, wondering if the operation had been a success after all, and Birdie was not pretending behind those dark glasses of hers.

'Course I can see it – sort of! Looks like a bird in a cage to me.'

'That's what it is . . . look, a little musical box, Birdie, isn't it sweet?'

'A very nice little one too . . .' Birdie said with a catch in her voice. 'Gold-plated, I suppose? You and Stuart shouldn't be spending your money on me, dear. You've given me enough.'

'Nonsense! Olivia pulled up the ring on the top of the tiny birdcage and the bird began to sing, "*I tort I taw a puddy-tat, a'creepin' up on me, tweet-tweet; I did! I taw a puddy-tat as plain as he can be, tweet-tweet*", and the faster the tune went the faster the little bird in its gilded cage twirled around on its perch.

'Now ain't that jest the cutest little thing!' Birdie drawled, playing it again and again, thrilled to bits with the pretty little novelty.

'Stuart brought it back from New York,' Olivia said.

'Well, I'm touched to think he thought of me in the midst of being a high-powered millionaire. Thanks, you two, a million – come here and give me a big kiss . . . now put it on the locker for me, Olivia, before some clumsy nurse lands a bedpan on it.'

Olivia put the bird in its cage on Birdie's bedside locker while Birdie asked, 'So, where is your husband, why isn't he here to see me?'

'Sorry, Birdie, he sends his love. We've had so

many invitations lately. Ever since the village fête, where I made a real fool of myself by slipping into someone else's grave, we've been asked out to dinner-parties and whatnot. Stuart's accepted an invitation to play golf with Dr Gareth and his cronies at the Midhurst Golf Club,'

'Now you've done it!'

'Yes, I know,' Olivia pulled a face, 'but I'm a grass window already.'

'Talking about your parents, they sent me a get well card and an open-ended air ticket to the South of France. That's the card up there along with all the others from the old firm, if you care to take a look. Didn't know they cared that much, except for poor old Dankers. Your Ma wants me to "recuperate" in Antibes, as I should be so lucky.'

'Well, that's great, Birdie!'

'No, it isn't. I'm no lady of leisure, Olivia, you should know that. I reckon you knew about it all the time. Wouldn't surprise me if you made the arrangements yourself, huh?' The dark glasses tilted up somewhat on her nose.

'Would I do that?'

'Yes! Anyway, I'm not accepting.'

'You are, and you're going. You need a good long rest after this.'

'I'm not taking any more charity from the Cotswolds or the MacKenzies, Olivia.'

'OK, throw it all back in our faces, I don't care. You'll be taking a pay-cut anyway, when you return to Lamphouse, if it makes you feel any better.'

She squeezed Olivia's hand tightly in her little

claw. 'You're sweet, but don't make me feel bad, dear. I've got my pride, you know.'

'I know. So much of it, it'll choke you one day.'

'It's the menopause – it makes a woman desperate . . .' She laughed her high-pitched cackle of fun.

A nurse poked her head round the door. 'No excitement, Sybil! Ten more minutes and then your visitor must go, lunch is on its way . . .'

Birdie waved her away. She made a face behind the nurse's back. '*Sybil*, yuk! Why they have to be so familiar, I don't know!' She asked Olivia to pour her a glass of water.

Olivia handed it to her. 'What's the food like?'

'Horrible.'

'Really? Don't they give you a choice?'

'Sure they do – pish-pash and mish-mash. Only kidding. As I said, it's five-star in this place. But breakfast was the only time I got anything to eat. They've starved me to death since Wednesday, just water without the bread. I wasn't even allowed to sit up to slurp my water, post-op and all that. If I got sick, that would upset the pressure in my skull, or something daft like that.'

Birdie chatted away brightly. Olivia was glad to see she was so perky after her operation.

'So I made up for being starved to death by having porridge for breakfast, and passed on the scrambled eggs to the night nurse who was more starved than me. She was welcome to them – they reminded me of the powdered stuff we used to get in the war. They're bringing me mashed chicken for lunch. There's nothing wrong with my teeth, I told them, so now I'm wondering if they operated on the right patient. Then they gave me back my teeth, so ask me again tomorrow what the food's like.'

They went on talking about this and that for a bit longer, then, when she could see Birdie was getting tired, Olivia said, 'Well, I'm out of here, Birdie . . .' She stood up.

'So soon?' Birdie whimpered.

'My half-hour's up, I don't want to be thrown out . . .'

'Visiting the sick is a real pain; my old aunt, who was my dead father's sister who raised me, died so many times I lost count of the hours I sat by her beside, so go if you want.'

'Birdie, remember the time I came to you as a horrible little teenager, begging sanctuary from my horrendous boarding school?'

'No, I don't!' She wrapped up tight like a cover on a hot-water bottle.

'Yes, you do. I skipped school and you shielded me from Pa's wrath by telling him you'd invited me to stay the weekend.'

'So what!' she added grudgingly.

'So, I'm telling you now what I told you then – how I could never repay you because I wasn't rich like my father, and you said, money wasn't everything – yes, you did, you said it! Up till then everything had been taught to me in Pa's language – pounds, shillings and pence, pre-decimalization and pre-Noah's ark. You told me to pass on a kindness for the next person to take it up, who could then pass it on to the next one and so forth, until the whole world was filled up with IOUs of kindness.'

'Did I say that?'

'You did.'

'Must have had a bad day at the office.'

'Birdie, stop whinging!' Olivia exclaimed, half laughing at Birdie's reluctance to be seen as a beacon in the darkness. 'You meant it, and I never forgot it – about the only thing I never forgot. Well, I'm passing one right on to you, right now. Shut up about hospital bills and convalescent bills in Antibes – IOU!'

'Get away from here, Olivia Cotswold MacKenzie, before you have me weeping in the aisles like a real snoockum!'

Olivia, her dimples deep, looked fondly upon Birdie's newly coiffured blue rinse – she was ever an old-fashioned gal! She bent down to whisper in her ear, 'Schnook, I'll come and see you on Monday. Sorry about tomorrow, but Stuart and I are spending the day in the four-poster. Sunday is the only day we get to being our truly decadent millionaire selves.'

'You tell that husband of yours if he thinks more of playing golf than coming to visit Birdie Gough, I hope I never see him again.'

'I'll tell him. I'll drag him over to visit you Monday after work.'

'Don't bother, I might be out of here by then.'

'No, you won't, you're here for another week at least. See you, Birdie, have fun with the canary.' She kissed Birdie's thin cheek and left her to her mish-mashed chicken lunch.

Olivia arrived home at just after two o'clock, and gave Ernest the rest of the weekend off. Stuart was still not back from playing golf, so she made herself some soup and cheese on toast to take up to bed with her. Dr Gareth had told her that she must try and put her feet up for at least a couple of hours every afternoon – some hopes, thought Olivia, who could just see herself with her feet up on the desk when someone walked into the office.

Weekends were her only chance to indulge herself. No sooner had she settled down on the bed and turned on a 1950's Doris Day film she'd seen dozens of times before, than the front door bell rang, followed by a hefty thump on the heavy iron knock-er. She wondered if Stuart had locked himself out, but it was Annabelle with her shopping basket.

'Hello, hope I haven't disturbed you. I've brought you some plants for your rockery.'

'Don't mention that sore subject. Stuart wants to grow grapes and breed racehorses,' said Olivia dourly, standing in her bare feet. 'Come in, I was just having some soup – tomato actually. Would you like some?'

'No, thanks, Olivia, I've just had lunch, but you carry on. I know Stuart is out playing golf with Dr Gareth, so I've taken advantage of his absence. I want to talk to you, alone.'

It sounded ominous, Olivia led Annabelle inside. 'OK, dump the plants in the kitchen sink while I nip upstairs and fetch down my lunch . . . as opposed to bringing it up again,' she added. 'Go on into the sitting-room, I shan't be a sec . . . help yourself to a glass of milk . . .'

'No, I'm all right, don't need a drink,' Annabelle said from the kitchen sink.

Olivia brought her belated lunch of tomato soup and cheese on toast downstairs again, stone cold by now. She curled herself up in her own favourite armchair, the tray balanced on her lap, while Annabelle occupied the Yuppie sofa. 'Fire away!'

'Well, I came to apologize for Max really.'

'Max? Why Max? Olivia asked, the soup-spoon halfway to her mouth.

'Well, you know how he can be a bit fanatical about his origins.'

More than a bit! thought Olivia.

'His silly remarks on the train home from work the other evening, about South African politics, were really in bad taste. He's always on about apartheid and people killing each other, only because he thinks the country will end up in a blood-bath if the ANC get control.'

'I didn't know you were a little fly on the wall, Annabelle.'

'He told me he thinks he upset you by his attitude.'

'He certainly did that. Your husband is a bigot. I wished I'd told him that too.'

'You have to understand Max's background in South Africa, Olivia, to know why he feels the way he does about South African freedom and . . .'

'No! Don't say it!' Olivia held up her hand. 'I don't

283

want to get on to that subject, I know nothing about South Africa – apart from MacKenzie having an office there. Anyway, why have you to apologize on his behalf? Why can't he come and do it himself, and say how sorry he is for being such a bore – as in boorish person.'

'Max is really quite a nice man, Olivia . . .'

'Sorry, we like you and the children a great deal, but forgive us please, Stuart and I honestly don't want to associate with Max, even if he is your dearly beloved husband.'

'He's not, actually.'

'Sorry?'

'Max is not my husband and I'm not here to defend him, Olivia. I think he's a pig too, when he goes on about black South Africa the way he does. But he was born and raised there and worked very hard for a homeland from which he was exiled. But he supports me and the children and without him I'd have no one else to turn to: I mean, little old me, three times divorced with six children of her own, I'd have to go it alone again, until I found someone else willing and daft enough to take me and my lot on. I couldn't go through all that again, Olivia.'

Olivia began to see the reasons behind Annabelle's blind adoration of Max.

'I was married and divorced three times before I met Max. He just the once – though they didn't divorce, she died quite tragically. Neither of us wants to go through all that married-divorced, dead and dearly departed scenario again. I use his name as it's simpler and more discreet to be known as Annabelle van der Croote – people gossip a lot in Midhurst. Neither would it have done my father's business much good – "the daughter of the firm, three times married and divorced and now living in sin", that sort of stuff.'

'Oh, Annabelle . . .' Olivia didn't know what to say.

'Max has two children by his former marriage, Sally and Sarah, and I've got two by my first marriage, Dicky and Gower, one by the second, Tandy, two by the third, Bryce and Lois, and the last one, Amy, is Max's and mine. We're a sort of extended family.' Annabelle made a coy hunch-shouldered apology for not being what she had seemed at the beginning of their friendship

An extended family – no doubt about it! Where had she found the time? Olivia wondered. They were now treading on very thin ice; she didn't really want to know about Annabelle's private life with her partner, it was bad enough coping with Max's bigotry.

'Annabelle, how you and Max live your lives is nothing to do with Stuart and me. It makes not the slightest difference to us whether you're married or not, but it *does* make a difference to us when Max behaves like a dictator.'

'Max says such things because he's still very bitter, Olivia.'

'I don't care how *bitter* he is, Annabelle.'

'I'm not going into details because you're having a baby and it's not fair to the baby to be depressed – they say everything the mother feels the baby feels too, and I don't want to upset you or the baby, but

Max had a really bad tragedy in his life during a race-riot on his farm just outside Johannesburg – his wife was killed. He and the two girls barely got away with their own lives. That's why he says the things he does – he's very bitter still.'

'I'm terribly sorry to hear about that, Annabelle, really. Neither Stuart or I feel comfortable in Max's presence, he has so much anger and resentment stored up inside him, so, if you don't mind, we'll pass on the bitterness and revenge scene. You and the children are welcome here any time.'

'I just thought I'd come and pour oil on troubled waters . . . because I don't want to fall out with you. Your friendship means a lot to me, Olivia. Well . . .' she got up and gave a feeble smile, not her usual airy-fairy self at all 'I'd better be off and leave you to get your afternoon rest. Sorry about intruding.'

'You're not intruding . . .'

Annabelle suddenly burst into tears at the front door, her hands covering her face. Olivia was so shocked, she could only put her arms around Annabelle and wait for the storm to subside.

'Come and sit down again . . .' she said.

'No . . . I'm all right . . .'

'Tell me what's really wrong, Annabelle?' Olivia patted her back in a motherly fashion.

Her face buried on Olivia's shoulder, she gulped miserably, 'I . . . I think . . . think the swine is having an affair with Ute . . .'

'Oh, no! No, I'm sure you're wrong, Annabelle!' Olivia felt helpless, unsure of how to handle this

286

situation. 'Look, come and sit down . . . I'll make us a cup of tea . . .'

'No . . . I'm all right now . . .' She sniffed and fumbled for her handkerchief. 'Now I've said it straight out, I feel better. I've had my suspicions about them for a long time. Sorry, Olivia . . . I . . . just had to tell you about it . . . I knew you'd understand, without . . . without gossiping to others.'

'Of course I understand. I'm just so sorry about it all, but I'm sure you're wrong about them . . .'

'Oh, no, I'm not – Tandy told me about the goings on behind my back.' Then Annabelle tossed her head back, sniffed and smiled defiantly, her handkerchief dashing away the last teardrop. 'Anyway, I've sacked Ute, she's gone, and I'm now lumbered until I get another au pair. I never did like her anyway. Max says I'm being neurotic . . . perhaps, I am. Sorry, Olivia . . .'

'Nothing to apologize for, Annabelle. You're welcome to stay and talk it through . . .'

'No, I won't, thanks. I don't want your husband to find me in such a state, not when you're the one who has to be taken care of . . .' She picked up her empty basket. 'I'll see you, Olivia.'

'I'll ring you, Annabelle. If I get home early from work one afternoon next week, I'll call and see you for a chat before Max gets home. Thanks for the rock plants; Andy and I will get planting. See you, Annabelle . . .' Olivia watched her go off with her empty basket. 'Annabelle . . .'

She stopped and turned round, her eyes still red from weeping. 'Yes?'

'Annabelle, tell Max from me that I'll knock his block off unless he grovels for forgiveness. He has an attitude problem and his umbrella has an even worse one – he'll know what I mean!'

She smiled and waved, her spirit lifting at once. 'Oh, yes . . .' The Ferrari roared up the steep driveway and Annabelle walked off into green pastures while Stuart swerved to avoid her. He also narrowly missed hitting the gatepost. Annabelle fled down the hill, her long skirts defying the incline.

He got out of the car and said, 'What the hell . . . was that Annabelle? She nearly got herself run over!'

'You shouldn't drive so fast around country bends, Stuart.'

He took his golf clubs out so the car. 'What did she want?'

'She didn't want anything, she brought me some rock plants.'

He grinned. 'Ganging up on me, you two women, is that it?'

'Not at all – you two women, a sexist remark if ever I heard one! If it's anyone we're ganging up on, it's Max van der Croote. Did you have a good round of golf with Dr Gareth?' Now she was sounding *just* like her mother!

He left the car for Ernest to put away, until she told him to do it himself, Ernest had the weekend off. He said he'd do it later and followed her into the house with his golf-bag. 'Owen said you missed your antenatal class.'

'Owen?'

'Dr Gareth.'

'Oh! First-name terms now? He's forgotten – I went to see him last Monday.' Olivia went into the kitchen with her tray of dirty soup bowl and cheese-toast crumbs. He followed her.

'Ante-natal class, not clinic – we were both booked in with the local midwife. A threesome is not my scene, honey.'

'*We?*'

'You and me, sweetheart – Wednesday.'

'Which Wednesday?'

'Don't ask me – last Wednesday, I suppose.'

'What have *you* got to do with it?'

'I'm pregnant too – or didn't you know?'

'Stuart!'

'Sorry!' He took a beer out of the fridge, while Olivia wondered idly if he'd ever end up looking like her father, all golfy, bald and cocky. Though bald men were supposed to be very sexy – according to the manuscripts she had read over the years, but her mother would no doubt have something else to say about it. 'Breathing exercises or something. It's called moral support for the new mother-to-be.'

'What did you tell Dr Owen Gareth?'

'I told the good GP . . .' Stuart gulped straight from the bottle 'he plays damn good golf, you know . . .'

Now Stuart sounded like a typical Englishman! 'Stuart, what – *what?*' Olivia wanted to know.

'I told him I'd done my bit of panting and writhing up and down and all over you; it was now up to the Baroness to do her bit for posterity.'

'You didn't . . .' Olivia took an apple from the fruitbowl and aimed it at his head. He ducked, and only the apple ended up bruised. 'Is this what professional *men* talk about on the golf course, us "women" having babies?'

'Yes, I did, and yes, we did.'

'Are you?'

'Am I what?'

'Coming to the next ante-natal class with me – the one I don't want to miss?'

'Sure, if you want me to. I'll hold your hand, pant and breathe and scream . . . talking about screaming, what's with Max and Annabelle?'

'If you don't know the answer now, I'll tell you later!' She kissed his rough, sexy chin. 'You need a shave, but before you disappear into our nice new Spanish-tiled en-suite shower,' she made big come-on-and-get-me eyes, 'I thought I'd tell you first how you brought me here under false pretences.'

'Howzat, my love?' He adopted a serious manner, one eye screwed to the bottom of the beer bottle.

'I thought living in the country would be a nice quiet countrified relaxation from the stresses of working in town. How wrong I was! It's like living in a jungle of dangerous animals!'

'Shall we turf out the lodgers and move back to the Yuppie flat?'

'Not on your life, Stuart. After what I've been through, we're making a go of this place if it's the last thing I do!' She shoved him up the grand manorial staircase, and each step of the way reminded him of what she had had to put up with since coming to Midhurst.

'From Mars Bars to Big Macs, big Maxes with

290

attitude problems and low tolerance levels, to un-
married mums with vegetable fetishes, from glaucoma to cess-pits, from roofers to tilers, ramblers to
Cleavers – meaning Ashton Dore – shut up, I haven't
finished yet, Stuart!

'From vineyards to racehorses, MD to pregnancy,
all in a short space of time, Stuart Lyon MacKenzie!
If I wasn't already a publisher's wife I'd be an author
and tell about all the deep dark secrets of the "county
set" sucking up to a millionaire with a shady past!'

She shoved him into their en-suite bathroom and
asked if he wanted his back scrubbed, 'Because that's
about as intimate as I can make it for the time being –
doctor's orders – *honey*!'

CHAPTER 17

As the weeks slipped into months and her waist began to disappear, Olivia took time out to have a new wardrobe made for her by 'Stork of the Town', an exclusive maternitywear designer in Bond Street.

'Lucky for some,' she overheard the girls talking in the cloakroom, without them realizing the boss was seated in style in one of the cubicles. She seemed to spend all her time sitting on the loo these days, were Olivia's exasperated thoughts. Neither Dr Gareth nor the midwife had told her about 'frequency of micturition', swelling ankles and the rest of the annoying discomforts of 'her condition'. Mercifully, the giddy spells and morning sickness, which had often lasted all day in the first weeks of pregnancy, had disappeared. A managing director throwing up over the boardroom table was just not on.

'Designer clothes – I should be so lucky. All I can afford is Mothercare.'

'Oxfam isn't bad, you can get some good stuff there. I like the maternity frock she's wearing today, very posh. You ought to get yourself a navy and white outfit like that.'

'I'm not married to a millionaire who can afford his wife to appear all tarted up at the table. She doesn't have a little Hadfield slopping tomato sauce over her – yet!'

'She'll have a nanny and a night nurse, just like Di. So, when's yours due, then?'

'January.'

'Got your maternity leave worked out?'

'What maternity leave?'

'I don't want to be lumbered with your work as well as mine. Accounts is in a real mess, what with our computers always on the blink: Royalties' excuse for not paying the authors on time. So, are they getting in a temp to do your work?'

'Personnel says I'm not entitled to maternity leave – haven't been here long enough. I'll have to give up when number two arrives, unless they can give me more maternally sociable hours.'

'You'll be lucky! What with Birdie Gough off sick, OM is going around like a headless chicken. How's she going to cope with a baby and all beats me.'

'Oh, she'll have someone else to change nappies and do the bottle feeding.'

'Suppose you're right.'

'I'll be glad when Hadfield starts at the Infants'. Private child-minders cost the earth – so what am I working full time for, I ask myself?'

'Well, I do it because staying at home listening to his nibs moaning all day in front of the telly would drive me more round the bend than he does already.'

'Me too. Soon as I finish here, I have to dash off to pick Hadfield up, do the shopping and then get home to cook Jim's dinner, seeing as he's on permanent night shift. Talk about being knackered at the end of the day, I'm really dead on my feet, what with this great lump I'm carting about like her ladyship. Only she's got a Daimler and a Ferrari to tuck *her* swollen ankles into.'

'What'd'you reckon she's having, then?'

'Who?'

'Her nibs – Olivia!'

'Oh, got be a girl – she's all out front. Boys don't show. That's why I reckon I'm having another boy.'

'Didn't you have an ultrasound to make sure?'

'Nope. Jim and me like surprises. As long as it's OK, we don't care what sex it is.'

'Well, you show enough to me, so it must be a girl. In fact, your lump is bigger than hers.'

'It would be, wouldn't it? I'm due a couple of months before her ladyship. At least she works alongside Stuwey, I never see *my* feller!'

'He must have managed it somehow!' Giggles outside the cubicle. 'Reckon printers get good money. I should be so lucky married to a redundant works manager. I'm only temping till Gary stops being a couch potato and finds another job with an engineering firm not in receivership.'

'It's the recession. It's got us all on the treadmill to nowhere.'

Taps were switched off and Olivia heard the two hand-dryers burring away and then the cloakroom door slammed. She breathed a sigh of relief, thinking that those two would never go, and that she really would have to get her own private loo installed in her office. But she did make a mental note to check into Lamphouse's maternity leave policy.

She sped back to grab her briefcase and coat and said to Natasha, 'Where are my notes? Thanks . . . see you . . .'

On her way to Blenheim Crescent and her meeting with the Book Packagers' Association, Olivia wondered if there was a life outside the Lamphouse Cross. She said to the back of Ernest's head, 'You wouldn't like to swop jobs with me, would you, Ernest?'

'Sorry, Miss Olivia?' Stuck at red traffic lights in the busy West End, he craned his neck to the frustrated voice from the back seat of the Dame.

'Never mind,' said Olivia. 'The lights have changed.'

At her next ante-natal check-up, Dr Gareth was worried about her blood-pressure. 'You've got to take it easy, Olivia. If it creeps up much more you'll be in trouble.'

'Trouble? What kind of trouble?' she asked, wondering if he was being facetious about his big stick method of getting the mother-to-be to toe the line.

'The baby might have to be induced early. Don't want that to happen, do we?'

Don't we? thought Olivia. But then, as a responsible mother-to-be, she wanted her child to have the best possible start, and that entailed nurturing it in situ for as long as her nine-month sentence decreed.

Olivia tried to curtail her hours at the office by going in at eleven and leaving at four, but without

Birdie to take her place, it was not easy. Even though she had set up her home-based office with fax, photo-copier and state-of-the-art computer, working from home was even more stressful than going to Farring-don every day.

Mrs Dannymott kept her gossiping for a start.

Then there was Mr Rapps and his team who were putting the finishing touches to the new extension which had to be architecturally in keeping with 'ye olde manor house'. Stuart's American-style swim-ming-pool, sauna, solarium, mini-gym and Jacuzzi still posed problems. He had envisaged the indoor pool opening wide to the gardens and sunshine during summer months, but modern electric sliding doors of aluminium and glass did not 'meld' with the rest of the house, even though the private leisure centre was at the back and did not detract from the façade.

The local planning department were not happy about the submitted plans, and nor was the building inspector: Mr Rapps had scratched his head and suggested ordinary French doors.

Stuart still wanted everything to operate at the touch of a button.

Negotiations were at a stalemate.

Then there was Annabelle with her domestic problems centered upon Max and his alleged affair with Ute.

Annabelle had moved into Tandy's room.

Max had apologized most profusely, had told Annabelle that she was silly getting worked up about nothing.

Annabelle had tossed a vegetable lasagne in his face.

The atmosphere in the van der Croote household was not good.

The children were suffering on account of the breakdown of Annabelle's relationship with Max.

She brought her troubles to Olivia, who, like a good friend, listened sympathetically if rather helplessly.

Annabelle herself was at stalemate: ought she to forgive and forget and move back into his bed? After all, he hadn't actually run off after Ute when she had tossed the girl, suitcase and all, out of the van der Croote back door.

They had a new au pair now, a Spanish girl who was very plain. But Annunciata was a 'real treasure', heaps better than Ute. Amy adored her and so did the other children. All Ute had done was paint her toenails and thrust out her Wonderbra in Max's face. Annunciata might be huge (hips not boobs) and nothing to look at, but she had a sweet nature and was definitely useful. She helped in the garden *and* she had made them a simply spiffing seafood paella the other evening.

'I suppose we're not fully fledged veggies,' Annabelle had gone on to add with a little self-conscious shrug, her blonde head sinking down onto her shoulders. 'The way I see it, calamares, prawns, mussels and things are the fruits of the sea, not the flesh.'

Or Big Macs, Olivia had thought. 'You must do what you feel is right, Annabelle. It's up to you whether you forgive and forget. I suppose you ought, for the sake of the children, but it's not up to me to tell you how to handle your personal relationships.'

'It would be simply awful if he upped and went because I refuse to give him his conjugal rights,' Annabelle had said. 'He does look after us all, financially. Decisions, decisions!' Annabelle had sighed.

And, thought Olivia, Annabelle, being a red-blooded woman, would be back in the bed of the Big Mac-eater sooner than she could say Christmas.

She was right; the van der Crootes settled their differences on Christmas Day when Max presented Annabelle with a fluffy little Burmese kitten.

Annabelle named it Reconciliation, or 'Recky' for short.

'My New Year's resolution is to try and be more tolerant of Max and his moods,' Annabelle declared.

Olivia's New Year resolution was to be less receptive to other people's personal problems; she had enough of her own.

Max was reinstated on his home-grown vegetable plot and behind the back of *de kleine vrouw* continued his carnivorous appetites. Olivia could not get away from him, even when she didn't travel first class. 'Hullow, Olivia, I hope you haf forgiven me for my slip hof the tongue about my sad bad homeland. I am not a wicked man by nature, just a very disillusioned one with our human race.'

Her determination to keep Max van der Croote as far away as possible from manorial lands was difficult. Despite his Boer self-esteem and bigoted politics, Max could be quite charming when he chose, *and* he was a pillar of the Midhurst golfing fraternity, as well as the Midhurst Arms, so avoidance was tricky. When Olivia happened to broach the subject of Max's first wife and the manner of her death in Johannesburg, the cause of Max's bitterness against black South Africa, Stuart said,

'I don't see why. She herself was black.'

'Oh,' said Olivia. 'Annabelle never mentioned it.'

'Owen Gareth told me. She was an ex-beauty queen or something, who died as a result of some kind of tribal vendetta. I didn't ask for details and Owen never went into them, apart from saying that van der Croote had his farm burnt to the ground and in trying to escape the blaze, his wife lost her life.'

Olivia said, 'I had always wondered about Sally and Sarah.'

'The beautiful Ms. Van der Crootes you mean?'

'Something like. They've both been accepted by a high profile "teenage" modelling agency in London because of their stunning looks – following in their mother's footsteps, I dare say. Annabelle only tells me what she wants me to know. None of our business anyway – the van der Croote saga, I mean. We've all got our cross to bear, mine being Lamphouse at this point in time.'

Dr Gareth continued to frown and cajole Olivia at ante-natal checks: she still wasn't taking it 'easy', as he would have liked.

A month before the baby was due he was not a happy man. 'I think we'll give it another week, and then, if your blood pressure is still way up on the rooftops, we'll have you in early and induce the baby.'

'Oh, no! Olivia said. 'Won't that hurt the baby?'

'Not a bit. He's almost ready to pop out of his own accord.'

'He? How do you know it's a he?'

Olivia had not wanted to know the sex of her baby before birth. Like the girl from Accounts, she and Stuart wanted it to be a surprise – a lot to be said for the old days and non-scientific pre-packaged deals. Knowing it all beforehand rather detracted from the surprise element. Had the scan shown up something awful, then of course she would have wanted to know, but taking pot-luck where the sex of her baby was concerned, she allowed the Almighty his dignity too.

Owen Gareth busily kept his back to her while he washed his hands. He maintained his memory lapse and resumed his seat behind the desk.

'You've seen the ultrasound,' Olivia said. One could not accuse a doctor of doing his duty, but he had let it slip, albeit unconsciously.

'Never saw a thing!' he growled as he wrote her out a prescription for more folic acid and iron tablets.

'Well, if it's a boy, I hope you *did* see a *thing*, Owen!' said Olivia while Janine Harvey, district nurse and midwife, helped get her bulk down from the examining couch. 'Don't worry, I don't care what it is as long it's a boy or a girl with every "thing" in order. Stuart was hoping for a girl, though.'

'I'm sure he won't mind one way or another.' Owen Gareth smiled, handing over the prescription. 'I shouldn't take my word for ultrasound authenticity; I can't read X-rays either. Anyway, we'll see you next Wednesday and decide whether to induce an early labour or not. I'll get on to the maternity hospital to keep a bed ready, just in case. But all that oedema in your ankles is not good, so put your feet up when you get home, Mrs MacKenzie!'

'Aye-aye, Doctor!' she said, the lump leading the way out of his surgery.

A week later the baby had to be induced because of the fear of eclampsia. Janine explained, 'One of the toxaemias of pregnancy, Olivia, which could be harmful to both you and the baby. Best just do as you're told by us medics, huh?'

Olivia was only relieved to know that Birdie was in the hot seat once more, now fully recovered from her eye operation and her six weeks' convalescence in the South of France with Harold and Maggie. Lamphouse would be able to manage without Mrs MacKenzie MD for a little while longer – she hoped!

Booked into a private room at the local maternity unit, Olivia was glad to know that Stuart had thought it all through beforehand, and would be there for her. 'Sweetheart, would I let you down in your hour of need after I have panted and oohed and ahh-ed my way through every damn ante-natal class you've dragged me to?'

'Much against your will. I've never seen a man so embarrassed when confronted with all those maternity lumps huffing and puffing fit to blow the house down.'

'How can you say that?'

Easily, she thought; he wasn't strung up like a chicken about to be de-stuffed. She wondered if all this was legal. Talk about hanging, drawing and quartering back in medieval times – this was the twentieth century, for God's sake!

The pain was like nothing she had ever imagined, when a couple of hours later her labour began for real.

Six hours later she was still groaning and gasping. Despite all her deep breathing, panting and ante-natal push-ups, with the moral support of her husband beside her, gowned and masked like a doctor, nothing had prepared her for this.

'You can do it, you can do it . . . deep breaths now, breathe . . . breathe . . . hooh, haah, hooh, haah . . .' Stuart grunted, sweating it out with her, anxiety in his eyes and not at all the image of the cool, sexy exec now.

'Who's having this baby, you or me?' Betcha sweet life you wish you'd never decided to be a caring-nineties father now, huh, darling? Olivia giggled hysterically, the stuff they'd pumped into her making her feel quite high.

He smoothed her fevered brow, perspiration plastering her hair to her face, 'You're doing great, honey, just remember all the breathing exercises and the counting . . . one and one, and two and two, and . . .'

'*Aahhh!* Get lost . . . get him out of here, I never want to see him again . . . I don't ever want to sleep with the creep again . . .'

302

'It's OK, she doesn't mean it . . . she loved it . . . me, she loves me, really . . .' He smiled at the medical team, but they never noticed.

'I'll kill you, Stuart Lyon . . .'

'Don't push, Mrs Mac . . . we'll tell you when . . .'

'Don't call me Mrs Mac . . . oh, my God . . . oh, my God . . .' She grabbed Stuart's hand. 'Get them out of here, Stuart . . . I . . . can't . . . *breathe!*'

'Come on, honey . . . not much longer . . .'

'Don't you *dare* say that! It's been all day already . . . hooh, haah, hooh, haah . . . and don't call me honey . . . *hooh, haah, hooh, haah . . .*'

An hour later, '*Puuussshhh!*' said the doctor and the midwife and the nurse, and Olivia wondered why on earth she had ever wanted natural childbirth when there was a zip-opener operation called a Caesarean that would have let her retain her dignity smoothly, elegantly and unconsciously. 'I can't . . . any more . . .'

'One last push,' someone said, it was definitely not her husband. 'We can see the head, now, Mrs Mac . . . *now!*'

'Oh, Godddd . . . !' She gritted her teeth and because she couldn't help it bore down so hard that the baby literally popped out. 'Is that it?' she panted in astonishment.

'That's it, my dear, nearly done . . . would the father like to cut the cord . . . where is he?'

'Gone out for a breath of fresh air . . .'

'Couldn't take it, you mean. OK, someone else cut the cord, then. All over, Mrs MacKenzie; not bad for a first-timer.'

'Huh!' she grunted. Seven hours' forced labour had been a lifetime!

It was all forgotten the moment they put the baby in her arms. Naked and slippery and pearly white, with blood on its head, it looked like a little alien from another planet until it started to wail. 'What is it?' she asked wonderingly, the agony swiftly replaced by ecstasy because it was all over and her body once more belonged to her.

'A little boy, Mrs MacKenzie.'

She could see it wasn't a big one: three and a half kilos was quite big enough, thank you, Stuart. She never wanted to go through *that* again! Annabelle had told her to have an 'epidural induction' which was far less painful than going into labour naturally, and now she believed it. But it was all well worth it, now! Olivia suddenly missed him. 'Where's my husband?'

'He went outside to get some air.'

'Coward!' She said it gently, because now that they had cleaned up her son and put him into his baby clothes (Birdie had crocheted the layette while recuperating in Antibes; she was good at that sort of thing), he really was quite sweet, as well as very hungry. She nursed him close, and because she too was exhausted, drifted off on the crest of a wave, satisfied because it had all turned out well.

When she came out of her dreams she was back in her private room. Stuart was beside her. There was a look of wonderment on his rather pale face along with the hint of seven o'clock shadow. 'How long have you been sitting here?' she murmured.

'You looked so beautiful and peaceful, I didn't want to wake either of you. Sweetheart, I'm so proud of you . . . of you both!'

'I'm proud of you too, Stuart . . . he's pretty, isn't he?' Their son sucked her little finger and Stuart was afraid to touch.

'He looks just like you.'

'No, he looks like you.'

'Well, I think he looks more like Pa, before he got really bald. Sorry you didn't get the girl you wanted.'

'There's always next time.' He said it very casually.

'You're kidding – you stay away from me for the next ten years . . . so, you chickened out at the last minute, huh?' She ruffled his dark hair, feeling closer to him now than she had ever felt before. Any man who wanted to sit watching a baby pop out of his wife's nether regions and still profess his love for her, surely had to be twenty-four-carat gold!

'I went to fetch this, actually . . .' He indicated the bottle of champagne and the two glasses on her bedside table, before putting a little gift box on the coverlet.

'What's this?' She opened it.

'Just a present.'

O-L-I-V-I-A – an exquisite ruby and diamond bracelet linking the initials of her name. She thought, in that wet-eyed moment, He loves me, he really does! How could she ever have doubted it?

Stuart cleared his throat, stood up and did the honours by next wetting the baby's head and told her one glass only. 'That's what the nurse said, not me, since she doesn't want a drunken mother and baby on

305

her hands.' He smiled, if somewhat wanly. 'Cheers, sweetheart, here's to us!'

'Thank you, Stuart. The baby, and the bracelet – they're both lovely. So are you, for being here when I needed you more than I've needed anyone in my life.'

For a moment and longer, he hung over her in a tender embrace that was sweeter than anything he could have said to her at that moment.

And then the female doctor and her medical team joined them in drinking to the health of the new mother and baby, and then the phone beside her bed started to ring, and the good wishes were faxed through, and the flowers started arriving, and Mac-Kenzie senior told her they were having a party out at Rhode Island, and sent congratulations to Stuart Daniel Geoffrey Harold Custor MacKenzie as well as the new parents, and her mother cried over the phone and her Pa said he was very proud of her, and in a little while Olivia drifted off again with her son in her arms.

She had done her bit for posterity; she just wanted to be alone now with her own little family, Stuart and Danny-boy.

CHAPTER 18

Annabelle admired the finished house in her usual gushingly girlish fashion. 'I love the decor – so in keeping with its character. Must have cost a fortune . . . and all this lovely new furniture – well, antique really, but you know what I mean.' Her head withdrew into her shoulders like a bashful tortoise.

'All these lovely old wood panels.' She smoothed her hand across the burnished oak, restored to pristine condition in the drawing-room. 'And this marvellous Chinese silk wallpaper,' in the dining-room, 'and these chairs – genuine Jacobean if I'm not mistaken.' She sighed the envious sigh of a woman not married to a publishing millionaire. 'You've done wonders to the old barnhouse, Olivia.'

Thanks to a private firm of renovators and restorers, and yes, it had cost a fortune, so goodbye mouldy old Yuppie sofa which had been tossed on to the last builder's skip; her home was her own, at last. Olivia felt nothing but relief, in much the same way as giving birth had been.

Stuart said, 'We ought to have a party.'

'Why?' Her concentration on her computer screen,

307

Olivia answered him distantly. He drifted out again, slopping about like a lost puppy in T-shirt, jeans and sneakers.

'A house-warming – now that the house is finished,' he drifted back on the perimeters of her concentration.

'The house itself was finished a long time ago. Your wretched bright ideas about swimming-pools and whatnot threw the original house-agenda into disarray.'

'A christening party for Danny, then.'

'Danny was christened three weeks ago.'

'I'm talking about a proper christening.'

'It *was* a proper one.'

'A village affair, Olivia. Hardly anyone else knows about our new son.'

'Everyone knows.'

'Annabelle as godmother, Birdie as great–god-mother, Owen and Dankers as godfathers – that hardly constitutes a real party on his account, does it?'

'Are you or are you not a Christian? We owe it to our son to give him the best start in this life, and the next, by being part of the establishment.'

'I'm talking about family.'

'Oh, really?'

'Yes, really!'

'Maggie and Harry were here.'

'Yes, but not my side of things.'

'Your father was too busy, your mother was too busy – not my fault, Stuart. You weren't meaning your ex, were you?'

'Come off it, Olivia!' He stormed out.

A little while later Stuart, as restless as a prowling tomcat, reappeared in her home-based office with a plate of cheese on toast and a mug of coffee. 'Thanks, darling,' she said.

'Did you want some?'

'Sorry?'

'I brought this for me – but if you want some too, I'll get it . . .'

'Doesn't matter . . .' She continued tapping, her concentration on her work absolute.

'Sweetheart,' he said, frowning at his own-made belated breakfast, 'we don't seem to be able to talk to each other these days.'

'Ummm?'

'You do know it's Sunday morning?'

'Yes.'

'We always used to have breakfast in bed on Sunday.'

'Lunch and tea too,' she murmured.

'Olivia!'

She pressed 'Save' and swivelled on her typist's chair to look at him, the tone of his voice indicating that he was bored and disappointed and had things on his mind. 'What darling?'

'You know what!'

'*What, Stuart*? I'm not a mind-reader.'

'No, I guess you're just a publishing mogul yourself! Dammit all, Olivia, can't you give it a break for once? Sunday is not the day to be doing this.'

'Oh, but it is. I have to work all the hours I get, Stuart. What with Danny taking up so much of my attention, I have to make time for Lamphouse. I can't let everything slip now, when I've worked so hard to keep us afloat. We're in a deep recession in case you haven't noticed, and no one knows *when* we'll hit rock bottom! I have to keep selling books on Lamphouse's behalf, in case you've forgotten! Until I can get back to the office, I have to keep control of Lamphouse from the outside-in. Tomorrow is another Monday, another week, I *must* know what's going on with the firm, and the only way I can do that is with my finger on the button!'

'What is so important that you have to do this to us on our one and only day off together?'

'If you didn't want to play golf with Owen and the rest of Midhurst G.C. on a Saturday, Stuart, we could have Saturday together too! So don't use that "little boy lost" tone of voice on me when I have to meet a deadline.'

'What deadline?'

'Lamphouse's financial returns before April 1st. Lamphouse's new spring list. Lamphouse's commitments for the forthcoming fiscal year. Merchandising rights, translation rights, the Copyright Licensing Agency, editorial, literary and production agencies, the new European marketing and press agencies . . . need I go on? Of course not, my dearly beloved husband wouldn't know anything about *real* MDship; he *delegates!* Whether you like it or not, I'm a hands-on person. I *like* to know what my staff are doing, where we're going, what next year's bookshelf contribution from Lamphouse is all about – those are *my* deadlines, Stuart!'

'Damn Lamphouse!'

She looked at him in utter astonishment. Stuart rarely reverted to such epithets; his line of attack was usually far more sophisticated – sarcasm skewered on the full beam of an executive scowl reducing the recipient to pinhead status was more his style.

'Come off it, Olivia. I'm sick of being ignored by you. It's five weeks since . . . since his birth. If it was all to do with Danny, I could accept that, but it isn't. It's Lamphouse – you've just stated your case perfectly plainly. Pre-Daniel even, you started to ignore me. We have no proper married life any more. Danny has to be fed, Danny's crying, Danny comes first. OK, but your depression is *nothing* to do with Danny. He has a good reliable nurse, he's made no inroads into our life; Lamphouse has. You're too tired at the end of the day because of Lamphouse's demands on your time, so don't use Danny as the excuse. All I can say, if you're itching to get back there that much, then do it, but don't blame Danny! And don't accuse me of not being around for you!' He stomped out in search of his Wellington boots to go and help Andy Grafter dig up the hillside in the absence of a JCB.

Olivia could only look at the drifting Screen Saver images on her computer with a tight knot of help-lessness inside her.

Annabelle was right. All a man ever thought about was sex, not a caring loving compromise!

Stuart hadn't actually said it in so many words, but his gripe was all about sex. Not enough of it. He was miffed because she hadn't felt like getting back to their old scenario of abandoned passion on Sundays

311

and every other night since! Never mind a new baby, up all hours of the night feeding, changing nappies, stressful days and catching up with endless mounds of office work; he was only concerned with *his own* physical needs. He was *jealous* of the time she gave to Danny and he was *jealous* of the time she gave to Lamphouse – just pure *jealousy* on his part. So now, when the boot was on the other foot, he couldn't handle it!

Well, damn you, Stuart, she thought savagely, just think of all the times you left me twiddling my thumbs because MacKenzie Publishing, USA & Canada came first!

The following day Olivia was back at her office desk, the baby beside her. Dr Gareth had told her she must have at least eight weeks off work; it was only five. Well, it was Stuart's fault she had been precipitated back into the market place before her maternity leave was up – she did not want to be accused of swinging the lead!

She was still breast-feeding and had to remain on tap beside her infant son. He was a very good little baby who only fussed when he was hungry. The rest of the day Verity York fussed over him. It made her feel better and less guilty to know that Danny was being properly cared for by a grey-suited paragon of virtue from the old school of certified nannies.

Verity York, however, might have been trained in the grey-suit image, but she herself wore blue jeans and tartan shirts. 'Daddy's a High Sheriff and has estates in Lincolnshire,' she had stated at the interview while crooning over Danny, only two weeks old at the interview, and the moment he had started whimpering she had given him her little finger to suck. 'It's quite clean,' she had stated with a little smile. 'I dipped it in Milton.'

Verity was a true-blue Sloane Ranger, but seemed to be a very grown-up and responsible young woman. She was twenty-three years old (mature enough), with three brothers and two sisters all younger than herself, Verity had looked after them all; she was used to children.

She had an adorable boyfriend – she had to be honest about it – an airline pilot called Steve. They didn't see much of each other as they were both saving hard to get married, 'somewhen' in the future. Meanwhile they didn't mind living apart; money came first, duty second, and love was relegated to the back burner for the time being. She and Steve were a thoroughly modern couple who had decided to plan sensibly for their future, rather than screw it up in the short-term. Recession, house-repossessions and unemployment made the future seem very insecure for all young couples like them, Verity had stated, so she and Steve were still 'putting by for their nest-egg'.

Verity had promised to do her duty most faithfully where Danny was concerned. And since they were on the same wavelength, Olivia gave her the contract for one year.

Three weeks into her contract Verity, with Danny in his carrycot, was peremptorily uprooted from the Midhurst nursery, to take their place at Lamphouse.

313

They accompanied Olivia in the Dame, driven by Ernest, while Stuart sat in the front, not talking to his wife because he thought she was 'mad' to have taken him so seriously – he hadn't meant what he had said the day before. Olivia glowered at the back of his handsome head – she would show him! 'You're going grey!' she told him, undermining *his* ego for a change.

'Honey, it's all to do with the trouble and strife in my life.'

Wife, that was what he meant! Olivia continued to glower from behind. But because she had more dignity than to make a scene in front of Ernest and Verity, she held her tongue from making further rude remarks about the person who had always supported her most in life.

Birdie, behind her tinted new high-powered exec specs, said, 'You shouldn't be here so soon after having Danny.'

'Time enough for my husband to give me my marching orders,' she huffily rejoined.

At lunchtime Stuart appeared with two bottles of champagne for Lamphouse staff, who drooled over the new baby, especially Natasha.

Birdie scowled at Natasha and told her to get back to work.

Olivia shrugged off her husband and told him not to 'butter her up' after his previous day's verbal assault upon her.

'Why are you behaving so stupidly?' he asked. 'Why can't we kiss and make up, in view of the fact I'm off to New York tomorrow?'

Olivia said, 'Oh, good, perhaps you'll feel happier

partying with Genesis March – go and kiss her, Jeremy Webber, Ashton Dore Cleaver, and possibly Legrand too, hot footing from Toronto once she knows you're in the Big Apple! After all, they're *your* crowd.'

'I don't know what's the matter with you, but I don't seem to be able to talk to you these days without getting into an argument.' He went back to his office on the top floor.

A few minutes later Stuart's PA buzzed down to say that Mr Stuart would be staying overnight in the executive penthouse suite as 'he was flying Concorde early in the morning, and not to save him any dinner.'

What was that old adage? thought Olivia wearily – never let the sun go down on your wrath? Oh, dear, suddenly she didn't feel in control any more, just all at sea regards marriage, husband, baby and work. 'Birdie,' Olivia said, as a means of diverting her thoughts elsewhere, 'surely you shouldn't be doing so much so soon? Shouldn't you still be careful not to overstrain your eyesight?'

'Hark at the pot calling the kettle black,' Birdie retorted, and turned to the carry-cot under an office-orientated flowering fig beside the computer, '*Chookie, chookie, choo*,' Birdie said to her great-godson and made him smile – or was that sleek, knowing baby smile merely wind?

Olivia observed from behind her seemingly disinterested façade; Verity had nipped out to do some shopping while in London. Birdie deposited a package at the feet of the baby in the the cot. 'Present for him.'

'Another one?' Olivia asked, diverting to the work on her desk. 'Thanks, Birdie.'

Birdie bustled back to her own office.

Olivia unwrapped a beautiful white crochet shawl. She went to thank her. 'It's gorgeous, thanks, Birdie.'

'You told me to take up knitting, but I took up crochet instead. I can do crochet with my eyes shut.'

'How did you know we'd be in the office today? I've still got another three weeks' maternity leave left, remember.'

Birdie tapped the side of her nose.

Olivia said, 'Stuart buzzed you?'

'At the crack of dawn. Told me to talk some sense into you since you were itching to get back to work.'

'He'll rue the day . . . you don't have to take on my agenda, Birdie.'

'I know that, but what are friends for? I told him I'd do my best, but you were a Cotswold even before you were a MacKenzie and you'd do just as you wanted – as always, and like your father before you.'

'It's really lovely, thank you, Birdie. Danny and I will treasure it along with the rest of the layette you made for him.'

She was on her way out again when Birdie said, 'How long do you think you're going to be able to bring little Danny boy to the office, Olivia? I mean, you aren't seriously thinking of subjecting him to artificial lighting all day, every day?'

'Verity took him to the park at lunchtime.'

'What park? The only parks in Farringdon are car parks. And in this office atmosphere, even the spider plants keel over from lack of oxygen.'

'Just until I stop breastfeeding, Birdie! His nanny is with me to see to the rest of his needs.'

'All his life, then. Tell me if I'm interfering dear, but you ought to be at home with my great-godson instead of subjecting him to bookmites and bad atmosphere.'

'I thought you'd got over your bad MacKenzie atmosphere ages ago.'

'I wasn't talking about the atmosphere, but you and Danny! Seems wrong to me to cart him along with you to the office every day – if you don't mind my saying so.'

'Well, I do – it's only the first day, he's hardly going to shrivel up in twenty-four hours, is he? I can't be in two places at once! Stuart's been lecturing me; don't you start.'

When her head felt as though it was bursting, when Danny started wailing because he wasn't getting enough attention, and when her husband did the same, all Olivia wanted to do was bury her head in the sand. She also knew it was time to cry 'help'.

'Post-natal depression,' said Dr Gareth, and prescribed an anti-depressant.

Now it was time to turn to a friend: Annabelle prescribed a swift solution too. 'If you're still dead keen to give Danny breast milk, then do it the easy way.'

'What easy way?'

'Mother's milk in a bottle. That's what breast-pumps are for. You can leave his daily feeds in the

317

fridge, which Verity can give him, and you can get back to the boardroom table with an easy conscience.'

'It sounds awfully undignified,' Olivia said.

'Is pregnancy and its aftermath ever dignified?' said Annabelle. 'In a parallel universe, maybe! Get wise, Olivia; men just don't understand what we women have to go through.'

'Point taken, Annabelle!' Olivia said with a smile. 'Dr Gareth's sweet and kind, but he's a man and doesn't really understand. Nor does Stuart.'

'Husbands rarely do. They've been put on earth to propagate, not equate.'

'Are you sure you aren't a reincarnation of a grandmotherly Midhurst witch, Annabelle?'

'Bitch, Max would say! Don't forget, I've been there six times before you, Olivia, so it's the voice of reason talking.'

'And very reassuring it is too!' Olivia felt so much better talking to Annabelle.

'Kids are like an insurance policy. Especially when you think they're there in their numbers the moment you get old – as like as not! But, having a handful, the odds are *one* of them might turn out grateful in the end, and do *you* a favour by not putting you in an old people's home. That's why I had so many – purely selfish reasons.'

'I'll bear it in mind,' Olivia grunted.

Janine Harvey, the district nurse, had also become her good friend. 'Forget about orgasms for the moment and think organization. Stuart will just have to appreciate that life has changed for both of you, not forever, but just until you are less at sea,

Olivia. You've got a little baby to think of now, who is utterly dependent on you. Organization is what is required in your life from now on if you're to be a successful working mother. Get yourself mentally and physically sorted out; do some post-natal exercises for a start. Go to the gym, the swimming-pool, anything, but try a little exercise regularly to release all those stagnant endomorphs of yours – they're the "good feeling" hormones. You'll feel so much better in yourself. Chuck out the pills for a start – only don't tell Owen I said so. You don't want to get hooked on tranquillizers.'

She listened and heeded all the good advice she received from her friends, without neglecting her infant son. Danny was able to get his 'proper' maternal nourishment from a bottle, supplemented by powdered baby milk – he was growing fast and greedy with it – and with him cared for by a doting Verity, Olivia was able to concentrate more on taking Lamphouse a step further towards the new millennium.

'*Oh, Danny boy, the pipes the pipes are calling . . .*' Stuart sang his heart out in the fully tiled en-suite shower, courtesy of a demolished Spanish castle. 'Honey, I think we're going to have to get Mr Rapps back, because the plumbing doesn't seem to be working as it should. There's no water pressure.'

'There's *never* any water pressure in England, Stuart. Even less now you've syphoned off Midhurst's water supply to fill your swimming pool.'

'*Oh, Danny boy, the pipes the pipes are ap-palling . . .*'

Stuart was off to Zurich; she was off to do her duty at Lamphouse. No time these days to let down one's guard for one moment. It was tougher than ever out there in the marketplace; recession was biting deep into everyone. You either had to perform and never play dead, or get buried.

'Danny, eat up your breakfast, there's a good boy,' Olivia placed a hasty kiss on his food-plastered forehead. At nine months, he was just about getting to grips with a spoon and bowl. Kitchen walls and floor suffered as a result of the learning process.

In possession of the ultimate in delegated child-minding facilities, nanny Verity York was the best solution to a working woman's answer to groping in the dark.

Stuart returned from Zurich, they passed like ships in the night for a little while, until one morning he came into her office with the daily newspapers proclaiming the downfall of yet another high-profile publishing empire. 'There but for the grace of God go we!'

'Oh, no!' Olivia said. 'That's awful! Don't say that, Stuart.'

He shrugged carelessly. 'Look at it this way: less competition from our point of view, huh, sweetheart?' He disappeared back to his own abode higher up the office building.

Birdie appeared with letters for her signature. 'Was that your husband I just saw descended from heaven?'

'Grass widower – that's what he think he is,' Olivia mumbled into her memo pad.

'Why? Aren't you giving him your undivided attention these days?'

'Not exactly. We both seem to be living on different planets lately.'

'Then I suggest a second honeymoon.'

'Do you mind? I've just got back here and into the swing of things. Neither do I need a brother or sister for Danny right now, Birdie.'

'Far be it from me to intrude upon your personal habits. Forget I mentioned it,' She bustled off with the boss's signatures.

CHAPTER 19

Choices: 1994

The gardener-cum-handyman made Danny a little wooden go-kart from all the old dead wood on MacKenzie lands – 'So's you can trundle him around behind you, ma'am, instead of carrying him around the garden, which ain't no easy feat on these slopes.'

'Thanks, Andy. He is getting a bit heavy for me.'

'Only make sure you hang on tight to the rope, won't you, Mrs MacKenzie – and make sure the brake is on tight when it's stopped with him in it. We don't want Danny-boy trundling off by himself, now, do we? I'd never fergive meself.'

Olivia reassured him utterly.

Mr Grafter had done a grand job of transforming half an acre of previously bramble-covered hillside into a proper landscaped garden (no further plans yet for vines and racehorses). Olivia had her rockeries and plants, scenic little waterfalls and pools (no danger to Danny), and Danny had a safe little enclosed 'nursery area' with sandpit to play in close to the house.

Ernest had married Jenny Stapley and they were well settled in the old tithe cottage which had been fully restored and renovated for them. Jenny was expecting their second baby – the first baby had been born soon after they had been married, hence the urgency of finding a roof over their heads, while Arthur Stapley, landlord, had given his daughter a right royal send off at the Midhurst Arms, with no hard feelings towards Ernest who had seduced his daughter.

The ramblers too had been accommodated and Theodore Grieves was well contented with the new 'right of way', which ran through the spinney and across manorial lands without encroaching on the family's privacy.

Danny was two and a half when Olivia had her second baby, the girl Stuart had always wanted. They named her Caroline Pears Olivia Margaret.

Olivia fought her way through her second post-pregnancy blues, and was still fighting her way through them as a working mother and executive wife, all the time asking herself why?

Why? for goodness' sake. She had a rich go-ahead husband, she had a wonderful home in the country – now that Mr Rapps and his team had disappeared at long last. She had everything a woman could want, a super-trooper hardworking husband who kept her in the style to which he had accustomed himself, two beautiful children, one of each to comprise the well-rounded family, good friends and neighbours, and yet she was still fighting the good fight – why? What was she trying to prove?

She could give up work tomorrow, and no one would miss her from the office. Birdie and Natasha and everyone else were doing their bit splendidly; she could let go tomorrow and Stuart would thank her. She could swan off to the South of France with the two children whenever she wanted, and never torment herself again by trying to be everywhere at once.

But – the big But – she could not let go because she had *earned* herself the right to retain her place at Lamphouse, because she *loved* her work, and because she became as depressed *as hell* whenever she stopped working.

Stuart suggested 'help therapy'.

'You mean a shrink?'

'If that's what it takes to get yourself sorted out.'

She told him she was a workaholic, not crazy. He was a workaholic too, wasn't he? OK, so he wasn't manic depressive about MacKenzie the way she was over Lamphouse. But he had pushed her into the hot seat in the first place; she refused to give up now when things were going so well with the company – despite the recession.

So all credit to her! He just wished she were less paranoid about Lamphouse and more like a loving wife – the way she used to be!

She was still suffering from post-natal depression; she'd cope without any shrinks or pills – just let her get on with things herself, thank you very much!

He didn't argue any more, but jetted off somewhere else on his own endless rour d of high-powered executive meetings. Olivia ended up talking to Annabelle and Janine again, remembering that she had had this same conversation with them after Danny was born.

'And don't suggest post-natal exercises – I hate exercising! Besides, I haven't the time.'

Annabelle said, 'Post-natal depression is awful. It seems to build up and up, and having one baby on top of another doesn't help. I went through it after Tandy was born. No one understands, not your husband, not your doctor, not your nearest relatives. They all tell you to pull yourself together. You spit at them and say, if I could pull myself together, then I blasted well would, wouldn't I? Try yoga.'

'Yoga?'

'Hatha yoga – it helped me enormously, still does when I get pressed and stressed. You lose weight naturally while your body gains strength and fitness; it gets rid of depression and teaches you how to relax, breathe properly, gets rid of aches and pains, improves circulation and concentration, makes you more sensually aware of yourself, improves your sex life and generally makes your feel heaps younger.'

'Sounds like magic,' Olivia said with a wry smile.

'It *is* magic,' Annabelle said. 'Dead simple. You can do it anywhere, even at your office desk. I'll show you how. In fact, combined with swimming, Hatha is the alternative answer to Prozac.'

It was the best therapy yet invented – and fun to do: Olivia wished she had taken up yoga after Danny was born.

'What are you doing, pray?' Birdie asked her one morning when Olivia, after a particularly nasty altercation with an author who really fancied himself, was found by her, sitting on the floor, cross-legged, hands on head, staring into space.

'Getting rid of my bad vibes, Birdie. It's called Hatha yoga.'

'Well, if you hatha moment, dear, Editorial would like your opinion on this blurb.'

Annabelle and her children occupied the swimming pool most of the day, and when Olivia got home from work there was Verity York and the children, Janine and Annabelle and the Spanish au pair, Annunciata, and Tandy, and the other younger children, all having a good time, so that all she could do was join in or be a real grouch by going to bed. They were all having so much fun, going up to bed or to her home-based office seemed like a poor choice.

Swimming and water and Hatha and children and like-minded company, Olivia dunked baby Caro in the pool even though she was only two months old.

'Sink or swim,' said Annabelle, while they all watched with bated breath to see if the baby would resurface ever again. 'Water is our natural element,' Annabelle assured.

She sat guru-like, in the lotus position, in command of someone else's millionaire lifestyle and perfectly at home on the edge of the blue marble-tiled swimming pool with its own air-conditioning and 'tropical atmosphere potted plants'.

'Better than a health farm,' said Annabelle when she had first sampled how millionaires truly lived. 'At least I don't have to pay.'

She had such an endearing way of speaking the truth, Olivia could not resent Annabelle and her brood for one minute, even though they enjoyed the Stuart MacKenzie pool more than did he or she.

French doors folded back to the newly built terrace and patio-cum-barbecue area – they had had to compromize on the French doors folding back manually instead of press-button aluminium and sheet-glass, and up till now, personally speaking, Olivia had thought that the swimming-pool idea and patio-barbecue tacked on to a lovely old building like the manor house was a bit 'naff', but not any more. Her dearly beloved husband had known all along the way to a woman's heart – as usual!

Late spring sunshine dappled the water and Annabelle's face. 'Ninety-nine per cent of our body is made up of it. We emerged from the murky edges of the great ocean, we are surrounded by pre-natal fluid in the womb, the priests baptize us with holy water and the Benares Indians send their dearly departed's ashes down the great Ganges – water to water instead of ashes to ashes. A far nicer concept of our destiny.'

Caroline mercifully resurfaced.

Olivia grabbed the baby out of the heated pool, infinitely glad to find that Caro was still alive and gurgling happiness not water. She wrapped a towel around her and handed her to Verity, hovering on the edge in her swimming costume. Verity had enjoyed looking after Danny so much, she had decided to stay on. Her contract had been renewed for another year. Jan Harvey said, 'Excuse me, Olivia, but I've got to get going for my evening stint at the surgery. Tomorrow we're trying out some aromatherapy on each other – will you be back by four?'

'Only if I skip a working MD lunch.'

'Well, try. Aromatherapy's great – Annunciata's got great hands, especially on the soles of the feet! I daresay *you* could do with a foot massage, being on your feet much of the day. Anyway, I hate to break up the mother and baby party – I always have such fun here, but duty calls.'

'I know the feeling,' Olivia waved a wet hand, feeling as if everyone else except herself was in possession of her household, children and swimming-pool.

'Mummy – mummy . . .' said Danny, his armbands squashed flat in the grip of Bryce and Tandy, 'Mummy, mummy, I can swim . . .'

'That's great, darling . . . excuse me everyone, but I hear my phone bleeping . . .'

Olivia grabbed her white towelling robe before grabbing her mobile phone: it was Stuart ringing her from New York, 'Olivia, honey, how have you been today?'

'Great. With a little help from my friends – yoga sessions with the girls. We've already mastered the Fish, the Lion and the Cat. Tomorrow it's aromatherapy – if I can get back in time. Only I've got meetings galore tomorrow morning and afternoon. But I rather hope to be back before Jan buzzes off to do her evening surgery stint. She's the big chief in our Midhurst mother and baby "self-help" programme without the aid of doctor's prescription drugs. Annabelle does the Hatha yoga bit, Annunciata does the aromatherapy massages. Yes, we are having fun . . . no, I suppose you can't hear me for the background noise going on . . . no, that's not music, that's Tandy practising the pan pipes. Dannyboy has learned to swim . . . what about you? No, silly! I know you can swim already – what? Yes, I'll be back in the hot seat tomorrow, as usual . . . sorry . . . I can't hear you, bad line . . .' Olivia pressed a finger to her ear.

'Yes, I know it's Wednesday . . . you'll be home the day after tomorrow . . . yes, I miss you, too, darling. You know how we used to take Wednesday afternoons off together for ante-natal classes? Well, now that I'm post-natally depressed again, I'm continuing our Wednesday afternoon tradition of taking it easy . . . yes, Sundays too. Seems like a lifetime ago, yes, me too . . . right-ho, see you when I see you. Ring me from JFK when to expect you, Ernest will be there with the Dame . . . bye . . .'

Olivia pressed back the aerial on her mobile phone, took off her towelling robe, found the bottle of champagne she'd asked Verity to locate for them, settled herself among the aromatherapeutic bubbles of the Jacuzzi with a glass of champagne in her hand and sighed a sigh of utter contentment. If this was living the lifestyle of a millionaire's wife, then why hadn't she discovered it sooner? she asked herself.

The following morning Olivia resumed her place at her desk. She had a lunchtime meeting with an agent who was keen to increase his client's royalty rate. A barrister friend of hers, Jane Fennington-Baines (of boarding school days), was also there to offer her advice as well as moral support. Olivia hated working lunches, and hoped to be away from this one by three-thirty for her foot-massage at the great hands of Annunciata and a yoga session at the small feet of Annabelle, Midhurst's guru.

She made her excuses when the working lunch was in danger of overshooting the three-thirty mark. 'Sorry everyone, must dash – I've got to get back to Farringdon. If you want extra drinks, they're on Lamphouse . . .'

'Don't know how you manage it all, darling, running a home, a husband, children *and* a major publishing company. Don't worry about us – or what we've discussed about you-know-who's relatives suing for libel damages. One can't sue the dead – relatively speaking, I mean. Bye, darling, see you, lovely lunch . . .' Jane waved her away, 'Family obviously takes precedence over business . . .' Olivia overheard the postscript when Jane thought she was safely out of earshot.

She caught a taxi back to Farringdon. Ernest was waiting to take her home in the Dame. Olivia said to Natasha, 'Where's Birdie? I must have a word with her before I disappear.'

'She's in Editorial, looking at the covers for the new list, Olivia.'

Olivia found Birdie among the girls of the old firm; they were looking through some photographs. At first Olivia thought that they must be for a photography book in production, the photos spread over one of the desks. Everyone looked a bit sheep-

330

ish at being caught 'hovering' by the boss, especially Birdie, 'Hello, dear, thought you were still at lunch . . . I'm just coming . . .'

'Don't worry, I'm off home, Birdie. I just came to tell you that the acquisition panel are taking up the option on Bernice Wintergarden's new romantic novel, which looks as if it's going to be another best-seller. Ring her agent and tell her what we've decided. Arrange a meeting between us and agent and author to discuss the contract.'

'Right you are, dear.'

'What's this . . . ?' Olivia caught sight of one of the photographs hastily being shuffled out of sight. 'That's Stuart, isn't it?' Olivia grabbed it up.

'Er . . . someone is over from Toronto Editorial; we were just browsing through their party shots, Olivia . . .'

'Faye Rutland's launch, you know, her new best-seller, *Hollywood Or Bust*, which MacKenzie-Toronto have bought in from MacKenzie NY.'

'Bust as in her new silicone image of a movie-star, Olivia. M-T had a big party in her honour . . . we were just looking . . .'

Olivia hardly heard the waffled excuses or the shuffling embarrassment all around her as everyone slid back to their own work-stations. Her attention was focused on the photograph of her husband cosily tucked between Faye Rutland and Vinny Legrand, one arm around Rutland's bare shoulders, too much cleavage jostling for attention and pushing him sideways into the arms of Vinny Legrand, with whom he was sharing a very non-professional kiss. The party at his table all looked very much the worse for drink, the big boss as the obliging millionaire so obviously hosting the occasion at some expensive nightclub. Caught in the camera's red-eye, Stuart, his bow-tie undone, was shown up in a very incriminating light, sans wife!

No doubt there were a lot more more of him in that state, the reason why the girls had all been giggling while ogling the photographs of Stuart MacKenzie 'someone' had brought over from Canada – no doubt the mischievous little person who had in all probability been a besotted party-guest too!

The photograph slid from her numb fingers. Olivia turned her back on them all and without another word, not even to Birdie, left the office.

Her legs were still shaking when she got out of the Dame. Ernest and she hadn't exchanged a word all the way from Farringdon to home.

He knew she was terribly upset about something, Miss Olivia had that 'locked-up look' she sometimes adopted when she had no desire for small talk. Ernest parked the car and went home to his wife and his own rapidly growing young family.

Olivia let herself into the house and went straight to the swimming-pool annexe where the neighbours and the nanny were entertaining themselves.

'Out!' she told the aromatherapy party waiting to give her a foot massage. 'Verity, give Danny and Caro their supper and put them to bed. Don't save me anything. I'm not feeling well, please see yourselves out,' she told the others. Then she went straight up to the master bedroom, slammed the door, flung herself on the four-poster and cried all night.

In the morning she felt awful, eyes red and puffy, her face swollen with tears. She looked and felt like death, with such a raging headache, she knew she could not go into the office today. She rang Birdie and told her she wouldn't be in, and to fax her anything urgent. Birdie said, 'Olivia, those photos . . .'

'I don't want to talk about it, Birdie.'

'I do. The reason why I was standing there like a dummy was not because I was interested in them – as you thought. I saw what you saw, a brief glimpse of people enjoying themselves. I was mad with the girls for passing them around. They really don't mean anything, Olivia – the photos, I mean. It was just a silly celebrity party, nothing sinister. Our Christmas office parties are just as bad. You've been to those do's yourself and know how stupidly everyone behaves when they're full of their own egos as well as drink, especially when someone else is footing the bill. It doesn't mean anything, least of all that he's being unfaithful to you.'

'*Don't* make excuses for my husband, Birdie. He had a drink-woman problem before – *and* it shows! Old habits die hard. I don't want to talk about it. Please just take control of things for me today. I'll see you tomorrow.' Olivia rang off.

She stood in front of her dressing-table mirror, looked at the pale, distraught, lank-haired image of herself. Her hair had grown quite long; she had to wear it up at work, a time-consuming job when she was in a hurry. She had let it grow because Stuart liked her with long hair, loved to run his fingers through its 'chestnut-dark silkiness', as he used to tell her in moments of tender passion between them.

Olivia went into the bathroom, found the scissors and chopped it all off. 'Sentimental buffoon,' she said savagely into the mirror, and she didn't mean *him!*

The day Stuart was due home from New York, Friday, she went to the office as usual. She felt and looked a mess, but Birdie did not comment upon her looks or her shorn locks – it was more than her life was worth.

During her lunch hour Olivia had her hair done properly at a nearby salon, and was back to her own self, the short, sleek bob as worn by the Ms Olivia Cotswold of her single days.

Stuart had promised to ring her to let her know the time he would be arriving at Heathrow. Olivia waited all day for his call, but none came. She left Farringdon at six-thirty and returned home for the weekend. There was still no message from him, no fax and no messages on the answerphone. Verity said he hadn't called person-to-person, either, to say when he would be back.

Mrs Dannymott had left supper for the family, Stuart's favourite, roast beef and Yorkshire pudding. Verity and Olivia sat down to supper without the master of the house, and Olivia hardly touched her food.

Ernest remained on standby to pick Stuart up from the airport, but when there was still no call from him by nine pm, Olivia rang MacKenzie New York. It was four in the afternoon over there in the Big Apple, everyone just about preparing to pack up for the weekend. MacKenzie senior's PA had gone home, and a junior staff member in the office told her that, as far as she knew, Mr Stuart had already left New York early that morning, after having dined with his father the night before.

In which case, Stuart ought to have been home by now. If he had left New York early that morning, three hours via Concorde or seven hours by scheduled airline, four o'clock that afternoon, UK time, should have been his latest arrival time home. Olivia wondered what had happened to him. He had always rung her from his airport of departure to let her know he was leaving and would be at Heathrow at such and such a time.

His flight was probably delayed – but he could still have rung her to let her know.

Olivia rang Ernest at the cottage and told him to go to bed; Stuart had probably decided to go straight to the penthouse suite at Farringdon, rather than disturb them at such a late hour.

The following morning, only a skeleton staff in on a Saturday morning, Olivia rang the front desk. Dankers was on duty. She asked him to check and see if Stuart was in the penthouse suite.

'No, Miss Olivia, he definitely is not. I would know. I went up to check the MacKenzie floor just a short while ago, the moment I came in for my weekend shift. No . . . no messages left, either.'

'Thank you. Let me know if my husband does come into the office today, Dankers.'

'I certainly will, Miss Olivia.'

Still no word from him all day, Olivia spent Saturday drifting aimlessly about the house and garden.

By Sunday she was beginning to get very agitated.

Her previous mood of anger and despair against her husband had diminished considerably. She was now very concerned. No good ringing anyone at the New York or Toronto offices; they would all be on their weekend break.

She was left wondering if Stuart had somehow got wind of her 'mad mood' concerning the photographs, and had taken matters into his own hands.

Perhaps he had decided to leave *her!*

Perhaps he had grown tired of her depressions, her heavy work schedules, her systematic thwarting of his bright ideas.

Perhaps he had just grown tired of her.

Cold fear and panic set in – she wondered if she had any anti-depressants left, and searched through the bathroom cabinet, but could find none. She must have thrown them out when she had opted for alternative therapy for post-natal depression and bouts of panic attacks – like right now!

So much for Annabelle's Hatha yoga. Olivia forgot all about deep-breathing and, fingers pressed to nostrils for the relief of stress, with shaking fingers she dialled the Plaza Hotel number, New York. She told Reception to give Mr Stuart MacKenzie an early morning call; his wife in England wished to have words with him. She was informed in due course that Mr Stuart MacKenzie had checked out in the early hours of Friday morning, confirming the original statement from MacKenzie's offices that he had left when he was supposed to.

She then she rang MacKenzie senior on Rhode Island, despite it being three in the morning, his time; she had always got on well with the old dictator. The MacKenzie butler took her call. 'I'm sorry, Madam, but Mr MacKenzie senior is not at home. He had to fly up to Toronto unexpectedly. Mr Stuart? Well, madam, I've no idea. He might have gone up to Toronto with his father in their private plane, but Mr Stuart did not confirm his personal itinerary to me. All I can say, Madam, is . . .'

'Never mind . . . thank you.' Olivia put down the phone – no joy from that end!

She rang Birdie at home. 'Birdie, I shan't be in the office very early tomorrow. My blasted husband hasn't shown up all weekend.'

'Dear, I am sorry! Can I do anything to help?'

'Not unless you know where the swine has taken himself.'

'Olivia dear, you sound very distraught . . .'

'I am, Birdie, I am! Why hasn't he rung me? Why hasn't he shown up? What on earth could have happened to him?'

'Olivia, I'm sure nothing has happened to him. Stuart is a good husband. He has probably been trying to get in touch, but . . .'

'No, he hasn't! *Someone* is covering for him, that's for sure!'

'I suggest you don't return to Lamphouse, dear, until you've sorted out your domestic situation.

Don't worry about a thing, the board, Natasha and I can manage. If he rings the office tomorrow, I'll let you know at once. Now go and get some rest, you sound all-in.' Birdie rang off.

To give him one last chance Olivia decided to telephone Christine, his ex in Toronto, but then decided against it. She put down the phone with a heavy heart; she did not want *her* to gloat over second wife's downfall concerning the unfaithful husband!

For the rest of that Sunday Olivia buried herself in work – the best therapy for depression and uncertainty and a whole host of other emotions engendered by the pace of modern-day living. Oh, yes, she really would like to have been a Victorian mama with a bunch of keys around her waist, the only worry on her horizon what to tell Cook to prepare for dinner in the absence of an undependable husband!

She gathered her wits together – too many historical novels (Lamphouse's forte), getting to her one hundred years too late, and went and had a swim all by herself.

Then she practised a full hour of Hatha yoga and felt heaps better. So much so, she cleaned the kitchen from top to bottom, even though Mrs Dannymott always kept it spotless. Then she took the children for a walk with Verity. Then she did some clearing out of brambles and bushes, trying to make a brave start on the rest of the twenty-seven and a half acres. What the gardener and she had already done looked good, with flowers and shrubs and rockery plants all ready to burst into bloom the moment May was out.

Did all that really matter now? she wondered. It

had been jolly hard work coming to grips with that half-acre of neglected ground: Stuart was right, perhaps they ought to give the rest over to vines or horses!

When she took off her gardening gloves that evening – a long spring evening – she was thoroughly exhausted, both mentally and physically.

It helped to sleep like a log. She woke up on Monday morning and forgot she even had a missing husband, until the cold light of day disabused her of any such illusions.

Verity was attending to the children in the nursery. Olivia kissed Danny and Caro and went downstairs with the Milton-sterilized bottles waiting to be filled for the baby.

Mrs Dannymott was bustling around in the kitchen. 'Someone has cleaned up my kitchen fit to be an operating theatre,' she said. 'I bet it was that nice gal Verity, God bless her.'

It was only ever 'her kitchen', never Olivia Mac-Kenzie's!

'Don't ask, don't say a word about why I haven't gone to work today, Mrs Dannymott . . . you know why we called him Danny, don't you? After you, who have been so kind to me – us! And yes, I've got a new hairdo. I've decided to be Olivia Cotswold again, not someone else's wife programmed to *his* tune! He should have been home by now . . . he should have rung me by now, damn him!'

The startled housekeeper did not know what to say or do, except, 'You've nothing on your feet, dear. You'll catch your death on these cold quarry tiles . . .'

'I hope I do!' Olivia said with passion. 'The bastard can go back to his other women with a clear conscience – not that he hasn't already . . .'

Now it would be all round the village that the MacKenzie marriage, like so many others these days, was on the rocks too! Olivia put the baby's milk bottles away in the fridge, neatly labelled with the date and time, took some yoghurt from the fridge and a banana from the fruit bowl and, because she didn't know what she was doing or saying, slumped down at the kitchen table, her head on her arms.

Mrs Dannymott said, 'There, there, dear, you cry it all out . . .' She rubbed the Lady of the Manor's back in a motherly fashion, as though she really cared about what was going on here. 'I'm sure it's not as bad as it seems; nothing ever is.' She put on the kettle. 'A nice cup of tea works wonders. You get back into bed, dear, you're worn out. Everything seems ten times worse when you're tired and run down. I'll fetch you up a hot water bottle and something warm to drink. I'm sure Mr Stuart is all right, and nothing bad has happened to him.'

'If it hasn't, it will!' Olivia stumbled up out of the chair and went into her office and shot off two messages in capital letters, one to New York, the other to Toronto – 'WHERE THE HELL ARE YOU?'

Then she took up the mobile and returned to the bedroom, but had to wait until the offices on the other side of the Atlantic were getting to grips with their own Monday-blues workday. The most frustrating part of doing business with Americans and

Canadians was that they remained a world apart in their different time zones.

Mrs Dannymott tapped on the bedroom door. Olivia took the tray from her hands. 'Thanks, Mrs Dannymott. If anyone wants me, I'm having a bath – a good long one!'

'Good idea, dear. Don't you worry about a thing. Verity and me can look after things. A good hot soak will make you feel heaps better.'

No, it won't, thought Olivia in despair. She did not touch the soup or the bread and butter Mrs Danny-mott had so kindly brought her, but took the cup of tea with her and the mobile phone, and locked the bathroom door. She just wanted to lie and wallow in hot suds and misery until her errant husband returned; and *when* he did, Stuart Lyon MacKenzie was going to wish he'd *stayed* away!

With sudsy bubble-bath hands Olivia pressed MacKenzie's New York numbers and was put through to MacKenzie senior's PA. 'Is that Olivia? Sorry honey, but there appears to have been an awful mix-up . . . sorry, honey, I can't hear you properly . . . a lot of interference on the line . . . oh, but I did! I left a message with my assistant to tell you that Stuart had rang me from La Guardia since he was re-routing to Toronto and to let you know . . .'

'When? When did he ring you?' The line was so bad, it was a struggle to make sense of what was coming through to her; Olivia put it down to using the mobile in a hot steamy bathroom.

'Friday morning,' said Mrs Steunbecker.

'I see. Did he leave any other message?'

'No, Olivia . . . sorry, I shall have to go . . .'

'No, don't!'

'All he said was, he was flying up to Toronto stat, and would I let you know.'

'Then why didn't you?'

'As I said . . . messages got mixed up . . . a lot of them coming my way on Friday morning; I was snowed under . . .'

'I rang Toronto, and he wasn't there . . . did he say why, or what he was doing?'

'Flying Toronto stat . . . nothing further . . . we're mighty busy . . . he's probably still with his father and mother . . .' The phone went dead.

A likely story! thought Olivia angrily. She got out of the bath and phoned the Toronto office again on the main telephone in order to get a clearer reception.

No, Mr Stuart was not expected; no, he hadn't rung in; no, he hadn't got a meeting with anyone; no, he had not left any messages – if he appeared out of the blue, they'd get him to get in touch with her immediately. She asked to speak to Davina Legrand. Vinny's assistant informed her that Miss Legrand had taken a few days' vacation; no, she had no idea where to, sorry, but Vinny would not be back in her office until the following Monday.

Secret assignations now, the swine! were Olivia's frenzied thoughts.

CHAPTER 20

Despite Birdie Gough's stricture to stay away from Lamphouse until she had sorted out her domestic situation, Olivia went to work on Tuesday morning with another bad headache which no amount of Hatha yoga could get rid of.

It was now four days since her husband had mysteriously gone missing; it had been the longest weekend of her life.

She continued to give him the benefit of the doubt; maybe he *had* seriously tried to get in touch with her and sent messages all round New York, Toronto and London telling her of his whereabouts; maybe the messages *had* become confused and mixed up over the weekend; she knew what it was like herself, eager to dash off home on a Friday afternoon, hasty and inattentive when last minute phone-calls and faxes sent one out of sync – late home again! Trains missed, dinner burning in the oven, kids who hadn't seen their parents all day . . .

Fact remained, why hadn't he called or faxed her direct?

He was a busy man, she reminded herself. Self-made millionaires did not grow on trees, they had to work at being millionaires.

Stuart was a *young* millionaire – all credit to him. With a young family, a wife who was always tired, depressed and somewhere else when *he* wanted *her*, he had to work harder, *much* harder than the average man.

She thought she understood.

She herself was trying to keep too many balls in the air at the same time – high-profile MD of a top London publishing house, the New Millennium businesswoman as well as unrecognized Citizen's Advice Bureau, Neighbourhood Watchwoman, nurse, wife and mother – it couldn't be done without something giving.

Beat the recession, beat the clock, beat the dead-lines, beat the next person to it, beat the system, beat the woman's role in the workplace, keep the home fires burning, keep everything in the garden rosy and flourishing and everyone else's life running smoothly; the only thing giving was her marriage.

Time to stop, she told herself; time to make time for herself, for him, ask herself what *they* really wanted from all this.

Just before noon Stuart's secretary rang down from the penthouse suite to say that he had just been in touch with her. He was about to board from Toronto Airport and would be arriving at Heathrow via Air Canada at round about six o'clock that evening, UK time. Could Ernest meet him?

'Thank you.' Olivia slumped back into her office chair with a sigh of relief. Must be five in the morning over there – time to take stock!

Olivia buzzed Ernest on his bleeper and gave him the message. She would catch the train home when she had finished at Lamphouse. Then she rang Mrs Dannymott and told her not to prepare an evening meal; she would do it herself.

Olivia told Birdie she was going home early. Birdie was quite happy about that; she and Natasha could manage, there was nothing urgent on their immediate horizon for Olivia to worry about.

Olivia caught the two o'clock train home – no danger of meeting up with Max, at such an early afternoon hour; she didn't think she could bear his company today.

She was back in Midhurst just after three, and walked the short uphill distance home. She gave Verity the rest of the day off.

'Steve's in London; we can take in a West End show together,' Verity said, happy to say the least.

'Take the next few days off with him.' Olivia felt generous.

Verity's boyfriend flew Scandinavian Airways – no danger of another hiccough to Stuart's transatlantic schedule. Olivia attended to her children before attending to the evening meal for Stuart and herself: *coq au vin*, with lashings of red wine.

She left the way to her husband's heart simmering gently on the Aga and went and had a quick shower, brushed her short sleek new bob until the static she generated was in danger of lighting up the bedroom, put on her backless black number which had first attracted Stuart's attention (amazingly it still fitted her, so she hadn't lost her figure to that extent!) and peeped into the nursery to assure herself that her two wonderfully good children had settled for the night.

They slept like angels from heaven, Danny with his pink nylon scrap under his nose, Caro flat on her back, breathing like an innocent in paradise. Olivia kissed them both, retucked them under their baby-tog duvets, re-checked the nursery-alarm which would buzz downstairs the moment either Danny or the baby awoke, before preparing herself to meet her Waterloo – with a barrage of well-prepared accusations to the forefront.

If she was to go down fighting, then she would do it in style – the style Stuart had so obviously found lacking in his high-profile life of late.

She allowed him time to get through baggage collection, Customs and a good hour's drive from London through rush-hour traffic. At seven o'clock he rang her on his car-phone to say he was on his way. At eight she lit the candles in the dining-room; the ambience was soft and seductive. She poured him a whisky on the rocks, and herself a double gin and tonic (Caro would just have to have ordinary com- mercial Baby Milk on the morrow), and waited.

At just after eight-thirty, from the kitchen win- dow she heard and saw Ernest draw up in the yard. In the long spring evening Olivia saw a very tired- looking husband emerge from the Dame, and dashed back into the drawing-room and zapped on the telly – he could let himself in! He came into the drawing-room, not with his usual happy- go-lucky tread, but with the world heavy on his

Savile Row shoulders. Served the blighter right, Olivia couldn't help feeling in that very taut moment between them. She tried to curb her emotions: relief at seeing him, anger because he had ignored her for the longest weekend of her life, and love that knew no bounds. She took some deep breaths and remembered what Hatha had taught her.

He leaned over the back of the Chesterfield to zap her a kiss but she dodged and zapped off the telly instead. She stood up, all very efficient and business-like in directing Ernest where to dump his lordship's executive baggage, upstairs, outside the master bedroom, golf-clubs in the hall cupboard. Ernest did so, and departed, carefully closing the great oak-studded front door behind him, back to the Dame to park her in the garage, all the time fully aware of the tension in the air of the MacKenzie household.

'I've missed you.' She handed him his drink.

'It's good to be home.' He tossed his briefcase on to an armchair. 'Sorry I didn't get to talk to you personally about what was going on, but I couldn't.'

'Couldn't or didn't want to?' she accused.

'I've missed you too. How have you been, sweetheart?'

'Anxious, worried, distraught. You might at least have rung me person to person!'

'I told MacKenzie New York and Toronto to let you know I'd be delayed. I wasn't sure how long I'd . . .'

'Why didn't you ring or fax me direct?'

'Why are you accusing me like this, Olivia? I was hoping you'd understand.'

'I can't understand messages I never received. I've been ringing round the whole of New York and Toronto, including Davina's office. Her PA told me Vinny was on vacation. Before that, I rang your father – *he* had flown up to Toronto, according to the butler. So why were you needed there when you'd already had your meetings with him? Four days, Stuart, so *where* have you been?'

'Toronto,' he said in a brittle, shut-down, non-informative way – sulking, she would have said!

Olivia took a deep breath. 'Can we be very civilized about this? I don't know who is lying to whom. I don't know what has happened, what you've been doing these past four days, and perhaps I'm not even sure I really care any more. Dinner is ready. You go upstairs and freshen up while I dish out. Right now I think I'm on the verge of making a scene – and you know how we both hate scenes of any sort. I'd take your whisky with you; you might need it.' She took her gin and tonic with her into the kitchen.

While he was changing out of his travel-weary clothes, she spoke to *coq au vin* on the Aga. 'Bastard! Skunk! Liar! Traitor! How *dare* he breeze in here after four days of silence – absolute, total, annihilating silence – as though nothing's happened? Leaving me to imagine all sorts of things!' She felt better, more in control after that.

He came downstairs in sweater and jeans, his hair still wet from a hasty shower. He helped himself to another whisky before following her into the dining-room. 'This looks lovely, sweetheart – you've gone to so much bother. God, I really have missed you . . .

348

come here and let's have that kiss I missed . . .' He put the whisky glass down, but once more she skilfully avoided his advances.

'Half a sec . . . these dishes are hot . . . let's eat while it's still edible and the candles don't splutter out. The red wine is one of your best, Stuart, I remembered to let it breathe . . .'

'Are you all right, sweetheart?' He gave her a peculiar look while pouring out from his exclusive stock laid down in his manorial cellar. 'These last few days have been a strain on everyone. The old man completely went to pieces . . .'

'I'm fine; eat up and then we'll talk.'

He looked at her in astonishment. She dished out hurriedly, watched him sit and eat with about as much difficulty as she had. Halfway through the meal he put down his napkin and let down his guard. He got up and replenished his whisky glass, a double Scotch, without ice, the ice in the ice-bucket had melted. He resumed his place opposite her, at the head of the table, both of them acting like the Lord and Lady of the Manor, stilted, artificial and definitely not at ease with each other. 'I'm really not that hungry, Olivia . . . I know you're mad at me, but I never knew you could be this heartless . . . neither do I think I like you when you want to be "civilized" concerning what's on your mind. I *hate* your chilled-out self-control!'

'And I hate your deception! I thought you were ill. I thought you'd had an accident. I thought you might have been . . . been hijacked! I thought . . .' Oh, God, how could she tell him that she thought he might have been with another woman? It would be too much of a humiliation. 'You've left me to pick up the pieces of our lives while you . . . while you swan around New York and Toronto with your *fancy* women! Getting your picture in the newspapers, peep-show photos and God knows what else!'

'Olivia – what has brought all this on?'

'You know perfectly well, so stop lying to me, Stuart! I never want to see you again in my entire life. I'm suing for a divorce, and it had better be a quick one. I'm taking you, Stuart Lyon MacKenzie, to the cleaners, for every cent you owe Lamphouse in the way of alimony – isn't that what Christine gets from you? Isn't it?'

His face taut and white, he downed the whisky in his glass in one gulp and then reached for the bottle of wine.

'Don't drink like that, Stuart,' Olivia said curtly from way end of the table.

He smiled, a cruel little twist of the lips when *he* was under pressure. 'I don't blame you, darling.'

'What?' Olivia said.

'I don't blame you. I've made a real hash of things, I know. I admit it.'

'You admit it?'

'Yes, I admit to everything you accuse me of.'

Unable to accuse any more, she attempted a two-way conversation. 'That awful Rutland woman and Vinny Legrand? Where have you been these past four days, Stuart?'

'Two actually, discounting travelling times – which I thought you were well aware of.' He too could cut to the quick when hurting like hell underneath that cool calm exterior of his. Unable to be demonstrative about his hostility, he only ever turned ashen-faced, only ever became sarcastically evasive, 'New York and Toronto, so chill out, will you?'

'Liar! I've rung around everywhere looking for you. MacKenzie Toronto told me you were not there and were not expected there, and Vinny Legrand wasn't there, either. What has been going on between you two? A cosy little cabin up in Bancroft, huh?'

'Boy! You sure present a mean case for the prosecution,' he drawled, adding fuel to the flames of her wrath by downing another glass.

'Answer me, dammit!'

'*Nothing* has been "going on", Olivia.'

'I don't believe you.'

'I don't expect you to; you've already jumped to your own conclusions. That is why I'm not saying anything until you've calmed down and apologized for what you think and what you've said.'

'*I, apologize?* You've got a nerve, Stuart! What about you? Aren't you going to tell me where you've been?'

'Yes, if you give me half a chance. I've buttoned my lip to accommodate your verbal assault upon me. You've been too busy accusing me with all your "holy mother at home and hard-pressed MD" spiel to make me feel like a heel for no reason.'

'I have every reason, Stuart.'

'If you want a divorce, that's up to you. But I want you to know that I still love you, no matter what . . .'

351

He had difficulty with the next sentence and turned his crystal wine glass round and round on the polished surface of the table, candlelight glinting ruby-red sparks. 'I don't know what all this is about, but Faye Rutland and Vinny are nothing to do with anything . . .'

'What about the photographs?'

'What photographs?' He looked genuinely out of his depth.

'Of you, and them.'

'What about *them*?'

'*Someone* from Toronto Editorial was hawking them around Lamphouse – you in some kind of drunken stupor with Faye Rutland pressed up close to you while you were in a seedy clinch with Legrand. What was more disgusting by far was the way everyone at Lamphouse and MacKenzie UK were looking at them, as though the big boss had some deep dark secret to hide from his wife: "*Unfaithful Spouse, USA, doing the dirty on Lamphouse's Wifey, UK*", courtesy Sigelle Hooper – not a very flattering gossip-columnist's footnote in a MacKenzie newspaper, Stuart!'

'I've never been unfaithful to you. I don't know what you're taking about. It's all in the mind: interpret what you've seen and read any which way you like. Newspapers lie to gain their readership – I'm in the business, I know. I've never seen the photos you, and others, are obviously making a meal of. They might have been taken at a party in New York for Faye Rutland – *she* did the honours, not me. I was invited by her own publicity promotion firm. Vinny too, as Toronto's rights manager launching Rutland's next book, *Hollywood or Bust*. Faye has got herself into some rat-a-tat Hollywood movie, and because she generates income for us, as her publishers, we accepted the invitation to her film launch party. Hype is what sells anything, from broomsticks to best-sellers, you must know that. Anway, that particular party was held ages ago and is nothing to do with *this* weekend, so however "disgusting" any publicity shots might have appeared to you, I guess you'd already made up your mind to think the worst of me.'

Olivia thought awhile, set her questions straight. 'Are you having an affair with Faye Rutland?'

'No.'

'Are you having an affair with Vinny?'

'No! Whatever gave you that idea? Vinny and I have the most asexual partnership ever. We're friends – working friends – so what's with a little peck on the cheek here and there by way of a thank-you gesture – publishing-speaking? You can't be that jealous, surely! She has her own agenda – a serious one, this time round.'

'Has she really?'

'I thought you knew?'

'I'm the last one to know anything.'

'Ashton Dore Cleaver.'

'Oh.'

'Now are you sorry for damning me out of context?'

'No.'

'What about Christine?'

'What about her?'

'Are you two getting together again? All your visits to Toronto?'

'I can't believe I'm hearing this from you, Olivia.'

'I have to be certain about *us*, Stuart.'

'Can't blame you, really.'

'You keep saying that. What's wrong between us, *really*?' Olivia asked in desperation.

'Two things *really*,' he answered, poised on the edge of the abyss between them. 'One, you are unable to trust me, and two, I'm sick of your thinking the worst of me, like my father!' Olivia swallowed. She passed her glass across the table to him, he poured her another glass of wine while the *coq au vin* was left sadly congealing on their plates.

'If it's not Faye and it's not Vinny, tell me who it is. You owe me that much.'

'My mother.' He passed the glass back to her.

Olivia stared at him. 'Your . . . your *mother*?'

'No one was given details of why Pa and I had to go to Toronto. I was going to tell you the moment I got home, hoping *we* could both fly out again together. I had to get back to London, for a day at least – but more of that in a minute. Pears became critically ill in the early hours of last Thursday night. She was at her sister's home in Toronto – my Aunt Clidhah, whom you might remember from our wedding. Pa and I had had dinner together at the Plaza Hotel on Thursday night, prior to my departure back to UK first thing on Friday morning. He went home back to Rhode Island, I went to bed, with an early-morning call from the Plaza receptionist to send me on my way home to you. But the early-morning call was from my father to tell me Mother had had a brain haemorrhage – a stroke – whilst at my aunt's house. She had been rushed into hospital. Dad and I immediately flew up in his private plane from La Guardia. That's where I've been all this time, sitting by her bedside – with my father – hoping Mother wasn't going to die.'

'Oh, God – oh, I'm so sorry, Stuart!' She looked at him with wide apologetic and terribly guilty eyes. Compassion too, and bewilderment – he hadn't given an inkling of it, kept it to himself even while taking a shower, even while listening to her rabbiting on, his manly emotions hidden away somewhere in the depths of masculine despair, quite unable to tell her what had been on his mind all along until she had precipitated his knee-jerk response of righteous indignation. She felt awful, and now she herself was unable to handle the situation, completely devoid of any idea of what to say to make amends.

'That's why you couldn't get in touch with me at the office. Neither of us, Pa or I, had time to do anything except get to her as soon as we could.'

The words stuck in her throat, she felt ill with her own foolishness and ghastly accusations against him. 'And . . . and is she . . . ?'

'Not yet – she seemed to rally a bit before I left. As soon as I knew she was out of immediate danger, I came home – to you!'

'Oh, Stuart . . . Stuart . . .' She scraped back her chair to go beside him, to comfort him, to make up for all the horrible, horrible things she had said and thought, but he held up a restraining hand.

'Sit down, Olivia. I've not finished yet – and I

don't want your arms around me right now; I don't *need* them.'

God! That was a chilling reprimand if ever there was one!

'Why, oh, why didn't you let me know what was going on, Stuart? Why didn't you ring me from the hospital – from anywhere? Why didn't you get your aunt to phone me, if you and your father were unable to? Why didn't anyone *say*!'

'I don't know why, Olivia. A message was left for Pa's secretary to get in touch with you while we were flying up to Toronto, to say I would be delayed home. She was supposed to ring or fax you. I couldn't get in touch with you personally, I didn't dare leave Pa even for a second – he was so distraught. I thought that MacKenzie New York would pass on the message Pa left with them. He didn't inform them of the reason for our hasty departure from New York, he didn't think it was anyone's business except family. He's funny about personal family matters. It unsettles everyone to know about family tragedy. We both assumed, I suppose, that Mrs Stuenbecker would get the message from the night security officer and pass it on to Birdie. Neither was the Toronto office informed; we went straight to the hospital. In the long run, I suppose, it was thoughtless of me, but I assumed such a message would get passed on to you somehow, and that you'd assume company business had necessitated my detour to Toronto. I was hoping to explain later should my mother's condition deteriorate further.'

'How? When the Toronto office didn't know of your whereabouts either?'

'I didn't think you would ring them, but just trust to what Mrs Stuenbecker relayed to Birdie. Nor did I want you to be unduly worried because you've been under a lot of stress yourself lately. Now I realize how wrong I was not to ring you person to person from the hospital, but all I could think of at the time was Mother dying. I'm sorry, but I was in shock, like my father. I was having to support *him*, in his own hour of need. But I promise you, someone's head will roll for not letting you know what was happening and where I was.'

'You can't blame Mrs Steunbecker or anyone else, Stuart,' she said gently, because he was still obviously very stressed out concerning the seriousness of his mother's condition. 'I'm sorry too, about shooting my mouth off to you so abominably. Let's just put it down to a lot of stress and a series of unfortunate blunders concerning mixed-up messages by harassed members of staff. I apologize too, most sincerely, for my part in all this – for not trusting you utterly.'

He took a deep breath and gulped down his drink. 'Before you say any more, Olivia, there's something else I have to say, and now is as good a time as any.'

She too took a deep breath – he was going to say that he was divorcing her for her lack of faith in him . . .

'Talking about blunders, I have to confess to a great many myself. I've made some appalling losses on my private investments, principally on the crash of a company called Peruvian Minerals in which I invested heavily. Basically, what I'm trying to say is,

I'm wiped out financially, unless I can recoup some of my losses, and that is why I had to return to London, to explain to you, and to my financial backers before they pulled the last plug on us, what has happened, hoping we could return to Toronto together tomorrow afternoon, after my meeting with them.'

At first she did not comprehend him fully. 'What do you mean, wiped out? What last plug on *us* – what are you talking about?'

'We own nothing any more. This house, the cars, our pad in Docklands, the income generated from the tenancy, our lifestyle, all wiped out overnight by my investment with Peruvian Minerals, whose shares plummeted overnight. They're now in liquidation. We . . . we are in financial debt up to our ears. Furthermore . . .' his voice seemed to stick in his throat '. . . I can no more guarantee any further financial backing as regards Lamphouse.'

It took a long time for the full extent of his words to sink into her brain. Appalled, she could barely get the words out herself. 'You pledged *Lamphouse* to prop up your falling shares with some South American company without saying a word to me about it?'

'I'm sorry, Olivia. I honestly thought I could redeem my losses and that PM-Mining assets would rally sooner rather than later. I'm truly sorry . . .'

She left her second glass of wine untouched and went up to bed, leaving him to blow out the candles.

You could live with someone for a million years and still not know them.

Olivia felt that way about her husband, her marriage, about everything.

She felt as though he had physically assaulted her.

In a way he had done just that; it was just as brutally painful and humiliating to know that he considered her unworthy of consideration, confidence, even his respect.

Marriage was supposed to be a partnership, a two-way trade in trust and honour and fidelity and truth.

Some time later Stuart came up to their bedroom to take his things out of the cupboards and drawers in his dressing-room.

She knew he had settled for the whisky bottle rather than her; she could tell it by his manner. Not the steady, sensible man she knew, the one she had married, but someone who was all at sea, like herself. 'I'll sleep in my dressing-room tonight,' he mumbled, groping around for his things, totally the helpless husband now, 'or else the Midhurst Arms – they have rooms for the night . . .'

'Stuart . . .'

'Yes?'

'Don't leave me now.'

'I thought you wanted me to.'

'I've never wanted you to . . .' Olivia switched on the bedside light and sat bolt upright. 'Please can we talk about this?'

'What else is there left to talk about?'

'Plenty. I know this is not the time, what with your mother still so dangerously ill – you should have stayed with her and your father in Toronto. You need only have rung me directly to let me know what was happening. I'd have understood. Instead, you left me in the dark and I imagined the worst. The worst for me would be that you walk out on me now. Everything else I can manage to come to terms with, if only you'll talk it through with me.'

The fight went out of him; he looked almost ten years older when he stood poised and lost in their bedroom, unpacked travel-bag and suitcase on the threshold of his dressing-room and a lot of dirty washing between them.

'Stuart, just don't lie to me and deceive me any more . . .'

'I've never lied to you, Olivia.'

'How bad is it with Lamphouse?'

'Taken in the light of having lost everything else, pretty shaky, Olivia.'

'Can you explain to me how shaky?'

'In order to buy my stake in Lamphouse, as a separate company from MacKenzie UK, I borrowed from the bank, using my shares in Peruvian Minerals as collateral. When PM-Mining went bust and all trading of their shares was suspended on the stock market, the banks financing me clamoured to be repaid. As a major stockholder in PM-Mining, my shares were worthless, so I had to sell off my shares in Lamphouse. What it basically means is, I can't put any more money into Lamphouse because there isn't any left.'

'You – we – are bankrupt, is what you're saying?'

'Not quite – there is one chance left – why I had to get back to London ASAP. But I have screwed up on you, Olivia, and my father – who knows nothing about this latest personal fiasco of mine. I was going to tell him last Thursday night over dinner, and then

I chickened out. It was too late then; he had other more tragic things to consider, like a dying wife five hundred miles away, who might possibly have passed away before he reached her. I couldn't do that to him, even when we were alone together for two days at the hospital, with plenty of time to tell him of my investment losses.'

'But all is not *irrevocably* lost with Lamphouse, is it?'

'No, not irrevocably. It just depends how much I can retrieve of my credibility in my father's eyes. He's the only one I can turn to now for independent financial help to keep Lamphouse solvent – as you have worked so hard to do.'

Pride comes before a fall, Olivia couldn't help thinking. She knew that was what was on Stuart's mind. It would simply tear him up to have to go cap in hand to his father and say, sorry, I've screwed it up a second time, Pa, but for her sake he could do it. If he loved her as he said he did, then he would do it, but she would not ask it of him. Nor could she humiliate her husband any further by offering to speak to MacKenzie senior on his behalf. All she could think of to say for the moment was, 'We'll manage somehow, Stuart. Lamphouse is on pretty firm ground at the moment. Maybe my Pa will buy back your shares, even if it entails a great loss for him. We'll think about what to do tomorrow. It's late now and you're exhausted; come to bed.'

In her nightdress she went to him then, standing so lost and alone, and so very weary. She put her arms around him tightly and whispered against his neck,

361

'Am I such an ogre that you were afraid to tell me about all these bad investments of yours?'

'Yes,' he said, 'Executive Wife.' He stroked her shiny short hair, and – a measure of his preoccupied thoughts – noticed the new hairdo for the first time. 'You've had your hair cut.'

'Yes . . . Stuart, I'm sorry – sorry for all the wicked things I've said and thought about you these past four days. I just need to sleep in your arms tonight, under the old Brig's tapestry canopy and curtains tight around us. I just want to know that you forgive me.'

'I'm the one who should be forgiven,' he said miserably.

'It doesn't matter, Stuart, it doesn't matter if we've lost everything; we've still got each other, and the children.'

In the darkness, neither of them able to sleep, but wrapped in each other's arms, heads and hearts close together, Olivia began to realize for the first time ever, that no matter how much you loved someone, no matter how close you were to that someone, in moments of deep and desperate calamity, each was their own person and each would act accordingly.

'Stuart . . .'

'Sweetheart?'

'You must go back to Toronto. Stay as long as you like – until your mother is fully recovered – and let's pray that she soon will be. I love you, and I don't want to see you torn between me and your other responsibilities.'

'I love you too.'

362

'It doesn't matter about the house or anything else. They're only material things. It's us – us as a family which matters most, you and me, Caro and Danny, my parents, yours, and of course dear old Birdie, who is part of the family too. Blow the Ferrari and the Dame, swimming-pools and acres of high hopes and dreams . . . we'll get along without them, just so long as we're still together.'

'I always knew my luck would change one day,' he murmured, his lips against her hair. 'Why did you have it cut?'

'Because I'm my own person too, Stuart: Olivia Cotswold before she became Olivia MacKenzie. Don't under-rate me, I asked you not to, once before.'

'I guess I never paid enough attention.'

'And I guess I never paid enough attention to your millionaire story,' she murmured with tears in her eyes, not for the end of their lifestyle, not for her happy-ever-after hopes and dreams, but because he had never been honest with her in the first place, nor she with him. 'I know how hard you've slogged, Stuart. So much so, I often wondered why a millionaire had to work so hard. Funny business, ours, huh? Would the money we could get by selling Father Lampion's Cross make any difference to bailing us out of bankruptcy?'

He chuckled. 'Not a bit. You keep it in its bank vault, sweetheart, but thanks anyway.'

Olivia yawned. 'Oh, well – a riches-to-rags story, just like Violet's! It's no big deal as far as I'm concerned – I never took our privileged lifestyle too seriously in the first place – just as well I didn't. As you said at Annabelle's dinner party, it's all paper money anyway.' She snuggled deeper into his arms and pressed snugly against his smooth bare chest, hanging in there because without him, for himself and not his millions, life would be a whole lot poorer.

CHAPTER 21

'*Up and down the City Road, In and Out the Eagle, that's the way the money goes, Pop goes the Weasel!*'

Stuart in the role of nanny was something quite outside her agenda. Olivia marvelled at his patience, adaptability and sheer ingenuity.

'*There was a young lass from Norwich, who refused to eat up her porridge. Come on, said her dad, don't make me mad, your Ma's the one with the Courage!*'

Olivia couldn't help laughing while Stuart scraped porridge off Caro's reluctant little face. 'I've got to be going . . . don't forget Annabelle's picking Danny up to take him to playgroup with Amy. Good luck. Fax me from here if anything important crops up on your daily agenda.'

'Go, woman, out of my sight! Do not presume that a man of my calibre cannot run a twenty-eight-acre farm-kitchen after he has headed a multi-million-dollar enterprise!' He blew her a kiss and directed his attention back to his favourite daughter.

Olivia was in danger of missing the eight-thirty to Charing Cross; she put a sprint on.

Max van der Croote panted a good hundred paces behind her to the station.

Once seated in her seat – a seat she had just about managed to grab before the other commuters like herself crowded in, Olivia hoped Max van der Croote would not overcrowd her too.

He too had come a cropper in the recession.

He too was fighting to keep his commodities brokerage business alive and kicking while the boom and bust years took their toll on everyone.

He too now travelled ordinary citizen class!

Olivia took stock of the situation.

Ernest and the Daimler had also been made victims of the recession. Ernest hadn't minded too much. He and Jenny and their children had moved out of the cottage and gone back to the Midhurst Arms, she as barmaid once more, and Ernest as novice landlord, 'Keeping it in the family'. Ernest's father-in law, Arthur Stapley, was in a better financial position to pay their wages and keep a room over their heads than she and Stuart were. Besides, the Stapleys senior wanted their grandchildren with them.

The cottage had been let to a nice young couple studying English viticulture. They paid their rent very promptly. The garage flat was occupied by an absent-minded artist who had to be reminded to pay his rent. The place in Docklands – no Yuppies around any more – had been sold to raise capital to pay off their debts.

The manor had been mercifully bought outright for them by her own Ma and Pa – the old mogul had insisted on it, if not for them, then for his grand-children. He had also sold the company yacht to buy back Stuart's shares in Lamphouse: in order to help it survive into the New Millennium, the least he could do in view of his daughter's courageous efforts to keep it alive and kicking, he had informed Stuart, who had taken his demise gallantly, right on the chin! Cotswolds were once again major stockholders in the company, much to her Pa's delight and cantankerous wisdom.

Her father's old Daimler Sovereign and Stuart's Ferrari had also been sold. She and Stuart now owned a second-hand Volvo Estate.

Verity York had also moved on.

Neither had she minded a bit – Steve had decided that money and living apart was not what life was all about, and they had decided to bring the wedding date forward. Verity was getting married from her father's 'estate' in Lincolnshire, and had promised that Olivia and Stuart would be included on the wedding-guest list.

Andy Grafter, gardener-cum-handyman they had to keep on as they needed him to superintend the growing of grapes; they made up his remuneration by making him a partner in the vineyard. They had been extremely touched by Andy's generous help. The half-acre of landscaped rockery and garden was kept as it was – too much effort had gone into it to dig it all up again to grow vines.

Mrs Dannymott continued to 'do' for them, but had taken a pay-cut for fewer hours and did not mind a bit – what were friends for? she told them. 'Besides, the real gentry round here never did have a penny to rub together, so you and Stuart are in good company, dear.'

367

Annabelle said, 'Golly-gosh, as bad as us! Max is really mad with the system.'

Stuart said, 'He told me he was really mad with his latest handicap.'

'Ha-ha, very funny! You and Max are as bad as each other.'

'I sincerely hope not!' Stuart had retorted, without loss of spirit.

'It's your turn to do the nursery-run tomorrow, Stuart.' Annabelle and Stuart were now pally-pally housemothers together – as long as they didn't share the Jacuzzi, pool, and aromatherapy sessions together, were Olivia's guarded thoughts.

And how was Stuart himself taking all this? Olivia continued to contemplate while the countryside zipped past her on the way to London.

Not bad, she supposed. He did not resent her being the major breadwinner now. They had had to cut their cloth according to their clipped budget, which was zilch when you analysed how much they had lost through Stuart's unfortunate investment in the Peruvian Mineral-Mining Company. But, all credit to him, he had not gone whining and pleading poverty to his father, who still continued to operate the way he always had, like a dictatorial publishing multi-millionaire with a dead loss for a son.

Stuart, without his playboy image and money-no-object lifestyle, did what she used to do in the early years of motherhood: he worked from home and travelled first class – never! He seemed to be enjoying his role as househusband, Olivia hoped.

As far as she was concerned, she now had to work

harder than ever to keep what little income she could generating for them; everything else of theirs was owned by the banks, apart from the house. Hers was the responsibility to take Lamphouse further than ever before, without let or hindrance, safe in the knowledge that her husband was getting to know his children instead of being the faceless daddy of her own childhood years when Harry had been in the hot seat at Paternoster Row . . .

'Ach, Olivia! How happy I am to zee you looking zo very young and beautiful zis spring morning!' said Max, looming large upon her after trekking the length of the train in search of her. 'May I zit beside you?' He indicated the seat next to her on which she had piled her briefcase, shoulderbag, mackintosh and umbrella.

She had a sneaky feeling, not for the first time, that Max fancied her.

Laugh! She tried to keep a straight face. 'By all means. BR is also being privatized, carved-up and sold off – like the rest of us. Be my guest in the New Millennium run-up, Max.' She removed her belongings to make room for him.

'Or zer run-down,' said Max, placing his big bulk next to her. 'Vun zing gute about zis recession is zat vee all pull togezzer, like in a war. Ven vee are down, zer is only vun zing for it, and that iz zer vay *up*!'

'Don't you believe it!' said Birdie, when Olivia mentioned the subject, Birdie being her daily listening diary of MacKenzie country and household happenings. 'In my experience there is a lot further to fall even when you *think* you're right down *there*.' She jabbed a spiky finger at the floor.

'Thanks, Birdie, for cheering me up no end, just as I was coming to terms with Stuart's being a house-husband instead of a millionaire, without feeling guilty about it.'

'Why should *you* feel guilty? It's his fault, not yours. It's not how low we sink, but how good we are at getting ourselves out of the gutter – still a gold-lined one in your case. Riches are relevant – so, you don't eat cake today but bread. His Pa still eats cake; ask *him* for a slice of the dough.'

'We both decided against begging. The old dictator would only have made Stuart feel lower than he feels already. With my own Ma and Pa it was different. They offered to help us.'

'So, what are friends for? OK, we don't choose our relatives, but lucky for Stuart, you did! So why don't *you* creep around the old miser MacKenzie? He knows *you're* good in your own right.'

'Am I?'

'Sure – we, meaning Lamphouse, have just received a spate of best-selling authors, courtesy the end of the net book agreement whereby "*Our Choices*" are being widely distributed from the book-shelves of every supermarkets throughout the country. Things are a-changing fast. Bet Florence Nightingale never thought she'd be packaged along with the porridge and Bernice Wintergarden's *O, Sole Mio*. We're not doing bad at all, dear.'

It was good to be back in the hot seat, now hotter than ever. She really did enjoy the cut-and-thrust of big business, and knew exactly how Stuart must have felt – like a gambler seeing his luck holding fast time

370

and time again, placing his bets time and time again, the winning streak, the toss of the dice, the flip of a card, the buzz which came with the name of the game, winner takes all. She did it with books; he had done it with his business investments, until his lucky streak ran out. She hoped hers would hold out a bit longer, long enough to get them out of their own personal financial crisis.

Maggie made the most significant contribution to their situation, not one bit zany now. 'Remember, Olivia darling, never make your man feel bad. A man never likes to feel he is not in control any more. Stuart might like playing the doting father *now*, but in the long term he's going to resent it – and you. If you want to keep your marriage safe, the wisest thing to do would be to put him back where he belongs – on his pedestal. He might have lost control of Mac-Kenzie UK in his father's eyes, but offer him Lamphouse instead. *You* can still be the power behind the throne, darling, but be wise about it, without sacrificing your husband and your marriage. A man's pride is a man's pride after all.'

Olivia thought about what her mother had said. She thought about it for a long time.

Andy Grafter and Stuart were planting vines alongside Pauline and Francis, the two viticulturists, while Danny performed happy somersaults and Caro gurgled in her pushchair right beside her father's muddy wellies, a dummy in her mouth and eyes only for her father.

Stuart dug deep on the one hand and replaced Caro's

permanently tossed teddybear into the mud with the other. Stuart had decided that the way out of their financial difficulties was to start planting with a little help from his friends and OU unpaid students, who still managed to pay him rent for their accommodation.

Birdie's idea to generate further income hadn't been quite so daft, after all, reflected Olivia. When the vines started producing grapes and they could make wine, and the profits from the wines business flowed in, *then* she would feel a lot happier: But right now it was early days yet and a bad year could once again set them back financially.

Stuart wiped a working-man's hand across his sweating brow. 'Nice to see you home early today,' he commented when she approached the work-party.

'Stuart, can we talk?'

'Right now?'

'Yes, please, right now.' She gathered up the children and took them back to the house, Stuart wonderingly following.

She settled the children at the kitchen table, gave them milk and biscuits, then made two mugs of tea. She handed one to him, 'I'm pregnant again.'

She saw the look on his face. 'You can't be . . .'

'I am – at least, I think I am. I'm throwing up again, all-day morning sickness. Point is, I don't think I can do what I'm doing a third time round. I'm getting too old to be a working horse – mother! I want to stay at home.'

His mouth opened and closed; he was unsure of himself, and her. 'What?' He looked into the middle distance.

'I know you're thinking we can't afford for me to give up work, but it's your turn now, Stuart – yes, again! You can get right back into MacKenzie tomorrow, only you don't want to because you've chosen to fight it out with Custor who had words with you over your bad investments. You should've ignored him and taken back your place at Mac-Kenzie-Farringdon instead of letting Custor put another MD in your place.'

'Olivia, the rift between my father and me goes far deeper than that . . .'

'OK, here's your chance – take control of Lamphouse for me and let me have home and family in return. I don't think I can endure another nine months of throwing-up at boardroom meetings. Lamphouse is doing well now, better than ever. We can pay back our debt to society within the next few years, if you will only trust me and not go investing elsewhere without telling me. I want to be a stay-at-home mum instead of a high-powered exec. I've done my share; now I want to call it quits. I know I can do it because I've done it – my way, if you'll forgive the cliché. After all, I *am* over thirty!' Her head on one side, she made a Bugs Bunny face, fingers as quotation marks for ears. 'Wot's up, Doc?'

The light came back into his eyes. 'You're doing this for me?'

'For better, and no worse, buddy-boy.'

'Lamphouse is your whole life, Olivia.'

'Not any more. I've done what I set out to do, and that was to pull it up by its bootstraps from a failing company to a thriving one.'

His arms came round her and he hugged her tightly. 'Did we forget ourselves again during our last throe of passion?'

'When was that?' she quipped. 'Can't say I remember it.'

'Oh, no? 'He began to tickle her and drag her off in a caveman stunt, much to the children's delight. 'Let me remind you then . . .'

'Stuart . . . ! Remember, there are young ones learning from our example . . . listen . . . *listen* to me! Let's be serious. You made your first million without anyone's help. The rest was easy after that, all your wheeling and dealing to raise the seventeen and a half million for Lamphouse, and then me to take Lamphouse from the red to the black. Now all that has changed; I'll settle for the bills being paid and no dicey deals behind my back. Deal, huh?'

'Do I have a choice, Madam Executive?'

'Only if you wish for another Madam-Ex on your agenda, Stuart Lyin' MacKenzie!'

'OK, let's have a party to celebrate the start of our vineyards. I'm bored with all this toiling for a living.'

Olivia groaned. 'You never learn, do you, darling!'

One year later they had a party, a great big party, marquee and all, adjoining the back of the house to make an open-plan ballroom leading off from the blue marble swimming-pool, even though they couldn't really afford it.

Their swan-song, Olivia reflected, or a Midsummer Night's Dream; it made no difference. She had suddenly switched to Stuart's own philosophy – play it good even when the going's rough. Everyone loves a millionaire, and despises a pauper. If you have it, flaunt it; if you haven't, pretend – that was how the real millionaires did it.

They had managed to pay off some of their debts – and another year would make all the difference in the world. Things were not as bad as they had seemed in the beginning. They still had each other. They still had good neighbours, friends and family – to which had been added Eliza Saffron MacKenzie, three months old and with her beautiful mouth, curly dark hair and speedwell-blue eyes as prettily charming as her father.

Stuart's mother had made a slow and painstaking recovery after her stroke, but at least she had survived that terrible misfortune. For that, they could be truly grateful too.

As for herself, this time there had been no post-natal depressions or anything else – she hadn't had time! She had regained her figure in a relatively short while, thanks to Hatha yoga, and, she was far less neurotic about Lamphouse; it was in good shape and in good hands; Stuart's, the board's, Birdie's and Natasha's. She had a *lot* to be thankful for. His arm around her newly trim waist, he said, 'You're looking lovelier than ever tonight, sweetheart.'

'Thank you, darling, you too.'

'Must be Chinese lantern-light in our eyes,' he murmured. 'Or Ma Hatha's.'

She dug him in the ribs. 'Annabelle is crazy in a different way from Max, but they're both the stuff of novels.'

'If they weren't so real and I hadn't seen them with

my own eyes, I'd have believed they were a figment of your Lamphouse imagination.'

'Some Lamphouse authors get Booker and Pulitzer prizes – MacKenzie still only get silicone boob implants,' she replied with irresistible glee.

Both of them dressed to kill, she in a long slinky silver-grey backless gown and boobs that were all hers (unlike Rutlands), he in white tux, crimson cummerbund and bow tie, the perfect host and hostess without a care in the world, he whispered in her ear, 'Sweetheart, do me a favour?'

'Now?'

'Don't stand too close to Max; I don't like him ogling your gorgeous cleavage.'

'Nor does Annabelle. You're jealous!'

'Too right.' He put his hand where another man might have got his face slapped.

'Stuart! Everyone is watching us, including the kids!'

'Who cares? Aren't you glad you married me now?'

'Sometimes.'

'Only sometimes?'

'Creep.' She smiled through her teeth while they stood with backs to the canvas, watching the party. 'Stuart, kindly take your hand off my posterior; the van der Croote girls are heading this way.'

'They're heading for the bushes with their boy-friends, sweetheart. Tandy is a man-eater!'

'How do *you* know?'

'I've seen it all before!'

'Oh, have you? Doing an Ute at her young age! I hope the ex au pair didn't encourage her.' 'Annabelle shouldn't give those two, Tandy and Lois, so much freedom. I never had it at their age.'

'Now you sound like your mother,' he said, and made her wince. 'Leave them alone; they're young men and women finding their feet.'

'As long as it's not crack,' she said, sliding a nervous glance towards his parents talking to her parents beside the swimming pool. Pears was still in a wheelchair, her private nurse at her beck and call. Her speech was returning slowly, plus the use of her right arm. She looked very bright and bubbly tonight, and, Stuart, who had followed her glance, suddenly turned away with tears in his eyes.

'You old softie,' she whispered, squeezing his arm and following him back on to the dance floor.

'Sweetheart, I'm glad we decided to go wild and have this party. And talking of wild, didn't Oscar Wilde once say, nothing succeeds like excess?'

'It was actually Dumas in *Ange Pitou* – "nothing succeeds like *success*" '.

'OK, I bow to your superior knowledge.'

'Get to the point, Stuart.'

'Not easy being the son of a multi-millionaire skinflint – nor the Prodigal Son. He's still judging me and mine.' He meant the old dictator, of course. 'Thanks to you, however, he has made us one of his charities.'

'What?' She inclined her ear.

'Come outside and I'll, tell you . . . it's too damn hot and noisy in this tent.' He grabbed her hand, 'One of Bernice Wintergarden's Arab Sheikhs I would *not* like to be . . .'

He wandered with her into the lantern-lit garden because it seemed a shame to waste such a beautiful night under canvas. Besides, the young ones were discoing to the most appalling music, so it was just as well the neighbours too had been invited to the Midhurst party of the year, because down in the valley no one would get any sleep tonight! 'We should have had the Midhurst violin quartet and pleased your mother,' Stuart said.

'Stuart, what do you mean, he's made us one of his charities?'

He tapped his breast pocket. 'O most worthy publisher's wife . . .' He kissed her hard under the bower of home-grown Philadelphus blossoms, commonly known as mock orange. Their fragrance was breathtaking, mock or not. The hot summer night was ripe with emotion everywhere, young and old. She tried to reach into his breast pocket, but he held her wrist. 'Naughty, naughty! Anyway, you won't be able to read it in the dark.'

'What? *What*? Tell me or I'll push you into the horse manure you ordered for your wretched vines!'

'A cheque for a million smackers, babe.'

'You mean a million pounds?'

'Yup.'

'Why?'

He shrugged. 'Who cares? I guess it's because you're so good at everything, including founding him a dynasty of grandchildren.'

'We can't accept it, definitely not.'

'Of course we can! *He* can afford it. About time he coughed up something for his three *English* grandkids. Your father did, by buying the house for us and salvaging my shares in Lamphouse, thus saving me a million grey hairs to boot.'

'Four.'

'What?' He shot her an anxious glance then. 'You're not . . . not again?'

'Not again, what?'

'Pregnant?

'It might be a phantom pregnancy, darling.'

'No . . . you *are* kidding, aren't you?'

'Yes, I'm kidding!'

He sighed with relief.

'As I said, it might be a false alarm, Eliza is only three months old – on the other hand, it might not.'

'Olivia!'

'Yes, Stuart?'

'I can't afford all these children.'

'*Our* children, dearest. Of course we can afford it – your Pa's just handed you *carte blanche* for a million quid . . . I thought we would stop at six – kids I mean, though six million quid would be even better. Children are our insurance policy for the future.'

'Did we discuss this arrangement, pre-nuptially?'

'Oh, yes, between black silk sheets – bedsheets not contract paper. I knew you would be a good father; it seemed a shame to waste you . . .' She dragged him out of the bushes and back to their guests. 'Smile . . .' She nudged him. 'Phantom pregnancy according to Dr Owen – go on over and ask him.' She nudged him in the direction of Owen Gareth, deep in conversation with Maggie, her mother, who was no doubt telling Owen and Mrs Owen all about Clipping Time Pudding. 'Annabelle says it's better to get them all done and over with in one go – starting a family, I mean.'

'I think she's definitely not a good influence on you. And Max is even worse – remember not to stand too close to him . . .'

'Too close to whom?' Vinny sidled up to them with a glass of champagne in one hand, a cigarette in the other. 'You two are truly disgusting, and make me green with envy. Creeping out of the bushes at your age, tut-tut! No wonder you're getting fat again, Olly.'

'Don't call me Olly.'

'Sorry. Anyone seen Ashton lately?'

'He's canoodling with Rutland.'

'Bitchy! Thanks, darling . . . lovely house, lovely party, Stuwey, as usual. Can't say much for your run-of the-mill neighbours.'

Over her Amazonian shoulder she slipped a cat-at-the-cream glance at Olivia before drifting off in Max van der Croote's direction while Annabelle swooned over Jeremy Webber, still a sales director, and Genesis March was captured by Theodore Grieves of the local Ramblers' Association, and Birdie and Dankers gazed nostalgically into each other's eyes, reminiscing over good old Lamphouse days of Doodlebugs and Scutari best-sellers while the abseiling vicar of Midhurst got waylaid by Molly Cartwright of the local teashop, and 'Violet', Lady Constance, sought the attention of the great publishing mogul himself, Custor, Father-in-law, and whoops, there goes another firefly bug, no doubt anxious to do a Faye Rutland on Lamphouse! The Stapleys and

Ernest dispensed beer and bonhomie to those who never drank champagne, and Tandy and Lois continued to pester the local boys, while Pauline and Francis, viticulturists, talked animatedly to Verity York, ex-nanny, now Mrs Steve of Scandinavian Airways, whose husband still looked to be flying high even though he was on terra firma tonight.

'Everyone seems to be enjoying themselves,' said Olivia, 'thank goodness!' She took another glass of champagne from the catering butler's tray. 'Stuart darling, do you get the feeling you've been here before in another life?'

'Often,' he replied laconically, sipping from his glass.

'You remind me of the *Great Gatsby* tonight,' she said with a wicked twinkle in her eyes.

'Who's he?'

'Never mind, ignoramus!'

'Here's to us, sweetheart,' Stuart clunked glasses with her, 'and to the old man who's footing the bill, Custor Stuart Mackenzie the First.'

Olivia intercepted a wink from Max's direction, even though he was still flirting with Vinny. She raised her glass to him and smiled and said behind her teeth, 'Max van der Croote just *wunked* at me, darling!'

'Shall I go over and thump him on the jaw?' Stuart replied, Gatsby-like.

'Better not; you might come off worst.'

'Then I won't.'

'And talking of *déjà-vu*, Rutland's on the move towards you, darling! I'm off . . .' Champagne bubbles tickling her nose, Olivia left her husband to ogle

Rutland's latest silicone implants, while wondering why one earth he had invited her *and* Vinny Legrand, her sworn enemies, to their neighbourly family party – like the Genesis March crowd, as far as she was concerned, gate-crashers, the lot of them.

But that was what publishing was all about: bestsellers built around the honey-pot of scandal, hype, tripe, instant fame and instant gain. It had always given her a tremendous buzz to be in the hot-seat of publishing, the heart of it all. Rather as a Hollywood producer or director must feel in launching a new starlet to mega-fame. Olivia wondered if she might not be able to launch Annabelle into a writing career, Annabelle had the background, the experiences, the verve, the nerve, the wit, the gift of the gab.

And then she remembered she was no more in the hot-seat, her husband was.

No greater love hath any women but to pass off her beloved inheritance to someone else, for better, for worse. But there was more to life than just the rat-race. Zany Mother had told her that she could still be the power behind the throne . . . Olivia went in search of Mrs Dannymott doing a superb job in the manorial kitchen – 'her' kitchen always.

'Not there . . . over here . . .' Mrs Dannymott directed the outside caterers. 'Those canapés are getting soggy; take them out to the guests at once. Who's in charge of this salmon? And where do you think you're off to with that Coronation chicken? That way . . . out there towards the marquee, not up the back stairs to her ladyship's quarters . . . Hello, dear, you should be taking it easy with your feet up.

Don't worry about a thing; Verity and I can see to these people. Nice man, her Steve – he's an airline pilot, you know – course you know, silly me! You were at the wedding too . . . now, what did we do with those profiteroles? Don't tell me the children have scoffed them all . . .' She put out a hand for the cooking sherry and found the bottle empty.

Olivia left them all to it, and crept upstairs to the nursery, which was really Stuart's old dressing-room, close enough to the four-poster, now that they didn't have a nanny and she had to be on tap night and day, instantly awake to their twenty-four-hour demands and desires.

Danny, Caro and Eliza were fast asleep, good as gold as usual, each one of them so different in personality and character and all three a blessing to say the least, even though she had suffered agonies of misery before and after their births.

Same for her as a million other repossessed house-wives and working mothers the country over, she reflected while watching over her little brood: what you had, you wanted to live up to; what you never had, you never missed. She had nothing to whinge about. At least she had a husband to love and stand by her, for richer, for poorer. And yes, they were a silly, soppy, sentimental couple who were more than ever in love with each other. Somehow, all the trauma of the last year, including his mother's shattering illness and slow, painstaking recovery, had drawn them closer together than ever before, had made their marriage stronger for it.

She hoped that number four would soon join these

three, but not just yet. It was not fair on baby Eliza, who still needed her so much.

Stuart found her there, leaning over their children in her shimmering dress and her Cotswold jewellery and her lifestyle still in hock to the powers that be. 'I thought I might find you here . . .' He sat down on the floor, his head and back and flagging spirits safely propped up by the toy cupboard which had previously harboured his Armani ties. 'I've got something else to tell you.'

'No more bright ideas, please, Stuart. Did I ever tell you how Lamphouse of the old days, way back about 1868, turned down *A Tale of Two Cities*?'

'I bet your great-great-great-great grandfather- as many as it takes to have that kind of publishing history – kicked ass.'

'In our case it's the proverbial triangle, *A Tale of Three Cities*; London, New York and Toronto.' She sat down beside him in her shimmering Versace sheath dress which had cost the earth, but never mind, and rested her head on his shoulder.

A quiet moment passed between them, as he ran his fingers through the sleek dark silkiness of her hair and breathed in her perfume. 'OK. Family are a liability – but family is what makes the world go round, and around and around. My mother, in gratitude to the Almighty for giving her back her life, has also donated to our charity.'

'Pears has given you another million? Things *are* looking up!' Olivia said sleepily. 'Why don't you take off your bow-tie and slip into something more comfortable, my darling . . .'

'I think we ought to frame it,' said Stuart, producing a roll of parchment tied with a red ribbon, again from what appeared to be a copious inside jacket pocket.

'What is it?' Olivia asked dreamily.

'A thirty-thousand-pound bus pass, sweetheart. You and I are now a *real* Lord and Lady of the Manor – Midhurst!'

Olivia jerked awake. 'You cannot be serious, Stuart!'

'Here it is – all authentic and valid.' He showed it to her.

Olivia began to laugh, her arms held tight across her stomach to keep the laughter inside herself and not wake any sleeping angels.

Stuart said, 'Listen to them all downstairs – why are we doing this to ourselves, Olivia? Do we really have to make a statement to the old folks at home? Let's go to bed beneath our manorial canopy, uh?' He raised her chin, looked into her eyes and kissed her full and strong and very energetically on her warm, champagne-flavoured, beautiful lips before approaching other parts of her anatomy.

A little while later Faye Rutland and Vinny Legrand passed by the open bedroom door, looking for the bathroom. Rutland paused on the threshold of the manorial master-bedroom. 'Now ain't that just the cutest thing . . . come here and look at this . . .'

Vinny looked, and drawled, 'Sweet! Excuse me while I throw up.'

'Betcha ass you wish you'd got him instead of Olly pipping *you* to the post, huh, Granny?'

'You betcha silicone ass, kiddo! Betcha wish it too, huh, Rutty?'

'You betcha! Anyone got a camera handy?'

'Cummon! We can't do that to them,'

'I wanna copy of the bed, not them! OK, but I'm spilling buckets of tears wishing I was in that smug guy's pocket-book of smiles, so where's the champagne?'

'That's why I persuaded him to publish you in the first place; you have such a neat choice of words, Rutty,' said Vinny, miles out of tempo with her ex-team-captain's voice. 'I wanna find Ashy and get him to propose roses to me too.'

'OK, but let's just find the manorial loo first.'

They drifted away down the landing, and in the subdued glow of the nursery light shining through his eyelids Stuart opened one eye and whispered against her ear, 'Poor Ashy!'

'Silly bitches,' Olivia murmured, 'drunk as skunks.'

'Pie-eyed as peewits and ugly as Cinderella's slippers . . . sisters!'

She giggled against his neck. 'You're drunk too!'

'Yes, but I'll be sober in the morning and they'll still be ugly.'

'That's not original!' She raised her head and kissed his chin, on the verge of becoming bristly. 'I'm wide awake now, thanks to those two.'

'Me too.'

'Shall we go downstairs and rejoin the party, or shall we have breakfast in bed? It is Sunday morning, you know.'

'Breakfast in bed – but shut the door first or we might never live happily ever after.'

She did exactly that, before slipping out of her tight-fitting backless silver-grey glittering gown, right down into his arms, like a mermaid slithering into the depths of an ocean of unconscionable desires. 'My Cotswold grandfather used to say – a good love story is like a well-worn carpet. Whoops-a-daisy! Your slippers slip, you land flat on your back, but you don't give a toss because you've already dog-eared the next page of happily ever after! I'm happy – are you?' She kissed his sweet-talking lips.

'Ecstatic-cally, my love! *"Oh, Yes! Love indeed is light from heaven, A spark of that immortal fire with angels shared, by Allah given to lift from earth our low desire"* – how low did Lord Byron's desire sink, I wonder?'

'Quite low, Baron Stuart – thanks to your dearest mother.'

'Baron Stuart sounds good enough to me.'

'I'm glad she's so much better and could make it here tonight, Stuart.'

'Me too. Guess what?'

'Ummm?'

'Byron was never the lover he made himself out to be, unlike me . . .' he said, sinking further down with her into the old Brig's incomparable four-poster. 'Promise me one thing, wife of my life.'

'What's that, silly old husband dear?'

'Now that you're a housemother, you won't end up like Annabelle, all flowery and countrified and vegetating. I like you just the way you are – sleek, sophisticated, sensible, successful and sexy.'

'You don't fancy her, then?

'Never have,' he fingered her silky hair, 'or Vinny or Faye or anyone else. Only you, my love. And as for this publishing lark, I used to think there was nothing to it, just hot air, nothing tangible, not like holding a cheque for seventeen and half million dollars in your hand. But now I know they're not just any old words, but magic words which can translate into other languages and other currency and live forever in the minds of others. A bit like creation, really.'

She was so glad to know that he was not all playboy but had actually learned something already from his spell in the hottest seat at the Lamphouse Cross.

'Yes, magic words,' he said, pleased with the discovery of other things besides making money. 'Creative words, like a beautiful painting, like a line of poetry, like a theme of music . . .'

'Like a piece of cake,' she murmured.

'No, not a piece of cake any more. I realize how hard you've worked to keep Lamphouse in the family, and how I almost wrecked everything by my foolish schemes and dreams. But now the dream is to be real about what we *do* have. The dream is *us*, Olivia.'

THE EXCITING NEW NAME
IN WOMEN'S FICTION!

PLEASE HELP ME TO HELP YOU!

Dear *Scarlet* Reader,

As Editor of *Scarlet* Books I want to make sure that the books I offer you every month are up to the high standards *Scarlet* readers expect. And to do that I need to know a little more about you and your reading likes and dislikes. So please spare a few minutes to fill in the short questionnaire on the following pages and send it to me.

Looking forward to hearing from you,

Sally Cooper

Editor-in-Chief, *Scarlet*

QUESTIONNAIRE

Please tick the appropriate boxes to indicate your answers

1 Where did you get this Scarlet title?
Bought in supermarket ☐
Bought at my local bookstore ☐ Bought at chain bookstore ☐
Bought at book exchange or used bookstore ☐
Borrowed from a friend ☐
Other (please indicate) _____

2 Did you enjoy reading it?
A lot ☐   A little ☐   Not at all ☐

3 What did you particularly like about this book?
Believable characters ☐   Easy to read ☐
Good value for money ☐   Enjoyable locations ☐
Interesting story ☐   Modern setting ☐
Other _____

4 What did you particularly dislike about this book?
_____

5 Would you buy another Scarlet book?
Yes ☐   No ☐

6 What other kinds of book do you enjoy reading?
Horror ☐   Puzzle books ☐   Historical fiction ☐
General fiction ☐   Crime/Detective ☐   Cookery ☐
Other (please indicate) _____

7 Which magazines do you enjoy reading?
1. _____
2. _____
3. _____

And now a little about you –
8 How old are you?
Under 25 ☐   25–34 ☐   35–44 ☐
45–54 ☐   55–64 ☐   over 65 ☐

cont.

9 What is your marital status?
Single ☐   Married/living with partner ☐
Widowed ☐   Separated/divorced ☐

10 What is your current occupation?
Employed full-time ☐   Employed part-time ☐
Student ☐   Housewife full-time ☐
Unemployed ☐   Retired ☐

11 Do you have children? If so, how many and how old are they?
_____
_____

12 What is your annual household income?

under $15,000	☐	or	£10,000	☐
$15–25,000	☐	or	£10–20,000	☐
$25–35,000	☐	or	£20–30,000	☐
$35–50,000	☐	or	£30–40,000	☐
over $50,000	☐	or	£40,000	☐

Miss/Mrs/Ms _____

Address _____
_____
_____

Thank you for completing this questionnaire. Now tear it out – put it in an envelope and send it, before 28 February 1998, to:

Sally Cooper, Editor-in-Chief

USA/Can. address
SCARLET c/o London Bridge
85 River Rock Drive
Suite 202
Buffalo
NY 14207
USA

UK address/No stamp required
SCARLET
FREEPOST LON 3335
LONDON W8 4BR
Please use block capitals for address

MACON/8/97

Scarlet titles coming next month:

DEADLY ALLURE   Laura Bradley
After her sister's murder Britt Reeve refuses to let detective Grant Collins write the death off as an accident. Britt suspects that the murderer could be someone with family ties, and soon she and Grant find themselves passionate allies in a race against time . . .

WILD FIRE   Liz Fielding
Don't miss Part Three of **The Beaumont Brides** trilogy! Melanie Beaumont's tired of her dizzy blonde image. She's determined to show everyone that she can hold down a proper job. And if that means bringing arrogant Jack Wolfe to his knees . . . so much the better!

FORGOTTEN   Jill Sheldon
What will happen if Clayton Slater remembers who he is and that he's never seen Hope Broderick before in his life? And Hope has another problem . . . she's fallen in love with this stranger she's claimed as her lover!

GIRLS ON THE RUN   Talia Lyon
Three girls, three guys . . . three romances?
Take three girls: Cathy, Lisa and Elaine. Match them with three very different guys: Greg, Philip and Marcus. When the girls stop running, will their holiday romances last forever?